MEDEA

PRIESTESS, PRINCESS, WITCH

By JJ Taylor

2024

Butterworth Books is a different breed of publishing house. It's a home for Indies, for independent authors who take great pride in their work and produce top quality books for readers who deserve the best. Professional editing, professional cover design, professional proof reading, professional book production—you get the idea. As Individual as the Indie authors we're proud to work with, we're Butterworths and we're *different*.

Authors currently publishing with us:

E.V. Bancroft
Valden Bush
Addison M Conley
Jo Fletcher
Helena Harte
Lee Haven
Karen Klyne
AJ Mason
Ally McGuire
James Merrick
Robyn Nyx
Simon Smalley
JJ Taylor
Brey Willows

For more information visit www.butterworthbooks.co.uk

CATALOGING INFORMATION
ISBN: 978-1-915009-51-7
CREDITS
Editor: Nicci Robinson
Cover Design: Nicci Robinson
Production Design: Global Wordsmiths

Acknowledgements

Like any epic journey, the writing of this book involved plenty of blood, sweat, tears, and assistance from a variety of stalwart companions who helped me complete the journey. What began as a love of mythology as a child has culminated in the writing of a story about a woman whose greatest desire was to life her life her own way. And isn't that the ultimate goal for all of us?

The part of the journey that was the doctoral dissertation where this began, as is the case in so many of these tales, went deeply awry. However, the challenge and ability to go to some of the places Medea lived will always be part of my soul. I travelled as much as possible in her footsteps, thousands of years later, and sat at the fountain of Glauke's demise. I knelt beside the grave of an unknown woman and two children, within view of the ancient castle at Corinth. I looked down at Athens from the Acropolis and wondered what she saw when she did the same. I studied geology, sociology, the climate change now being theorized with regard to the changes in that era, and the archaeology of ancient Greece as well as of the areas around the Black Sea, and I devoured every scrap of information about Medea that I could find. Eventually I put together a picture of someone far, far ahead of her time.

Did she exist? Like many of the heroes of the epics, and of many ancient tales in general, I believe there's a kernel of truth mixed into the larger-than-life characters we continue to hear about centuries later. The fountain at Corinth has a plaque which reads, "The temple where Medea killed Glauke." That's a statement of fact, not a quote from a story, which leads me to believe that there was, once, a woman who was brave enough to forge a path for herself in a way that led to her name being passed down through the generations. A reminder, perhaps, that we can all forge a path for ourselves, if we're willing to do whatever it takes...

As I said, there were many, many companions on this journey of mine, and I don't have the space to mention them all. My mother bought me books even when we were so poor, there wasn't much money left. If I wanted books, she found a way to get them, and she cemented my love of stories right from the beginning. Bret Johnston, my creative writing professor at CSUSB, convinced me I had a modicum of talent I should dig into, and he sponsored my time at the Iowa Summer Writing school, which was an invaluable and deeply humbling experience. That started the process, however slowly it would gain momentum. Once I made the leap into doctoral territory, Professor Gregory Woods said, "We know you can write a novel. That isn't in question. The question is how you can make it special." I hope I've managed to do so.

After several years passed and this story languished in the metaphorical bottom drawer, I decided it was time for Medea to finish her journey. Without my wife's support, encouragement, occasional cajoling, editing, and relentless questions, this work would remain only in my mind. She has been my rock, my adventure companion, my way out of the darkness.

To everyone else involved in the journey whom I haven't mentioned, thank you for your support and patience. And to all the readers who take this journey with Medea: I hope you find your own light as you live your adventure in all its fullness.

Dedication

To all the women who have fought for the right
to live authentically, freely, and without fear.

CHAPTER ONE
Memories

Today, an old woman remembering.

I'VE PAID FOR MY freedom in blood that drowns me in my dreams. I see it on my hands as I walk through my days, I smell its fetid heat when I pass the candles in the palace. And yet faces I saw so clearly as I ended their lives are now vague impressions, and that is a blessing. The gods may not forget, but we do, and I, with the bodies piled at my feet, can take some comfort in it.

Granted, the days are less saturated with it than they were. As the lines have appeared on my face, a map of waterways and roads I've both willingly and unwillingly travelled, the blood guilt has diminished somewhat.

I studied the oak and beech trees blanketing the hills around me, and took in their varying greens, their size and solid presence. The Athenians were wrong to strip the hills for their temples. Better to be here, in Egrisi, flanked by lush trees and mountains rather than out in the open on a sterile hill, wondering why the gods had forsaken them.

"You'll catch cold, Medea." Alkippe shuffled into the room and laid out my clothes for the day.

I glanced at her, unwilling to look too long, for the old woman I saw was not the young companion who had set out with me on my journey so long ago. I too was moving closer to Hades' hearth. Grey threaded through her once raven hair and lines travelled her once smooth skin. Fear of seeing the same kept me from the looking glass most days. "If the gods haven't taken me for what I've done, they'll not take me because of a chill."

"You of all people know better than to speak of the gods' will." Alkippe made a sign against evil. "And what has you staring so?"

"I was thinking about our trips across the sea. How long they were! And how different."

Desma, my newest young servant, looked up from where she sat sewing in the corner. "What made them so different? Surely it was the same sea both times? Sea is sea, after all."

Alkippe cuffed her. "Have you no more sense than to question your betters? Learn your place, girl."

Desma dropped her head and let her tears fall, though she had the sense to cry without sound.

"They *were* different, though, weren't they, Kip? We are not the women we were."

Alkippe made a grunting sound but didn't reply. There was no need. After so many years together, and so much horror, there was little need for words.

Words were dangerous.

"Do stop crying. You'll ruin that linen with your tears." I snatched it away from Desma and examined it. "You have a neat hand," I said before I handed it back and turned to Alkippe. "Where is my son this morning?"

Alkippe snorted. "Likely lazing with his pile of whores. He hadn't been to the hall yet when I was last there."

I rubbed my temples. I'd spoiled him, cosseted him, because I couldn't let anything happen to my remaining child. When we'd returned to Egrisi to find my father dead and my uncle Perses in his place, my dream of having a child on the throne had finally come true. Once I'd dealt with my uncle, obviously. My son was the rightful heir but still too young to rule. I'd met with each of my father's advisors individually, many of whom I had known as a girl. The ones I deemed too old or too attached to their ways, I had removed from their posts. More than one couldn't forgive my actions of so long ago, and they had been quietly taken to the hills and sent to the afterlife. This kingdom belonged to me now, and anyone who lived there would bow or leave. I may not get my hands bloody anymore, but age hadn't dimmed my understanding that sometimes there was only one way to do things.

"Very well. Desma, tell Daminanos to wake his master and get his day under way. I'm to be informed when my son is decent so I may discuss the day's plans."

The girl scurried from the room, and I turned to the bed where my clothes lay ready. Once again, I was pushed into a memory of a time before, far away. Such a strange custom, in Mycenae, to have the women wear garments which covered their backs and left their breasts exposed. Of course, I could see how it would be appealing when looking at the young women. I lifted my own heavy breasts and sighed. It was not nearly so appealing after children and time had ravaged one's body. Better to be covered, modesty and ego intact.

Alkippe removed my robe from my shoulders and set it aside before replacing it with a light linen robe woven with reds and golds. Even now, ruling beside my son in the home I never should have left, I couldn't help but think of my time in Achaea and how different even the smallest things were. Here my robes were linen, threaded with colour instead of the pale, undyed blandness of theirs. In Corinth, women were used as vessels for their men's seed, used to bring up children and be domestic drudges. I'd soon put an end to that expectation. I'd followed their customs but refused to kneel, refused to bend, refused to obey blindly. Though why Jason had thought I'd ever be such a wife, after having been in my homeland and traveled with me, continued to puzzle me even all these years later.

"Do you think he's still alive?" I'd once had a vision of his death, but that was long ago, and no word had yet come to me that he'd left this life.

Alkippe sighed and gave an indifferent shrug. "Who knows what plans the gods had after you happened to him. And what with the droughts and earth shaking... Do you suppose the men who leave women on every shore wonder what happened to them? They've the right of it. Forget him. He was never worthy of you."

I shared a rare smile with my old friend. "No, but my journey wouldn't have been the same without him, would it?" I closed my eyes and blood washed over my vision. The flippant comment nearly bent me double as I heard their screams, a sound that chased me through the years like the dark-winged Erinyes doling out their punishment.

CHAPTER TWO
The Beginning

I LAUGHED AS THE butterflies startled from their thin perches and swarmed, multi-hued and frantic, into the air. I released the branch I'd been swinging from and dropped to the ground, the semi-solid mud cool beneath my bare feet. The warm forest air was thick and heavy, the sound of the river Phasis pounding below as it made its way to the sea beyond. From my vantage point at the temple, I could see the black waters of the sea in the distance, a place that beckoned and chilled me all at once. It had been too long since the last rains, and the forest seemed a little duller for it. Nevertheless, I adored it.

The scenery shifted, spun and tilted, and my stomach lurched in response. Instead of the sea, I saw men, clambering to shore from their galley, making all sorts of noise as they floundered in the water and splashed grime from their skin. Among them, one man stood out. His shockingly light hair, the colour of wheat, offset his strange eyes, the blue of the river in spring. As I watched, he seemed to look straight at me. He wasn't much older than my own twenty years, and his body retained the limber litheness of youth instead of the burly bulk of manhood. He raised his hand as though to summon me.

The vision jerked and faded, leaving me alone among the trees with the sounds of temple life behind me. I dropped to my knees and retched as I always did when such visions came on me. I wiped the putrid bile from my lips with the back of my hand before rising and stumbling to the small creek, where I splashed cool water on my face and rinsed the foulness from my mouth. I rested against a tree and contemplated my vision as my stomach settled, and my trembling ceased.

The visions had begun when I was a child. A gift from my grandfather Helios, the Sun God. When my parents had realized my power, they'd sent me to be raised at the temple, which was fine with me. Not once had I seen my father's expression in anything less than a scornful sneer, even when he spoke with my mother and siblings. I despised him almost as much as I despised my eldest brother, whose cruelty had often driven me to hide in one of the palace's many rooms. His fists brought me pain, but it was his words that hurt the most. He called me unnatural and said that my visions were a curse rather than a gift. It was only when I'd been at the temple for some years that I felt confident in gainsaying him when he harangued me in the palace courtyard one day. After a particularly vicious blow, I'd threatened to curse him, and whatever he had seen in my eyes must have convinced him of that truth. From that moment he stopped speaking to me entirely rather than risk my ire.

I'd never fathomed why he hated me so much. My younger sister, though we weren't close, seemed to have no such prejudice. But Absyrtos had hated me practically from birth. Any praise I garnered was coveted and any punishment I received he took great delight in. Once, in a rare moment of truce while we were playing together by the river, I asked him why he was always so angry with me. Instead of striking me, as he normally would have, he looked sad when he said, "Because I know what you're going to do one day. I know, but fate can't be changed. If only Father hadn't told me, maybe I could love you as the sister I have instead of the witch you are."

With that, he'd left me there by the river, his shoulders hunched as he made his way back to the palace, as though waiting for a blow to fall. From that time, his cruelty developed new terrors for me, and I'd never been able to ask him what he meant that day. I had tried to question my mother, but the look of despair on her face when she said not to ask such questions was enough to make me desist. Still, I asked the temple priestesses, I asked my maid, I even asked the servants in the kitchen who always spoke freely around me. Not one of them would tell me, though I sensed that most of them knew the answer I sought. Over the years I learned to avoid Absyrtos and my father whenever I could, and instead immersed myself in my training at the temple, where I was not only at peace but always felt the goddess near.

I shook off the meandering thoughts and focused on the strangers I'd seen in my vision.

I reached out mentally and caressed the seeing, almost like one would feel a fine piece of linen. No, it wasn't something happening right now. But the strangers were coming, and the fair-haired man was coming for me, of that I was certain. A noise in the thicket across the river drew my attention. There, amongst the oaks and maple trees, a woman stood watching me, her head cocked and a small, twisted smile on her full lips. She was tall, too tall, and her skin was so flawless she looked almost like a carving. As I watched, she took a step back and faded from view. I shivered and pressed myself against the tree, taking comfort in its solidity. Visits from the gods never meant anything good, and the fact that she'd been watching me as I received the vision spoke to its importance.

I pushed myself to my feet, keeping the tree at my back. I scanned the woods, but the birds continued their silly songs and the distant sounds of daily life at the temple sounded as they always did. Routine, dull, demanding. I left the safety of the tree and hurried to the protection of the temple, though why it felt better there, in the goddess's own sacred space than in the forest beyond where I was free from prying eyes, I couldn't say. As I left the canopy of branches, I thought I heard a woman's laughter behind me. I picked up my skirt and broke into a run.

By the time I got to the temple entrance, I was sweating and filled with dread. I shut the door behind me and slid to the earthen floor.

"Medea? Whatever is wrong?" Alkippe, my handmaid and only

friend, hurried to my side. She swept my hair from my face and searched my expression. "A vision, then."

I nodded and gripped Alkippe's hand. "Men are coming. Foreign men. Kip, I think they're coming for me."

"For you? Why would they come for a priestess of the temple? Surely they seek your father?"

I pulled my hand away and stood. "Is it so hard to believe I might be wanted?" I walked away without waiting for an answer. I didn't need one. I knew I was both cherished and despised as the granddaughter of Helios and of Perseis, a powerful ocean nymph noted for her beautiful cruelty. My gifts were coveted and feared, and my refusal to act like less of a person simply because I was female went against all my parents desired of their middle child. I knew they worried about who they might marry me to, with my fierce desire for independence and an even fiercer tongue. Fortunately, because I was a priestess of Hecate, they couldn't force me to marry, but there was no question it was expected I'd do my duty. I hated the thought of it.

"You know I didn't mean it that way. But how would strangers know of you?"

I entered my small room in the temple and stripped off my damp, mud-covered linen. I handed a wet sponge to Alkippe and raised my arms so she could wash the sweat from my body. Though we never spoke of it, it was a routine we both enjoyed and one that had ended between the sheets more than once.

"I know you didn't. One of the men... It was as though he could see me." I turned and faced Alkippe and sighed happily as she moved the sponge over my stomach and breasts. "But that's not all, Kip. After the vision, I saw the goddess. Right there in the grove, watching me."

Alkippe's hand stilled. "If so, you should tell your mother these tidings. The gods only wander among us if there is something in it for them." She frowned and continued sponging, though far faster.

"You're right, of course. I'll go see Mother, if she's not busy being berated or mounted by Father."

Alkippe finished drying me and slipped a new linen shift over my head. "You shouldn't say such things. You know it fuels his distrust and anger to hear you speak in such a way. And it infuriates your brother all the more."

"I'll speak when I want to, and no man will tell me I can't simply because they feel themselves superior. The gods don't hold themselves higher than the goddesses. Why should we do differently than they do?"

"Shush! Don't, Medea. You know better than to compare yourself to the gods. You know what they can do, how terrible they can be to those who would rise above their station."

I leaned against the window. Below the temple sat the palace, a group of large wooden buildings surrounded by a massive wall. My family lived in the largest, full of rooms where they could spend the days avoiding one another. The outside, painted with beautiful red designs, was a stark contrast to the dim, quiet interior. And beyond that was the city, where the people of the kingdom of Aia lived out their daily, simple lives far below both the temple and the palace. The colourful city buildings went right down to the river's edge, where small boats docked and left. I and my sister had enjoyed playing with a small skiff on the river before I'd been sent to the temple and even now, surrounded by dense earth and whispering trees, I could remember the feel of the water beneath me, bucking and churning, ready to wash me away to new lands or pull me into its depths. I shivered again as the image of the strangers flashed before me.

"Change is coming, Kip. I can feel it in my blood."

CHAPTER THREE
Strangers

"I DON'T KNOW. YET again, I don't know." I threw my hands up in frustration. Would he never listen?

"You must. The gods wouldn't give you so little information. You're being stubborn, as always. I demand you tell me why they're coming. I swear by the goddess I'll have you beaten if you say nothing further."

I spun to face my brother. "You? *You* would have me beaten, would you, brother? And who are you? A fledgling prince, barely grown, under his father's thumb. A boy with nothing to recommend him would demand the beating of a priestess of the goddess, because I shared my vision and it isn't good enough for you?" I stepped close enough to smell his rank breath, my unusual height allowing me to meet him eye to eye, something I knew he despised. "Even you wouldn't dare, brother."

The thick silence hung for a moment as I stared into his angry, mud-hued eyes. Beneath the burning hatred, beneath the anger, I saw fear. I could feel it vibrating from deep within him. "What is it you fear?" I murmured, searching his expression for answers.

His palm came up, and I refused to flinch. I'd taken enough blows at his hand to know bruises healed but respect was harder won. Fear created bullies in men who might not be such and kept women from speaking as they ought. I'd long ago decided fear had no place in my world. His jaw clenched in anger, and we stood frozen, neither willing to back away first, and I knew the only reason he didn't strike was because we had an audience. But with his hand ready, he couldn't lower it without losing face either. I gave him the faintest grin, knowing I'd won.

"Enough." My father stood and waved us apart. "Do you at least know when they're arriving?"

I finally looked away from my brother's hard gaze and turned to my father's scornful one. "Within the fortnight. The leader is fair; he doesn't look like the usual traders from the east. They'll put ashore below the village."

"Very well. I'll send scouts along the shoreline and see if we can garner information. If you should deign to provide more information, it would be appreciated." He turned to Absyrtos. "Come. We'll question the artisans first. They always seem to have information."

He swept from the room without looking back, clearly expecting my brother to follow. Absyrtos stepped close, his jaw clenched. "Watch yourself, little sister. You haven't won yet."

"What is there to win? I've never known what we're competing for."

For a flicker of a second, his guard slipped, and I saw the boy I'd once known, a boy who played in the woods and laughed freely, though rarely if I was around. He looked desperate, as though he would say more. But the moment passed, quickly submerged beneath the usual façade of insouciance.

"That's because everyone is afraid of you, Medea. Since you showed what an unnatural creature you are, they've always feared to tell you all they know. But not me. I'm not afraid of you, and I will fight for my life when the time comes."

Taking a chance, I placed my hand on his arm. "I don't understand. If you would just explain—"

"The time for that is long gone."

He shook off my hand and I winced at the expression on his face, an image of my father's. He left without a glance, leaving me puzzled and frustrated. I startled when there was a light touch on my back. I'd forgotten my mother was in the room.

"The gods have their own plans, daughter. We do but live the lives they've set before us to play their games."

I put my arm around my mother's slight waist. The rare times we spent together made clear our differences. My lovely mother, so slight, so retiring, so submissive to my father was my opposite in every way, and it was hard to believe she'd given birth to me. And yet, I could feel the tides in my blood as surely as my sea nymph mother could. "I know that better than anyone in this house, Mother. But it doesn't mean we shouldn't try to live as well as we can and hope we can escape their notice for as long as possible."

My mother's smile was sad. "Daughter, you were never beyond their reach. Before you were born, we knew you were their own tool..." She drifted off, as she was wont to do, looking like she was staring at a horizon no one else could see.

I gripped her shoulders. "What? What does that mean? Was there an oracle? Is that why Absyrtos hates me so?"

My mother refused to meet my eyes, and she rested her hands on top of mine. "Come with me, daughter. It is beyond time you knew. If your father found out I told you, he'd be furious with me, so you must keep the knowledge to yourself. But I feel this vision means more than even he can fathom. You must be ready."

I followed my mother down the long hall and across the dirt courtyard to the women's quarters. This was the moment of knowledge. Whatever I was about to find out would change things. So why did I want to run, to block the words? When we were seated with cool drinks, my mother waved the servant girls away. She was lost in thought for some time, but I knew better than to try and get my mother to speak before she was ready. The creatures of the water have their own timing.

"You know that when I married your father, I was given no choice. My father decided I would marry a mortal king after he received a grand sacrifice, and so I did. Believe it or not, your father wasn't always so...well, what he is. When we married, he was young, full of ideas. It was later, after Absyrtos was born, that he changed."

"After a prophecy?"

She sighed. "Yes. When the gods gifted us with the golden

fleece from Thessalonia, it came with a prophecy. The kingdom would only stay in the family as long as we kept the fleece. If it were stolen or lost, terrible tragedy would visit our first-born son, and our daughter would be the cause." She wiped tears from her eyes, which had turned the eerie watery blue of the shallow sea at sunrise, as they always did when she was emotional. "We were told that sending our daughter away would do no good, as the gods' plans would unfold no matter our actions. Sadly, we were told nothing else, and your father decided that when your brother was old enough, he would know what was foretold as a way to protect himself from whatever might come to pass. Absyrtos has always assumed you would be his downfall, though we've never known that for certain. We considered your sister, of course, but she's too much like me to be a threat. You, however." She twirled a piece of my hair around her finger, the dark earth contrasting with the pale moon. "You have always been more like the goddess you serve than any woman living in your father's house."

I contemplated my mother's words, unsure what to say. What does one say when it's revealed you're to be the destruction of your family? "Why wasn't I told, Mother? Perhaps I could have done something differently. Prayed to the goddess for change or left to live elsewhere? At the very least I would have understood why my own brother despises me so."

My mother was already shaking her head, the tears flowing freely. "The gods set our fates. If you are to fulfil the prophecy, then we will deal with it as we must, and nothing you could do would keep it from happening. It could be that it doesn't come to fruition for many years. But if the goddess walks among us and you've had such a clear vision of strangers, then you must be ready."

"But ready for what? I don't understand."

"Nor do we. I must go and see to dinner. Return to the temple and pray for guidance. Perhaps the goddess will be merciful." She splashed cold water on her face to wash away the remnants of her tears, though the sadness remained. Her eyes faded back to their usual afternoon sky blue. "Know this, daughter. I do not hold you responsible for what is to come. We are but pawns and as women, even more so. Whatever happens is their will, and I will forgive you whatever you do at their behest."

She held up her hand to silence me when I would have spoken and left the room silently, leaving me more alone than I'd ever been.

***

"They're here!"

Chaliope came racing into the room, her hair loose and her robes flying wildly around her. Two years younger than me, she was the essence of spring, of beauty and optimism, and life. Where I was earth, my sister was water like our mother, always able to flow around our father and brother's tempers, soothing them with her sweet laughter and kind spirit. She was also already betrothed and unlike me, she saw it as a fresh journey and was glad to make a good match for our family. I saw marriage as another cage, a transfer from one prison to another. As a priestess, I had the freedom to wander the woods, to visit the market, and walk among men without fear of reprisal because I served the goddess. The goddess and the mother priestess were the only beings to whom I need answer, which gave me a sort of freedom. And I would choose freedom over anything else. My mother had once said neither the sun nor the ocean could be tamed, and as I was a daughter of both, I would be twice as fierce and equally untameable. I don't believe she meant it as a compliment, but I took it as one just the same.

My sister disappeared as the room swam and jerked. Instead of the cloth-covered walls of my room, I was in the sun-dappled oak grove halfway to the palace. The group of men followed a sheep herder leading them up the hill, the canopy blocking out the unusual heat of the day. At the entrance to the sacred grove, their fair-haired leader stopped and pointed.

"What in god's name is that, man?"

The sheep herder looked up. "What mean you?"

"That...thing, hanging there, wrapped in linen. Is that a man?"

"Of course. You handle your dead in another manner? Like butterflies, we prepare ours to fly once they have shed their spirit."

The men stared at the several dead hanging from the trees in their thick linen cocoons and were visibly taken aback. They moved carefully past, sure not to touch the lightly swaying masses.

Their leader looked distressed. "We would not handle our dead so. How can their spirits rest if left unburned? Are you not harried by them because they cannot cross over?"

The herder stared at the stranger, uncomprehending. Without responding, he turned away and continued up the path with the men following closely behind him.

Spinning, shunting, the room came back into focus, and I opened my eyes to find my sister kneeling beside me, a bowl ready for the inevitable retching. She wiped my brow with a cool cloth and gave me water to rinse my mouth.

"Did you see them?" she asked.

"They're at the grove. Does Father know?"

"He received word as soon as they were spotted off the coast. He's readying the palace, but he says sending an envoy to meet them shows weakness. He says they must come to him."

"Help me up. I must go to the palace."

My sister helped me up, brushed away the dirt from my skirt and smoothed the creases out. "Wait. Let me dress your hair quickly."

I sat and closed my eyes, trying to get my stomach to stop churning. Anticipation rode me hard, and I clasped my hands tightly to keep them still. My sister was expert at taming my wild hair, her way soft and skilled. Few others would touch me at all, afraid of inviting the god's attention. Or that of my father and brother. Or even my own, which could be as volatile as a meeting of the sun and the ocean, overseen by the goddess of the underworld I served. A woman thrice touched by the gods wasn't someone you invited for wine. Sometimes it was lonely, but mostly I enjoyed the sense of power it gave me.

"Done. Can I come too?"

"Silly swan. You know father wouldn't allow that. But use our secret spot, the one we had as children. You should be able to see from there, and I think you're still small enough to fit as you did when we were little. Stay quiet." I caressed my sister's face fondly. "And remember that I love you, above all."

Chaliope hugged me tightly and together we made our way to the palace. Once there, I continued into the main hall, and my sister skirted the walls and entered the tiny hidden passageway that led to the small alcove. What I wouldn't have given to trade places with her as I felt the battering wills of the gods beginning their assault. My skin was on fire, energy threatening to burst from my hands, and I felt too small.

I steeled myself and stepped inside. My father and mother were on their thrones, talking softly. My brother stood to the side, his palm white-gripped on the sword resting on his hip, his jaw working as he ground his teeth. His eyes were tight, angry. Scared. And though I now understood what there was to fear, I still couldn't quite forgive him his brutality over the years. Fear need not make a man a monster.

"Father," I said, bowing my head slightly to appease him. "I understand the strangers are on their way."

"Yes. Stand behind your mother. I want to know what the goddess says, if she chooses to reveal anything about our visitors. I'm told they're Thessalonian. Men who would come so far must have good reason indeed."

"Of course." I refrained from saying the goddess didn't speak simply because he wished her to. But the air crackled with possibility, with change and expectation, like the wood walls were alive with it. My mother's eyes were wide and fearful, my father's sneer more devious than usual, the crease between his brows more pronounced.

A shadow passed in front of the door, and eerie gold eyes looked directly at me before disappearing. My mother made a tiny noise of distress and gripped the chair rests. Although we'd only spoken about it a few times, I knew my mother had been given gifts she'd chosen to deny, though she'd never said why. That she'd seen the goddess told me whatever was about to happen involved my mother as well. I gently rested a hand on her shoulder and was glad when she let go of the chair to rest her hand on mine. We would face whatever followed the goddess through that door, together.

Chapter Four
Hospitality

"Welcome to our home. Be greeted as my honoured guests. Eat at my table. After, we will discuss your reasons for coming to a shore so far from your own."

The strangers nodded respectfully and move to the tables laden with food. They were quickly surrounded by my father's advisors and the nobility. The laws of hospitality meant no one could ask the strangers their reason for being there before they'd eaten at their host's table, but suspense hung heavy in the air. When they'd entered, I'd kept my eyes on the ground, unable to look at the man who could change the course of my life. Somehow, I knew that if I looked at him directly, things would be beyond my control, and as much as I wanted something more than life in the temple, if events were being dictated by the dark goddess I served, the journey would be hard. The damp on my palms and the moisture on the back of my neck said I wasn't as ready as I wanted to be. *Fear is weakness. I will not be afraid. I will not.* I repeated it over and over, a chant, a prayer, a plea.

"Well?" My father spoke softly without looking at me.

"Nothing yet, Father."

He grimaced and gave me an irritated glance. My father was given a platter of food, which he ate quickly and efficiently, without spilling a crumb. My brother, standing behind my father, waved the plate of food away. His eyes narrowed as he watched the strangers converse with the Kolchian nobles. His expression changed from guarded to furious and back again. He clearly struggled to stay still. My mother's expression revealed nothing, though she seemed like a puddle, small and still, boneless in her obvious wish to be anywhere else. While my mother's emotions were usually clear, at the moment, her eyes were their normal blue and her mouth was neither glad nor grim. The only suggestion of her inner turmoil was the death grip she kept on the arm of her chair.

The feasting slowed and the hall quieted in anticipation. My knees went weak when I heard a chair scraped back in the silence of the room. The fair one stood, and he glowed with the radiance of the god-touched. I couldn't look away.

"Good King Aeëtes. Thank you for the generous feast you have provided. If you will indulge me, I will explain our presence in your kingdom. I am Jason, prince of Iolcos, kingdom of Thessaly, and I have sailed here on the Argo, a ship gifted to me by the goddess and built from the sacred oak from her forest. My men are the Argonauts, strong sailors who have pledged to make this dangerous journey with me. Together, we have sailed hard to get here, facing rocks that move, monsters on shore, and sirens who tried to sink our ship. They are brave men any leader would be proud to sail with."

He motioned at the men seated around him, and I saw their devotion in their eyes.

"I was raised by Chiron, wise centaur of the forest, because a prophecy foretold my uncertain path. In an effort to save me, my father had sent me away. But while I was gone, my uncle forced my father from the throne and took it for himself. When it was time, Chiron sent me to reclaim my throne, as the oracle said I must. My uncle has promised the return of my throne on the condition that I bring the golden fleece back to Iolcos, from whence it was borne by Phrixus and Helene. You, King Aeëtes, are my distant cousin through good Phrixus, who was borne here by the god's will on the back of the golden ram, though our cousin Helene fell to the waters below, to my mother's eternal lament. I apply to you, on the bonds of family, to gift me the fleece so I may return and claim my throne, as is my right. In return, the warriors of Iolcos will fight at your side against the Scythians, whom we have been told harass your borders and murder your people. We will help you defeat them, if only you will grant us what we seek."

A tsunami of emotion gathered in the silent room. All faces were turned to the king, waiting for the wave to break. It was a simple, plain speech without artifice, and it wouldn't be nearly enough.

My father stood slowly, his face a thunderstorm. "You dare? You dare come to my palace seeking what is rightfully mine, because you are unable to fight for your throne as a true king would? If it weren't for the laws of hospitality directed by the gods, I would have your tongues ripped out and your sword hands fed to my dogs. But I will not incur the wrath of the gods by breaking their laws. Leave. Go back to your boat, and do not step foot on the shore of my kingdom again. If you do, I will be within my rights to send you all to the underworld."

In the ensuing silence, I looked at Jason of Iolcos and found him looking directly at me, as though waiting for my intercession. Behind him the shadow of the goddess gestured towards me, and when Jason raised his hand, the others in the room saw a gesture of supplication to the king. But I saw it for what it was, a request for me to move to his side. I stayed in place, though my chest ached and my limbs trembled, pulled by a million threads that connected our souls. I wouldn't give up control, not without understanding what I was agreeing to. Desire, passionate and terrible, flooded my body and the urge to go to him was physically punishing. My mother turned over her hand and I took it, drawing strength from her calm assurance. She must surely see what I did, and she was letting me know I wasn't alone.

When I refused his simple demand, when the goddess faded behind him, he lowered his hand and returned his gaze to the king. "We will go. No offence was intended. Thank you for your hospitality." Jason bowed slightly and backed away, his shoulders stiff and his jaw working. He motioned and the rest of the Argonauts followed him from the hall. A chaos of noise erupted the moment they were gone, and my body trembled with exhaustion. Fighting gods was not meant for mortal flesh.

"Kill them all before they return to their ship. Be done with them." Absyrtos stepped forwards, his sword half drawn. "I will take men and do it myself."

My father turned to me. "Now. What says the goddess?"

I closed my eyes and tried to think past the desire to run after Jason. I focused instead on the politics of the situation. "If you kill him, you invite the gods' anger. He is favoured, and a goddess stands with him. But sending him away without entertaining his request makes you seem intractable. You must test him. If you do so and he fails, you have not violated the laws of hospitality, and you've given him a chance to claim the prize he seeks. If he passes the test, you must abide by the rules you set or incur the wrath of the gods." I opened my eyes, unsure if the words had been mine or someone else's.

My father considered my suggestion, his gaze on the far wall, and I wondered if he was trying to see beyond the oracle foretelling our family's disaster.

"Very well, I will devise tests and make certain of his failure. Send an envoy to tell them I've reconsidered and will allow them the chance to gain what they seek."

I intervened, sensing the foolishness of the idea. "If you send an envoy, they will fear attack. Allow myself and other priestesses from the temple to inform them. Tell me what tasks you will assign him, and I will relay your message."

My brother's rage nearly kept him from being able to speak at all and he sputtered. "You? Send a woman to deal with men from a foreign land, whom we are set to kill anyway? You are clearly mad. Surely you won't listen to her, Father?"

Father stared at me for a long moment, clearly searching my expression for betrayal. He frowned and waved my brother aside. "He will yoke the fire-breathing bulls. He will sow the seeds of dragon's teeth in the field, and when the dragon's teeth give birth to the men of earth, he will slay them all. If he fails in any of these, he dies. If he succeeds, he may have the fleece." He stood and clapped his hand on my brother's shoulder. "He will not succeed. And if, for any reason it looks like he will, you will make certain he and his men die before they leave these shores. I will do what I must to keep the gods happy, but if I have to suffer their wrath because I want to keep my kingdom, then so be it." He turned to me and held up his finger in warning. "Make sure the guardian is well. If this stranger is truly favoured by the gods, he could pass the trials. But you can make certain the guardian is ready. No matter what, he does not leave our shores."

Absyrtos smiled, a mirror image of my father. "As you will it."

"That kind of treachery will not please the goddess." I wrapped my arms around myself, god-touched desire flaming through me, painful and unwelcome.

And unexpectedly exciting.

"Then he had better die in the tests, hadn't he?"

CHAPTER FIVE
Meeting

I MADE MY WAY down the forest path to the shore, quickly skirting the narrow stone streets. My sister and two young priestesses followed behind. Shadows shifted and blurred, and I knew we weren't entirely among the mortals. We left the shabby line of houses and moved into the soft reedy areas near the shore. I stopped and turned to the women behind me. "Wait here. I will go to him alone."

Chaliope grasped my gown. "Surely not? You cannot go among strange men alone. Our father and brother would not approve."

"When did I last seek their approval? And equally, I would not subject any of you to possible harm, though I do not believe they would do so."

"Please, sister. Bring the leader to the temple and tell him there. He will not threaten you if he is alone, and surely even strangers would not anger the goddess by distressing her priestess in her own temple."

I looked closely at my sister. Chaliope wasn't a worrier nor did she usually have any interest in strategy. When I stared into my sister's eyes, another looked out at me. Chilled, I looked away.

"Very well. All three of you, ask to speak to their prince. Tell him to meet me at the temple. I will ready myself there."

We separated, and I got a last glimpse of my sister's unearthly eyes before the women made their way to the men camped on the shore by their boat. I hugged myself against the cold inside me as I made my way through the sultry night to the temple. My life was in the hands of the goddess now, but I would try my best to keep my wits about me. *What game do you play? And why do you use me to play it?*

Because you are the key. And as my priestess, you do my will.

I gasped as the words whispered through my mind. To hear a goddess's voice in your head is to hear thunder in a cave. Yet, I stood my ground. Fear is an enemy, no matter who you're facing. *I don't wish to be anyone's key to anything. I am my own.*

Tinkling laughter, at odds with the undercurrent of malice behind it, was like fingernails on granite. *Your own? Or your father's? Your brother's? You serve me, and if you serve me now, you will know true freedom. You will fly your father's palace and know what it is to move freely through the world, just as a man does. Serve me, and I will give you freedom. Your name will be known on every shore. Deny me and end up a carcass hanging in the trees for the birds to feast upon.*

The feeling, and the voice, faded. The temple I'd served for most of my life, a sanctuary from my family, suddenly felt ominous and promising. Freedom. A man's freedom, no less. To be away from my father and brother, to sail and live as a bird on the wind.

The rustle of branches was quickly followed by the scent of crushed pine.

"Princess Medea? I understand you have words from your father?"

Steeling myself, I turned to face him, only to find him on his knees, staring at me with his palms up in supplication. My heart lurched, and I nearly dropped to my knees with him.

"Princess, I believe you felt it too. You know the goddess has brought us together. I know it. I felt it the moment I saw you in your father's hall. I've seen you in my dreams, and I know that you are the key to my destiny. Will you help me, princess? For surely I am lost without you."

Pity gripped me, and though I knew it was not my natural feeling, I gave in to it. "You are to face three trials. I can help you pass them all, and I can get you past the guardian who watches over the fleece. With the knowledge the goddess has given me, I will help you."

He held the bottom of my robe to his mouth and kissed it fervently. "May the gods bless you and give you all you desire, princess. I will make your name known throughout Thessalonia, and you will be immortalized."

I studied him like a witch studies the mushrooms under a full moon to see if they're what she wants. Moonlight slid off his hair like liquid gold, and his fair blue eyes seemed kind. Key. I was the goddess's key, and now he wanted me to be his as well. If someone was always using me for their own purposes, what freedom would I truly have?

Better than marriage. Better than trapped within temple walls as you decay, day after day, until you are nothing and have never been anything.

The words were chilling, filled with dark promise, and they made me consider my own words in return. "I will help you, but you must take me with you when you go. For my father would surely kill me if my brother did not do so first. I heard your tales at dinner, about your travels here and some of the horrors you had to overcome. I can help you with those trials on the way back, if you'll take me with you."

An unnatural breeze stirred the leaves, and when he looked up at me again, I recognized the goddess's touch in his eyes. "Yes. Of course, I will take you with me. You will come to Iolcos and be my honoured guest, always. For your beauty would stir the loins of a man without sight and your wisdom shame even the most learned of the wise."

I heated at his words, though I knew them to be god spoken and false. In Aia, the priestesses were untouchable, virgins who served the goddess and no man. I could marry if I chose, but I never wanted to be a pawn, traded to a man's bed for a bit of land. But to be wanted, with the kind of passion I heard the servant girls whispering of in their beds at night, the kind of passion I occasionally shared with Alkippe in the darkest of moonless nights...

"Come with me." I turned, expecting him to follow.

I led the way through the dense wood around the back of the temple and into a long-forgotten hidden passageway I'd discovered when I was a child roaming the temple on my own. It opened into the small courtyard near my private rooms, which I was accorded as a senior priestess as well as a princess of the palace. We moved silently, both barely daring to breathe. A man in my private quarters would mean death should anyone find out. But the goddess wanted this, so surely we were protected.

Once in my room, I closed and locked the door. "I must prepare some things for you. When you have completed the trials, my father will set a feast for you and promise you the fleece when we gather for the evening meal. But he has ordered your death before you lay hand to the fleece, so the first moment you are alone, you must meet me, and I will take you to the fleece."

I poured herbs and unguents into a bowl and mashed them together fiercely, thinking quickly. "Your first task will be to yoke my father's fire breathing bulls. Wear this on your skin, and they won't be able to get their horns on you. It will deflect their fire, but only for a short time, so you must move quickly. Once you've yoked them, you will use them to plough the field and plant these." I held up a bag. "They are dragon's teeth. When planted, they will grow into warriors of the earth who will try to kill you. Throw a boulder in their midst, and they will grow confused and fight one another. When they do so, kill them all."

I handed him the potion, though he looked bemused. "Once you have accomplished those three things, you will have passed my father's trials and he will have no choice but to honour his offer. But know this," I said and looked him in the eye, "the oracle told my father he would rule only so long as he held the fleece. If you take it from him, someone else will rule in his place. Breaking the laws of hospitality is worth the price of keeping his kingdom. But to keep the goddess happy, you must abide by his challenge and so not break the laws yourself."

Jason watched me quietly. "You are truly a wonder, Princess Medea. I will honour you, always."

As with his other words, they felt false and empty. "Do not make promises you cannot keep. But you must take me with you. Now, return to your ship. Be at the palace at first light. The moment you have completed the trials, meet me here, and I will take you to the fleece. We will have little time, for my brother will be upon you the moment my father lets go his leash. I will bring what small riches are my own, as well as my handmaid."

He took my hand and kissed my knuckles, his hands callused and large. "I will do all you say, and more. Trust in me to be true."

He turned and disappeared into the woods.

Freedom. Can you feel it coming for you?

I closed my eyes and tried to block out the voice. Until I was far from my own shores, I would not let myself believe.

CHAPTER SIX
Escape

THE CROWD ROARED AND stomped and dust flew from beneath their sandals, creating clouds of noisy chaos. It seemed as though all of Aia had shown up to watch the strange foreign man die for having the gall to ask for their country's precious fleece, which none of them had ever seen. For, of course, word had spread throughout the kingdom that the fleece was the reason the strangers had journeyed to the edge of the world they knew. At least part of the oracle that had defined my life was about to come true, and there was no question now of which people knew and which didn't. Those from the palace stepped back when I drew near and wouldn't meet my eyes. I'd known them all my life, and now they were strangers. I'd been promised freedom but right now, only terror filled me at the thought of the unknown racing towards me like an inferno.

I stood behind my father's throne, fear roiling my stomach. If Jason missed a spot on his body, the bull could gore him. If he died, however, no one would ever know I had tried to help him. I would be safe. Trapped within the kingdom and under my male family members' hands, yes, but safe within the confines of temple life. And the oracle would have been proven wrong...but what would that mean for me? If, on the other hand, Jason succeeded, my father would surely wonder if I had helped him in some way, and my life would change forever. Not only would I have to flee, but I would also be leaving my home, my family, my temple, everything I'd ever known and loved. I watched the prince stride confidently onto the sands of the stadium, and never before had I been so unsure what outcome to hope for.

The passion I felt for him had waned with his distance. Now, as he stood waiting for the bulls to be released from behind the enormous iron gates, my heart stirred and my breath caught at his beauty, at the wide, smooth expanse of his naked back and his firm, taut legs below the sand-coloured chiton. I found women's forms more pleasing, generally, but in Jason I saw the truest form of male beauty.

Distantly, the thought crossed my mind that those feelings were not my own, but as soon as it occurred to me, it fled, leaving only a mist of desire in its wake.

The iron gates began to lift, and the crowd quieted in anticipation. Aeëtes' bulls were renowned for their fire-breathing and ferocity but rarely were they seen. When the gates were high enough, the beasts came raging forth, their hooves covered in iron, their heads encased in heavy metal hoods, and fire streaming from their nostrils, looking like the bastard pets of Hades himself. They charged and Jason spun to the right, the massive horns sliding over his glistening skin and leaving barely a red skim mark. Father leaned forwards and scowled. The bulls charged again, and Jason whirled away yet again, his movement as lithe as any dancer, graceful and smooth like water as he waited for the right moment. When it came, he made it look effortless as he swung the yoke over one bull, then the other. He jumped in the chariot attached to the yoke and waved to the king. The king held out his hand to indicate the direction of the field to be ploughed, and Jason raced away.

When everyone's attention was focused on following the prince, my father spun to face me. "What have you done?" He gripped my arms tightly, making me wince. "Have you betrayed us, witch?"

I stared back at him, unflinching. "Can you not see that he is goddess-touched? That she stays at his side and guards him? What power could I possibly have that would make a man move so swiftly and easily? There is no knowledge in the temple that could give the kind of gift only the gods may bestow. This is not my doing."

He shoved me away. "Then go pray to your goddess and ask that she remove her favour from the pale stranger. If I have to kill him, at least the gods will know we prayed for it to be otherwise."

I refused to look at my brother, but I could sense his smug satisfaction as he followed our father from the stadium to the fields.

"Medea, come. We will go to the temple together. If the goddess walks at his side, then there is no more you can do. We will pray and wait for news."

My mother took my hand and led me from the stadium. I looked over my shoulder and saw the chariot racing away in the distance. Beside Jason, the goddess stood ethereal, a glowing giant among insects who couldn't even see her.

You don't need me. He has you to help him through the trials. I sent the thought out, a prayer as much as a plea, a demand to be let go, and strangely, I knew she'd hear me. I followed my mother down the wooded path, and I paid attention to the feel of the dense earth beneath my sandals, the heavy oak rustling overhead, the scent of woodland on the breeze, the sound of the rushing river below them. I wanted to remember everything, down to the colour of the pebbles and the whisper of the willows as they spoke to the water below them.

You will serve my purpose for many years to come. Do not question.

I closed my eyes and stumbled. *What freedom do you offer if I'm never to be free?*

You would be free of the goddess you serve? Do you take the vows you made so lightly?

I stayed silent. There was no answer to give. The vows I'd made to serve the temple were given freely. Temple life meant a certain amount of freedom compared to life in the palace. And when I had made those vows on the night of Thesmophoria, dedicating my life to temple service, it was freedom I had been thinking of, not so much of the goddess. Clearly there was a price to be paid, and I and the Thessalonian prince were pieces in a game that mortals could never hope to understand. I reached out and pulled my mother to a stop. I hugged her tightly to me and let my tears fall. My mother held me before pulling away to look at me.

"Remember, daughter, that you are the granddaughter of the sun god, but so are you the granddaughter of the sea god and daughter of a sea nymph. I wasn't gifted your visions, but I know when the gods walk among us. Whatever is about to happen, bear it the way you have always borne your life here: with courage, strength, and knowing your own will. The gods may use you, but you can perhaps carve something out of their plans for yourself, the way water will shape the stone that attempts to block it." She kissed my hands, her tears cold as they slid over my wrists. "Know that you are always my beloved daughter, no matter what the heavens rain down on us."

We walked hand in hand to the temple, where we knelt and prayed, but I noticed my mother speaking to Alkippe, who glanced at me, wide-eyed, before moving swiftly off to do my mother's bidding.

Not long after, as my knees began to ache, bells brought us to our feet and a breathless messenger stumbled through the doorway. "He did it. The stranger passed all the trials. They're going to feast him tonight, and the king will hand over the fleece as promised." The man turned and left as suddenly as he had come.

I kissed my mother's cheek. "I must go. Remember me well, Mother."

CHAPTER SEVEN
Medus

Today, an old woman.

THE WALLS OF THE temple hadn't changed since the day I'd left them behind as a young woman. Unlike then, the skin on my hands was looser, with more lines and the dark spots of age. I opened the temple doors and stepped inside the cool, dim room. The massive stone altar sat stark in the centre of the room, the grooves in the floor at its base dyed rust red through years of sacrificial blood running down the runnels to the grove outside the temple, where it returned to the earth to nourish the plants that gave the temple food. Such was the way of the goddess.

I knelt before the altar, the earth hard beneath my aching knees. I raised my hands, palm up, in a motion I felt I'd been making since my birth. It had long been an empty gesture, made only so I didn't face further retribution and not because I venerated the gods whom I'd served. Those days were past. *I am here to do your bidding.* For the first time in many years, I received a response.

What bidding would you do? You have served your purpose. Your son is on the throne, and you are where you began. Your time is done, and we have made certain your name will live in men's memories forever. Others are serving our purpose now.

I rocked back on my heels. Done? I had been in the service of the gods, doing their will for so long, that I didn't fully understand what that meant. Though they'd mostly left me alone since the night of my everlasting nightmares, I'd always felt tied to them, felt them under my skin.

I'm free? You release me from service?

There was no answer. For the first time in my life, I felt...alone. Completely and wonderfully, terrifyingly alone. There was no waiting, no anticipation, or sacred breath on the back of my neck. No pressure on my shoulders, pushing me ever forward to do what must be done. Not only in the service of the gods, no, but to further my aims as well, of course. Of course. But those two things seemed to go hand in hand more often than not. Where they led me to do their will, I found a way to make it gainful for myself. For a while, it had been for the gain of my family. But then that had all come crashing down, like so much stone after the raids and earth shaking. After that terrible day, as I fled Corinth for my life, I had seen it in a vision at the temple. The people, the village, even the animals, all wiped out by the invaders who would follow the breaking apart of the earth and the fire falling from the sky, bringing with them centuries of darkness, spoiling everything the Thessalonians thought fine. My part in it, the blood that stained my dreams, was barely a grain of sand in the shores of eternity.

Free. It was all I had desired, once. To be free to live, to fly and explore. I had given up everything. Everyone. But in my search for freedom, I had found power, and when one had enough power, one had all the freedom they could devour. I learned to wield that power, to caress and mould it, to hoard and develop it. But ultimately, I paid the price, over and over again. I'd been given visions of what would come but nothing of the terrible cruelty the gods would punish me with for demanding they let me go. Had I known, I would have fought them. I would have tried to find another way. Not that anyone who fought the gods won. The wyrd sisters began weaving a human's shroud the moment they were born, and only they knew what threads crossed and which would be cut. Cut so soon.

I looked around the empty, cavernous room and saw it for what it was. A dark, damp cave with a massive piece of stained old stone in the middle of the earthen floor. Carved figures sat in niches around the room, their likeness to the goddess minimal. Empty of the goddess's presence, it was a room like any other in the palace but even more barren. I closed my eyes. Empty. Like the temple, I was bereft of the goddess. Now *I* was a used chalice, stained and with no hope of ever being full again.

I stood, shaking and tired, and left the temple. Standing in the sun, I thought that freedom tasted sour, like berries left too long on the tree. What was I if no longer a vessel to the goddess? My son was on the throne and needed my council only when I forced it on him. I was the mother of a king in the kingdom I had abandoned in search of freedom. Now, I had the freedom I always wanted, but it was too late to do anything with it. The goddess had kept her promise, but the price had been too high and too long in coming.

***

Medus reclined on a couch in the courtyard like a young, indolent god waiting for a new game. He looked so like his father, the king of Athens, that a brief pain surged through my chest. I hadn't loved Aegeus, but he had been strong and kind at a time when most anyone else would have turned me away. And he'd given me the son to replace the one I had lost.

Lost. I pushed the thought away.

Medus should have ruled Athens after his father, but then Theseus had shown up, a man ready to follow his father's rule, and although I had tried to keep it from happening, the fates were set against me. I'd left with my head held high, as I'd been the queen of Athens briefly, and no one could take that from me, but this time I'd taken my child with me. When we reached the boat, I had a vision of Egrisi, and I'd known it was time for me to take my son home. Over the years in Athens, word had reached me occasionally about the things happening in my homeland. My beloved sister, Chaliope, had moved to her new kingdom with the husband she had been betrothed to when I left, and she, of all of us, had been left alone by the gods to live in mortal contentment. She had a bevy of children running through her home, her husband cherished her despite the darkness that surrounded her god-touched family, and she remained blissfully unaware of what it meant to be used as a pawn in a game too large for human understanding. Of the two of us, I have often wondered which of us gained the freedom I coveted.

"You will get fat and lazy," I said to my son, watching the way he caressed the leg of the slave girl sitting beside him. I waved the girl away, and my son watched her go with lust in his eyes.

"I am quite sure you will keep that from happening, Mother. What brings you here on this fine day? Am I to meet another pig farmer who has a land dispute with the goat herder? Or shall I put on my ceremonial robes and meet with the councillors to discuss trade with the East? What is your will, dear Mother?"

His deceivingly respectful tone made me wince internally, but I wouldn't show it. If there was one thing I'd taught my son, it was to spot weakness and feed on it until you got what you wanted. I would not show him how strangely weak, how adrift I felt knowing the goddess had left me. I watched him eye the serving girl and realized I needed to give him something to keep him occupied. Perhaps a quest, like the one that had brought Jason to my doorstep and overturned my world. There were rumours of heroic journeys being taken by young men everywhere these days. It had been Jason's nature to journey, to seek. I looked at my son and tried to divine his true nature. He lacked the kindness of his father or my ambition. In fact, he was more like his uncle, my brother Absyrtos, with his penchant for cruelty and his quick temper. If my brother hadn't died... No. That wasn't right. He didn't just die. I had murdered him, as surely as I had murdered the others. With the goddess gone, it was time to accept what I had done.

If I hadn't murdered my brother, what would he have become? If he hadn't known I was going to, from the time I was born, would he have been so angry? So cruel? Had there been anything redeeming in the monster he had been? As I saw his likeness in my son, I doubted it. I should have left Medus in Athens. Between the king and Theseus, maybe he would have turned into something more than the spoiled wretch that lay before me. If I sent him away, I could set the kingdom to rights. I could rule in his place while he went on a journey that would either make him grow up or kill him. Either way, he would be better off.

CHAPTER EIGHT
Flight

My youth, when I made my choice.

JASON WAS WAITING IN the shadows outside the temple when I emerged, leaving my mother behind. I took his large, rough hand and led him down the forested path hidden behind the temple. Neither of us spoke. He was covered in sweat and mud from the trials, but he was glowing as a man victorious and powerful, confident in his ability to overcome even things not of this world. His hand fit perfectly in my own and I wondered if he thought so too.

We came around a corner to an open field with a single massive willow tree in the middle. Curled around its base was the pet snake given us by the gods, covered in black and red diamond scales, its massive triangular head resting on a fallen branch. It was longer than two galleys and larger than two men standing on each other's shoulders. It was magnificent. Jason stopped and pulled me so my back rested against his chest.

"What is this? Another trial? Are you loyal to your father after all and would feed me to the beast?" he whispered fiercely and his hand crushed mine.

I pressed against him, liking the way he felt solid, like a tree, and spoke softly. "If I wanted you dead, I wouldn't have helped you at all, silly man. And you will find no trial here. I am a priestess of the goddess, and this snake has known me from a child. I will charm it, and while I do so, you will climb the tree and take the fleece. When it's done, go back to your ship and be ready to sail the moment I arrive, for we will have little time." I squeezed his hand in return and heard his surprised intake of breath at my own strength. "But do not play me false, hero. For if you do, the gods will not be pleased, and I will see to it that you do not make it home." I felt his slight tremor and understood, for perhaps the first time, the truth behind my power.

"I will wait for you to arrive, unless your father's men come down on me and I must flee to save my men. I will not have them die in this harbour because I wait for you."

I pulled away and went to the snake without another word, motioning for Jason to stay in place. I knelt before the giant and rested my head against its own, the scales smooth and cold beneath my forehead. It opened one great black eye and stared at me before closing it again. I scratched the point below its enormous mouth, and it raised slightly to give me better access. Of all the people in my father's kingdom, I had always been the only one to dare its company. Many times growing up, when loneliness had assailed me in both the temple and in the palace, I had made my way to the snake and slept curled in its massive coils, protected by the protector of the fleece. A thick, terrible chain wrought by Hephaestus himself wound around its neck, pulled so tightly it couldn't writhe free. I scratched along its jaw with one hand and motioned to Jason with the other. He moved silently to the tree, climbed it quickly and pulled the fleece from its place, which he draped over his shoulders before descending. When he was down, he looked at me and raised his hand in question. I motioned him away, back to the path. He looked at the snake, its head bigger than my body, and I saw his moment of fear, as I saw it with all people who saw the true nature of what I could do. He took a few steps back while watching me pet the guardian, then he turned and loped down the forest path out of sight.

I rested my head against the snake's and placed both hands on the cold metal chain around its neck. *Goddess, you brought the man here. I have helped him gain what he seeks, and I will do with him as you have decreed. But before I do, release your creature from the bonds my father has placed on it. Do not let your sacred snake bear the brunt of my father's anger. Let it go free now that the fleece is where you wish it to be.*

I pressed on the chain as hard as I could and with a glowing, rending pop, it split open and fell away. The snake's dark eyes flew open, and its tongue snapped out of its mouth as though tasting the air of freedom. It rose and rose, higher and higher above me. It stretched its length for the first time in my memory, a beloved and sacred pet of the goddess. It gave a mighty hiss and lurched forwards, away from the tree that it had been captive to for so long, away from the temple into the deeper blackness of the forest beyond. I thought it might look back at me, might acknowledge that I had been the one to free it, but no. It disappeared almost instantly among the foliage. I watched the protector go with a heavy heart, glad that it wouldn't feel my father's wrath but extra aware that a soothing piece of my life had been swept away as easily as leaves in the winter rains. I placed my palm flat against the tree and felt the life in it, life that had been a part of mine since my memories began. It was sacred, magical, guarded. It was lonely and safe. Now, it was a tree like any other, though tainted with my memories. I rested my forehead against the rough chestnut bark for a breath and whispered goodbye.

I lifted my peplos and ran down the forest path to the temple, where my mother and Alkippe had already packed essential belongings in a small trunk along with riches my mother had gathered from the palace which might help smooth my way into my new life. I quickly donned my thickest cloak and left with Alkippe, who had insisted on coming with me when I'd rushed through an explanation of the situation. I'd said I would understand if she had chosen to stay behind, but I set off down a rarely travelled path to the river where we would make our way to Jason's ship unseen glad that I wouldn't be making this leap alone. Two servants who had always been loyal to my mother walked behind us, carrying the trunks.

Before we'd gone far from the temple, the goddess appeared before us on the path, blocking it from my sight. I stopped abruptly and bowed my head, causing Alkippe to crash into me from behind and send us both sprawling into the damp earth. I looked up and saw the goddess's mirth before she spoke, though I was never certain whether the words were said aloud or only in my mind.

Go back. Send the others to the ship without you. You must gather your potions and herbs, as you will need them for challenges you will face on the voyage. Though you will mostly rely on your wit and the gods' grace, there will be moments you need that which you have trained for within the temple walls.

She disappeared, and I felt a well of frustration begin to boil. Why hadn't she told me this before? I turned to Alkippe. "Hurry. Take the chest and make your way as fast as you can to Jason's ship. I will be with you shortly, but I must return and gather items the goddess bids for the voyage. Tell Jason I will arrive as quickly as I can, and that he is not to leave without me."

Alkippe did as she was told without argument, as she had been my confidant and maid long enough to avoid questioning things she had no desire to understand. I turned and ran to the back door of the temple, where I made my way quickly to my rooms and gathered everything I could, dropping it all into a sturdy woollen bag. As I was about to leave, I heard voices in the main room. I stood pressed against my wall and listened with my eyes closed.

"He has no right. No temple priestess can be forced into marriage. It is against the laws of the gods. The goddess will take her vengeance if he takes against one of her servants, mark me."

"You know as well as I the prophecy. If he can remove her from the city, her brother may yet live. He should have done it long ago. Surely the strangers have made him think it better to have her gone after all, rather than where he can keep her under eye, as he thought."

"The oracle didn't say when she would kill Absyrtos, only that she would. Even if he marries her off to some foreign prince, who is to say she won't do it from afar? You've seen her power. There is no other priestess of the temple with the power the gods have given Medea. Better to have killed her as an infant so there was no chance."

"If it hadn't been for the queen, he would have. But she told him she'd seen the goddess over Medea's cradle. You don't kill a god's chosen."

The priestess's voices faded, and I fled to the exit and down the hidden path. Married? My father was planning to give me away without even speaking to me first. Like a chalice, or tripod, or a goat. I would never be a pawn in another man's game.

I continued down the path, breathing deeply the nutty pine and heavy earth, trying to remember the distinct shape of leaves and flowers, of bird calls and animal noises. My father wished to take away the last vestige of freedom I had, but I would be gone or dead before that would happen. At the edge of the wood, before I stepped beyond it to head to the ship, I looked over my shoulder. Although it was bright daylight, the path was shrouded in darkness. No, there would be no turning back. My fate lay with the man on the ship; he would take me on an adventure. A journey to new lands, to foreign people...to freedom.

I pulled up my hood and held the bag of herbs and mixtures closely to my stomach. No one stopped me as I walked quickly down the beach to the ship swarming with men getting ready to set sail. I strode up the gangplank without being questioned, though several of the men moved respectfully out of my way. Once on board, Alkippe took my hand and led me to a small bench at the rear. We kept our heads down so no one on shore would see us leaving and raise the alarm. A pair of dusty sandaled-feet appeared beneath my gaze.

"We're ready. Are you certain this is what you want, princess? For I would spread your praises throughout my travels even if you did not accompany us. You leave much behind and if you do, there will be no returning. The river will carry us back to my home, and you will live among strangers."

I raised my eyes to look at him and enjoyed a small thrill of victory when he caught his breath. "I would not be on the ship if I were not sure of myself. You have the fleece and because of that, my life here is forfeit. You promised to take me away and to secure my safety. I held my part of our bargain. Now you must do the same." I touched his hand with my own and a single shock ran through us, making us both jump slightly.

He ran the back of his rough knuckles down my cheek. "I promised, and I will see to it my promise is kept. Keep down, and we will be gone shortly."

We sat even lower, hunching forwards as the ship cast off. Strangely, there was no one on the dock to see us leave, the whole area deserted as before one of the late autumn storms. They must all be helping get the feast ready. Or they'd been ordered elsewhere... I jumped up and met Jason at the tiller.

"Something is wrong. I feel it. Treachery comes."

He looked at me, and whatever he saw in my expression was enough to convince him of my truth.

"What do you suggest?"

But it was too late. We rounded a bend in the river and several of my brother's small, swift skiffs were waiting. My brother was first to grab a line and swing himself aboard, and his men gave a shout as the skiff he'd been on slipped backwards, pushed by an unnatural wave. The other skiffs, too, were pushed towards shore and no matter what the men did, they couldn't get any closer. They shouted to Absyrtos, and although he glanced at them and saw the state of things, he stayed aboard. He was alone. Jason's men lurched forwards but stopped when Absyrtos's blade touched Jason's throat.

He looked at me.

"Since you were born, we knew you were nothing but deceit in woman's form. But Father thought if they killed you, he would bring on the wrath of the gods because you are the granddaughter of the sun and sea. If he sent you away, he wouldn't be able to keep an eye on you, and he wouldn't know what evil you might get up to. So he sent you to the temple, you and your goddess-touched mind. He should have killed you and sacrificed in apology. But no matter. I will kill you now and be done with it. We will prove that an oracle can be wrong. I will take the fleece back to Father, and we will be rid of anything to do with prophecy." He turned to Jason, his sword causing a trickle of blood to make its way down his alabaster skin. "And you, filthy stranger, you would take the help of a woman, a witch, over abiding the king's decision? You are no better than a common thief, a milksop suckling at the teat of my whore sister."

I stood and approached slowly, noticing the way all the men on the ship were waiting for an opening to save their leader. Some stayed at the oars, while others stood ready, their swords in hand. "Brother, let us leave. I am aboard a ship, heading to new lands. I would not touch a hair on your head if you would let us leave in peace. The Prince of Iolcos has passed Father's trials, and yet we both know Father was not going to allow him to leave our shores except to enter the underworld. Do not incur the gods' wrath for the sake of his pride. It was not I who helped the prince take the fleece but rather the goddess who rode beside him." I kept talking even as I moved closer. Closer, until I could almost touch him and could smell the potent combination of his fear and desperation emanating into the salty air.

"Stop. Stop speaking, sister, or I will cut your tongue out before I kill you so I can watch you suffer silently."

"Brother, think. Do you really think that once you have killed their leader, these men surrounding you will simply allow you to leave? Do you think they won't take vengeance for their prince? You have left your men below, and they cannot help you. See, even now, that the goddess keeps your men from helping you. If you back away now, I will give you the prince's word that you will not be harmed. Is that so, Jason?"

Jason's eyes were tight with anger, and his hands gripped the wheel in white-knuckled fury. "You have my word. Leave the ship, and you will not be harmed."

I watched as my brother processed all we had said. But truly, he was trapped. If he left the ship, my father would kill him for not following through. If he followed through, he was dead anyway. His men waiting below couldn't help him. He had acted rashly, rushing in, thinking only of victory, and instead found himself at the gates of Hades. I saw the moment he made his decision and knew what he was thinking. Better to kill the foreign prince and die trying than to die a coward. And though he might die, my father's men on the boats could overpower Jason's and therefore keep us from fleeing. I'd be taken back and sold off in marriage like a cow to a farmer.

Before he could push the sword through Jason's throat, I flashed my hand out from beneath my robe, and Jason's face was covered in blood as it pumped from the gash I opened in Absyrtos's throat with my curved sickle blade. I looked into my brother's terrified eyes as he dropped to his knees, his hands slick as he clasped at the gaping hole in his throat.

From outside myself, I watched the gruesome dance. "It was not me, but you who caused your death, brother. Had you not acted so, your death would not have been certain. But I will not allow you to take my life or endanger my freedom. I will not be caged."

He gasped out his last breath, and his filthy nails clawed at the deck in the throes of death as he crossed to the underworld. Power, suffocating and terrible, flooded me. The goddess I served had a dark face but only certain priestesses were allowed to see it. As my brother's blood bubbled at his lips and his breath stopped, I knew the power of that dark goddess. Terrible, horrifying, and yet, in that moment, I knew what it was to control my own destiny, to be a man among men and take life so easily in the name of something I believed in. The stunned silence of the men aboard the ship surrounded me, and only the sound of the water lapping against the boat filled the space, though I could hear my brother's men crying out near the shore. Even Jason looked bewildered, and he stared at me with more fear than desire.

Was this what it was to be a god? To move as I wished, to know no consequence, and have men fear me?

I liked it. I liked it very much.

I sheathed my blade after wiping it on my brother's cloak, and it was from afar that I noted my lack of remorse or horror. "I suggest we sail quickly. His men will get word to my father, who will come after us with proper ships to reclaim the fleece and claim our lives as payment."

Jason stared at me for one more moment before turning to his men and giving order to row for their lives as he wiped my brother's blood from his face. I stepped closer to Jason so I could speak with him quietly. "When my father comes after us, we must slow him down. If we drop pieces of my brother in the water, he will have no choice but to stop and get them so he can give Absyrtos a proper send off to the afterlife. It will allow us the time to get far enough away, and he will not be able to give chase."

He looked at me in dread. "You would desecrate the body of your own brother? Your own flesh? The gods will destroy us for such treatment of the dead. I will not do such a thing."

"Then you condemn us to death at my father's hand, for his ships are larger and faster than yours. He will overtake us, and he will not even bother to bring us to shore to kill us. He will do it here and burn the ship until the water puts out the last of the flames. Our bodies will be food for the fish, and we will stay unburied for all time. Jason, please, listen to me," I said and placed a hand on his arm. Once again, desire flooded me. His pupils contracted and his arm tensed under mine. God-driven desire was a dangerous thing. "The goddess has brought you to me. Not to another, but me. Because I have the knowledge to save us and to get you home. But you must trust in me as you trusted me to take you through the trials."

He breathed hard as he considered my words. "Very well. But I will do it myself. I would not have my men cause the gods such anger. If there is justice, the gods will not punish our entire voyage for what I am about to do."

He motioned to another man, who took the wheel. Jason dragged Absyrtos's body to the rear of the ship, where he used his razor-sharp sword to quickly hack my brother into several pieces. It was grim. The smell and sight truly awful as blood filled the floor of the boat and swirled around the men's sandals, dying their leather and feet crimson. The stench of punctured entrails and loosened bowls sent several of the men to vomit over the side. These were not yet warriors hardened to the reality of death. Alkippe kept her face hidden in her cloak, but I forced myself to watch the entire process, though my stomach quaked and I wanted to retch as well. But this was my idea, and I wouldn't show weakness. I would see it to the end.

Absyrtos's insides flopped to the deck, covered in bloody slime and excrement. Was man anything more than the animals which roamed the forest and were then laid out on the nightly tables?

When he was in pieces, Jason dropped each stinking, gory piece into a thick bag. "We will leave him in this until we have need."

The sight of the blood-drenched bag made me ill and memories of the few happy moments as we were children assailed me. "You should expect my father within the hour. As it is in large part my sacrilege, I will drop the pieces overboard. He is already aware by now that it was I who helped with the entire plan and because of the prophecy, he will be expecting the worst. I will provide him that as thanks for the destruction he made of my life, as well as the destruction he was planning. Had he not prepared my brother to hate me, perhaps this moment would not have come."

Jason returned to the wheel without another word after cleaning himself of detritus, and I returned to Alkippe's side. I stared at the bag of Absyrtos, my disgust and guilt etched into a memory that would stay with me forever.

"What have you done? Medea, what have you done? Your own brother."

I squeezed Alkippe's hand in my own, choosing to ignore the slight hesitation I felt in her grip. "I have done what the gods decreed I would do, and nothing more. You know we cannot go against the gods. If I were not meant to do what needs must, we would not be on this ship." There was truth to it. But if I'd had a choice, if there had been another way, would I have taken it? We'd never know anything except that the gods had said I'd kill my brother, and I'd done so, whatever the motives, whatever the options. Did it relieve me of blame? My mother thought so, and I was inclined to agree.

We remained quiet for some time as the current moved us swiftly down the river towards the Bosphorus, where we would move into the open sea. The men eyed me warily, but I was used to that. What I wasn't used to was the pull toward someone, the desire to stand beside and fight for them. Giving in, I went to the railing by Jason, wanting to be closer to him, but not so close I couldn't think. He'd relinquished the tiller to someone else, and he remained at the front looking like a young god, or at least, the paramour of one.

The boat swayed under me, forcing me to plant my feet in a wide stance so I didn't tumble overboard. I'd been on small boats before but never a boat this large on open water, where the shorelines on either side seemed too far to swim to, should anything go wrong. The boat was beautiful, though it looked weary from its journey to Egrisi. Fifty men sat at benches, rowing easily in the current. A wide path separated each side of rowers, allowing for movement between so no one felt overly cramped. At the front and rear of the ship were thin benches for those not rowing to wait their turn, with several men there to give others a break. On one of those benches cowered Alkippe, her shoulders shaking as she cried silently into her cloak. I looked away, knowing my friend and servant would still do as I said, no matter how she felt about what had happened.

I allowed the view of the quickly passing shoreline to distract me. Sea birds dove and called to each other over the wake behind the boat, as though singing for our escape. I took the first deep breath since Jason had landed on my shore and stretched, my spine popping as the tension of the past week began to lift. I inhaled the salty air, the speckled moisture dotting my face and cleansing the dirt of my escape from my skin. I felt like laughing, like throwing my arms up and hugging the bright blue sky.

"It will be night soon."

Jason's arm slid around my waist, and I couldn't help but smile back at him. His optimism was contagious, and though I knew my feelings were false gifts from crafty gods, I couldn't help but be glad of his good nature and that he seemed no longer wary of me. Perhaps he too was being ridden by gods, forced to feel things he did not wish to feel.

"The more distance we have the better. My father will be raging." I shivered at the memory of my father's glare, and Jason pulled me closer.

I didn't recognize any of the land around us, and my fear and sickness at what I'd done receded to the shadowy realm from which it came. Freedom tasted like wind and sea salt, like water's gentle embrace as the river swept me to new shores. I had escaped my father and brother's cruelty, escaped my mother's mournful visage. I had helped a hero and was on an adventure of my own. I looked down at Jason's hands, clasped over my belly. My life was my own, and this man was the key.

"We'll outrun them. There is no faster ship than the Argo, built by Athena herself. You don't need to worry," Jason said.

"We should all worry."

We turned at the bitter tone and saw the one they called Eurytus leaning against the bulkhead glaring at us. He pointed at me. "You've cursed us all, princess. You've got us the fleece, but you've brought down the wrath of King Aeëtes and his gods. We'll be lucky to make it home."

"Come now, Eurytus. We'll be fine. Medea is a chosen one of the goddess. Hecate won't allow us to perish."

A vision of Eurytus, his limp body being pulled from the water as his sightless eyes watched the sky, flashed before me, and I quickly turned away. He was right. There was still much blood to be shed but telling him so would not indebt him to me. As I often did, I kept the fleeting vision to myself, knowing there was no way to avoid that which the gods had decreed. Why had they gifted me with prophecy when there was no way to change the future set before us? This time there was no retching or dizziness, and I hoped that it would remain that way in the future.

"Don't let him bother you. Most of the men on the ship are superstitious. We all want to be heroes, but no one wants to die to become one."

"He's right. He won't make it home." I looked at the water rising and falling, rising and falling, and knew it was like life itself. Rising only to fall once again a moment later.

"What? What do you mean by that?"

I turned my attention to him and noticed how pale he was, how childlike. Surely the gods could have given me feelings for a more heroic man. Even as I thought it, I felt the tug of the gods' choice on my heart, and the idea drifted away like smoke. I rubbed at the gooseflesh on my arms, disconcerted. "I see things, sometimes. I see what can happen to people, what the fates have decreed. The future."

He leaned forwards and grasped my hand tightly. "Always? Do you see all things, like the oracle at Delphi?"

I pulled my hand away, strangely bothered by the moistness of his palm. "No, not always. Sometimes I see things I can't make sense of. And I only see what the gods want me to, when they want me to. But if I do see it, it never changes."

"What about me? What do you see when you look at me?"

I wanted to tell him I saw a child with grand sense of himself, a boy who wanted to be a man but had the backbone of water. I wanted to say I saw a young man who needed to bathe more and eat less. But that strange golden leash, that firebrand burning in my chest, stopped me and twisted my words. "I see a man who will be a great hero. A man who will be remembered forever."

His face lit up and for a moment, I was glad I said what he wanted to hear.

Typhus shouted from the rear. "We've got friends."

We joined him and looked in the direction he was pointing. The ship behind us was still far enough away I couldn't tell if it was my father, but there was no question it was gaining on us.

Eurytus moved to Jason's side and flicked a brief glance at me. "There's an island ahead. Leave the woman there. It's her head they want. She's the one who betrayed them. Leave her behind, and it will give us enough time to get away. We'll be gone by the time they're done with her."

Jason stiffened and I could smell his fear, could sense his desperation. He couldn't be a true coward, for he had sailed through terrors to arrive in Egrisi, and he had faced my father's trials willingly, though with my help. But I already knew he would fight only if forced. He wasn't the kind of hero to go in search of bloodshed. I had guessed as much when he stood before my father and asked for the fleece as though my father would simply hand it over. He had looked supremely confident, as though it were the most natural thing in the world to ask a king to turn over the one item that legitimized his kingship. Even with the vision of him I'd already had, I had felt contempt at his naiveté. But from the moment the goddess had forced her way into my heart, I would have gone to Hades and back just to bring him an apple if he wanted one. The love I felt was not my own, but I would kill and die for the child-man in front of me. I had denied all I was, turned against my own family and gotten him his heart's desire, and the weakling was afraid to stand up to his men for me. My chance at freedom could slip away like the water under the galley. I looked at the approaching ship and an anger born of years of loneliness and captivity screamed to the surface, burning my blood as the goddess choked me with indignation.

"You would dare?" I screeched, and my voice was not my own.

The men around me looked as insignificant as leaves on a forest floor. "If it weren't for me, would you have yoked the fire-breathing bulls? Would their horns have slid from your body instead of impaling it?" I stood in front of Jason, my face inches from his own hairless cheeks. "Would you have known how to kill the men of rock? Would you have put the serpent to sleep on your own? Would you be on your way back to your throne with the Golden Fleece in hand?"

My body grew painful with power, aching and stretching with an infusion of unearthly dominance. In a distant part of my mind, I knew the goddess was using me, that the Medea who usually used my body was nothing compared to the deity using it now. Everything was so vivid, so beautiful, the colours of the ocean and sky making my human eyes throb with their brilliance. I could smell every grain of salt in the ocean. I could feel every breath of wind on my skin and every sliver of hard wood under my feet. Never had I felt so alive. All at once I was standing on the boat, but I was part of it, part of the air, part of the ocean, part of the sea breeze sweeping my hair around my face. I was myself and everything around me. I looked at Jason and took pleasure in his fear as he watched me.

"If you do this thing, if you leave me, forsaken on the shore, you will live to regret it. I will curse your house and the houses of your children. You will never have a day's peace, your music will be harpies screeching, your food will be filled with maggots, and your only comfort will be a bed of thorns. No woman will want you and no house will have you. You will die a coward, and no one will remember your name."

My voice echoed off the masts, darting back at the men around me who cowered like children. Jason held the rail, clearly to keep from stepping away. The silence of indecision made the air thick. He finally looked into my eyes, and then he did step back.

"Keep the course. Medea brought us this far; I will take us the rest of the way."

The men jumped as though released from a cage, scurrying

about the deck to complete their tasks, rowing with all their might to put distance between themselves and the ship behind them. Pulled by instinct, I looked at the water as an uncommonly large wave rose beside us, the white foam forming into the massive half-man, half-sea serpent body of the sea god. My mother's kin stared at me from whirlpool eyes, his enormous trident flashing gold before he dove back into the sea to become one with it again. The men cried out and Jason dropped to his knees, his hands over his head. The boat leapt forwards, carried on the shoulders of those who swam below, quickly leaving our pursuers behind.

I felt the goddess's power drain from me, as though a hole had opened in my heels. It slipped from my body and the vibrant night, with its deepest black and unfathomable blue, with stars I felt belonged in my palm, returned to mortal levels and distance, and I despaired at the loss. I trembled and fought to stay on my feet, my body heavy like wet clay, like the damp wood I stood on, like the creature of flesh and blood I was. Being the vessel of a goddess was double-edged. There could be no better feeling on land or sea than being filled with holy essence, but there could also be no starker reminder of the frailty of being human when they left you. I sank to my knees, my body too heavy to bear, the weight of being used too much to understand all at once.

The playful adventurer was gone. In his place was a child frightened of the unknown. Jason backed away from me and disappeared among his men. I had glimpsed some portion of the goddess's intentions for him, but only enough to understand we were caught in a web not meant for mortal survival but for godly pleasure. I found an empty corner and pressed my face to the cool wood. Soft hands brushed my hair from my face, and Alkippe lifted my head and cradled it in her lap. She held my hand tightly, and I looked up into her soft brown eyes.

"Had the goddess appeared so while you were in the temple, perhaps our fates would be different." She smiled down at me and continued to stroke my hair. "Your father and brother would never have dared go against you if they'd seen what we just saw."

"It seems they have plans of their own. I would not have you suffer for the choice I made though." I kissed the back of Alkippe's hand even as sleep began to overtake me, exhaustion sweeping through my body and mind.

"My place is by your side. Always. The fates may decide what will happen, but they cannot choose the path we walk to get where they would have us end."

***

Shouts accompanied the fingers of morning light that reflected pinks and oranges over the still waters. No breeze filled the sails, and the men were tired from rowing all night. Behind us, a ship was moving closer, quickly. I stood and stretched the kinks from my cramped spine and went to Jason's side.

"Much as I loathe it, it may be time to put your idea about your brother's body into position. We're close to the currents that will draw us quickly into the mouth of the Pontus, but your father's boat will catch us before we can get there."

I narrowed my eyes, searching the swiftly approaching boat for my father. He was at the front, shouting direction, his hands raised as he implored the gods. But I knew full well they'd stopped listening to him long ago. "Wait for them to get a bit closer. The moment I begin sending my brother to him, he will slow."

Jason gave the order to stop rowing and they waited. I could feel their resentment, their fear and anger. Their worry about affronted gods, and angry kings, and beings who rose from the water. I knew from my brother's mealtime stories that having a woman aboard a ship was considered unlucky by many sailors, and although these men were from a land far distant, it was likely they too harboured such nonsense in their heads.

Before the end of the voyage, they would respect me.

My father's boat pulled close enough he could see us, and he started shouting curses. Men with bows stood ready to shoot, while others held their spears high. Our eyes met, and I saw that no longer was he the imperious, superior ruler I'd grown up with. In his gaze I saw madness, raw and devastated. His shoulders were hunched forwards as though protecting himself from a wound to his chest. Though my focus had been freedom, at any cost, rather than causing my father pain, I wasn't sorry. He'd never shown me an ounce of love or compassion. He had used me and looked to me as a pawn in a bigger game. He had turned my brother into a copy of himself, one who despised me and treated our mother with disregard. In a way, he'd set all this in motion.

I reached into the bag and pulled out my brother's head. It was surprisingly heavy. The dried blood matted his hair, and his unseeing eyes bulged from slack facial skin. He wasn't the little boy I'd grown up with, but rather the tormentor who'd made my life misery for so long. Now, he was a game piece ready to be played. I held it high, the gruesome mask facing my father. I raised my voice and felt the goddess respond to my plea.

"This is what you seek, Father. My brother, whom you so cherished over me. I will give him back to you, gladly, and rid my boat of his stinking carcass, which is nearly as bad as it was while he was breathing. If only you had sent me away. Or allowed him to love me instead of loath me, maybe I would have had more kindness in my heart towards him. But instead, I gift him back to you so you may hang him in the trees to be reborn." My voice boomed across the water, ripples in the water's surface the only movement in an unearthly stillness encapsulating the drama enfolding between us.

I threw my brother's head into the water to the sound of my father's agonized scream. A spear was launched and found Peleaus, one of the oldest of the crew, waiting. It went through him, and he fell into the water with barely a splash.

I quickly added several other pieces, leaving enough space between them that it would take time for my father to manoeuvre the boat to reach them. When the bag was empty of all but entrails,

I threw the sack into the water and watched the froth from the boat turn pink.

I turned to Jason. Clearly uncomfortable, he refused to look at me. "Tell your men to row hard and move us to the river. When we've left our shores, my father will likely give up."

My father's boat stopped alongside another of my brother's pieces. Their ship quickly grew smaller as we pulled away. I turned my face to the sun. "We're free."

CHAPTER NINE
Detour

BY NIGHTFALL, WE WERE nearing the mouth of the Pontus, which would carry us into the next sea and closer to Jason's home. But something stirred in the air, making me uneasy.

Kip held my hand, which she'd hardly let go of since my father's ships had fallen so far behind. She squeezed. "What is it?"

I shook my head, unsure, and continued to scan what little of the horizon I could make out in the dark. I felt the sting of flying water a second before the wind hit, and there were shouts around me as the boat, which already rode low in the water, tilted dangerously from one side to the other. A flash of lightning in the cloudless sky told us what was happening. Zeus himself was angry.

"Can you do anything?" Jason shouted over the howling wind as the men fought against the wind, their arms straining to hold the oars steady.

My words stuck in my throat and once again the fire of the goddess filled me. "Kin-slaying must be atoned for. We befouled the water with my brother's blood, and so we must pay the price. Release the oars."

Jason stared at me, and he seemed such a long way off, like a man on a shore left behind. He turned away and gave the order, and the men pulled the oars in. The boat turned, spun, dipped, and rose, and then under the power of the wind, it flew across the water like Helios's chariot dragging the sun across the sky. We all held on, white-knuckled in the face of a god's fury. Remotely, I considered how it was unfair to be punished for something the gods said you were going to do before you were even born, meaning you had no choice but to follow the path they'd laid before you. But those thoughts scattered under the power of the goddess filling me to bursting as we sped towards the clear inlet of a large river ahead and away from the strait that would have taken us into the sea leading to our destination.

Alkippe, beside me, said, "The River Ister."

I glanced down at her, easing my grip on the rail. "How do you know?"

She continued to hold on tightly as the wind buffeted us. "My family lived in one of the villages along this river. I grew up here, until I was sent to serve you."

I'd never once considered what Kip's life had been like before she'd come to me. We weren't so far apart in age and when we were children, she was more playmate than servant. The line had become clearer as I'd gotten older, but still, I'd never stopped to wonder where she came from or if she had a family too. The thought disturbed me but before I could ask her any questions, Jason moved to my side.

"My lady, do the gods give you any indication of their desires?" He looked at the swiftly passing shore, which was becoming rocky and sparse. "I fear we're far off course."

For perhaps the first time, I really looked at him through my own eyes. He was pale and nowhere near as muscular as his shipmates. There was a weakness to his chin and his eyes darted everywhere, not in calculation or strategy, but in fear. He was not the hero of bard's tales and disappointment welled in me. I felt the stirrings of desire and pushed them away, irritated. *I'm not going anywhere. Leave me be.* The feeling faded and the knowledge that I could converse with those using me was something to consider later.

"I fear we're trapped in a game we can't win, with players we'll rarely see." It was truth, but I didn't want to terrify him. "We can but go where the winds lead and pray for guidance from any gods who would hear us." They were the kind of priestess platitudes I'd learned in the temple, and they were as useful now as they'd been then.

The waves carried us up the opposite coast and settled only when we reached a smaller river where the Cucuteni and Yamnaya people, who came across every few months to trade with us, lived. In the dark of night though, no one called out to us as we pushed into the new river.

The wind dropped and the men slowly picked up their oars again at a word from Jason. He looked to me, and I shrugged slightly. The goddess was gone, leaving only exhaustion and a strange emptiness in her place. I sat beside Kip, who draped a blanket around me and pulled me close. I rested my head on her shoulder and drifted to sleep. It seemed we were in the hands of the gods in full now, and there was nothing to be done but follow where their whims led.

By morning, the men had been rowing for too long and were exhausted. I had never been across the sea, though the many different tribes often came to trade with us. Our languages were similar, and I'd taken the time over the years to learn what I could when I didn't understand someone, so I wasn't worried about communicating. Jason gave the order to land, and they pulled us to shore. It was hot and humid already, and I noticed that the change in weather seemed a little more pronounced. It was even drier, and the water had pulled away from the shore. I wasn't sure it meant anything and dismissed it. There were other things to consider.

The men quickly moved off the boat and Jason helped me down, then lifted Kip down behind me. His concern for my maid made me kinder towards him.

"Do you know where we are?" he asked, looking around.

His men had fallen to the sand, and many were already asleep. I looked into the trees, searching, and found what I was looking for. Two men watched from the tree line, the markings on their faces telling me what I needed to know. "Periprava, I think. They're one of the tribes of the Cucuteni." I thought of the times they'd come to trade at the port. "They don't speak much, and I think they like to be left alone for the most part. They won't give us any trouble." My words carried more confidence than I felt. Although I'd studied all the tribes along the sea, as it was fit for a priestess and a princess to know these things, I wasn't completely conversant with all their customs.

"Good enough." He spread his cloak on the sand and motioned to it. "We should sleep while we can."

I didn't argue. I lay down on his cloak, and Kip lay curled against my back. Jason lay facing me and gave me a small, shy smile before he closed his eyes. As I closed mine, I wondered if my father's ships would think to look up this river. It was unlikely, given that they'd seen us headed for the Pontus, which was the quickest way out of the sea. We had time.

I slept and stirred again only when I heard the men around me beginning to move. I sat up and ran my fingers through my hair. I'd need Kip to tie it up for me. Sailing with it loose would leave it unacceptably tangled.

Jason sat beside us, looking at the river. When he noticed I'd woken, he nodded in greeting.

"Princess, you named the village we've come to. Do you know the rest of this river? Do you know where it leads?"

I shook my head, still trying to comb out my hair. "I've studied the tribes in the area and met some people who have come to trade at our shores, but that's the limit of my knowledge." I closed my eyes and tilted my head to the sun. "But if I concentrate, I can feel the goddess telling us to keep going." I opened my eyes and looked at him. "What do you feel?" After all, he too was goddess-touched when it came to this venture.

He frowned and stared at the Argo for a long moment. "You're right. We have to keep going." He stood and told the men to get ready before he turned back to me. "If you had to guess, would you say there's a harbour near? One where we could get supplies?"

Kip leaned close. "Izmail."

I looked at her and smiled, motioning for her to go on.

"Izmail is a harbour port not far away. The Yamnaya people are welcoming, if a little different." She kept her eyes downcast, but her voice was sure.

He gave one of his quick, easy smiles. "Izmail it is."

I shook out his cloak and handed it back to him.

We got on board, and I nodded discreetly at the tribal people still keeping an eye on us from the trees and was gratified when one nodded back as they faded into the shadows. Kip and I took our seats at the front, and the men pushed hard to get the boat into deeper waters. Once again, I felt the surge of excitement. I was away from home, and the men turned to me for advice, not to give orders. It was a novel feeling, and one I'd easily get used to.

CHAPTER TEN
New Paths

Today, as I remember.

THE MIDDAY SUN BEAT down on the earth. Pine trees and wild onion scented the air, carried on Boreas's breath to the windows of the palace. I inhaled and took the earth into me as I touched the memories of my youth almost like they were happening before me. My power had grown from that day. My intuition and wits served me well but none who came across me had any doubts I was god-touched, though my visions pertained to others and never myself, which seemed a grievous oversight by the gods. Had I known many things, I would have tried to walk a different path. And had I known about Theseus, I probably would have left Athens far sooner. Nonetheless, I was glad the goddess had taken the direction she had. With my son on the throne, I was free to live out my final days any way I chose.

I shuddered at the emptiness of the thought.

"May I get you anything, your highness?" Desma looked up from her needlework.

I sighed. What a question. Was there an answer? What did I want? I'd worked all my life for power, to gain my children the respect and standing they deserved, that was their birth right. I was born a princess and had fought to become a queen. Now I was the mother of a king. My son had power, and I unquestionably ruled beside him. But without the goddess beside me, inside me, I felt adrift, and the power felt vapid.

"No, Desma. There is nothing you can get me that would be of any use."

"Perhaps you would tell me stories of your journey? The other servants say you were the most powerful woman in the world, that men and women feared you, that the gods kept you in their hands."

"Do they say so?" I thought about my time in Iolcos, in Corinth, in Athens. The things I had done, the men and women I had enjoyed and the ones I had sent to Hades. "I *was* power. I wasn't just a woman or a priestess. I was power itself. Kings knelt before me and begged for my help. My husband wept when I left in the palm of the sun god."

Desma looked awestruck, like a child being told an enthralling bed story.

Alkippe stood in the doorway, linen folded over her arms. "You leave much out of that story. It was not nearly so neat as all that." She bustled around the room, straightening the bedsheets and patting out the indentations in both pillows. "No mistake, there was much blood. Much screaming and terror. Times you did things that no mortal would ever do because the goddess herself spoke through you. It was terrifying, and you had the temper of Hades and the wrath of Hera when someone crossed you."

"Quiet, old woman." I waved Alkippe's words away, but Desma looked even more enraptured.

It was true. There were still nights, even so many years later, when my dreams were tidal waves of blood, of pleading and screams of agony, of begging and bartering. I would wake drenched in sweat that I would swear was the blood of those I'd lost or killed, my reasoning irrelevant in the face of their shades as they chased me through the underworld of my nightmares. No other mortal, woman or man, was so afflicted. But then, no other had been so used by the gods either. I heard stories, and I knew the gods walked among humans more frequently now, playing with their mortal toys. Eventually they would get tired of their fragile playthings and move on to other pursuits.

"Were you like Helen of Sparta, your highness? They say she's the most beautiful woman in the world. The armies in Troy have been fighting for years just to get her back to her husband."

Alkippe snorted. "Beauty is fleeting. Armies of men will not fight for a single woman they cannot bed. If there is war at Troy, it will be over the riches of Priam, which he flaunts to the world, and for access to the Marmara Sea, which he regulates. The gods may have decreed war for their own reasons, but man will always find his own within their game. Won't they, highness?"

There was no judgement in her tone, solely the tinge of memories. "We did. The gods started us on our path and in their hands, we played our parts. But still, we made our own way, created our own riches. We took what we could to make life under the god's dominion worthy."

We turned at the knock on the door.

"Come." I sat on a stool and smoothed my skirts around me. I straightened, ignoring the twinge of pain in my back caused by too many long trips over the sea, months spent lying on benches or wooden floors under an open sky, in fair weather or foul, nights spent sleeping on ruined temple floors or even in ditches on the sides of roads on beds of pine needles and moss as the world trembled around us. My son's advisor swept in. I didn't always like him, but he had proven loyal upon our return, unlike so many others. More blood. Does the river of Hades overflow with the blood of those I've sent there?

"Your highness. Your son would have council with you if you would favour him with your presence?"

He bowed, and his obsequious, weak nature was like the smell of rotting fish in a small room.

"Of course. Tell him I'll be there shortly. Make certain none of his whores are present."

The man flushed, still unused to my direct way of speaking, as so many others had been. Often to their detriment.

"Yes, your highness." He backed out of the room, still bowed.

When he was gone, Alkippe bent low. "Yes, your highness. Of course, your highness. Would you like me to spread my ass cheeks for you, your highness?"

Desma put a hand over her mouth to hide her laughter, her eyes wide.

I patted Alkippe on the head. "Good dog. Go lick your master's feet, and fetch his mother, and his whores, then lie at his feet until he kicks you to do else."

Alkippe panted like an animal and licked my hand. My breath caught slightly, and I traced Alkippe's mouth with my finger. She gave me the small, secret smile reserved only for me, and I returned it before turning away. It wouldn't do any good to give Desma food for the gossips in the servants' quarters.

"Desma, come. Leave Alkippe to attend her work. Accompany me to my son."

I saw Desma flinch and wasn't surprised. Women in my son's presence often ended up in his bed, whether they were interested in being there or not. So, too, did some of the boys. I had spoken to him about it several times but seeing my own maid's reticence told me it was a conversation that needed more force behind it. The goddess may have deserted me, but no one knew that but me. And while my son wasn't devout, he'd been with me on enough occasions when the goddess rode me to know I wasn't to be trifled with. What he didn't realize was that I wasn't to be taken lightly on my own merit either. For the first time since I'd left the barren temple, I felt a flicker of passion return. Living as a wholly mortal woman didn't have to mean going quietly to my grave.

I motioned for Desma to follow me and ignored her hesitation. We walked quickly through the halls and across the beautiful gardens of the courtyard. The palace had been much smaller when I was a child but over the years, it had expanded to mirror some of the palaces travelling merchants had told me about in the East. I preferred the palaces of Egrisi to those of Corinth. All that heavy stone and marble was stifling, like piling the earth all around you so you couldn't breathe and were just waiting for it to fall, to collapse on you and push you into Hades.

Here, hard-packed dirt lay beneath ornate rugs, so it was always possible to feel the living earth. The wood walls breathed the forest into our living space and even though it was too hot, too dry, and the earth still shook beneath us, we weren't as devastated by the changes as were our neighbours, who'd lost so much so quickly.

Truly, temples weren't needed, as we lived in spaces full of the goddess in every way. Ornaments full of colour, of spices and smells, of shapes and sizes that varied like those found under the sky, my palace was alive with the personalities of the people who lived within, balancing the celestial with the mortal.

But of course, the gods must have their portion of temples, their sacred sacrifices. They need to feel special.

I entered my son's rooms and was directed to his private courtyard. I found him pacing, and alone. "Son?"

He gave me a slight bow, his glance briefly flicking to Desma before returning to me. "Mother. Thank you for coming. I have need of your council."

"In more ways than one, I think. Come. Sit and drink with me and tell me what makes you pace so." I turned to Desma. "Go to the kitchens and get us drinks and food." The girl's relief was palpable as she hurried away. I turned back to my son and sat on the couch facing him, shifting so my grandfather's light shone directly on my face. I closed my eyes, glad of the warmth when so often I felt a cold that had nothing to do with what the sky or air held.

"Mother, I have news from the West. There are rumours of Troy falling. When it does, someone needs to be there to take it. If the Achaeans win, they'll extend their borders and be nearly unstoppable. If Memnon takes it after it falls, and his warriors are already there fighting for Priam, then Aethiopis will control the river's mouth to the sea. I fear if we do not move quickly, we will be outflanked and appear weak, and then we'll have no defence against the Scythians."

He ran his hands through his thick, dark hair, and I was reminded of how like his father he was and how unlike my other children. I pushed the thought away and considered his words. It was good he was taking an interest in affairs of state, though somewhat surprising. He waited patiently, knowing from experience I wouldn't speak until I'd thought everything through. I closed my eyes. Whereas once I would have called on the goddess for guidance, I knew there was little use to it now. Just as I'd needed to use my wits in the breaths between the goddess's strategies when I was young, right now, I needed to think as a queen rather than a priestess.

Cities everywhere were falling. I'd seen the beginning of it first-hand and nearly two decades on, it was only happening faster. Everywhere, it was too hot. Rivers had dried up, crops had failed. The rains stopped, and no matter how many people knelt in temples begging, no water issued from the sky. Mountains in the sea were causing the waters around them to boil and with every noxious breath, they expelled flaming boulders that fell into the water, and then the water rose up only to crash down on villages that were wiped away when the sea calmed. Death and destruction were the only things being given by the gods now, and people were travelling in masses to get to cities further inland, anywhere that still had crops and water. The war on Troy was a way to escape, for the men to find something useful to occupy their time instead of waiting in their cities and villages to starve to death.

But, perhaps in the chaos we could find our own way. Expanding our territory would give us more leverage when the Achaeans returned and tried to take what didn't belong to them, as I knew they would, if there was anyone left in their cities to come for us. If Priam held Troy, we need not fear, as we'd always had a good relationship with the kind and forward-thinking king who controlled the entrance to our sea. But if Troy fell, the land would be overrun, and we would have to hold our own. We had an army and knowledge of the terrain that would mean we could defend what was ours. What was more, it would make clear that our kingdom was a force to be considered, and tributes would arrive in overflowing carts. Riches meant respect, and respect meant power, especially in times when people needed rulers who could keep them safe and fed. Though all of those were interchangeable, none of them were optional when ruling a kingdom. Unlike my son, I had enough experience to know. I studied him. His stomach was soft, his hands unbroken by the sword. It was good he'd come to me, that he was concerning himself with issues of state without me badgering him to do so.

Yes, it would be good for him to be more than the coddled son of an infamous queen. I'd wanted to send him on a quest like Jason's, and this was the opportunity I'd been waiting for. It was time for him to take a journey of his own, even if it would be perilous with all the changes happening to the world around us. And while he was gone, I would turn the kingdom into what it should be, what it should always have been. It would be my legacy. I would rule as queen in my own right.

"Gather your men. Take only half and leave half to defend the city. If you take too many, you leave us vulnerable to attack by those who think we're ripe for picking. Choose well; take men who are strong and wise, not foolish and wild."

Desma followed two servants who brought in food and drink and set it on the table between us. The servants bowed and left, and Desma moved to stand behind me, keeping her eyes lowered. My son stared at her as he bit into a fig and the juice dripped off his chin. Once again, I was reminded how vile I found men in general. Jason had been different. At first. He had glowed with godly grace and elegance, with beauty and intelligence, particularly by the time we'd reached Corinth the first time. He'd grown into a man on that voyage, and I'd come to respect him. It had made it easy to follow him for so many years. Until the end, of course. Then he had appeared as any other mortal man with wounded pride and a broken spirit.

"Another thing, before you leave. No women go with you. It is the nature of war camps that some will eventually make their way to you, followers to fill your needs who expect certain rewards in return. But keep your mind clear and away from what dangles between your legs. Remember this, son," I said and leaned forward to make certain he paid attention. "No woman will ever be what I have been, what I am. But that does not mean you treat them so disrespectfully. Never forget that any man with a woman at his side also has her in his ear, and what servants say often makes it to my chamber. When you mistreat women, you risk the wrath of the men who keep them company, and you risk the woman placing a knife in your back while you sleep." I raised a hand to forestall his argument. "I am not saying you should not keep your bed warm. Kings are given to higher passions than common men and must use those passions. But they must also control them, not be controlled by them. If nothing else, I have taught you to use your head, child. Do not become the kind of man I fought against. You do not wish to anger me."

He winced at the clear warning. He knew the blood that stained my hands, knew of what his mother—his strong, ruthless mother—was capable, and that blood relation had no bearing on my actions if I decided on a course that didn't include those relations. His jaw set in the way it had when he was a child, showing the stubborn nature I had exhibited as a little girl as well.

"I am a king. I don't have to listen to my mother tell me how to run my bed." He raised his chin and looked at me, but I saw the fear in his eyes.

I held his face in my hands, letting my long nails rest on the tight skin next to his eyes. "My heart, you will listen to me not as your mother but as the woman who put you on this throne. You will never have a greater ally than me." I let the implied threat hang in the air. Sometimes fear was a stronger motivator than love. I felt his jaw bunch under my hands and noted that his hands were clenched at his sides, his pupils were wider, his breathing faster.

"Yes, Mother. By your leave, I will begin gathering men for our journey. Thank you for your wise council. It is, as always, invaluable."

I gave his face a gentle squeeze and let go before standing and offering him my hand, which he kissed quickly. "I am always at your side, waiting to help you in whatever way I can, my son. I always have been, and I will always be."

He flinched slightly and bowed before leaving the courtyard. I sat and finished my food and drink, thinking of a future that suddenly had more potential than I had anticipated.

CHAPTER ELEVEN
The Gods and Their Games

WE STOPPED IN IZMAIL for supplies, and at no point did I forget to watch for Kolchians in search of dus. It's a busy port, full of Cucuteni tribes, where the Yamnaya and Kurgans mix with everyone else. While the men got food and water, I went to the temple on the hill. Alkippe left me there to find out what she could about our route, though I was sure Jason would be doing so as well. The temple was simple stone with a red design in the floor similar to the one in my own temple, but in the crevices were small carved pieces, stones with holes bore in the middle, wooden carvings with whorls and red ochre smudges. I touched one, an almost perfectly round wooden carving with an intricate design cut from the middle and caught my breath at the power I felt pulsing in it.

"Child of Hecate, we've been expecting you."

Startled, I turned and found a woman standing only a foot away, though I'd not heard her approach. Her eyes were a spring green, glowing in comparison to her deep olive skin. I wasn't sure how to respond to her statement, though with her head tilted and amusement in her eyes, I could tell I didn't need to.

"There is a better place to talk." She turned and walked through a well-hidden door at the back, an optical illusion that made it look like part of a single rounded wall.

I followed, intrigued. Why would they be expecting me? I faltered. Had my father's men already arrived? Was she leading me to them?

"Temples are no place for men's politics," she said softly, her voice echoing in the stone hallway.

What kind of power did a priestess have to read someone's

thoughts? It was both fascinating and worrying. Cool air caressed my face as the hallway opened into a large cave. A trickle of water ran through the back of it, diamonds sparkling on its surface from the candles lining the walls.

She sat cross-legged in the middle of the cave floor, and I sat opposite her, somehow knowing it was expected of me. She held out her hands, and I placed mine in them. She closed her eyes and began to hum softly. My eyes drifted shut, and I began to see something else...

I stood beside her on a plateau, a large river far below us and the sea on the horizon. Smoke rose from the ocean, and the sky was unnaturally dark. Cries, pleas, and shouts rose into the air around us from all directions. My heart pounded and my knees were weak as desperation and fear surrounded me, pressed against me. She held up her hands, and the sound muted like a pillow had been pressed over the world.

"The world as we know it is ending. And when something ends so completely, it takes a long time to rebuild."

"What's happening? Are the gods angry?"

She smiled, a small enigmatic expression, and continued to look at the view ahead. "Who is to say what the gods feel or think?" She glanced at me. "Except when they're in your head. Then we have some idea, but we still don't know *why* they play the games they play, do we?"

I understood, then, that she too had been goddess-ridden and understood. "I hate it. I hate that they can use you that way, that you have no freedom or control."

She nodded slowly. "You don't consider it an honour, priestess of Hecate?"

I flinched. Any good priestess would be glad to be chosen. But lying wasn't an option, not here, in a sacred place where I was being shown a future I didn't understand. "I would, maybe, if it meant I could serve well. I helped a thief and murdered my brother; how is there anything good or godly in that?"

Her sigh was like the wind blowing through the oaks. "The gods we serve made us in their image, and as we're often violent, petty, and cruel, so too are they. Being a priestess of the goddess, any goddess, means accepting their plan as the one you follow, whether that makes your life here better or not." A pebble fell from the plateau cliff to the river below. "I said we were expecting you. I saw you in a vision, and I understood what you are."

I waited but she stayed quiet. "And what am I?"

She turned to me, her surreal eyes glowing in the sun. "You are power. You are change. You are an avenger, a fury in mortal form, born of the sun god, the goddess of the water, and serving the goddess of the underworld. And that makes you more dangerous than any priestess in any temple. Between your own power and that of the goddess filling you, you will burn through this life like a fire started by lightning in a land parched of water."

Once again, my heart began to pound, but this time it was from anticipation. That kind of power meant freedom.

"But there is always a price, princess, when it comes to power. Mortals aren't meant to wield the kind of magic you have running in your veins, and you will pay the price, over and over again. Never forget that when you're forced to use it, as you were with your brother and with the man attached to your destiny."

Her words were like cold water, dampening my excitement. I could feel the weight of my brother's head as I held it up to my horrified father, and I began to shake.

She nodded again. "When you forget to feel, when you are unashamed and the power overwhelms you, you've lost your way. Grieve for those you've lost, those you'll lose, and those you send to the underworld. Never take for granted your power over life and death, Medea. It's a burden not placed on your shoulders lightly."

She turned away and the cacophony of noise hit like a wall. I dropped to my knees and covered my ears, and emotions I'd not taken the time to feel swallowed me. My brother, who'd grown up angry with me, had died because of me. The little boy who had climbed trees, stolen apples from the kitchen and who had often left one where I could find it, was gone. What I'd done had been foretold, but that made it no less horrible, and the taint it would leave on my spirit would be there until I could drop to my knees and beg his forgiveness in the afterlife.

My mother and sister. I'd left them behind with barely a thought. Chaliope would be okay; she'd marry and leave my father's wretched house. But my mother, my sweet, gentle mother, would be alone. She'd known, and she'd already forgiven me, but what would happen to her now? I pictured her as I last saw her, and I knew. She'd return to the ocean now, her part in this drama complete. A sea nymph understood the ways of the gods as we mortals couldn't.

I wept. I pulled at my robes, I tugged at my hair, I screamed to the sky, and I cried for what I'd done and already lost. And there was still so far to go. I knew that, though I didn't know where I was supposed to end up or why.

Eventually, my weeping stopped. Exhausted, I listened to the cries. I smelled the strange burning in the air and watched as boats moved erratically along the far away seashore. We'd heard stories from travellers who said strange weather was sweeping over cities. Terrible drought in some places, deluges of rain in others. How bad would it get before the gods were satisfied? Had people been remiss in their sacrifices? Had not enough sheep been slaughtered or incense burned? I thought of the temple priestess. She was right; there was no way to reason the gods' actions. I could only play my part.

I got up and closed my eyes, and when I opened them, I was sitting in the cave, stiff and numb. In my hand was the beautifully carved wooden circle that pulsed with power and in front of me was a small basket of jars filled with various herbs and liquids. I was alone and couldn't ask what they were for. Somehow, I knew I'd figure it out when I needed them.

I stood and stretched. How long had I been here? A momentary pang of worry went through me. Would Jason leave without me? Destiny, she'd said. No, he'd wait. He was tied to me, like I was tied to him. So be it.

I made my way out of the temple to see the sun setting, sending purple shadows over the cliffside. Alkippe sat in the shade of a pine and smiled when I came out.

"I was afraid I was going to have to become a priestess in order to be at your side again." She stood and brushed off her skirts. "I'm glad to see we're not staying."

What it would be like, to stay here, in a temple so sacred to the gods that you could see into the world beyond it? But the thought passed. My calling to the temple had been a way out of my father's house, not a true calling, and to stay in a place like this would be sacrilege. The goddess had her own plans for me, and they didn't include a simple life in a cave.

"You might not feel that way when we're through," I said. "But I hope you know what it means to me that you're beside me." The catharsis I'd felt on the plateau remained with me, as did the warning. "If I ever forget to show you, to appreciate you, tell me." My eyes welled up. "You've given up everything to be with me on a journey with no certain end, and that kind of friendship is something written about by the travelling singers."

She pulled me into a hug. "I'll be beside you always. And if you get too full of yourself, I'll kick your feet from under you."

I laughed, the moment eased, and we headed back to the port together.

CHAPTER TWELVE
Stories

THERE IS NOWHERE TO hide on a ship. Bodily functions for men among men are barely given any thought. But when women are aboard, it becomes a different matter. Rations and water were stowed in the shallow area beneath the benches where the men rowed. There was no privacy, nowhere to go where you couldn't be seen. Jason and another of his crew hung a carpet meant for trade at the prow, attached haphazardly by rope to the mast and sides, and this allowed us some small bit of space. We used a makeshift pot to take care of our needs whenever they arose and we weren't near enough to land. She would then take it and dump it overboard. Of all the things I missed about living on land, privacy for that kind of thing was perhaps highest on the list.

Between Jason and Alkippe, we had an idea of the route ahead. They'd both talked to different people in the marketplace, especially to the traders who came in contact with people from all along the river. We had names of villages that would welcome us, and we had names of places we should avoid, people who weren't happy about strangers on their shores. We also heard that the river was dropping in places and that it might be difficult to get the Argo through some areas. Jason felt certain the crew would manage and given what I felt of our future together, I was confident as well. We bypassed Galati at the first large bend in the river, as we'd been told there was an illness among the villagers that caused extreme weakness. Instead, we once again stopped and slept on a deserted beach of soft white sand. Jason decided that as we were still far from home and had no idea how long the journey would take, he wouldn't ask the men to overtax themselves. Slow and steady was the best way, he felt, and it created an easy calm among the men.

And because of that ease, there was another aspect to living on a boat I hadn't considered, and as the men rowed against strong currents day after day, sometimes making little headway by the time we dropped anchor again in the evening, they began to relax around us.

Battered by wind and water, the division between sailor and princess quickly dropped away. Alkippe and I were soon included in the men's banter, and we enjoyed giving as good as we got. They told stories of their journey, of the crashing rocks they narrowly avoided by following a dove between them, nearly foundering when one of the boulders bumped against the prow. The story of the women of Lemnos had Kip and I in thrall, as the men told us how the wives had killed their husbands because the men had taken Thracian wives instead. It had left the island full of widows and bereft of men. One of them had fallen desperately in love with Jason, who had fled in the dead of night to get away from her bed and to avoid her tearful pleading that the Argonauts stay and help them repopulate the island. The bluster and crude jesting directed at Jason made him blush, and I couldn't help but like him a little more for the company he kept. I learned many of the men's names and family histories and did my best to remember them. Though some of them remained aloof and suspicious, most let down their guards, and I made an effort to speak frankly, directly, rather than in the tempered vague words I'd grown up uttering. That, too, brought down the barriers between us, and although they remained respectful, the laughter and conversation made for a far more enjoyable journey.

The men enjoyed asking us questions and were happy to oblige us in return. I asked about Thracian customs, about family life and food. I asked who they prayed to and where, filing away all the information for use when we arrived. The men were happy to reminisce, telling us of mothers and wives left behind, of their favourite foods and the gods who watched over their cities. In turn,

Kip and I talked about our home and the kingdoms surrounding Corinth. At some point, a few of these men might journey back and perhaps the information would help them along their way. I liked to think so anyway. In the evening, after we dropped anchor, I asked Jason about the future. I didn't share with him what I'd seen at the temple; that was for my knowledge only, a sacred gift. But that didn't mean I wouldn't live in the present.

"Will you miss being a shepherd with so little responsibility?" I asked as the clouds were turning pink and we'd laid out some makeshift bedding on the shore. He'd described sleeping under the stars, the basic meals he'd enjoyed with the herder's family, and the simple sweet taste of long grass in the spring. To give that up to take his place in a kingdom he'd only been to once seemed odd to me.

He glanced over his shoulder but no one was listening, and he turned back to look out over the water. "I already miss it, a little. It was simple, but it was good. Like...like an apple. Sweet, and you know what you're getting. But when we were going through the rocks, when we were escaping Lemnos...I worried about every man on this ship. They're here because of me, because they believe in my ability to rule my kingdom. This isn't war, where they'd gain great glory in death. If they die on this journey, it will be only as sailors helping a dispossessed prince, which isn't nearly as noble."

I considered the truth of that. Did they care about how he'd rule? I'd come to know that they came from a variety of kingdoms, widespread throughout Thrace, Thessaly, and Epirus. No, I thought, they came for the adventure, for the opportunity to see the world and to have a grand story to tell. They were mostly young men in search of more than they could find at home, a way to be remembered, a tale for the fireside when they were old and grey. I didn't blame them at all, and I didn't disabuse Jason of his notions. If he wanted to believe they were there for him, so be it. It didn't hurt anything and perhaps it gave him a feeling of support to bolster his spirit.

I was learning to like him, to some degree. He wasn't strong, like Ancaeus, or terribly smart, like Castor, but he was kind. His men liked him, though I wasn't sure they respected him as a fellow warrior. Was it better to be followed because your men liked you or because they knew you were fearsome? In this case, it didn't seem to matter. They followed his orders, and they had a vast array of experience between them that meant they often didn't need directions to sail well. There was a prevailing sense of optimism, and though we were off course, none of them seemed in a hurry to get back. Other than Jason, who spoke of being duty-bound to return and put the kingdom to rights. Sometimes those felt like platitudes, though, like a script he'd practiced during his time with the centaur. Like any young man, his eyes were turned toward any new things we might see. He, too, took turns fishing and was better than most of the other men at catching the evening's dinner. It was easy to see the pride he took in being good at something that didn't involve his title.

The River Ister was beautiful: sometimes swift and choppy, other times smooth and slow. But the rowing was hard because the current was pushing back towards the sea we'd come from. We had no idea how long it would take or what we'd face along the way, but no one seemed to mind. I certainly didn't mind at all. The future held chaos and sadness, and there was no escaping that. But here on the river, I was free to watch the shore, to stare at the birds, to let my hair flow freely in the breeze. Never did I worry that the men would behave in a way they shouldn't. Jason had chosen his crew well in that regard. They were men of simple, genuine honour. Though I saw Neleus glancing at Kip more than once, he kept his distance. I don't think it was fear of me but rather, his awareness of her position. I wasn't sure how I felt about sharing her should it come to that but decided I would deal with it when the time came. If it did.

Chapter Thirteen
Istros

W<small>E STOPPED AT THE</small> small harbour of Braila for fresh water. Jason wanted to get fresh food whenever we could, as we were unsure what we'd find further downriver. Kip and I stayed in a small inn, and it was heavenly to be able to wash properly. They even managed to clean our robes and when we got on the ship the following day, I was refreshed and ready.

The rowing was slow, and the men were tired by the time we reached Ghindarsti, though we knew well before we reached it that we were near. Boats lined the shores and the city spread along the shoreline like weeds in a field. There were fewer trees here, mostly browning pines, meaning we could see the strange way the houses were built on individual small hills where the tops had been flattened. Each house had a bright yellow painted sigil beside the door, the kind of colour you got from mixing turmeric with paste made of beeswax. Kip and I leaned against the rail and pointed things out to one another, and Jason studied it with a quiet intelligence I was coming to understand meant he was planning.

One thing that became clear was that the people around us were as interested in us as we were in them. When we pulled into the harbour, a small crowd was already waiting. I hadn't paid much attention to the Argo, but I turned to look at it when we got off and saw people pointing.

Kip had her head tilted, and I knew she was listening.

"They sound like us, but there are differences." I could hear it too.

She nodded. "It's more like the language I grew up with. A kind of river version of what we speak at the palace."

A boy was staring at us shyly from behind a dock post, and she knelt down and waved him over. He ran forward and touched her robe, looking impressed.

"Can you tell me what your people are called, sweet child?"

She used the dialect around us, but I understood it well enough.

He puffed out his little chest. "We are the Coslogeni, goddess. Born of the river god, Istros. We're the most powerful people on the river."

She smiled and gave him a coin. "Thank you, little one."

He clasped the coin to his chest and ran off into the crowd.

"Well, now we know who they are, not that it helps us overmuch."

Jason moved up beside us, his second in command, Neleus at his side. "I'm going to leave a few men to stay with the ship, but the rest will stay in the city. If it pleases you, princess, I think we should stay at the same inn. I'd like to know you're safe."

It hadn't occurred to me to worry about my safety, but he was right. This was a large city, and the mound houses at the edge didn't extend here, where houses were close together on narrow streets. Men here wouldn't care where I was from; they'd only know we were women alone. I appreciated his thoughtfulness, and then realized it might have come from Neleus worrying about Kip. Either way, it was well done.

The little boy we'd spoken to came out of the crowd, pulling a woman along behind him. She was young and fair, and her smile was open.

"My boy came home telling me of beautiful people on a beautiful ship who might need a guide." She looked down at him, and they shared a smile.

Jason bowed slightly. "We are strangers to your land and would be most grateful for a guide if it wouldn't trouble your family."

He may have grown up as a shepherd, but his mentor had done well, I thought. He spoke like someone brought up in a palace.

She smiled but didn't quite make eye contact, as was appropriate when speaking with a man you didn't know. It was something I never wished to adopt. There was truth in people's eyes even when there were lies on their lips. If you didn't look them in the eye, you might miss the truth of who they were.

"It would be my pleasure." She looked around at the many men of the Argo. "Do all of you need a place?"

Jason laughed. "The four of us would appreciate your help, lady, but the rest of my men will find their own beds for the night."

She looked relieved. "Come with me."

Kip fell in step beside her, and they began talking like old friends. I stayed behind, walking between Jason and Neleus. The little boy slipped his hand into Jason's and skipped along beside him, peppering him with questions that Jason answered with ease.

"Princess—"

I shook my head. "Neleus, I think we should perhaps do away with that particular title, especially in public."

He looked around. "Of course. Priestess, then?"

"I think that would be safe, but maybe we could try my name?"

He looked surprised, and then he smiled. "Medea, could I ask you something without giving offence?"

"I think you'll find very little offends me." It was true, at least to this point.

"The lady Alkippe, is she spoken for? Or rather, was she, before you came away with us?"

It was sweet, the way his cheeks turned pink and he looked at the ground when he asked. Apparently, I'd have to deal with this sooner than I'd thought. I concentrated on what I was feeling and was glad when there was nothing ill there. "Not that I'm aware of, Neleus. But there may be things she didn't tell me." I considered the question further. "I know when we're in the palace or among people who judge how things are done, we have to behave a certain way. But we're on a boat, taking a journey that includes danger and many miles. I think you should consider that Alkippe is a person, and as a person, she can speak for herself."

He frowned and kicked a pebble. "That would be acceptable

to you?"

"I would like nothing better for Alkippe to have the freedom to be with who she wants, when she wants, and to find love where she will. That's all any of us can hope for." A sense of melancholy rose at my words, but I pushed it away. I wanted the freedom, not the love.

He walked in silence for a moment and slowly his smile grew wide. "You speak like an oracle without the frustrating parts."

That made me laugh, and I thought I might have a friend in him. We stopped in front of a large stone house with a yellow sigil by the door that looked like an eagle in flight. Our new guide turned to us as the little boy let go of Jason's hand and ran inside.

"There are more elegant places, but they don't cook as well as I do." She smiled and opened the door. Kip and the men went inside, but I stopped beside her.

"Can I ask about the symbols? I've seen them on most of the houses."

She looked at the eagle. "Every family born to Istros takes courage from the spirit of one of the animals or plants that grow in his land. My family is one of the oldest of the Coslogeni, and we took the eagle. We believe in flying free and being brave."

They took their gods seriously here then. It was good to know. "Thank you."

She touched my robe. "This is beautiful work. You wouldn't find better in the craft halls here."

It was the work of the temple priestesses, and they were known for their deft hands and intricate designs. Other than being clean, I hadn't given them much thought. "They come from a temple far away." It was all I could say without feeling like I'd given away too much. It was unlikely my father would search this far up this river, but people travelled, and you could never be sure how far words could go on the wind.

She searched my expression, and I saw understanding.

"Things said in this house will stay in this house." She motioned towards the door. "If you'd like, I'll have a bath drawn and you can soak while I cook dinner."

The house was clean and cosy, and the windows let in a welcome night breeze. The little boy had already taken Jason and Neleus upstairs, and Gestia, as I learned her name was, showed us to our own room. It was spacious and had two soft looking beds as well as a copper bath.

"I'll have someone fill the bath and bring you something cooler to wear, if you'd like?"

We thanked her and made ourselves comfortable by the window as a stream of young women bearing hot water made their way into the room, filling the tub quickly. When it was done and they'd closed the door behind them, Kip and I quickly stripped down and took turns washing. I wouldn't want her to have a cold bath simply because I wanted to luxuriate myself, and her smile told me she appreciated it. There was a knock at the door, and someone passed Kip some clothing.

It was far lighter than the robes we'd been wearing, a fine linen that was beautifully dyed. Mine was a blue that reminded me of my mother's eyes, and Kip's was a deep green like the trees of the grove below the temple. It felt unnatural but was far more comfortable, and after tying the string that bound it closer to me, right below my breasts, we went downstairs and followed the aroma coming from the kitchen.

Jason and Neleus were already there, and there was no mistaking the look in their eyes when we entered. It was a reminder of a different kind of power, one I'd had yet to use though the goddess had certainly given me a taste of it. We sat at the table and Gestia served us herself, with her son and some of her serving girls helping. The food was delicious, better than any I'd had at the palace, and the conversation was easy. Neleus seemed relaxed but continued to take subtle glances at Alkippe throughout the meal. She didn't seem to notice, focused as she was on asking questions about the customs here.

"We passed houses on the way in, built on mounds." Jason

picked up another dolmade. "I've never seen anything like it."

Gestia looked at her son, who answered as though taught to recite it. "The mound houses are from the time before, when the river was so high every person had their own little island, and they took boats from house to house. Then, later, the river got lower, and they couldn't take boats between the houses anymore. Now, the river is where you found it, and no one really lives in the mound houses anymore, because it's too tiring to climb up to them all time."

He looked proud of himself, and Jason told him it was a tale well-told, making his smile grow even wider.

"The river has dropped so low?" I asked, thinking of my vision.

"It's taken many, many years, but yes. We seem to get less fish too." Gestia's expression turned serious. "I've heard that upriver it's getting worse. There isn't enough food to feed the people in the villages, and they come seeking help. We get more and more in the city, and we have the room. But when it gets bad here..." She shrugged. "Istros will provide."

The conversation turned to other topics, and she described some of the places we might pass, though she only knew of them through the words of travellers who had stayed at her inn. Her husband, we found out, had been crushed in a rockslide in the mountains above when he was gathering limestone and small gems to trade at the market. Her son had only just been born, so she started the inn.

In that, I saw her freedom. She'd married and done what was perceived as her duty, and she had a son she could be proud of. She was running her own business, making her own money, and living as good a life as she could. No one told her what to do. I admired what she'd done, though she probably would have traded that freedom to have her husband back. Still, it proved it was possible, and without a goddess using you as a toy.

The night wore on, and I knew I needed to make a trip. "Could your son lead me to your temple, Gestia? I feel the need to say thanks for our safe passage and hospitality."

She looked a little surprised. "Of course, lady, though it's very late. Would you rather go in the morning?"

I felt it, the pull in my blood, the pressure on my neck. "I'd rather go tonight, please."

Jason looked at me, and I saw sympathy in his eyes.

She called her son and handed me a thin, long cloak. "There's a slight chill in the air. Please take this."

I put it on gratefully and followed her son. He looked tired, and I felt a momentary pang until I remembered how exciting he found the beautiful strangers and their beautiful boat. This would be an addition to his story, the foray to the temple at midnight.

When we got there after a short hike up a grass covered hill, I gave him a coin. "I can find my way back, sweet one."

He looked undecided for a moment, then waved and set off at a run back down the trail. I entered the chill temple and knelt beside the altar piled high with shells and handmade jewellery. I closed my eyes and let go of all my questions. I let the silence fill me, sliding over the danger, the blood, the choices I'd made like a blanket smothering a fire. The stillness settled me, and I could breathe again.

I heard a noise and opened my eyes. In the shadows was a figure covered in a robe that seemed to shimmer and move. His eyes were pools of blue, and his beard looked like seafoam.

I bowed my head, my heart pounding. Would I ever become accustomed to the gods appearing before me? Did anyone?

"Speak." His voice was a cascade, the sigh of water over a cliff edge.

"I came to thank you for our safe passage, Istros, god of the great river and its people, and to ask for your continued blessings as we make our way further."

He shifted, moving towards me, and I swore I could hear the tide as it hit the shore. I wasn't prepared when he touched my cheek, his hand cool and soft.

"You have my blessings, daughter of the dark goddess, granddaughter of the sun and daughter of water, and I'll grant you a gift as one of our chosen. When the rivers diverge, when you must make a choice about which way to go, think of me and you'll know the way."

Knowledge poured into me, the tides, the shifting of the currents becoming one with my blood. I gasped as water, cool and fierce, rushed through my body. His hand left my face and when I looked up, he was gone.

CHAPTER FOURTEEN
Blood Tides

I STUMBLED BACK TO the inn, the feeling of rushing water almost too much to carry. Alkippe caught me on the stairs and together, she and Gestia helped me to bed. I heard Kip telling Gestia not to worry, that I was god-touched and sometimes things like this happened. It was vague and would have made me smile if I didn't feel like I was drowning. I slept and dreamt of water: waterfalls, rivers, tides, oceans. Of life in and around it and how it connected all living things, and I tumbled along, powerless against the currents.

When I woke, I felt refreshed and full of energy. I wanted to take the world to me and never let it go. Kip and I had an early breakfast with Gestia and her son while Jason and Neleus went to the port to see about supplies. Gestia drew a map for us, showing us where she thought villages were. She wasn't sure how we'd get to the sea she'd never heard of, the one where Jason's kingdom lay, but there was no need to worry. After my visit to the temple the night before I had no doubt that we'd find what we were looking for.

The feeling of rushing water in my body had subsided, and yet I could still sense it if I concentrated. The ebb and flow and the way life on land mimicked it in the rhythms and routines of the people were a part of me now. And I very much liked it. Once again, I felt bigger, more powerful, more...knowing. I wouldn't say it out loud, of course, even though Kip kept looking at me quizzically. The gods don't like braggarts, though they themselves had no such scruples.

We went upstairs to take advantage of a wash, since there was no telling how long we'd go without one again, and Gestia brought in a bag with our robes in it.

"It only gets warmer from here, and it seems to me you'd be

more comfortable in our type of clothing than yours."

Kip went to protest but Gestia shook her head firmly. "Jason has paid me well for your stay, so well we'll be fine if I don't take in another guest for the rest of the season. It's the least I can do, and it gives me some pleasure to think of a gift travelling so far."

I thanked her, surprising myself by hugging her. I rarely touched anyone, but this woman and her child had been so kind. Kindness had been a rarity in my life, and I knew enough to treasure it. She hugged me back, and then Kip and I set off in the light robes we'd worn the day before, and there were two more in the bag with our original robes. It felt like excess, which was novel given that I once had the wardrobe of a princess.

When we got to the port, it was teeming with life and noise, and Kip and I took the time to buy small things from the marketplace that caught our eye. From where we stood, we could see the ship, and it was clear the men were still loading supplies.

Kip studied a bracelet. "Will you tell me about last night?"

I knew she'd ask, but what could I say? But then, this was Kip, who understood that I saw things others didn't. "Istros has given me the gift of understanding the waterways." It was bland, put that way, but that was the essence of it.

Her eyebrows raised, and she shook her head slightly. "A woman with less spine would be terrified if the gods kept appearing to her the way they do you."

I pondered that as we made our way to the ship. Why wasn't I terrified? Yes, in the moment it was breathtaking, and I worried about their capriciousness. But terror...no, that wasn't part of it. Maybe it was because I was the granddaughter of the sun; Helios, certainly, wasn't afraid of anything. And the goddess I served, of dark hearths and things unseen, she had nothing to fear either. So it made sense, maybe.

Or maybe I was foolish and should be far more concerned about being one of their pets.

We boarded the ships, received welcome from various crew,

and made our way to our seat at the front. As the boat pulled away, we waved to the people on the shore, and there was more than one woman who looked disappointed that the men were sailing off. As princess in Egrisi, I would never have enjoyed the freedom to wave to people; it would have been too common. But here I was a woman on a boat, a priestess, yes, but someone people could relate to in some way. All my life I'd been an outsider, and this new sensation of being on the inside, created simply by being among people, made me understand with new insight that the palace, any palace, was a cage.

And how I abhorred cages.

We moved onto the middle of the river, the men rowing hard, and Jason came to join us.

"You returned late, Medea. Is all well?" he asked, and there was no judgement in his tone, simply curiosity.

Was it well? I could feel the water rushing below us like it was part of me, and it created a strange sense of vertigo, of being in two places at once and falling in both. "Yes, thank you. I went to the temple and prayed for assistance on our journey. I believe I was heard." There was little point to telling him about my meeting. The men were only now becoming at ease, and I didn't want to put another wall up between us.

"That's very good news. There were many traders who told us of villages to watch for but only for the next several days' journey. Beyond that, there weren't answers." He looked out at the river. "But I have to believe the gods are with us." He looked at me sidelong. "We know they have been, at least."

I nodded and didn't say anything else. There was no question they wanted us on this journey, although we might never know why or what dangers it entailed for us. For now, we were on our way and that seemed to be enough. The improbable passion I felt for him had ceased, as, I believe, had his for me. Neleus took his place at the oars in such a way he could continue to catch glances of Kip, though she still seemed oblivious.

The day passed quickly, and the mountains flattened out and became plains. We stopped at a village called Silistra, where we found simple housing for the night. I was tired but not overly so and only managed to sleep lightly.

And so, I was awake and out of bed at the first tremor of the earth, and I pulled Kip down the stairs and outside as it grew in strength, until we fell to our knees with our hands in the earth as it flung us to and fro, a sickening roar making me feel ill. Screams and cries were all around us and the roofs of houses collapsed in, creating more screaming. Or in some cases, cutting it off. Plumes of dust clouded the dry air, making it hard to breathe.

It probably wasn't very long, but it felt like it went on for an eternity. It stopped, and Kip and I looked at one another wide-eyed. Slowly we both rose and looked around. We headed back to the house we'd been sleeping in and found much of the roof on the bed we'd left behind. The owner lay under half the wall, and it was clear he wouldn't be getting back up. Kip let out a small cry and turned away.

Jason came running up the hill, his expression wild. "You're well?"

I nodded, still looking around. "The men?"

"I can't find three, but the rest are with the ship. If you'll gather your things, we'll go. The gods aren't happy here."

Kip and I got our bags and followed him to the shore. I couldn't help but think that fifty young men could help rebuild, or at the very least help with the dead. But the gods never spoke quietly when they did choose to speak, and here they were shouting. By the time we made it back to the ship, the three men Jason hadn't been able to find were in place, and we set off quickly, leaving behind wailing, cries, and the unquestionable sense of desperation.

It was dark on the water, and the men rowed slowly so we didn't slam into any unexpected rocks. Kip and I huddled together against the black morning cold, and it was a relief when the sun sparkled across the water. We floated along in the current as the men took a break, letting the sail fill and carry us forwards with Jason steering at the helm. I noticed the men looking at us, and it wasn't long before Neleus made his way over.

"Priestess, the men are wondering if you have any godly knowledge of what happened?"

Would that I had words of comfort or some prophetic saying. But I wasn't a liar and wouldn't pretend to knowledge I didn't have. "I'm sorry, Neleus, if the gods are angry with the people of Silistra, they haven't seen fit to tell me why." I thought about it. "But every Argonaut is here. No matter where he slept, he came back when plenty of others around him died. I think that speaks to someone watching over us."

He looked a little surprised, but then nodded in that slow, thoughtful way of his. He flicked a smile at Kip. "That's very true, priestess, and I think the men will be glad to hear it." He returned to his seat and spoke softly, and the relief in the men's body language was clear.

Kip tugged at my sleeve. "Careful, Medea. They already expect great things of you. The last thing you want to be is an oracle."

"Why not? Oracles are sought all over the world. They're the height of knowledge, and everyone knows they play at the gods' feet."

"They're also the first ones people turn against when things go wrong." She squeezed my hand. "I'm counselling caution."

I let go of the pique and squeezed back. As always, she only had my own best interests at heart. "I'll rein myself in. Thank you."

We sailed on and slept on a beach, foregoing the small harbour. I think most of us felt that we'd had enough of people for the moment. The following morning was bright and beautiful, and one of the men began singing in a low, strong voice and others joined in. By evening, everyone's good humour was back and so the jesting and singing continued. We came to a fork in the river, and Jason looked at me from where he stood at the wheel. I closed my eyes and asked the question, and the water surged in my blood, making me lightheaded. I motioned, and he moved the boat onto the left fork, and it wasn't long before we came to another small, quiet harbour.

There was nothing terribly interesting about the place, and yet I couldn't help but feel the ghosts in it. Not, necessarily, the ghosts of those who had been, but rather the ghosts of those would come to be here, long after we'd gone to the underworld ourselves. The ground itself seemed to groan under the weight of the future, and I don't think any of us slept well that night. We were off early.

As I looked at the receding shore the world spun and tilted, and it was another time. The clothing was strange, and the buildings surrounded by patchy, shiny fencing were ominous. The cries of despair rose into the sky, and the shades of the people within nearly blackened the sky as they left in groups too large to be natural.

The vision faded, leaving me retching over the side. Kip rubbed my back soothingly and gave me a waterskin to rinse my mouth. She didn't ask but when we sat back down, I didn't miss the stares from the men, some of whom had stopped rowing to watch me. I closed my eyes and concentrated on the feeling of the water, flowing and cleansing, and soon felt better. A shadow fell over me, and I opened my eyes to see Jason squatting in front of me.

It took him a moment to meet my gaze and when he did, I was reminded how very young he was. Still, he was here, and that was something.

"Is there anything we should know, lady?" he asked softly.

"Nothing that concerns this world, no." I thought of what I'd seen and how to explain it. "Sometimes I see things I can't explain but that have little to do with us. I saw what that place will become, a kind of feeding ground for Hades."

He shuddered. "I'm glad the gods don't see fit to show me those things."

No, I didn't imagine he would have handled it well. I simply smiled slightly. "Are we on the main river?" I didn't need to ask. I could feel it, but there was no point in saying so.

He stood and stretched. "We are, and the wind is good. But we could use supplies if there's a village ahead."

We'd gone further than we had information for, so there was no telling where the next place would be. We sailed swiftly and as evening hit, it became oppressively humid, a condition I'd only felt a few times at home. Our robes stuck to us, even thin as they were, and the men rowed in nothing but their tunics, pulled as high as they could go without putting themselves on show. I have no doubt that had we not been aboard, it would have been a ship of naked men.

Once again, we slept on the shore and used our supplies sparingly. There was plenty to go around, but these men had sailed all the way to Egrisi and understood the importance of taking measure. I wasn't hungry, nor was I thirsty. The water surged and plunged in my veins, an odd, unsettling feeling, and I wished we were back on the boat.

Though Jason slept near, he never tried to sleep beside or with me, and there was never a point when I worried we were unsafe among the many men surrounding us. I imagine had I not demonstrated my powers, as well as what I was capable of, that perhaps it mightn't have been the case. While Jason had chosen his crew well, we were still two women on a ship of many men, and young ones aren't known for their ability to withstand temptation. But the men mostly kept their distance, though Neleus slept nearby. I wondered why he didn't make any motions towards Kip, but I didn't want to put anything in her head if she truly hadn't noticed. I doubted it; she was one of the most observant people I'd ever known.

We sailed for two more days without seeing another village, stopping only to sleep and eat before moving on once again. I woke in the early hours of the second day and felt the earth trembling lightly under my fingertips, and when I looked at Jason, saw that he too was awake, his palms pressed to the ground. When it stopped, we stared at one another for a moment longer, and then I rolled over and pretended to sleep once again. I didn't have any answers for the questions in his eyes. Was the earth goddess herself angry? What would appease her?

The following night brought us to a large harbour which, while not as busy as some of the others we'd been to, had plenty of supplies and beds. In Orezov, we heard people talking about the earth shaking and a village not far away that had been nearly destroyed. After the earth had stopped shaking, the waters had risen as though pushed forwards by Poseidon himself, drowning many who had survived the initial destruction. I caught Jason's eye and he frowned, shaking his head slightly. It was good that although he hoped I had answers, he wasn't cross with me for not having any.

We spoke with the innkeeper, an older man whose wife had died the previous year. He was surly and not terribly talkative but when sitting with Jason at the table, he was happy to give us a sense of what was ahead.

"Here, we are." He set down a small wooden carving that looked like an egg. "Here, you come to Artanes. The River Lom is big and strong, and the fishing is good." He tapped the table with another little wooden egg. "After that, you should be watching. Old magic lives in the crossing of the three rivers, and people have been in those two villages for longer than we can remember." He looked at me with his narrow, yellowed eyes. "You should do the talking there, if you want good beds and prices for food."

The first village, he said, was called Lepenski Vir, where the Lepenian people were unusual and fiercely independent. The second village was Vinca, where the Vatin people made things out of beautiful black glass and copper. It was also, he said, a place where many of the people looked and dressed like Jason and his crew.

"A Thessalonian settlement? On the Istros?" Jason seemed bewildered, as did Neleus.

The old man shrugged. "They call themselves the Vatin. I don't know about the other thing you said." He stood and placed a bowl of barely good fruit on the table. "You can find supplies here, but I suggest you wait until you get to the other places. More choice." He poked at the overripe fruit. "And better options."

With that he left, and the four of us remained at the table.

"I think he's right. We get only basic supplies, and we row until we reach Lepenski. He said it's at the centre of three rivers." Jason turned to me. "Will you know which to take?"

I nodded without hesitation. It was exactly what Istros had given me the gift for.

"Good. Then we can sail to each village in turn and get some rest in between." He stood and Neleus stood with him. "Yassos."

We bid him goodnight and watched as they went. I turned to Kip and saw her watching them with a small smile.

"So you have noticed his affection?" I asked.

She tilted her head. "Of course. How could I not with the way he looks at me like a lost lamb?"

"But you don't find him attractive?"

"Of course I do. And if we were at the palace rather than on a ship of fifty men, I might be interested in pursuing it. But we're not, and therefore I won't. But he's from Jason's city, so it might be that I see what happens when we get to where we're going." She smiled. "I have enough to do looking out for you. I don't need a man's hand under my chiton to distract me."

I laughed, and we headed to bed. My dreams were vivid, and my pulse raced as I felt the water ahead, saw the people who almost seemed to be watching for us, and above it all, the eyes of the goddess watching, always watching, my every move.

I woke drenched in sweat, with Kip mopping my brow with a cold cloth.

"You've been talking in your sleep," she said.

Remnants of the dreams slipped away, leaving me with only the sense of something looming, something dark and despairing. "I can't make sense of what I saw."

She wrung out the cloth. "Then you don't need to. They're very clear when they want to be. You'll know what they want you to do when it's important."

"So wise, my sweet friend." I got up, and we quickly gathered our things to head to the boat. Most of the men, including Jason, were already in place, and he welcomed me with a smile and nod. News of the Achaean settlement had gone out, and the men were clearly eager to see what it was like. We left the harbour, and I felt the tug in my soul. We were sailing back into the hands of the gods and as the man had said, it felt like older magic, like the earth and sky mingling in my blood, and the taste was like the best wine on a cool summer day. It called to me like a shepherd guiding his flock.

I can hear you, and I'm coming.

CHAPTER FIFTEEN
Vodena Vila

I COULDN'T STOP SHAKING. The closer we got to Lepenski Vir, the harder it became to breathe. I slipped in and out of visions that made no sense, snippets of things I didn't have time to understand before they shifted again, leaving me elsewhere. I was a stone tumbling downhill towards a cliff edge, and then we were beneath them for real.

The cliffsides were high, so high we could only see a strip of sky. And as we drew closer, there were enormous faces carved into the stone, three times the height of a man and again as large across. They wore serious expressions as they looked down on those travelling the river. Every man on the boat stopped rowing as we sailed beneath them, two godly visages on each side of the canyon, and we floated past in expectant silence. It was as though none of us wanted to disturb them, to draw their attention. And more than one man looked towards me, watching. Would I provide safety? Would I jerk and fall unconscious yet again?

I did neither. I watched the enormous carvings and felt that the gods themselves observed through those eyes. But they were gods older than the ones I served, a chilling and startling thought. How could that be? Were they gone? Had they passed the world on to their children? Where were they now? As we passed the final face, I looked into its eyes and felt myself analysed and found wanting. Every breath was a struggle under the weight of those who understood that magic and gifts from the gods required a price few mortals could pay. I closed my eyes and answered a question that I felt asked deep in my bones. Yes, I would pay it. I would pay whatever the gods required if I could stay free, if I could live my life under their guidance, taking steps I chose instead of those they determined. Should you barter with the gods? Especially with those far more ancient than any we knew? A smell of apples surrounded me, and I knew my bargain had been made. Now I had to pay whatever price they'd exact at their whim.

I opened my eyes and could breathe again. Once more, power surged through me, making me feel as big as the faces in the stone, and I understood things, ancient things, as I never had before. The mountains lifted and fell, the rivers were swollen and dry. The very bones of the earth cracked, broke free, and floated away from each other. Plants grew, animals changed, and at some point, we began crying to the gods for help. Throughout it all, they watched the way a king watches his children grow—from a distance, dispassionate and vaguely interested in how they'll be of use. I felt all this in my body and soul and let it flow through me, holding the knowledge tightly like a child holds sweet figs. It was mine, and it would make me stronger and wiser than those around me.

But I felt, too, the darkness of the gift. The light requires the dark, and the knowledge given meant that yes, I would be stronger and wiser, but it pulled on the part of me that had looked on at Absyrtos being thrown overboard in pieces and not railed against it. It pulled at the part of me who had cut his throat, felt the knife slip below his taut flesh and sever tendons like bands pulled too tightly. That part of me I had to acknowledge in the face of the ancient ways that knew blood spilled was the greatest gift the gods desired, and I would give it, again and again.

I shuddered. So be it. If that was the cost, I would pay it.

When one of the sailors shouted and pointed at the water, I looked down and pulled Kip over to see too. The water beside the boat leapt with colour thanks to the shapes of women clothed in strips of pinks and oranges that seemed to dance with the music of the tides, their arms and legs more fin-shaped than limb-like. They were small things, no larger than the length of my forearm, and they were beautiful.

"What creatures are these?" Jason asked, standing beside me.

"Vodena Vila." I pulled the name from the new knowledge given to me. "Ancient water fairies who protect the waterways. If we meant harm, they would sink our boat before we got to the gate." I watched, smiling as one leapt from the water, twirled, and dove back beneath the boat's plume. "They exist here and nowhere else on earth now."

I saw Kip glance at me, her brow furrowed, and I shook my head slightly. I'd speak of these things to her one day but not within hearing of the men. The rise and fall of power often balanced on the pinhead of secrecy and a lack of understanding. Power was my foothold in this world, and I wouldn't diminish it by explaining how I knew these things. Although gifts from the gods were something to be admired, gifts I had because I was chosen and powerful within myself were far better for gaining, and keeping, respect.

A shadow fell over the ship, and the Vila dove and didn't come up again. I turned to see a gate larger than any I'd ever seen. Each panel on the side of the river was made of iron inlaid with intricate designs that surrounded the same faces carved into the rocks behind us.

Jason leaned over and studied them closely. "Remarkable." He looked at me, and I nodded for him to continue. "Do you see the frame, the piece of iron along each side? It's made so the main door attaches to it and will allow the gate to swing over the water, effectively closing the river off to anyone sailing into the city. No one could attack by water, and they'd be ready for you to attack by land."

It *was* remarkable, and I knew it was a design created long ago by people who had more understanding of these things, people who were now long gone. In my mind's eye I saw their city, full of these types of wonders, and I felt their despair as the water crashed over their beautiful world, taking the whole thing into the sea, along with their amazing creations. A few things, like this, were left behind. It made my eyes well with tears to know what was lost, how we could have learned from such people.

Beyond the gate, the shadow dropped away and once again, we were in the sunlight. A breeze picked up, the sail was let down, and we fair flew along the water to the harbour at Lepenski Vir. The old inn owner had been right. Three rivers met beyond the mouth of the harbour, creating whirling tides that seemed to meet, take over one another, and flow off again elsewhere. But the only city on the crossing was Lepenski, with the other coasts looking empty but for trees and wading birds.

We docked and I waited, though I wasn't sure why. I knew I shouldn't get off the boat yet, and Kip waited beside me, used to not asking questions. Jason, busy with his men and discussing what provisions were needed, paid no attention. I waited, watching.

It was when many of the men had already left the ship that I felt what I'd been waiting for. Not that it was subtle. The crowd on shore, interested in the beautiful ship full of men chiselled with muscle from hard days of rowing, were welcoming and open. Chatter was high and children ran among the adults, touching scabbards, caressing leather, and giggling when someone went to swat at them before they dashed back into the crowd. Slowly, the locals grew quiet and moved aside. Our crew watched, confused and wary.

And out of the midst of the people came a woman who exuded the kind of power few humans held. Her long grey hair was tied in intricate braids that became a kind of crown, and no queen would have commanded more respect. People bowed their heads as she passed, but her eyes met mine and never wavered. Her linen robes were finer than anything I'd had at home, and they floated around her, highlighting her elegance.

"By the gods," Kip breathed softly beside me.

The woman stopped by the ramp of our boat and waited, and I made my way to her, trying to look like the poised temple priestess I'd been trained as but after days on the water, I feared I looked more like a beleaguered peasant. I felt the stir in my blood and remembered the strength I'd been given and raised my chin. I was no peasant.

When I reached her, I bowed my head respectfully and saw Kip go to her knees reverently beside me. It irked me for some reason I couldn't name. She certainly didn't revere me that way.

"Welcome, Princess Medea. I've been waiting for you." She stepped back and motioned. "The temple is ready."

I gave her a small smile as though I understood, and I fell in behind her as she led the way. Ready for what? How did she know my name? I considered what the old innkeeper had said. "I'm sorry, my lady. Could you give me a moment?"

She turned and nodded, her hands folded in front of her. I searched for Jason and found him watching us from the edge of the crowd, who still hadn't gone back to what they were doing. I raised my voice to be heard by everyone listening. "If you and your men could see which traders offer the best deals, my prince, perhaps I can assist you with the transactions upon my return." He looked surprised, as they'd certainly never needed my help before, but then I saw his understanding. The old innkeeper had said I should do the talking if we wanted the best trade deals, and now that I saw their reverence for the woman I assumed was their High Priestess, it made sense. He gave a respectful bow and turned to his men.

I smiled at my guide. "Thank you."

She resumed her walk and I followed, looking around as we climbed a steep path through the village. The houses near the shore were like none I had ever seen. Arrayed in a fan shape, the front of every house faced the river. Some were small, little more than a single room. Others, especially as we got higher, were much larger. All of them were covered in a beautiful red clay of some kind, inscribed with symbols, and they all had large firepits outside the front door. The path narrowed and the trees grew sparser, and then I spotted doors cut into the hillsides. "Are those houses too?" I asked, unable to curb my curiosity.

She glanced at one of the hillside doors. "Once, they were used only for storage of food and wine. But the earth trembles, the sun god shines down until we gasp with thirst, and the water falls lower each day. There's been sickness. Now, our pit houses are used when it becomes too hot to be outside and for those who become ill. We leave the river and fall into the earth mother's arms for protection." Her tone was heavy with the changes they faced.

I looked over my shoulder at Kip, who stared back wide-eyed. All along the river it had been the same. Earth trembling, water changing, illness, and heat. What did it mean?

We arrived at a beautiful building, the largest yet, covered in the red clay with an enormous fire pit surrounded by triangular stones all tilted slightly towards the pit. They had holes bore into the tops of the triangles, as though to hollow them out. I was so struck by the set up, I failed to notice how I was feeling until it nearly buckled my knees.

I reached out and steadied myself on a pillar, and the priestess walked inside the temple. Two acolytes came rushing out bearing water and a cold cloth, and I was quickly restored, though my head continued to buzz with the nearness of the gods. Not mine; these were the ancient gods, those of the faces carved into the canyon rock.

The priestesses stepped aside, heads bowed, and I made my way into the dim, cool space. Kip stayed outside, and I understood why. She served me in the temple of our gods, but we were guests here in this sacred foreign temple. The priestess I'd followed up the trail was waiting by a low stone altar set in the middle of the room. Black glass reflected and swallowed the firelight coming from the rushwick lanterns burning a sweet moss that scented the air in a delicate fragrance that made me unsteady.

"Drink." She held out a beautifully worked stone chalice.

The honeyed wine was sweet and earthy, the finest I'd ever tasted. Beneath it, though, was something else. Something herbal, a potion meant for sacred things. I handed it back to her, and she splashed some on the altar, where it beaded and shifted, running together and apart, and I couldn't look away from the patterns emerging. I sank slowly to my knees.

I saw myself, running through the trees towards the Argo, my hair flying behind me, my arms clutching my few belongings, and moving swiftly beside me was the goddess, laughing. I watched the water turn red and heard my father's wails of sorrow, and I felt despair. I saw us on the boat, among the people we stopped to speak with, and I felt wonder. I saw Jason looking at me when I wasn't aware, his expression one of awe, fear...and desire, which surprised me. I saw the men who looked at us, but never for long. Some were curious, some were afraid, some were lecherous, some were angry. So much emotion, it threatened to overwhelm me. I felt it all, every moment. Not the experience, but the emotion behind all of it, the ones buried and the ones let rein.

I wept.

Tides of impressions washed through me, and I understood. Power, love, hate, desire... Emotion drove us, all of us, forwards. Fear of death, of being lost, of being nothing, of being forgotten made us strive for more. And each feeling, no matter what it was, drove us in different ways and for different reasons, even if the base sentiment was the same. We were creatures of feeling, the way the old gods had created us to be. The further we grew from the old gods, the more complicated our desires and needs became, the more confused and desperately we lived our lives.

There was no telling how long I sat in the blood cave, but at last I felt it coming to an end. I saw Jason, older and heavier, his shoulders slumped and his hands over his face. He sat alone with his back to the Argo, the picture of defeat and despair.

My stomach clenched and bile rose in my throat. That would be his end. What of mine? Nothing but shapes in slick, grey mist, and the emotions were taut like lines pulled by heavy fish.

My eyes felt full of grit when I opened them once again and found myself lying on the cool, hard floor. It was dark beyond the temple entrance, so I'd been there for some hours. Hearing a sound, I slowly pushed up from the floor to see the beautiful priestess sitting in a niche in the wall, like an exquisite statue carved of redwood. She motioned and a temple priestess brought me water, which I drank gratefully. When I was done, she stood and tilted her head, and I got up and followed her through a back door of the temple. It led to a beautiful garden lit with candles and burning moss. She sat beside a pond, and I sat next to her.

She took my hand and turned my palm up, then traced the lines with her fingertip. It made me shiver as the power she exuded seemed to flow across my palm.

"Daughter of the new gods, the old gods have touched you as well." She traced the long line that ran in a half circle around my thumb. "Some of us are placed in their hands to do their bidding, to be the ones who lead others to their worship." She moved to the long line across my palm. "But we are never at ease."

She continued to hold my hand but with her other hand, she touched my forehead, and I gasped and arched at the sudden flow of voices and emotions that slammed into me. I tried to pull away, but she held tight, her grip surprisingly strong.

"Listen to them. Hear them. These are the people I serve, the way you will serve others. Feel what they feel, and you understand what your own sacrifice must be in order to serve the gods who need you. Never turn away from what others feel, even more than what they say. Wisdom is found in understanding the emotion that drives both gods and humans alike."

She released me, and I nearly fell forwards. Once again, a glass of water was pressed into my hand, and I drank deeply. We sat that way for some time, and when I could finally speak again, when the voices went silent, I turned to her. "Why use us at all?"

She shook her head, understanding the deeper question I couldn't voice. "The gods only know. We can but live as true to them and to ourselves as possible. But to deny their gifts is to insult them, and we both understand what comes of that."

I remembered the goddess's eyes in the forest when she told me what to do, when she looked out at me through my sister's eyes, and I shuddered. The old gods might understand how mortals were created of emotion, but the new gods embodied that emotion in its varying forms; while one of them might be love, she wasn't compassion, and while another might be war, he wouldn't be desire. The old gods were all things of heaven and earth, the new gods were...less. It didn't make them any less powerful, but perhaps I could live with them around me a little easier.

She nodded as though divining my thoughts, and I wondered if she could read them. Her small smile gave me the answer. What a power, to read the minds of those around you.

"Knowing what others think is a curse, not a gift," she said softly. "You rarely want to know what things they're capable of considering. There is beauty, but it's often threaded into a blanket of mud." She stood and held out her hand. "Your road is long, and I admit I don't envy you; no mortal should bear the weight of the gods as you do."

I bowed my head and tried to keep my thoughts clear, but I couldn't deny the flush of pleasure I received from being found worthy by so many gods.

She sighed quietly and let go of my hand. "But perhaps they know when there's a mortal who can play their game with ease."

She led the way from the temple and stood to the side. Kip was sleeping against a tree, a light blanket draped over her. I tapped her shoulder and when she jerked awake, her relief in seeing me was clear.

She walked down the path with me, and I contemplated what I'd seen and learned this day. There were gods older than mine. I now served them all. I understood emotion in a way I never had before, and I knew it would serve me well. I had seen Jason's end, but it looked many years away. My own future remained a mystery.

I was a tool of the gods and with every gift, I took one more step towards being one myself.

I shook the thought away. Hubris was judged harshly and to compare oneself to a god was certain to get you turned into a plant or bird. Gifts given could be taken away, and then I'd be as I was in the beginning: a girl in a cage.

We slept at an inn a temple priestess had suggested to Kip, and I woke after a fitful sleep. The earth shook slightly again in the night, and fear was quick to find me in the multitude of people in the village. Many were taking flight, leaving the river to go somewhere the gods weren't angry. Buffeted by their feelings of fear and anger, I stayed in place, unable to stop the barrage and find my footing. From downstairs I could hear Kip telling Jason I was ill after a difficult night at the temple. He, perhaps better than anyone, would understand what that meant.

I moved in and out of sleep, the pillow pressed against my ears though it did nothing to drown the feelings I seemed to sense from the entirety of the village, if not the world. A shadow fell over me and a cool hand pressed to my forehead. It was the High Priestess, and her touch dimmed the voices to a bearable level. I sat up slowly, and she kept her hand in place as I settled against the cushions.

"Gift or curse?" she asked.

I considered it now that I could think. "I don't know yet."

She nodded as though that was the right answer. "Because it could be, and probably will be, both. Nothing from the gods comes without cost, and I would guess yours will be high."

"What am I hearing?"

She tilted her head as though listening. "The old gods are about what makes us human. Joy, sorrow, suffering, love. As a priestess touched by them, you're feeling what those around you feel. It's important to remember the world is so much bigger than you, but your actions affect those around you, like ripples in the water that grow. You've been shown this as a reminder. The voices will fade but don't forget what you've learned." There was a knock at the door and the priestess stood. "Good journey, child. May the gods smile on your steps."

She opened the door and nodded to Alkippe and Jason, who bowed respectfully as she passed. They came into my room and to my side.

"You look better. I thought we might end up burying you here in one of their odd houses." Kip smiled at me and handed me a glass of water.

"My lady, I'm sorry to intrude, but the men are eager to trade, and the villagers here won't do so until you make an appearance." He shook his head, looking bewildered. "I've never been to a place where the temple priestesses are held in such high regard."

"This isn't like any place you've ever been." I closed my eyes, still tired. "Let me dress, and we'll join you shortly."

He studied me, and, curious, I mentally touched the tree containing the emotions I was holding at bay. I thought of him and felt what he felt, though it was muted rather than clear, as it had been before. Perhaps that was because our fates were bound, and I wasn't allowed to see my own path. He was wary, yes. But he was also kind, his emotions leading him to compassion and worry. And, as I'd thought when we met, he was soft, not meant for warfare and glory but rather for a field and a sky full of stars.

He started back slightly, his eyes wide. "You are god-favoured once more?"

Surprised, I nodded. "Can you tell?"

He frowned and rubbed at his arms. "It's as if you've opened a door in my head, like you've gained access to my thoughts. I can feel you there, taking me in your hands and letting me fall through them, like salt." He tapped the centre of his forehead.

It was an apt image, and it was interesting to know he could feel me. I'd have to work on my subtlety. "Thank you for explaining. As with the other gifts, I will have to learn to use it."

He took a deep breath. "You may want to keep it at bay on the ship. I don't think the men will like it."

I gave him a small smile, and he left the room so I could get ready. Kip, seeming to understand my mood as she often did, helped me bathe and dress quickly. When we went to leave, I stopped at the door and put the barriers in place the way the priestess had said to, and then we joined Jason and Neleus for a walk to the marketplace.

People along the way bowed, and I noticed something. "There are jaw bones in the walls."

Kip laughed softly. "That's what I meant about burying you in a house here. They bury their most revered under the floor of the house, and they put the jawbone in the wall so the dead can continue to speak to them from the underworld."

Neleus shuddered. "To treat the dead with such disrespect. It's unthinkable."

I shook my head. "But to them it's the ultimate respect. Burning them would be disrespectful. Death is honoured in so many ways." We hung ours from trees, the Thessalonians burned theirs, and here with the old gods, they kept their dead close. Did we all go to the same afterlife? Or did the old gods, the Kolchian gods, and the Thessalonians all have their own lands in the place of the dead? It seemed odd to think of geographic boundaries in the afterlife.

We got to the marketplace and began our bartering. I had to say very little, as my presence seemed to be enough to get the goods for a desirable price. A few, in an attempt to gain my favour, asked too little, and I encouraged Jason to give more than asked. It wasn't right to take advantage of these people and would dishonour the gods who had given me something special.

We stopped for honeyed bread and wine beside the river, and the food stall owner was happy to provide information on the river. We didn't need directions, as my blood coursed stronger and I grew almost dizzy when I considered what section of the three rivers we needed to take. I said which we'd take, and the man looked surprised.

"There are few villages within several days' journey on that river, priestess. The larger one has more to offer."

I touched his emotions like I would touch a leaf on my mental tree and watched his skin shiver. He was being true, and his emotions were simple. He was proud we'd stopped at his stall for food, happy that we'd spoken to him, and more than a little in awe. The emotions were clean and light but as I considered him, I felt his discomfort and fear begin to rise. I pushed away from the tree and stayed in the moment.

He took a step back and bowed his head. "If I may be of service?"

Jason, clearly thinking of the fact that our way might mean nowhere to get new food, engaged him in a search for dried food. The man called over a child and gave him a small list of names and the child ran off, excited to be part of the mysterious strangers' quest. He returned shortly with traders who carried baskets with them. Neleus and Alkippe engaged with them, deciding on what was best and how much they would need. It made me smile to see them arguing like a good-natured old couple. Soon they had arranged for everything to be delivered to the ship and the traders hurried away.

"I'd like to give the men another day of rest and set off in the morning, if that's acceptable?" Jason ate another fig and wiped the juice from his fingers on the grass at his feet.

"Thank you."

"For?" he asked.

"For asking." I saw Neleus and Kip a little way away, talking and laughing by the water. "We both know we had little choice in what has happened." I smiled when he sighed softly. "I think it's safe to talk about it. We were chosen, and we don't know why. But you've been kind and respectful to us. Whatever may lie ahead, whatever it is the gods have planned for us, I want you to know I'm glad to be on this journey with you." An image of smoke and destruction flashed in front of my eyes, and I blinked it away. The future would have to wait.

"I..." he began. "You frighten me, sometimes. I see the goddess in your eyes, feel her beside you. I watch the water god rise to speak with you and feel you inside me." He shivered. "Yet, I'm comfortable with you as well. I can speak to you without fear in a way I can't speak before the men. Mayhap that's because the gods have bound us, as you say. But we could find a way to enjoy one another in the face of the gods' interference..." He shrugged, looking like the shy young farm boy he was.

"Indeed." I smiled at Kip when she turned to look at us. "I'd like to look at some of the craft stalls, and then sleep early."

He held out his hand to me, and I took it. Desire flared so hot, my knees went weak, and I saw the same in his eyes. He moved towards me, his hand raised as though to pull me to him, and I closed my eyes. I pushed at the emotion and shoved it away, and then felt him and did the same for him. When I opened my eyes, I saw the relief in his expression and his hand had lowered.

"The gods play a game I don't understand," he said, his gaze searching mine. "Should the day come that we...we come together, I would like it to be because we wish it and not because they force us to it."

It was the first time he admitted to an attraction, and it thrilled me. Knowing what he knew, having seen my power, he still wanted me. It was a heady feeling. I smiled and turned away, unsure how to respond. I'd never been wanted only for myself.

We wandered the craft stalls and traded some of my smaller bracelets and jewels for the strange but beautiful carvings of fish created from pebbles, many of which had the heads of the old gods formed in smaller pebbles on their sides. I was told they were charmed, blessed by the gods and would give us safe passage on the river. The trader of the nicer, more intricate ones was a woman with long, lank hair. Her eyes were intense, and she didn't lower her gaze like most others did when I arrived. I touched her emotions and nearly jerked back. They were a mass of confusion, whirling and dipping through her mind, making her unstable and unpredictable. I saw how others shunned her, driving her to despair. She made a small sound, like a rabbit in a trap, as I pressed.

Praying for guidance, I mentally touched the writhing shapes and gently tugged at them, pulling them apart and soothing them, like I would the snake who'd guarded the fleece. Tears ran down her cheeks, but she didn't look away, and I concentrated on untangling the emotions and putting them right, in as much as I could. She felt...damaged. But as I stroked the threads and imagined cool water soothing the flame of her madness, I knew she could heal. I wondered why the temple priestess hadn't done this and realized she'd never gone to them for help. I'd simply pressed and forced the help on her, which perhaps wasn't right. But her shoulders dropped, and she breathed easier, and I didn't regret it.

When I pulled free of her mind, I was tired, but when she took my hand and pressed it to her tear-streaked cheek, I understood fully what the gods had given me and what the priestess had been trying to tell me. I could do things that mattered, that changed people's lives but as mortals, we're tied to our emotional coils and those are what drive us. I proceeded to buy a carving for every man on the boat as a thank you for having us on board and as a way to give this woman a way to begin again, as I'd been given the same.

And so, we made our way back to the inn, where the outdoor firepit was burning brightly, warming the area, and the small internal firepit glowed softly as it cooked a spit of meat. Behind the inn was a personal altar, and I left a gold bracelet on it as sacrifice and thanks. I fell to bed that night knowing I was changed, that what had happened here would dictate the course of my relations with people from this point forwards. Instead of being frightened, I was exhilarated. I would leave my mark on this world, no matter where it took me.

CHAPTER SIXTEEN
A Glimpse

A KNOCK WOKE ME, and Alkippe opened the door to the high priestess.

"You should see this before you go."

I slipped on my robes and followed her down to the harbour. The silence of pre-dawn was broken only by the few boats setting out for the morning catch. Sailors looked at us and then away again, going about their business and leaving us to ours.

We waited, and I didn't question what we were doing there. Shortly, the sky began to lighten, growing beautiful with pink edging the few clouds, and the sun was nearly blinding as it rose over the mountain before us.

"Look," she said, motioning.

I was made breathless by what I saw. The sun rose before me, but on the other side of the mountain peak, a second sun rose at the same time, slightly higher and equally as brilliant. "How can this be?" I whispered. "The sun god takes only one across the sky."

She watched it as well, a small smile on her lips. "Not all is magic." She pointed to the one in front of us. "That is the true sun, pulled by Helios across the sky." She pointed to the other. "That is an image of this one, created by the combination of the way the mountain is shaped and the waters below it. A traveller once called it an illusion, a trick of the light on the mind, and I think that's right."

The explanation may have taken the magic from it but not the beauty. As the sun before us rose, the other grew lighter and disappeared completely when the real sun rose above the mountain's peak.

"I wanted to show you this to remind you of two things.

Sometimes you must look deeper and find what is real and what is not. Other times, you must be a person to create two suns so others see what they need to. Such is the life of a priestess." She gave me the kiss of departure and left me.

I walked back to the inn thinking of her words, which would stay with me for the rest of my life.

I was refreshed after my long sleep and sunrise surprise, and Kip helped me dress for the day. We gathered our things and headed to the ship early, and I wasn't surprised to see Jason directing the men and getting ready for the trip. His smile lightened his eyes when we boarded.

"We won't be sailing far today, at least I don't think so. The next village is Vinca, and it sounds as though it's a Thessalonian settlement. It would be nice to be among our own for a little while, and it will introduce you to our ways."

I nodded and got settled, my mind on the two suns and the words of the priestess, but once we were underway, Kip motioned to me and I followed her to our makeshift private space, behind the hung tapestry.

"We may be in the next village as soon as midday. If they're like the people we may settle with, you should look your best."

I hadn't even considered it. I felt in my blood that we were still a long, long way from where we needed to be, and it was unlikely we'd ever see any of these people again. But she was right. Impressions mattered and if I wanted to be taken seriously, I would have to seem like the priestess and princess I was.

I sat on a barrel of wine and listened to the waves lapping at the oars outside while Kip brushed out and braided my hair. She pulled one of my lighter gowns from my trunk and fastened the necklace marking me as a priestess around my neck. It was reassuring, wearing the things I knew best, and I pulled my shoulders back and lifted my chin.

"Ouch!" I rubbed at the spot on my head Kip had tapped hard with my brush.

"You've been given so many gifts, and your beauty is something to stun the birds from their branches." She moved in front of me and waved the hairbrush. "Don't allow it to make you arrogant."

I frowned and pushed the hairbrush aside. "So what if I am? Men are never accused of being arrogant when they walk into a room and expect others to listen."

"Silly seedling. Of course they are. It's kings and gods who aren't accused of that, and only because it would be dangerous to do so."

I laughed and hugged her. "With you at my side, my feet will never leave the ground."

I waited while she changed and smoothed her hair, then we went back onto the deck, and more than one man seemed to catch his breath. I couldn't help but raise my chin, and Kip simply shook her head.

We listened to the men sing and laugh, and it wasn't long before we came across other boats on the wide waterway, who hailed us. Indeed, they sounded very much like the men we sailed with, and there was no denying the joy in the crew's faces as they slowed and joked with passing boats. When we docked, there was a flurry of activity as the men hurried to unload, and the welcome we received was genuine.

I watched it all, my façade of arrogance gone. They were open, these people, and they dressed very much like the men with us. They barely glanced at us, and I saw few women on the shore, which was odd and disturbing after the many villages we'd passed where that wasn't the case. I looked at Kip, who shook her head slightly, also frowning. The priestess was right; I could no longer hear the emotions of those around me, though I could still sense them to a small degree. I wished I still had the gift now, but I had learned the lesson the gods wanted to teach, and their way of speaking to me was gone.

When most of the men had gone ashore, Jason and Neleus escorted us onto the dock, where men who seemed to be of rank were waiting.

"I am Jason, son of Aeson, rightful king of Iolcos. This is my second, Neleus, and the priestess and princess, Medea, with her servant, Alkippe."

The man looked us all over, his smile wide and his expression curious. "I am Vuk, high council leader of the Vatin people. Welcome to our city. Word has come down the river of your arrival, and we've been waiting." He bowed formally. "Rightful king means you're not currently one, which means I welcome you to my humble home without fear you'll find it lacking." He bowed slightly. "Priestess Medea, if you'd like to join us you are, of course, welcome. I can send to the temple for someone to lead you there for your prayers, if you wish."

It was the best option, and one given with good forethought. If I found their company distasteful, I could leave without causing offence, but if I didn't, then I could stay and be welcome. I nodded and gave him a slight smile but said nothing more. Sometimes there is more power in silence.

We set off, following him and Jason, who talked of sailing and weather. We walked past houses with thick grass tops, all circular, and all facing the water. At the top of the hill, we came to the largest house yet, with walls painted in vibrant blues and reds. Odd figurines, unlike any I'd ever seen, sat in niches in the wall. I stopped to stare at one with a long triangular head and eyes set widely apart. The body was squat, the arms and legs seeming out of proportion. It was eerie, unlike any person or animal I'd ever seen.

"The Annunaki," Vuk said, seeing what I was looking at. "We believe they were here long before us and disappeared, leaving only their images and ideas behind." He motioned at the houses ranged in semi-circles below us. "We built on the remains of their buildings, which have things such as we've never seen in Thessaly. Hot water runs beneath each house, bringing heat through the floor so people are never cold." He looked at the sky. "We believe they came from somewhere else. Maybe one of the gods' earlier creations."

Jason shook his head. "If I could take that knowledge back to my kingdom, I'd be a hero indeed."

They entered the house but I remained behind, staring at the odd statue. I felt the tug and pull of a vision and yet, what I was supposed to see was too distant, too far away to reach me. It was like looking over a cliff and knowing I could fall but being firmly on solid ground. Kip lightly touched my shoulder, and I blinked the feeling away. Perhaps a trip to the temple was a good idea after all.

We were shown to our rooms and given light linen gowns, and the servants requested that we follow them. After several corridors painted with bright murals, and down more stone steps, we entered a cave such as I'd never seen. Behind me, I heard Kip gasp softly.

Steam rose from crystal clear water, and the scent of roses was heavy in the air. Fountains tinkled in the middle of several individual pools, and the light of candles flickered against damp black walls that sent the light scattering over the ceiling.

The servant in front of me bowed. "If you would like to bathe, mistresses?"

Kip and I quickly disrobed and handed our borrowed gowns to the servant, who hung them from a peg in the black wall. Lusciously warm water flowed around me as I stepped into the nearest pool. I sank gratefully into it up to my neck and reclined on a shelf that seemed built for the purpose. Kip rested her head on the lip of the pool beside me and we remained there, silent, for some time. My muscles relaxed, and I was nearly asleep when the servant softly touched my shoulder.

"It is customary in Vatin for servants to wash their betters. Would this be acceptable?"

I blinked, aware of how lethargic I'd become, and nodded. She entered the pool and pulled up my leg to rest against hers, and she proceeded to scrub it with what seemed to be scented sand. It hurt, but it also felt oddly good. Kip, too, was receiving the same treatment, and I was glad for it. As a servant herself, this would normally be her job, and it was good to see her being treated well.

As the servant continued to scrub me down with the strange sand, I decided to ask the question foremost on my mind. "Why did I see no women as we came here?"

The servant glanced up but looked away quickly. "You are headed to Mycenae?"

"Beyond, I believe. To Iolcos."

She nodded. "They have similar customs, and among the Vatin are many from Thessalonia." She switched legs, leaving my other tingling. "In these cultures, women and men live very separate lives. The mistress of this house has her own rooms, including where she eats and entertains. The master, too, has his. There is a common area should there be celebrations or dinner where they mingle, but those times are rare."

She finished my leg and moved to my stomach, which felt deeply intimate, especially as she moved over and around my breasts.

"It is a woman's place to run the home. To raise the children, to see to supplies and meals. She is the one who makes the home beautiful."

Her words felt practiced, rote. There were things she wasn't saying, and I needed to understand what they were. I tilted her chin slightly so she'd look at me. "Do not hesitate to give voice to truth."

She searched my gaze, and I could see her fear, subtle as it was. She moved her hands over my chest and shoulders, the sand scraping away not only the journey, but almost who I'd been before I arrived here.

"Women are property in our culture. They do as they are told, and when they belong to someone, they are to remain behind the walls of their husbands, or their brothers if they aren't yet wed. They may travel to visit one another, but they must have a male with them at all times, so they don't stray or get taken by another man who does not have honour."

I considered her words and glanced at Kip, who also looked like she was thinking. Women as property wasn't unusual. Had I not been a priestess at the temple, my life would have been dictated by my father and brother as well. But to not be allowed the freedom to leave the home? To walk through the woods alone or down by the river?

"Women are prisoners." I'd left my home, my golden cage, for one made of four walls where I wouldn't even be able to see the world properly. Breathing became difficult until I felt Kip take my hand under the water.

"Many women have very good lives. They are loved, and they enjoy taking care of their family and home." Again, what the woman wasn't saying was clear. Many women meant not all.

"Do these rules apply to all women? To servants and merchants as well?" Kip asked as she turned around so the servant could begin the sand process on her back.

"All women belong to a man, but those who provide a service may go unaided into the marketplace." She smiled slightly and motioned for me to turn. "The lower your worth, the more freedom you have, for no one cares for your safety or virtue."

So it wasn't that different from my home, but I wasn't going to be someone of low status, of that I was certain. How solid would the bars of my cage be once we reached where we were going? I would make sure I had the key, if that were the case.

Once we were scrubbed down, including our hair, the servants dried us, and we put on the gowns once again. I tingled from head to toe and mentioned how much I enjoyed the feeling.

"The sands of the Sava are known to have healing properties. They help the blood run freely through the body and make the skin healthy."

As we made our way back to our rooms, which I now understood were in the women's quarters, I slowed to look at the enormous murals on the walls. The women were often in a state of undress, with at least one breast, if not both, uncovered.

A man often stood over them in some kind of heroic pose, or at least one of benediction. There was a sensuality about the figures, though, that I found pleasing. The women's breasts were heavy, their hips rounded, and the men were muscled and well-hung, but not grotesquely so.

"In Mycenae, it is customary for women to bare themselves." The servant motioned towards the clothing in one of the paintings. "To show one's breasts is to revere the Mother Goddess, to thank her for fertility, and to remind a woman, always, that she is to be taken care of."

I narrowed my eyes at the painting. To remind a woman of her place, that meant. To obey, to submit. Kip touched my arm, and I saw the smile on her lips. She knew well what I was thinking and what fight lay ahead of us. "And do they dress this way here in Vatin, as well?"

She tilted her head. "The most important women do, but merchants and servants are allowed to remain covered, as it can be difficult to work with our breasts in the way."

"And the priestesses?" Kip asked.

The servant led us to another mural, where the priestess wore a long white sleeveless robe gathered below the breasts. It was simple, understated, and far preferable to walking around baring myself. If I had to dress that way for my time in Jason's palace, so be it.

"Would you like to wear your own clothes, mistress? Or would you like something from the lady's wardrobe?"

My trunk hadn't been brought up from the ship. It seemed silly to have the men drag it so far, only to drag it back tomorrow. "Can you get me a priestess's robe, please?" Her eyes widened, and she began to bow deeply. I let her. "And can you please get my woman something to wear as well? Something similar to what you're wearing?" I glanced at Kip for confirmation, and she tilted her head in acknowledgement. Because she wasn't a priestess, wearing the robes would be an insult to the gods, whoever they were here. But like me, she would never want to parade herself either.

The servant opened the door to our room and then backed away in a half-bow. "Yes, priestess. I'll be back shortly."

Kip and I entered the large, sumptuous room. Long rectangular windows looked out over the city, with the river glistening in the distance. Heavy tapestries hung from floor to ceiling, hiding the thick, mud-coloured walls behind them. These, too, portrayed scenes of valour and women in reclined or supine positions.

Kip stood beside me, also looking at the tapestries. "All the women look ready for mounting, and all the men look like they're about to go fight a beast. They like their bare skin, don't they?"

I agreed and went to lay on the couch by the window. "I dislike the idea that we'll be seen as belonging to someone. If Jason doesn't say we belong to him, does that mean someone else can lay claim to us?" It was an ill-making thought.

"Not to a priestess and her servant. We'll go straight to the temple when we arrive and make certain to dedicate you to the goddess they serve. We know she'll hear you." She rolled her eyes. "You might wish she didn't, since you're already god-ridden as it is." She sat down on the floor beside me. "But it will keep us safe."

Something about her words made me shiver and that sense of foreboding came over me, but before I could fall into it, the servant returned with our clothing and helped us dress. Kip quickly dressed my hair and threaded in a long white ribbon that stood out beautifully.

"You've been invited into the communal area to dine with your prince and the master." She led the way, walking gracefully and silently, her skirts brushing the floor. I was reminded how lovely women are and took in the way Kip moved too. She was sturdier, a little heavier on her feet, but she was still graceful and beautiful. She raised her eyebrow at me, and I gave her the smile that we often shared when we lay in bed together. She shook her head and looked away after returning my smile.

We entered the room and the men stood. I saw the flare of

appreciation in the master's eyes, as I did in Jason's. Were they genuine, though, or were they pushed by some god or goddess? It didn't matter, as long as I kept my wits about me. Neleus was there too, and I had no doubt his desire for Kip was genuine. He swallowed hard, and his smile was almost sickly. Kip gave him the kiss of greeting, and I wondered that he didn't melt at her feet.

"Vuk has been telling me about the things they do here that differ from home. Did you enjoy the baths?" Jason asked, and his boyish excitement was palpable.

"They were truly works of art. What are the walls made of?" I asked and was glad when Vuk looked me in the eye to respond.

"Some distance from here, there's a mountain that belongs to the god of fire. There's a great crater at the top where smoke is constant and the melted earth flows. Sometimes the melted earth flows away from the mountain, and when it cools, we brush it off and find the same thing the walls of the cave are made of." He held up a piece of the shiny black rock. "We believe that once this area might have been a fire god's mountain too, but he gave it up for a new one. The baths are heated by the melted earth that remains below it, and the cave walls are what is left of the inside of the fire mountain."

It was an extraordinary idea, that we could be bathing inside the hot core of the earth, and yet it felt true. I held my hand out, and he passed me the black rock. I turned it over, caressing it, the smooth beauty of it calling to me. It felt like looking into a mirror. Polished, dark, light reflecting away from it. Made hard from fire and still beautiful.

Conversation continued and Vuk talked about the problems they were facing. The mountain of fire groaned more often and sent more rock and ash towards the heavens, sometimes fouling the air for days. For several years the river had flooded the low-lying areas every spring, but now it was receding, moving away from the land. Crops were dying as the sun baked the earth and rain fell less frequently. Many of the Vatin and the Thessalonians had left, moving north to the seashore where it was cooler and they might still be able to grow food, which was becoming scarcer in Vatin.

"It could be that we have to abandon our beautiful city." He sighed heavily and played with the black rock. "If we don't, we may starve. We try to store as much as we can for the hot months, but each year it gets worse. By next spring I will likely have encouraged everyone to leave so we don't starve to death."

It was a strange thing to hear, given the beautiful pools beneath our feet, but it wasn't so different a story. We'd heard much the same from many of our stops along the way. "And the earth shaking," I said.

He nodded. "That too. We can rebuild but for how long?" He smiled as the woman of the house entered. "The gods require us to take care of our people, and so we will."

She moved to his right side and gave us a small bow. Her skirt was long and full, but her top was cut over the shoulders, allowing for sleeves, but baring her breasts and stomach, though it covered her back. It was extremely disconcerting, and I found it difficult to look at her.

"My apologies for not being here when you arrived, honoured guests. I was in the kitchens overseeing the meals being prepared for the group leaving for the coast tomorrow."

Jason leaned forwards. "You supply them food, lady? Instead of them taking their own?"

She picked a date from the bowl and nibbled at it daintily. She reminded me somewhat of my mother in small frame and delicate nature.

"Daily food, they provide themselves. But as they're taking a dangerous journey and getting the settlement ready for us to arrive, we feel it our responsibility to make certain they are provisioned."

Her slight smile and hair the colour of oak trees were lovely, and I was sure I saw the men falter slightly. I had power, yes, god-given and intense, but she, too, had power of her own kind. We all used it in our own ways. She caught my eye, and I saw that she knew what I was thinking, and I gave her a small smile of acknowledgement in turn.

"Enough talk of destruction." Vuk turned to Jason. "You know the tradition. Tell us the story of your journey, Prince of Iolcos."

Jason shook his head. "I'm afraid I'm no gifted orator, kind sir. But my brother by sword, Neleus, son of Agestus of Sparta, can tell a tale better than any bard."

Neleus laughed and stood. "I will vouch for my friend's lack of storytelling. He's too humble by far, you see. But I will gladly recount our adventures."

I listened as Neleus began and smiled with the others, my heart racing at the moment of them going through the crashing rocks, of them narrowly avoiding the sirens and having to escape the island of women. I'd heard the tale before, but Jason was right; Neleus had a gift and held us all enthralled. When he got to my part in it, I was fascinated by what he'd perceived and how he described me. I'd never thought myself beautiful, or exotic, or particularly brave. But he gave me all these qualities and more, and I admit to a sense of swelling pride as Vuk and his wife looked at me in admiration and, when Neleus described the way I'd taken the goddess into myself and the water god swimming beside the boat when I prayed for help, no small amount of awe and fear.

He finished the tale and received applause that made him blush. Kip's expression was one I'd seen before, and I knew I'd be without her that night. There is little more intoxicating, I've come to learn, than someone who can use words well.

The door opened and a servant entered. When Vuk acknowledged him, he turned to me. "The priestess at the temple wonders if the visiting priestess would like to join in the moon celebration this night."

I pushed away from the table and held up my hand to stop Kip from joining me. "Thank you, yes. Alkippe, please stay and make certain Neleus doesn't take back any of the things he's said about me once I've left."

She smiled at me as the others laughed, and I turned to follow the servant. In truth, though the evening had been lively, I was ready for the quiet of the temple and for any knowledge the goddess might impart. We walked the path behind the house that led further up and around a hill, and though it was late, the way was lit by the beauty of the full moon. When we came to the temple, I stopped to stare. It was enormous, by far the largest building I'd ever seen outside the palace. Large, black pillars made of the black rock held up a long triangular roof, and at the end of the long, wide terrace was a group of priestesses in a circle. The high priestess turned to me as I approached, her hands held out to receive me.

"Welcome, princess and priestess. May I ask who you have been dedicated to?"

It was a heavy question, though she had no way of knowing it. But a temple was no place for omissions. "I am Medea. I was dedicated to the goddess Hecate and became a temple priestess. But another goddess touched me when I left my land, Athena of the Thessalonians, protector of the man I travel with. The sun god is my grandfather, and he too has watched over me throughout our trip, as have the kin of my mother, who is a water nymph. While at the temple in Ghindarsti, I was given the gift of feeling the currents in my blood, so we always know which way to sail." It was odd to say it all out loud, and I made sure to keep my voice soft and without boast.

The high priestess looked surprised and thoughtful for a long moment, and the others kept their eyes down. "To serve one goddess is a privilege and can be a strain. To not only serve but be touched by several gods..." She drew in a shaky breath. "We are honoured to have you here."

She turned away and I followed her into the circle, where a space was made for me.

She invoked the goddess by splashing blood from a chalice on the low altar at our feet. In the middle was one of the strange figurines, this one clearly female and painted red, long hair stretching down its back, away from its strange triangular face.

"Manassa, goddess of the night star that lights our way, of the light that sees into our darkness and refuses to let us hide away those parts of us we don't wish to see, be with us tonight."

Perhaps it hadn't been a good idea to come after all. I had no desire to see into the dark parts of me. The god at Izmail had already shown me the pain I'd caused and given me a sense of the pain to come. If there had been a way to leave gracefully, I would have done so, but to leave once the goddess was invoked could incur her wrath, and that wasn't something I was prepared to endure. The chanting began, raising the energy around us, echoing off the hills and into the sky, and though I didn't know the words, I joined in with the tune. The reverberation became almost unbearable, and at the moment when I felt like my heart might burst from my chest, it stopped all at once.

The priestesses dropped to their knees, as did I. My body ached with power, and I trembled at the need to contain it. I heard a noise and looked up to see a young priestess looking behind me, and I turned slowly to look over my shoulder.

I wished I hadn't.

A figure stood in the shadows watching me. It looked very like the small statue on the altar, the face angular and odd, the red hair flowing around it, all the way down to its knees. It motioned to me, and my body reacted though my mind screamed for me to run. I stood before it, looking into its thin, long eyes. It raised its hand and placed it on my head, and I shuddered at the weight of it, like a boulder placed there.

Do not be afraid of your darkness. Where there is darkness, there must also be light. And where there is light, there must be darkness, for you cannot have one without the other.

It pressed harder, and my neck ached. I wanted to push it away, this strange creature that felt so very, very ancient. Older than any of the gods we'd come across, older than those at Lepenski Vir, who had given me knowledge of ancient things. Those gods, too, had spoken of darkness, but more of the price it required than of control. I'd been willing to pay it there, and I was willing to pay it now.

Controlling your darkness will be your challenge, for you are arrogant and full of hubris. If you do not seek the light and be sure of your intentions, the darkness will rule you. Look for the balance, for the meaning behind what you do. Dark deeds must have light intentions, and light intentions may create dark deeds. This is our gift to you, child of the gods. May you always seek balance.

The pressure left my head and I fell to my knees once again, exhausted. Someone moved to my side and gently lifted me. She guided me to a seat and pressed a chalice of wine into my hands, but I was shaking too hard to hold the cup, so she held it to my lips, and I drank deeply. Soon I was calm once more and able to look around me.

The priestesses were gone. Only the high priestess remained, and her expression was one I was becoming used to seeing. Awe and fear, but this time, tinged with envy. Most priestesses went their whole lives without ever once seeing the face of the goddess they served. And here I was, a stranger already god-touched, and their most ancient deity had come to me. I understood jealousy, as I'd feel the same.

"Did you see her?" I asked, my throat raspy.

At this, she smiled. "I did. We all did. She was..." She shook her head, unable to find the words. "You brought us a gift we will cherish for all time."

"She's so different from the other gods. The ones I've been touched by, the ones from home. So much older."

She nodded and sat beside me. "We believe the people here long ago came from a world that wasn't our own. They were from somewhere else, and for some reason, they left. But they keep watch over us, hear our prayers, help us when they can." She tapped my arm. "We've never heard of them bestowing a gift directly to a mortal."

I frowned, uncertain how she'd known I was given a gift, and she looked at my chest. I reached up and found a necklace I hadn't been wearing when I'd arrived. On a thick black cord was a simple round stone, made of the black rock I'd seen here, but it was shot through with white, like the moon lighting the night. It would serve as a reminder to always look for balance, and I knew it was a directive I'd never forget. Nor would I ever forget the strange creature, though I'd never see one again.

I held the rock in my hand and took in its warmth. "I'm not worthy of these gifts." It came out unexpectedly, and then I understood why I was there. "I'm afraid. I want these gifts and the power that comes with them. I want to be feared, and loved, and sought after. But at the end of the day, I'm simply the daughter of an angry king, who fled to the temple to find freedom, not service."

"Knowing our darkness allows us to fill it with light." She laid her hand on mine. "Continue."

"I'm travelling to a land I don't know, and what I've learned here worries me. What if it's terrible? What if I hate it and I'm forced to serve in ways I don't want to? What if they steal my voice?" That was the deepest truth. "What if I can no longer make myself heard? If I'm silenced simply because I'm a woman?"

She nodded, staring at the statue on the altar. "Men have twisted things, and we are the unwilling sheep being herded towards the cliff if we misbehave. And so we find our voices where we can, take control of what we can, make changes where we can." She turned to me, her smile enigmatic. "And Medea, I feel that you, god-touched one, will never be silenced unless that is your choice. Unlike many of us, you have been set on a path nothing like that which a man would have set out for you."

Unburdened, I thanked her and bowed low before I headed back down the path to my quarters. I considered all I'd learned, and I wanted to scream to the skies with power, with joy, with... something I couldn't name. She was right. I would never be silenced, and for whatever reason, the gods had seen fit to give me the tools I would need to be heard, no matter what land I went to or where I lived.

CHAPTER SEVENTEEN
Embers

THE NEXT SEVERAL DAYS were spent in Vinca, where trade was fierce. I attended the marketplace with several of the temple priestesses, and though some people stopped and stared, for the most part we blended in as part of the vibrant life of the city. There were foods I'd never seen that Jason and Neleus encouraged us to try, and there were gems and urns, tripods, and cauldrons made of copper. There were even small pots made from the black stone, and Kip and I traded some of my smaller jewels for them. The sailors were welcomed, and there were rumours that many a woman would bear a child of our adventure in the coming year. Goods were loaded onto the ship, ready to be taken back to Jason's homeland, gifts and offerings to cement his rule there.

Beneath the newness of it all, however, there was a sense of urgency. The earth trembled, not hard but enough to make my breath catch, and I saw the worry in our host's eyes as he began to put together another group to journey to the coast. Massive amphorae were stored in every house, containing grain, water, and wine in preparation for the hard times they knew were coming. Darkness and light. Was that all the world was? Years of building and prosperity followed by hunger and fear. Must it be that way? It seemed unfair, and knowing it was all futile left me angry but with nowhere to deliver my anger. So I pushed it down inside me and let it burn as embers in my soul, where I could let them flare once I was in a place to scream my fury.

On the day of our departure, the temple priestess came to see me. We stood by the water in the dawn light, and she helped me pray and give an offering to the old gods and to the river gods.

She told me to keep the robes, as they were light and would travel well, and I thanked her warmly. When she left me, I looked at the ships, at the marketplace coming to life, at the smiling and kind people, and I was heartened. Their ways were different, yes, and they might be more different yet when we reached Iolcos. But different didn't mean unliveable and had this been our final stop, I would have been happy here. These people, though, wouldn't be here much longer either, a thought that made me ache for what they were leaving behind. The rich history, the gods who were like no others. What would become of them when there was no one left to sacrifice to them? Would they be wraiths who haunted the deserted temple, mourning the loss of adulation? Or would they move on, go somewhere else where they'd be called by new names? Those were answers no mortal would ever have. All I could know was that it was time to leave the beautiful spot and begin the next stage of our trip. It was all wonderful, even with the impending sadness.

Darkness and light. I understood.

We were underway once more as we turned onto the River Sava, and there were women weeping on the shore as the men rowed into the current, more than one of them looking back and waving. It seemed I wouldn't be the only one who could easily have stayed in Vinca.

"The Vatin were interesting, were they not?" Jason asked, taking his place beside me at the front of the ship.

"Their gods are so different." I'd never forget the face of the one I'd knelt before. "But if that's what your country is like, I think I'll like it there."

He laughed and spread his arms. "That was barely a taste of it, and it was very much combined with their own ways. My land is bigger. You could wander the agora for days, and the palace has hallways you might never come across in a whole lifetime."

His face was lit with joy, and I truly hoped it was as he remembered it by the time we made it back. He had, after all, only been to the palace once, when he went to claim the throne. He'd been sent away as an infant, so he must be going by what others had told him and not his own memories.

The men rowed until nightfall, and Jason watched the land for the markers Vuk had told him about. Vuk hadn't sailed the way we were going, but he'd gone far enough to have an idea of the next, short river, that would take us to the larger one. From there, it would be down to my gifts, which hopefully wouldn't fail. The gods weren't always trustworthy when it came to depending on something they'd given you.

We stayed overnight at a small village called Provo, where their pottery was made almost entirely of animal bones. They kept their distance, traded a few items, and then left us to sleep under makeshift tents by the river.

Once more we set sail, bypassing the village of Sirmium as we had no need for supplies, and when we'd drawn close, the people had faded into the shadows to watch warily. Jason looked to me, and I shook my head. Darkness pulsed from the trees and the black stone on the necklace from the temple was hot against my skin. It was a place out of balance. I said we should continue rowing. We moored and slept, though several men stayed awake to keep watch, and I believe we were all glad to be back on the water come daylight.

And so it was we came to the crossing of a massive river, far larger than the one we were on. When Jason asked, there was no question. "It's the River Dreinos. Row with the current."

He gave the order, and it was likely a relief to the men that they wouldn't be rowing against the strength of the river god. As soon as we were in the current, the men stopped rowing and they let down the sail, giving them a well-earned rest as we shot past the shoreline. The wind was chill, which was odd as it had been hot all the way here. It would drop and then suddenly whip up again, yanking us forwards. The water had a greenish tinge, reflecting the luminous green stone that lined parts of the shore. It was exhilarating and beautiful and I drank it in, taking it as part of me, feeling the current in my blood.

We covered many miles thanks to the wind and current and when nightfall came, we had to go slightly longer until we found a small port. I was strangely exhausted and glad we were able to find a bed for the night in the village called Drinum. There, the innkeeper informed Jason that villages were sparse beyond theirs, and it would be wise to stop when we encountered one so we could get fresh water. I listened and knew his words to be true. I could sense the journey getting more difficult, and I suggested we get any dried fruit and fish that we could. Jason made the arrangements, and then I slept as though it had been weeks since I'd last done so.

I woke refreshed, and we set off once more. There were no villages even after a long day of rowing, and we made camp on the beach. Jason set his blanket beside mine, slightly away from everyone else, and Kip walked off into the shadows, closely followed by Neleus. I lay on my side facing Jason.

"Is this the adventure you wanted?" I asked.

He smiled that sweet, gentle smile of his. "And so much more. We've seen monsters and gods. We've met new people and sailed down rivers no one in Iolcos even knows about." He stopped and lightly touched my cheek with his knuckle. "And there's you. No one else in history has sailed away with a princess who was beloved by the gods. A beauty whose strength and wisdom will get us home."

There was no god in his eyes, nor was anyone bothering me. I kissed his hand. "I am glad the gods saw fit to make me part of your adventure." I studied his face. "You're very kind, and your men love you."

"They love adventure, and I was the one to bring them to it. I thought it was for the kingdom when we first set out, but I know better now." He shrugged. "But kindness is never a bad thing."

I brought up the one thing that had been on my mind since Vinca. "When we arrive in Iolcos, what will become of me? And

Alkippe? You own your women, do you not?"

He winced. "I would never presume to own a woman like you. And I would hope that any woman to marry me would be my partner, not my servant." His gaze touched my lips like a caress. "What would you like to do? Would you go to the temple and serve?"

"I don't know. I don't know your gods. I suppose I'd have to...feel it." I knew he understood what I meant.

"You could always be my palace priestess. We have one, you know. An advisor who lives in the palace and helps us with our prayers to the gods. You'd have your own rooms and the freedom to come and go as you pleased." He took a deep breath. "You could stay with me."

I very much liked the sound of his offer. "Thank you. My mind will be at ease knowing I will not be caged or used."

I could tell it wasn't quite the answer he was hoping for, but I wasn't willing to give him false hope. He was sweet and kind, but my heart didn't ache for him. I was given elsewhere, and there's a reason most priestesses don't marry. Service to a god means serving a single person is almost impossible, as they both have conflicting needs and get jealous of your time. He wished me goodnight and closed his eyes, and, feeling bad for his disappointment, I reached for his hand and held it as I fell asleep.

CHAPTER EIGHTEEN
A Queen

Today, as I take my place.

WAR IS INEVITABLE. AS is death. How often these two things coincide depends on who is ruling and how well. But it also depends on how easy it is to live. And right now, times are hard. The world has changed, and people are hungry and thirsty. They're afraid. The gods walk among them and distract them with war and pride, and I wonder if that's because there's nothing they can do to help. For all their interference in our daily lives, in our loves and woes, they can do nothing when the mother goddess herself is angry. She, of all of them, has final say and for whatever reason, she is angry.

We're lucky, here in Egrisi. Since we returned, I've ensured that our crops are safe and that we built up a reserve of water by damming a part of the river the way the Hittites did when they saw the drought coming. I sent troops to help clear lands so people spread out further into Aia, creating less demand in the city, as I learned to do when the great palaces began to fall. It will make the people harder to defend if war comes, but at least they won't be starving to death in the meantime.

I had learned so much on my journey with Jason, and as I listened to my advisors with my son at my side, I was reminded that through all the madness, it gave me this. A way to rule well when my son leaves to go to war. Which he would, and if he did not come back, he would die the death of a warrior. For although he was too much like my brother in many ways, he was also like him in that he wasn't a coward.

"Go to Dioscuris and speak with their king. See if he will add

JJ Taylor

men to your ranks. Among all those who share our lands, I trust Pankaja the most."

The advisors nodded in agreement, and they went on to speak of ships and provisions, and I said my piece when needed. But in truth my mind was elsewhere, on the things I'd put in place when my son was gone.

"Who will be king in my place, Mother? Who will sit at your side and make the decisions for me?" Medus leaned forwards to look at me.

I couldn't help it. I laughed. "Do you think I need a man to sit in your place, Medus? Putting someone on the throne would make it very hard to take it back when you return. Best to leave me to make the decisions while you're gone, so your seat is ready for your victory." I heard a few murmurs of protest and he frowned slightly. "Consider. While all the men are fighting at Troy, while Odysseus and Agamemnon fight for a woman only one of them can have, who is making decisions in their place? Their queens, Penelope and Clytemnestra."

There was silence, and I knew I'd won the point. I hadn't met the queens of the other cities which had been much diminished by the changes in weather and the destructive force that the Sea People had become, but I knew it to be true.

"And the Sea People? What if they raid while we're gone?"

Once again, I laughed. "Do you not remember when they came last spring? They ate at our table and left peacefully. They are old friends of mine and would never lay a false hand on anything to do with me. Leave me enough men to secure us against the Scythians who aren't fighting at Troy."

It seemed they had little else to say. I stood and looked down at them. "Gather your supplies and men and set off soon. You want to be underway before the heat becomes too unbearable to march."

And so it was that my remaining son left Egrisi, and with a small army at his back, began his own quest in search of glory and honour. I knew, with the powers I'd been born with and which the goddess hadn't taken from me, that I wouldn't see him again. Why then, didn't my heart ache? Why didn't I weep and wail as I had the first time that I'd lost my children? Was I so empty and cold? I would speak to Kip about it later. Perhaps she could help me make some sense of it.

I spent my time after my son left speaking with my advisors and to the people. I talked to the temple priestesses who looked so young and sweet, and I couldn't imagine having been such myself. I had the temple scrubbed and renewed, and I sent to the nearby villages for new acolytes. I was busy and possibly happier than I'd been in my lifetime.

Were the other queens who were ruling in their husbands' absence as happy as I? Rumours had reached Egrisi that Clytemnestra had taken a lover, though Penelope remained steadfast, even beset by suitors who waited outside her door like hounds in heat. Spontaneously, I gathered a few items for each queen and sent two envoys out, young men who'd been left behind as they weren't of age to fight.

"Tell the queens that Queen Medea of Egrisi sends her highest regards, and that she hopes they will remember her as a great ally, should they be in need when the war at Troy is over."

The youths set out, and I had no doubt they would find their way to their destinations, even though Ithica, Penelope's kingdom, was far away. It wouldn't hurt to cement a friendship between the queens who ruled different seas.

I also sent a young couple across the shore to the River Istros. I instructed them to go as far as they could and see what villages remained populated along the river. It could easily be that they'd all been abandoned as the earth shaking and heat had driven them to find safer places to live. But I wanted to know what had become of them, those vast and varied tribes and old gods who had been so large a part of my journey. Once I'd settled in Corinth, the gifts of the old gods had slowly faded, and I could barely feel the currents anymore. My sense of things being balanced between dark and light had faded too. That city had taken far, far too much from me.

CHAPTER NINETEEN
Scodra

My youth, as the world tips over.

THE VILLAGE OF SKELANI was nothing much to speak of, except that the Dindari people were very much like the Achaeans but also like no others we'd found. They considered themselves part of the Scordisci, a large, scattered tribe made up of a mixture of Thracians and Illyrians. They had no king and few warriors, though there were some. The innkeeper was a quiet man who told us most of the village had already left to live with other tribes. In Skelani, they were "neither sky nor sea," which we took to mean they were too isolated to truly be anywhere and getting supplies was becoming harder as the crops dried out.

It was becoming a common story, and Jason confided in me that he wondered if it would be the same at Iolcos. As before, my vision swam and my heart thundered in my ears as I saw a world unfamiliar. Palaces lay empty and crumbling, and the world shook as it was covered in grey snow that buried everything beneath its suffocating blanket.

I turned and vomited into the bowl Kip had ready, and after she'd cooled my face with a wet cloth, I turned to see Jason staring, wide-eyed as always.

"I'm sure all will be well." I didn't want to lie, but there was no point in diverting him from his path either. There was no telling how soon what I saw would come to pass, though it felt closer than I'd like.

Disappointed, he gave a quick nod and turned to sleep. Kip searched my eyes and sighed softly. "It's in the hands of the gods," she said as she soothed my brow, and I fell asleep beside her.

When we left Skelani, the innkeeper told us the next village was far away, but we were well provisioned already. We set off, and the walls of rock beside the river seemed to grow taller with every hour. It was suffocating, being so far from the sky and so deep in the earth. There were no beaches to stop at and the current was swift, making dropping anchor to sleep in the river overnight unwise. And so we sailed, the men mostly at rest as the current pulled us ahead.

It had long been nightfall by the time we saw the fires of Pijavice, where the river widened, and I felt like I could breathe again. The mountains remained tall on either side, and the water moved strangely here. I could feel it swirling, catching, almost playing beneath us, and part of me wished to dive in and play too.

The simple mud and wattle huts were open to the night wind, and the people were polite but kept their distance. I could feel their curiosity, and when I asked for their temple, they didn't understand me. I thought perhaps I was using the wrong words, but then I realized not only did they not have a temple, they also had no gods. They turned away from me, shaking their heads and looking wary.

Kip watched them with that look I knew so well. Neleus, as ever, was nearby and joined us when the villagers went away.

"Imagine, no gods." He almost sounded wistful.

"No one to call to when you need help," I said.

"No one to blame when things don't go right." Kip glanced at me and then back at the villagers.

"No one to bind you, control you, confuse you." Neleus kicked at a rock. "No one to dictate when you live, how you live, or when you die."

Their words flared through me like lightning, and I turned on them. When I spoke, my voice was not my own. "No one to care about your pitiful lives, to give you the gifts of wine and fruit, of love and fair winds."

They both lowered their eyes, and Neleus dropped to his knees.

The lightning receded and I, too, dropped to my knees. He looked at me, and there was no fear in his eyes. Worse, there was pity.

"I cannot fathom, princess, what it is to be filled by them at their whim."

There were no words to explain it, so I didn't try. "Best that you not know, if you truly feel that way about them."

He nodded and got to his feet, then helped me to mine. Kip dusted off my gown, and we made our way to the largest mud hut, where the villager had offered us a place to sleep for the night. Kip covered me, and I was aware of her moving off to sleep in the shadows, and not alone.

I wouldn't begrudge her passion. I could have it as well; I simply didn't have the energy or desire for it. But I had a feeling that if I'd turned to Jason, he would have taken me in his arms as surely as Neleus did Kip. Something was bothering me, though, and I needed to understand it.

My conversations were never private. The gods heard everything I said, they watched what we did. Was there any control here? Did it matter if we rowed or if we slept? Would they still take us where they wanted us to go? Where did our actions matter, if at all?

And if the people around me truly understood that the gods were always listening and could talk to them through me, that they didn't only listen when they were spoken to, would they keep their distance from now on? I would deeply regret losing the easy camaraderie we'd built up over the last weeks. I would have to ask Neleus not to say anything.

I slept, and my dreams were of the river and wind, bending and unfolding beneath and around me, sweeping me along one way and then the other, no matter what direction I wanted to go. I woke to Jason gently shaking my shoulder, and judging by the stars above him, it was too early to be awake. He put his finger to his lips and motioned for me to follow.

I wrapped my shawl around me and followed him through the trees to a high point above the river. He pointed to the distance, and I gasped softly.

The water was flying, spinning in a tight funnel from the clouds to what looked like a large lake in the distance. No water seemed to move at the base of the funnel. There was no splash, no disturbance.

"What does it mean?" he asked, never looking away.

I could only shake my head. I felt the power of it, the raw intensity of the sky calling the earth to it. But strangely, I felt no gods involved. Or if they were, it wasn't given me to understand. Perhaps, if the gods weren't worshipped in an area, they simply stayed away from it. So who was travelling between the sky and the earth?

The middle of the funnel seemed to break like a branch, and the bottom half fell back to the lake with barely a splash. The top of it lifted into the clouds and disappeared completely. The clouds shifted like they were being stepped on from above and then faded away, leaving only the constellations to see us through the night.

My heart pounded, and Jason took my hand. We walked back to the hut together in silence, and the feel of his hand enclosing mine was unusual but...nice. Yes, I decided, I liked it very much. I liked him. And that was more than I'd ever said of any man I'd been saddled with. When we woke in the morning, neither of us said anything of what we'd seen. There was no explanation, and there was no reason to worry the crew. It was something shared, a minor secret, and Jason's shy smile showed it meant something to him.

We couldn't get any information from the villagers about what lay ahead. Either they didn't understand us or they didn't know because they'd never gone beyond their village. We sailed until the river narrowed once again, and we came to the village of Hotca. Surprisingly, there were many boats in the port, covered with markings I'd never seen before.

"Why would there be a trade route here?" Jason asked, leaning on the rail and surveying the many boats and people around us.

"Surely there's nothing to sail here for."

It wasn't long before the water told me that it was the last place for trade before the river narrowed and the rock walls grew even taller. From here, we would likely be sleeping on the boat wherever we could, and for some time. The men went about making sure the ship was ready.

The gods were numerous here, but the priestess of the temple was an old woman who looked uninterested in our presence, though I felt like she could see directly into me and stare into the eyes of the goddess if she'd wanted to. I was glad she didn't.

I said my prayers, including to all those who had gifted me along our journey so far, and spilled wine as offering. I knelt until my knees were numb and my back ached, asking for guidance and abundance as we entered the next section of our trip.

No one answered, and I wasn't sure whether to be grateful or disappointed.

We left the next day, and the tension rose as we headed towards the unknown. But what I also felt was the crew's attention. They looked to me, their ship priestess and the god's chosen, to guide them. It was a burden, but it also filled me with pleasure.

I would lead, a desire that burned hot. A sense that I would do so flitted past and left me with a smile.

We sailed with the current, and the days were long and hot. The cliffs rose steeper and higher beside us until there was nowhere to stop. Calais began to sing, his voice as strong as the winds, and I closed my eyes to listen to what must surely be his own god-given gift. For some time, he sang alone, of heroes and love, of war and loss, and his voice echoed over the water, bouncing back to us from the walls. Sometimes a few of the men joined him. And sometimes he went silent, and we listened only to the ship cutting through the water. In the night, we lit a small fire in a cauldron and in the lanterns that hung alongside the ship to better see our way through the moonless night. We dropped anchor at a bend in the river and the men slept.

JJ Taylor

I'd been sleeping throughout the day, made drowsy by the songs of water and men. Now I stared at the stars and wondered where the gods lay among them. Hecate was below the earth, in the depths, and I understood that better than I did the sky gods, who felt so very far away.

"Is all well, Medea?" Jason asked softly.

I noticed that he too slept rarely, snatching small moments rather than long hours. It didn't surprise me that we were awake together. Kip gave me a brief smile and then slipped to where Neleus sat at his oar. He opened his arms and she slid into them, and they were quickly asleep together.

"Do you ever consider such comfort?" he asked, also watching Neleus and Kip.

"No." My answer was instant but perhaps not honest. "A priestess isn't given to marry, and a princess doesn't have a choice. If I could find a man who didn't wish to keep me as property, who respected my thoughts and appreciated my voice, then perhaps." I turned to him and looked at the moonlight playing in lines over his fair hair. "It is likely too much to ask. Do you?"

He looked at them again and nodded slowly. "One day. I'd like to raise children, hear them laughing and teach them how to hunt and fish. I'd like a wife who smiles at me when I come home and is happy in my embrace."

His words were simple and sweet. And yet the shiver they sent down my spine nearly made me step away from him. I pushed the feeling away, as no vision came with it. "A king isn't usually given to such a life, is he?"

He leaned on the rail, staring out over the water. "I'd like to think that a king becomes the person he wants to be and creates the life he wishes to live. A good king, a kind one, makes the people happy and therefore has the life he desires."

Such beautiful naivety. "Maybe that is so. I hope for you that it is."

He turned to me with that small smile of his that was his most genuine. "And I hope you find such a man as would make you happy. But, if I may speak freely, I don't feel that any man would be so blessed to get your love."

I frowned at him, taken aback. "Why is that?"

He turned to stare at the water again. "Because to marry is to give the other person a piece of yourself. To trust them to be the moon in your sky as you are the sun in theirs. You have to lose some of who you are to make room for them in your heart."

"And?"

"And, princess, you are made of the pieces of the gods. There's none you can lose to make room for a mere mortal man. And based on what you've said..." He tilted his head. "I don't think you'd want to give up a piece of yourself to anyone, because that gives them the power to hurt you."

I wanted to be angry at his bluntness. I wanted to be hurt by his assertion that I would rather be alone than share myself. But he was right, and I saw the truth in his words. "Your centaur wisdom is deep."

He looked at me and laughed at my jest. "They are exceptional creatures. I hope you get to meet one someday."

"I fear I wouldn't hold my temper if they were to give me such bold answers as yours."

"No, and I think they wouldn't come out of it for the better." He touched my arm gently. "I'm to bed."

I wished him fair sleep and stayed at the rail. Alone with my thoughts, I closed my eyes. I felt for my gifts, for the gods who rode with me, for the pieces that Jason spoke of. He was right. I was cobbled together, a patchwork of desires, power, experiences, and ambition. I wanted everything the world had to offer, and I wanted it in my hands. And what man or woman could compete with that? His insight shook me, but it shouldn't have. He was deeper than he seemed and perhaps craftier because of it. Where others saw a young man who looked out of his depth, he was actually cunning, and intelligent, and could see into the truth of what men were.

I considered our meeting and the goddess's hand in it, and I was glad she'd chosen me to undertake this adventure with him. I went to the front of the ship and curled up on a blanket placed between the slats where Kip and I sometimes relaxed when the heat of the day became too much. I fell asleep with the sound of the water soothing me as it stroked the hull of our ship like a lover.

I woke to feel us already moving once more, and Kip rested beside me.

"Do you mind?" she asked.

I blinked the sleep from my eyes and stretched. "Mind?"

"Where I sleep."

I understood then. "Take your pleasure where you can. When we arrive in Iolcos, we don't know what awaits us. We know the gods are volatile and capricious. Enjoy all he is and gives you."

She nodded and her shoulders dropped, then she moved behind me to brush out my hair. "I'm going to braid it. The heavy air is making it wild."

I nodded, glad to have it off my neck. And Kip's braids were always beautifully done. I wondered briefly if Jason would like it and then chided myself. After our conversation last night, any romance between us would be foolish.

Once we'd splashed some water on our faces, we pulled aside our makeshift privacy curtain and moved into the already warm sunshine, where we were greeted by the men. Though some were still wary of me, they all seemed to adore Kip, and I tried not to let my envy show.

I stood at the tiller beside Jason, who himself looked like a virile young god in the morning light streaming between the high walls. I gripped the wood as the world shimmered around me.

"Medea?"

Jason's voice sounded far away, submerged beneath the way in front of me. But this time I was in two worlds at once: on the ship and seeing what was ahead. "There's a large lake with a village where we'll be welcome. We're nearing the end of our river journey. One of us will not make it further than the lake."

The shimmer faded, as did the lake, and we were once again standing side by side. Kip stood ready with a bowl, but I shook my head, puzzled that I didn't need it.

Jason stared at me, his eyes wide. "Do you know who won't make it home?" he asked softly.

"No. I didn't see a face."

He gave a curt nod and turned his attention back to the crew. "A song, men! Calais, make the morning goddess blush with your songs of love and lust."

There was plenty of laughter at that, and the men took up singing bawdy tales that made everyone else laugh. I appreciated that Jason wanted to make the men happy before one of them died.

By nightfall the men were tired, and we all wished to step foot on land once again. Jason asked my counsel, and I felt the waters and let myself drift with the currents. "If we continue on until the moon rises ahead of us, we can sleep in the village tonight."

He pushed the men further and told them what I'd said, and they rowed harder. The sliver of moon rose ahead, shining a path down the middle of the water and before she went further, the cliffs gave way to a massive lake, where villages were clearly seen on the shores around us thanks to their torches and lit homes. A temple high on a hill across from us had an enormous fire burning at the top so that it almost looked like a ball of fire sitting in the night sky.

I motioned to the village to our left. "There."

Jason steered towards it, and we passed a large carving of a serpent looking out at the water. It made me ache for my old companion, and I felt even more clearly that this was where we were meant to be.

On our arrival, we were met by a small group bearing torches. Jason announced his name and, surprisingly, mine, and a young boy ran off, presumably to let their leaders know. A man stood at the front of the group, and as our crew finished securing the ship and received Jason's permission to go, the man directed them to various inns that could accommodate us all. As usual, Jason, Neleus, Kip and I were the last to leave and by that time, the boy had returned with a woman draped in a beautifully wrought peplos.

"Prince and priestess, our king and queen request that you receive their hospitality at the palace." She bowed low and waited in that position.

Jason glanced at me and I nodded, having no feeling of foreboding.

"Thank you, we gratefully accept."

She stood and gave him a shy, winsome smile that made me frown.

"This way, please."

The four of us followed her up a well-lit path to a fairly large palace tucked among the trees. Servants were waiting to show us to our rooms.

"The king and queen will be glad to see you at the morning meal. If you have need of anything further, servants will be outside your doors."

We all knew what that meant, and Jason gave me a wry smile as he and Neleus entered the room across from ours. There would be guards outside our rooms to make certain we made no trouble. A steaming bath had already been filled, and I sank into it gratefully while Kip shook out our clothes and hung them by the open window to air in the woodland-scented night breeze.

While I soaked, I took in the room. Heavy stone walls were covered in thinly woven bright tapestries. The bed had posts at each corner and a sheer net curtain over and around it that puddled on the floor, making of the bed a sort of shrine. Figures of herons and snakes were intricately worked into the stones along the floor, sometimes entwined and sometimes separate. It wasn't unlike my home in Egrisi, and it made me think of the forest and sounds of my old room.

"Down." Kip pushed on the top of my head.

I slid beneath the water and let her quickly wash my hair before

I got out so she too could bathe while the water was warm. I sat wrapped in a towel on the wide window ledge and looked out over the flickering lights of the village below us.

"Are you ever sad we left home?" I asked.

The water swished as she moved around. "Sometimes. But mostly I'm glad we left. We've done things no women at home could do, and I wouldn't have met Neleus."

"And if what lies ahead is darkness?"

"If we'd stayed under your father's roof, it would have been dark there too." She came and sat opposite me on the window ledge. "There are no guarantees anywhere. At least this way we get to see the world."

It was a simple way of looking at it and if I didn't have pieces of the gods in me, perhaps I would have felt the same. As it was, I knew the next stage of our journey was coming, and there would be more challenges. Dread grew deep in my soul like an itch I couldn't scratch.

Chapter Twenty
Moonstone

In the morning, Alkippe answered the door when someone knocked softly and announced the morning meal was ready and being served in the great hall. She quickly braided my hair and hung one of my finest Kolchian necklaces around my neck. If I was going to stand before royalty, it wouldn't be as a pauper.

When we entered the hallway, Jason and Neleus were waiting for us, and I fell into step beside Jason.

"Were you able to gather information?" he asked.

"None. The servants stayed away. You?"

He shook his head, and his eyes were troubled. "We were told it would be servants outside our rooms, but Neleus checked and they were warriors instead. What are they afraid of that they'd treat guests so?"

I didn't have an answer, but it made me wary as we entered the dining hall. At the far end were seated a man and a woman, talking quietly. As we made our way towards them down the long table, I saw the intelligence and uncertainty in their expressions. These were people expecting trouble but who didn't know which direction it would blow in from.

"Prince Jason, it is a pleasure to have you in our home." The man stood and clasped Jason's hand. "Be welcome and eat with us."

The woman turned to me, her hands held out in front of her. "And Priestess Medea, be welcome. I'm looking forward to your tale about how you came to be on this journey."

I searched her eyes for anything malignant, but there was only open curiosity. Still, it wasn't a tale to be told in full. I gave her a brief smile and then sat down to eat. Kip and Neleus sat beside us, and I could see the puzzled look in the king's eyes. Servants didn't eat with their betters, but Kip was my friend as surely as Neleus was Jason's, and I wouldn't have her demeaned.

The man placed a thick slab of melon on his plate. "I am King Dorieus, first of my name. I built the palace under the blessing of the sun god." He looked at the woman and smiled.

"I am Queen Agave, first of my name, daughter of King Cadmus of the tribe Ardiaei."

Jason stopped eating for a moment. "And the name of your beautiful city?"

"You've arrived at Scodra, home of the Labeates, Ardiaei, and Dorian people. And you've come at the festival of the harvest goddess as we give thanks for what we've received this year." The king's expression was neutral, but he didn't seem very festive.

"I noticed the heron and snake symbols. Are they for your gods?" I asked, hoping this wasn't like some of the other cities we'd been to where the women weren't supposed to talk.

Queen Agave laughed, a tinkling sound like a creek in summer. "They are the animals our gods hold sacred. Here in Scodra, you will see more birds than anywhere else in the world and snakes so beautiful only the gods could have gifted them to us." She raised her hand and moved it gracefully through the air. "The heron's beauty is second to none, and yet it is as swift and fierce as any bird of prey. Like the heron, we too are beautiful and fierce."

They were pretty words, and the meaning of them was clear.

The meal was soon finished, and Jason told a version of the story he'd been telling throughout our journey. Neleus remained quiet. This wasn't an evening meal meant to entertain but a simple breakfast with royalty who wanted to understand our journey. My part in it was far less brutal and far more helpful, and it irked me to be placed in a less active position. But then, we didn't need word to get back to my family that we'd come this way nor did we want to be turned away. An echo of the god's warning about hubris and balance sounded in my mind, and I listened, suitably chastened. I tilted my head and listened impassively, and the king and queen looked impressed and empathetic.

"Imagine, you've travelled so far from home to help this young prince take back his throne." Queen Agave pressed her hands to her chest and smiled, but I saw the shrewdness in her eyes. She knew there was more.

"The gods chose, and it's thanks to them we've come this far safely," I answered, not looking away. The minute tip of her chin acknowledged what we weren't saying.

"If it's not impertinent of me, may I ask why you seem wary of strangers?" Jason asked. "There's a feeling of impending war."

King Dorieus pushed back from the table. "These things are best discussed under the open sky."

He motioned towards the large double doors, and we followed him and the queen into beautifully landscaped gardens. They led us on a leisurely stroll past bushes of every colour flower I could have imagined, as well as past trees ripe with fruit being plucked by servants and placed into large woven baskets. Eventually we came to a table and benches placed in a large, open clearing.

It seemed odd to me that they'd sit beneath the blazing sun with no shade when there were so many trees, and I looked at Jason.

He bent his head towards mine. "So they can be certain no one is near enough to hide behind anything and overhear them."

I could see then how clever it was and how concerned they must be. But that also meant they didn't trust the people in their own palace.

We sat around the table and drinks were quickly placed before us, and then the servants left.

"You're familiar with war?" Queen Agave asked as she poured us scented water with pieces of orange in it.

"All of us from Thrace are familiar with war, my queen." Neleus spoke for the first time. "And the feeling in the air is the same no matter where you go."

King Dorieus laced his hands behind his neck. "True, young warrior. We are fortunate to be one of the most important trading stops from the Ionios Sea to the river people. People from all lands come here looking for fortune and glory. It's one of the best things about us." He frowned. "But the earth shakes, and the crops die, and the water turns sour. People fear we've angered the gods by mixing with people from other tribes."

I took a sip of my water, weighing my words. "We've come a long, long way. We've passed villages on three rivers, and they all say the same thing. There are areas where the river has receded so much, we feared we wouldn't get the ship through. If the gods are angry, it isn't only at you."

The queen closed her eyes and breathed a sigh of relief. "That is good to hear, although also worrying."

"People are leaving, heading north to where we've heard things are better, although the northern people don't speak our language." The king took the queen's hand in his. "And we've heard rumours that the people wonder if taking us from power will make the gods happy once again. With your news, spread by your crew in the marketplace, perhaps that worry can be put to rest."

"And you?" I asked. "If things get bad enough, will you head north as well?"

He shook his head. "We'll stay. This is our land, and these are our people. We won't abandon them, even if the gods refuse to help us." He leaned towards us and said softly, "But beware, young prince. There are sailors of chance here who have been raiding villages all along the coast, taking their wealth and women and leaving death in their wake."

"And so you have guards outside your doors." Jason made circles in the condensation on the table. "Are the raiders headed upriver, from where we came? Or are they going back to sea?"

"We don't ask. It's best not to speak to them if you can help it. They trade and don't make trouble here, but they bring their stories with them, and we watch them closely until they row away again.

They call themselves the Sea People. They lost their lands years ago and turned to the sea as a home."

I shivered slightly as a shadow passed over the table. Jason looked at me, but I shook my head and returned my attention to my water.

"Now you understand why the city feels like a knife edge." Queen Agave smiled. "But it is also festival time, and you and your men are welcome to compete in the games." She turned to me and Kip. "And I hope you'll join my women in the games as well."

I knew I looked as surprised as Jason did. "Your women play too?"

She laughed that sweet laugh again. "We are equal here in the city. We even have some female warriors who choose that life over one in the home. Zeus and Hera are equal, why shouldn't we be?"

It is hard to describe the elation that flooded through me. I'd had that same thought so many times myself. Here was a place I could be myself, where no one would expect me to belong to anyone. I swallowed at the possibility this could be the end of my journey with Jason. Perhaps this was where I was meant to be.

King Dorieus looked over my shoulder and motioned. A young woman dressed all in white bowed her head respectfully when she came up to the table.

"The high priestess would like to invite the travelling priestess to the temple ahead of the festival celebration this night."

Strangely, I didn't want to go. I wanted to sit here and ask more questions about how their city worked, how women who didn't marry made their way. But refusing the invitation would be rude and would bring dishonour on our hosts.

"The festival goes on all week," Queen Agave said, squeezing my hand. "I hope we'll get more time to talk."

I smiled in thanks that she seemed to know what I was thinking, then followed the priestess out of the palace and down the hill, back towards the port. This path was laid with beautiful white stones shot through with grey veins. They glittered in the sun, and

I stopped to touch one.

"Moonstone," the young woman said. "Beautiful in the day, and magical in the moonlight."

I nodded and continued to follow her, though I was surprised when we got in a small boat that she then rowed to a small island not far offshore, where the temple stood, made of the moonstone and shining like a beacon against the still water. The temple had large columns at the front, painted with blues and reds and images of trees that matched those on the hills. Inside were numerous rooms falling away from the main circle. In the centre was a large altar, but instead of being stained rust-red with blood, it was stained a strange yellow. The room buzzed with pre-festival excitement such as I'd felt when I was getting ready in the temple at home. Women's quiet voices laughed, talked, and gave orders. It was another reminder of home that made my soul ache.

The high priestess came forwards and kissed my cheeks. The small jewel on her forehead was clearly made of the same stone along the path, and the chain holding it to her hair was the most delicate work I'd yet seen on this trip, almost as good as that done in Egrisi.

"Be welcome, sister." She looped her arm through mine in a strangely familiar gesture and led me through one of the back doorways. "We are always happy to have a new priestess with us, and it happens all too rarely. I'm sure you're used to the festival madness."

I nodded, out of my depth. People had been kind in many places but never this open.

"We have a quiet area where you can pray and give offerings for as long as you like. We will open the festival at sundown by the shore if you'd like to join us."

I nodded again, still unsure what to say. This temple felt so light, so easy. It was nothing like my own back home, nor the others I'd been to along the way here. I wasn't sure how to handle it. She left me in a slightly darker room with one open window. Incense, fruity and clean, burned in one corner. In the centre was a small altar with bowls of fruit, multi-coloured pebbles, and flowers nearby. They'd even provided offerings.

I knelt beside the altar, forgoing the pillow so I could feel the cool tiles under my knees. I bent my head and breathed deeply, focusing on the water I could feel on the shore, on the ancient knowledge pulsing in my neck, and the images of the future that pressed like thumbs against my skull. My shoulders fell and my jaw relaxed. Birds chirped, but there was no other sound.

I am here. I wasn't sure what else to say.

A breeze wafted across my skin, and I lifted my eyes to see a woman sitting across from me. She wasn't old, but there were lines at her eyes. *Harvest goddess.*

Medea. You've done well, coming so far. You have far, far to go yet. But as autumn is here, you too can rest for a moment before you move on.

My heart sank. *Can I stay?*

No. Your destiny lies with Jason's, your threads intertwined by the gods. You will know when the time comes that your threads are no longer twisted.

Her cat-like eyes were soft, like she understood, and I wished she was the goddess who had called to me in the first place. But then, would I have gone to her like I did to the other?

Find joy where you can. Breathe in life and all it has to offer. A mortal's life is swift and must be appreciated.

I blinked, and she was gone. It was far less interesting than the meetings I'd had at the other temples, but that wasn't a bad thing. After all, I didn't need another power, another god who wanted something from me. And she'd appeared to me, which I knew was a rare thing and something to be cherished. So why did I feel despondent?

I stayed a while longer and made offerings from the bowls, giving thanks for our safe journey so far and asking protection for the rest of the trip, but my mind was elsewhere. I couldn't stay because of Jason. Not surprising, certainly, given the way we'd begun. But how long would I be with him for? How long would it be before I could find the place I wanted to be, where I belonged? There would be no answer, of course. So, as the harvest goddess said, I would need to enjoy all I could, draping myself in the experiences as I went along.

The priestess was as kind when I left, and she let me know how things would proceed so I could meet them at the right time. I met Kip back at the palace, and we discussed what she'd heard of the upcoming festivities. New gowns, gifts from the queen, had been delivered and looked very fine. Kip was excited the way she'd been as a girl when we were still allowed to run, and the feeling was infectious. To feel like a young woman, free and able to laugh, was a gift.

CHAPTER TWENTY-ONE
A Favoured Toy

TOGETHER WE TRIED TO figure out the best way to pin our new clothing, but there was simply too much material. A knock at the door came as I was losing my patience. A servant came in carrying an armful of cloth.

"The queen suggested you might like something to wear for the games." She held up a simple gown beautifully decorated with a heron.

Kip went over and examined it. "How do you wear it?"

The servant blushed sweetly. "If you'll disrobe, I can show you."

It turned out to be wonderfully simple. There was a front and back piece, and they were held together with beautifully worked pins at the shoulders. The material overlapped at the sides and a belt was tied below our breasts, and then the material was pulled out to cover the belt. It left our legs free to move, and she placed two more small pins at the sides of our thighs to keep the material from opening too much. It came to just below our knees, which meant we wouldn't trip over it in the games either. It was perfect, and nowhere else had I ever been where a woman could exhibit her legs so freely. Her breasts, certainly, but not her legs. The thought made me laugh.

My gown had a stunning snake in red and blue that ran from between my breasts all the way down my stomach and so intricately was it done, that the blousing over the belt still allowed it to look as though it could slither off the material. On the back was a heron, its wings spread over my shoulder blades.

Kip looked impressed with her own, less intricate but still beautiful, version.

We took our afternoon meal in the bustling market spread throughout the city. Unlike other areas, the sections here were clear. The jewel workers were deep in the heart of it, lined up along narrow cobbled streets. Here I traded a few small pieces of Kolchian jewellery that were eagerly sought once I'd traded the first one. We traded a ring for a thin bronze arm band for Kip, and it looked beautiful on her. I found a diadem similar to the one the queen wore, with a chain that showed up nicely against my hair and a black stone for my forehead like those we'd seen elsewhere. But my new stone had something special. The jeweller stepped into the sunlight and held it high, and the red sparkle in the middle of it looked like a heart. I would have traded several pieces for it but fortunately Kip was better at bartering than I, and it cost us little.

Walking through the market, I could feel it against my forehead, my third eye pulsing under it. I considered going back to him to see if he had any other interesting pieces but when I turned, he was gone. Not even his table was there.

Kip looked around the area and then sighed deeply. "Will they ever leave you alone, I wonder?"

I shook my head. "Gifts from the gods aren't something to scoff at." I pressed the stone and nearly dropped to my knees when the world shifted beneath my feet.

Flames burned my skin. Smoke choked me. Cries of fear and pain deafened me. And beneath it all was my own rage, consuming me from the inside just as the outside threatened to. I crawled along broken stone towards the lake but stopped at the sound of children screaming.

The world turned right again, and I knelt in the street, retching into a bowl Kip held for me. Men stood grouped nearby, watching, waiting, their expressions wary and curious. A foreign priestess kneeling in the street and vomiting wasn't something they were used to.

I watched numbly as my tears created dark spots on the hot stone. I never saw anything to do with myself and now that I had,

I knew the depth of the darkness I was being led to. I allowed Kip to help me to my feet, and she kept her arm around me as moved quickly back to the castle. Once there, she ordered a bath and got me washed and redressed and sent my peplos to be cleaned where my knees had crushed it to the dirty stone. I heard all of this from a distance, unable to get the images from my mind, everything else dimmed by the sound of the children's cries.

Kip answered the door to a soft knock, and I heard murmuring but didn't turn from the window to see who it was. But when a hand gently touched my shoulder I turned.

"Would you walk with me?" the high priestess asked.

I nodded and followed her from the room, down several hallways to a long open terrace that overlooked the lake beyond the walls. We sat on a long stone bench that provided a perfect view across the lake, where another small white city could be seen on the far shore.

"A runner told me a story. He said you were speaking with someone no one else could see and when you walked away, you wore jewellery you hadn't been wearing before. And then you collapsed as though in prayer and let your tears wash the street."

I wrapped my arms around myself and nodded slightly. She was silent for a long moment, and I longed for her to give me advice, to tell me not everything I saw would be true.

"Have you been god-touched before?"

Again, I simply nodded. How to explain I was a favoured toy passed from one to the next?

She sighed softly. "Many serve but few get spoken to. I'm guessing those of us who get to serve in ignorance are better off." She took my hand and held it and didn't ask anything else. She simply sat with me, and soon I felt my despair begin to lift.

I turned to her. "But you're god-touched as well."

She tilted her head. "Not like you, thankfully. Is there any way I can help?"

"Do you believe we create our own path? Or do the gods

dictate all? Are the Fates always weaving? Have they already spun our threads and know where they'll end?"

She stared at the lake, her brow furrowed. "We're taught to believe that our paths are laid before us, and all we do is give thanks to the gods." She stopped to nod to a passing servant, who gave a shy smile and continued on. "But I think they leave most of us alone. There are few the gods cradle in their palms, and those are the ones we tell stories of, whose tales will be told hundreds of years from now."

"But it never ends well for them, does it?" The effects of the vision were nearly gone, but it left an oily heaviness behind.

"No." Priestesses don't lie, even when the truth hurts. "But they're not forgotten either. Just as I don't think you will be."

Once again, a shudder ran through me, but she squeezed my hand and pulled me up from the bench. "Come, sister. Let us open the festival and invoke the goddess, and then we will drink and tell stories and pretend for the night that we aren't chaste and sweet."

Her genuine smile reached through my gloom, and I smiled back. "Thank you for coming."

She cupped my cheek. "I won't pretend to understand the burden you bear, but the gods wouldn't have chosen you if you couldn't live with it."

They were simple words, but they worked as intended. I straightened and gave her a brief hug. "Thank you, sister."

She walked me back to my room, and the buzz in the castle was infectious. "I'll send an acolyte to get you shortly."

There is little to say about the rest of the night, or even most of the days that followed. Jason was kind and often sought me out for a talk about how things were there, and I enjoyed the music and games. Kip won one of the races and received a beautiful bracelet. I was appalling at most things but still enjoyed the ability to run, and throw, and be part of the festival. Word had spread about my experience in the market and though some stayed away, many sought to touch me and even left small things for me at the palace, asking me to pray on their behalf. I must admit to it being a welcome feeling, and one I wanted more of. The warning of hubris and balance faded under the weight of appreciation.

It was on the day before the end of the festival that the accident occurred, bringing our enjoyment and ease to an end.

Eurytus, a boisterous, energetic sailor who often sparred with his brother, took part in an unusual game. An extremely long pole was given to a runner, who ran as fast as they could to the shoreline. There, they planted the pole into a shallow indentation in the ground and used their body weight and the pole to launch themselves into the river. The person who landed furthest away was the winner.

It was a silly game, one the young men took great joy in, and Eurytus desperately wanted to show his strength. His brother, Echion, quieter and more thoughtful, cheered him on. His leap was impressive, his body arching through the air gracefully, his yell and smile like those of a young god in flight. He hit the water cleanly, but when he failed to come up right away, his brother stood at the edge of the water, scanning. Was he playing a prank, as he was wont to do?

When the water became laced with red, Echion dove in, quickly followed by others. Eurytus' body was pulled from the water after being dislodged from the rocks. An unlucky jump, he'd landed where two boulders came together. He'd cracked his head and his arm had caught in the crevice. Even if he'd been awake, which he likely hadn't, he would have drowned.

It put a pall on the festivities and by nightfall, there were whispers of the gods' anger once again. The priestesses joined me as I prepared his body for the kind of burial done among his people, while the men of the city prepared his grave. I could have left the preparation to the priestesses, but he'd been with us, played and laughed with us, and he'd never said an unwelcoming word to us. I owed him, both as the ship's priestess and someone he'd trusted. Now I would ask for guidance for him into the underworld.

Jason and Echion wept openly and kept vigil throughout the night. The sailors gathered around a campfire on the beach and told inflated stories of Eurytus's adventures in war and love, making him out to be one of the greatest. At sunrise, they bore him on a litter and took him across the water and up a hill. There, a tomb had been erected out of stone, and he was laid inside along with his weapons and jewels, bowls, arm bands, and pottery donated by the villagers and taken from our ship. I anointed his head with oils and prayed, but I didn't feel anyone acknowledge me. I wished otherwise, so I could give Echion some relief, but I wouldn't lie. Not about this.

The rest of the day was muted as the festival came to a close. I went to the temple and prayed. For the first time in a long while, I prayed simply for comfort. I didn't ask for anything other than Eurytus's safe passage and an easing of the grief of the men, especially his brother. I was surprised, therefore, when I found myself with the harvest goddess once again.

"It is time for you to go." Her golden wheat eyes were bright in the dim stone room.

"The men will want to take a week to mourn." In truth, I wouldn't mind leaving now.

She spread her hand and passed it over the alter, and it shimmered and took shape. Waterways and landmasses became so clear I could see deer moving through mountains and tiny fish swimming in the shallow water by the shore. Was this what the gods saw when they looked down on us?

"You will follow this river until you reach this curve." She pointed to each area. "And then you will sail on, stopping here." She pointed to a large island. The magical map disappeared, and she looked at me once more. "You will have to choose and choose again. Remember you are beloved by the gods, and human rules will not always apply to you."

With that, she was gone. Her warning made me shudder and irrationally angry. What did that mean? And if rules didn't apply to me, then shouldn't other humans know that? Because what happened when I chose wrongly and had to face the wrath of one or the other of my oppressors?

I rose and left the temple, glad once again to be in the sunlight. I said a soft prayer, thanking my grandfather, Helios, for the warmth and comfort it always brought me.

And then the world crumbled.

CHAPTER TWENTY-TWO
Agave

I FELL TO MY knees, unable to keep my balance as the world shook and roared. Stones collapsed, people were screaming, and ancient trees born not long after the gods came crashing down. With my hands in the earth and my knees bruised by the stones under them, I held on and looked through the plumes of dust rising in the air. It seemed to go on forever and when it stopped, the priestesses stumbled from the temple, covered in dust and wide-eyed. The temple remained standing, which was good since it would be needed to tend to the injured.

Two of them helped me to my feet, and I dusted myself off. Blood showed through the white material where my knees had been scraped by rocks. I ignored the sting and turned to the high priestess, who looked as shaken as the others.

"There will be injured and trapped. Send only two to pray and gather everyone else. Take supplies into the city and begin assisting those in need."

She nodded and did as I said, and I left to check on my own people.

The palace had been hit badly. Walls were half broken teeth with towers of blank eyes open to the sky. Inside there was wailing and calls for help. I turned away.

I needed to find Alkippe. Above all, she had to be okay. I closed my eyes and used my powers, any and all I had, and I moved in the direction where she'd be. Indeed, she was at the harbour, helping Neleus place stitches in one of our crew's arms.

She stood when she saw me, and I embraced her hard before holding her at arm's length. "You didn't come to look for me?"

She gave me a small smile. "No one but the gods will take you, and we know they have much to do with you yet."

I couldn't help but laugh, drawing startled looks from those around me. "True enough. Have you seen Jason?"

Neleus stood, stretching his back. "He said he wanted to discuss something with the king. He was going to the palace."

I flinched and looked over my shoulder, though I couldn't see it from where I was standing. "The palace is broken."

He pushed past me and ran up the path, and Kip and I followed. In that space the goddess had created inside me that existed solely for Jason, I knew he was okay. But there was darkness, and I thought of the goddess's warning.

When we got to the palace, servants were already bringing out the dead and laying them beneath the trees. Others were digging beneath heavy stone to pull out the crushed and mangled bodies of others. We picked our way through the rubble to the main hall, where Jason knelt with the queen in his arms as she wept. The king lay before them, his head a pulpy mess. The pang of regret I felt at his death was overshadowed by the deep irritation that came over me at the sight of Queen Agave in Jason's arms. It occurred to me I didn't know who he bedded or if he did, and it bothered me more than it needed to. And yet, I didn't feel the goddess's hand in it.

Kip knelt beside the queen as Neleus laid a tapestry over the king. She gently pulled the queen up and led her away, and Jason turned to me, his eyes stricken with grief.

"We were about to walk out to the gardens, and the stone fell before I could move him. I barely managed to get the queen away."

So he'd saved the queen and not the king. Had he consciously chosen, or had he simply reacted? He stepped towards me, and I opened my arms. He fell into them, holding onto me like a man drowning. I soothed him as best I could, somewhat puzzled by the depth of his emotion. They'd been kind, yes, and hospitable. And the queen and I had several talks about women's place here. She was intelligent and charming, and I was sorry for her pain. But I felt far more deeply the loss of one of our own than a king we barely knew. Yet Jason wept as a child cries when a beloved one dies.

But I held him anyway, and when he was done, he dried his eyes and shook his head.

"You feel nothing?" he asked, looking at me to see no tears.

"Man going back to the gods who created him is nothing to mourn. We cry for our loss, not theirs." I cupped his cheek, hoping my words would cover my lack of womanly wailing.

He sighed and put some distance between us. "Wise words, as always, Medea. The gods have gifted you with wisdom, if not depth of heart."

The words stung, more so because I recognized their truth. "I received a message from the gods while I was at the temple. We're to leave right away and continue our journey." When he went to protest, I stopped him. "The people here will put their world right, and they'll move on as they'd planned to. We have given Eurytus his funeral rites and he is with the gods now. We must go."

His gaze was searching as he studied me. I held my ground.

"Fine. But we can't go today. I need to check the ship and make sure the Argo wasn't damaged, and we need to see if any of our crew are hurt."

I nodded, feeling it was best not to say anything further, and he left me. I'd forgotten Neleus was there until he moved out of the shadows to stand at my side.

"It could have been Jason, hit by that falling rock. I would never have forgiven myself."

I shook my head. "The gods have much to do with us yet."

He, too, left me. I stood there in the ruin of the palace, alone and angry. No, perhaps I didn't wail and weep, but that didn't mean I didn't feel. I wanted to tear down the rest of the stones with my bare hands. I wanted to light a flame and watch everything burn. These people were nothing, they meant nothing. I heard a noise and turned to find Kip watching me, her eyes narrowed. She made her way towards me, and she seemed so small. She took my hand.

"Leave her," she whispered. "Leave her alone."

Emptiness surged through me, and I dropped to my knees once again. Kip caught me and held me there as I took long, shaky breaths.

"How did you know?" I asked when I could speak again.

"How did I know you were being inhabited by a god?" She grinned and swept my damp hair from my forehead. "Your body changes. You look bigger. Scary and powerful. More than you do normally." She pulled me to my feet, and I leaned on her as we left the ruins. "I'd know you and your body anywhere."

Why was the goddess riding me when there was no reason? She hadn't been speaking to anyone through me. I wasn't doing her bidding. Was she responding to my own anger, helping me overcome the loneliness brought about by her presence under my skin? Did she not see that by doing so, she pulled me away from the people around me? There was no answer to my silent question, and I let it remain unanswered, too tired to plead for answers.

Once we were in the garden, we sat at the table, a strange oasis in the midst of chaos. "We have to leave."

We watched a servant scurry past, his arms laden with bronze items from the palace.

"We won't be the only ones." Kip nodded towards him. "The city was on a tipping point when we got here. This will force the people to run."

"I didn't know."

She looked at me quizzically.

"I didn't know the goddess was using me. I always know. I can feel her, like I'm looking through two sets of eyes at once. But I didn't know this time." I picked at a splinter in the table until it made my fingertip bleed. "What if it happens more often? What if I lose myself?"

Kip covered my hand with hers. "Then I'll bring you back. I'll always bring you back."

We stayed there until nightfall, hardly talking, watching what was happening in and around the palace. Our rooms were likely destroyed, but we would have to go to them to gather our things. I could have gone to the temple, but it would be busy with the priestesses tending the injured and praying, and I didn't want anything to do with either right now. We waited, out of the way, until Kip finally shivered as the air grew cooler and the light began to fade.

"Let's get our things. Then we can head to the ship and sleep there overnight."

We made our way through the palace, stepping over large stones and around broken pottery and mosaics burst into pieces of a picture that would never look right again. In our room, we hurriedly put our things together and carried the trunk out, where we found several of the crew waiting. They took our things, and I told them of our plan to sleep aboard the ship, and they seemed to take heart at that. They'd been waiting for Jason, but Neleus had been the one giving orders.

I knew in my heart where Jason was and what he was doing. He and the queen would both need solace, and a warm embrace with someone else who was in pain would do well. Once again that feeling swept through me. Was I not good enough? I'd held him, but he'd turned from me. But then, I didn't want him that way, did I? That was the gods' doing, not my own. Wasn't it?

Kip linked my arm in hers and pulled me away, down one corridor and then the next, though I paid little attention to where we were going. But then we entered the baths and I stopped.

"You're covered in dust and scrapes. I am too. If we're leaving tomorrow, we should be clean and ready."

I didn't say anything. I let her undress me and lead me into the warm cavern baths. "I feel so alone." I didn't mean to say the words out loud, but there they were, echoing off the damp stone walls.

"You hold yourself away, Medea." Kip rubbed my skin with the cleansing salts. "I know what you're thinking, just as I did when you were a child. You want to be wanted; you want people to flock to you. But you never reach out to them, and then you get angry when they don't come to you anyway."

I turned on her. "What do you know of it? To be born with an omen, to be chosen by the gods?"

She sighed and slid beneath the water to wet her hair. "You would have been this way without an omen or any gods. Perhaps that's why they chose you."

Between her words and Jason's earlier ones, I wanted to lash out. I also wanted to cry. Instead, I quickly washed my hair and scrubbed myself down hard, including the scrapes on my knees. I relished the pain it brought and by the time we got out, I felt a little better. Still, we dressed silently, and Kip did my hair with little patience. I swatted her away when she tugged too hard and finished it myself.

Clean and dressed, we made our way in the darkness, following the moonstone path to the harbour. The city was quiet except for soft crying. Community fires were common as people gathered to share their sorrows. When we got to the Argo, Neleus was waiting and his relief when he saw Kip was clear. At least one of us would be missed, I thought unkindly, and walked past him onto the ship. I went to our place behind the tapestry and curled up in a new blanket. I was fine. I didn't need anyone. Kip could have Neleus, and Jason could have the queen.

Kip didn't join me that night, and I slept fitfully. In the morning, I was cross and took my morning wine sullenly. Jason walked towards the Argo and was greeted by his men. I watched him greet them by name, giving thanks to the gods they'd all been spared, and I watched as he searched among them until his gaze finally landed on me. He tilted his head and his smile faltered. He motioned towards the beach, and I glared at him over my wine cup. But he didn't look away and with a sigh, I made my way off the ship and to his side. We walked along the beach until there was no one nearby. I wanted to ask if he'd had fun, if he'd enjoyed her. But there would be wrath in my tone, and I didn't want him to think

I cared.

"Medea," he said softly. "I need your guidance."

Surprised, I stopped walking. "What is it?"

He picked up a handful of pebbles and began throwing them into the water, one at a time. "The queen has asked me to stay. They're without a king, and they had no children. As a prince, I'm able to take the throne."

My stomach lurched but not the way it did when I had visions. Initially I had considered staying myself and ending our journey together if I could be free here. But to hear him say it, to have him take the choice from me, from us all, was unthinkable. And to do it for a queen, another woman... I wanted to scream and claw at him.

Instead, I touched his arm. "Is it what you want?"

He continued throwing his pebbles. "A kingdom of my own to rule, with a queen who is beautiful, wise, and kind? It would be foolish to say no." He glanced at me. "But it isn't my choice to make, is it?"

You must choose and choose again. The warning echoed in the canyon of my soul. I could choose to tell him he could stay, that he had that option. Or I could tell him otherwise. The gods said I would have to choose, not that he would. His happiness was in my hands. Once again, I heard the whisper about the balance of light and dark.

"I don't know, Jason. You know as well as I that we were brought together. I was told only yesterday that we had to leave. But if you stayed, would the gods punish you? Or would they find someone else to torment me with?" I smiled when he looked at me quickly, and he smiled slightly in return when he saw I was jesting. Mostly. "Perhaps you should go to the temple. Pray on it and see if they answer you." I thought of the day he'd shown up in my palace in Egrisi and he too had been god-ridden. "I think they will."

He kissed the top of my hand. "Thank you, princess. I'll do as you say."

"We'll wait at the Argo for your decision." I watched as he

practically ran up the path towards the temple, and I knew what the gods' answer would be. In truth, I couldn't blame Queen Agave for asking him to stay. But she'd have to find another. Jason was mine.

CHAPTER TWENTY-THREE
A Mother's Love

WE SET SAIL SHORTLY after midday. When Jason had come back, he'd looked like Atlas with the world on his shoulders. He gave me a small smile, and I nodded. He'd been answered and so we were leaving. The crew were already in place and the ship was stocked, thanks to Neleus. There was no leaving party nor group of well-wishers on shore. They were busy preparing their dead and fixing their homes, and ships were being prepared for trips north. I didn't speak to the queen again, as I feared my anger and jealousy would get the better of my tongue. It wasn't well done, but I didn't care. I knew I'd never see her again, and so it didn't matter.

"We take the Bojana River to the Cape of Rodon." I drew lines in water on the rail for Jason. "From the Cape of Rodon, we follow the shore to this island."

"We stop at Scheria? That may not be wise. They've been at war with Corinth for a long time."

I shrugged. "I don't know why, and I don't know the name. But I was told."

He sighed. "Anything else?"

I shook my head. "Did you love her?"

Startled, he turned to me. "Does it matter?"

"It might."

It took some time before he answered. "I'm not sure if I know what love is. What you and I have...it can't be, can it? Because we had no choice. Queen Agave gave me a choice, and I could see a future with her. But if I'd loved her, I would have stayed and be damned, whatever the gods said. That's what the poets would have us believe."

So he didn't love me and felt I'd been forced on him. I suppose I hoped we'd gained more than that throughout the trip. But he saw no future with me either. I turned away and went to the front of the boat, behind the curtain, and when Kip would have followed me, I waved her away. I needed to be alone with my pain, to let it burn through me, so I never needed anyone again.

The river ended and the Argo entered the Aegean Sea. The men cheered and sang and lit fires of thanks as nightfall came to us. I slept alone beneath a strand of trees on the beach, and in the morning, I kept to myself once again. The crew seemed to sense the unrest between Jason and I, and it smothered the good humour we'd sailed under to this point. But I couldn't seem to break from my despair and anger.

The next day, I was standing at the rail watching the water give way before the bow of the Argo when a flash caught my eye. A tail, a strand of hair, a flash of eyes, and then it was gone. I leaned over and watched more carefully and nearly fell overboard when a river nymph leapt from the water, her body shiny with soft scales, her faint green hair flowing over her shoulders. It was her eyes that caught me. They were exactly like my mother's and my chest tightened.

Shouts rose behind me as the crew saw what I'd been seeing. River nymphs played in the Argo's wake, their firm breasts catching the crew's attention, and the men pleaded with the woman to jump aboard. They made promises of forever and threw coins and jewels, which the nymphs largely ignored.

"Your mother sends her love." A beautiful young nymph rose in front of me, her tail dancing in the water as she stayed ahead of the ship. "She says not to forget where you come from."

I felt the unfamiliar burn of tears begin to slide down my cheeks, and my anger and frustration left me as easily as the nymph slid back into the water. I was not a god to demand that people love me. I wasn't a human either, allowed to live and love as I wished. I was something in between, a godly toy, and allowing human emotions to warp my mind wouldn't do anyone any good.

The nymphs disappeared, leaving us to play elsewhere, and I let the water soothe me. I closed my eyes and tried to recapture the feeling of freedom and ease I'd had before we made it to Scodra, and calm spread through me. A shadow blocked the sun and I smiled. "I can always tell when it's you."

"And I know when you're near me too." Jason leaned on the rail beside me. "Medea, I speak honestly but sometimes without thinking. I hope you understand how much you've come to mean to me. If I had stayed in Scodra, I would have begged you to stay with me." He swallowed hard, his eyes sad. "You could've told me I had no choice, you could have forced my hand in any direction. Instead, you told me to pray, to ask the gods. You guide me, and I wouldn't have wanted to be without you."

My heart swelled, and there was room for it now that I'd let go of the other things. "I would have stayed, though it might have broken me to share you." The words were unexpectedly honest, but they were true. I saw his surprise, and then his softening.

"I think we have far to go, you and I." He raised my hand and kissed it lightly before going back to the wheel.

There was deep truth in the words, and I shivered at the shadow lingering beneath them.

CHAPTER TWENTY-FOUR
Chaon

WE'D LEFT THE LAND of the Ilyrians and were moving into the land of the Chaonian people. One of our crew, a Chaonian himself, told us of their customs and of the fractious relationship with the Ilyrians. He cared little for politics and had gladly left to take the voyage when he heard Jason's call for men. He directed us to Chimaira, named after Hades' three-headed guardian of the underworld. It was ruled by King Chaon, a benevolent king who spent much time among his people.

This was the biggest body of water I'd ever seen. Though we had the shore within sight on one side, on the other, there was no end of water. It looked as though the sky and water met and bounced off one another, neither merging nor giving way. It made me breathless, and I held on a little tighter to the rail. The world was so much bigger than I had imagined. What other lands were out there? What people, living their lives, equally unaware of us? It was unfathomable and made me tremble to think of it.

The men rowed hard as there was little wind for the sails and were ready to step ashore by the time we made it to Chimaira. The port was busy, and no one seemed to take notice of another ship arriving, and I was both grateful for the reprieve and somewhat irritated that we were so easily ignored. Kip tsked at me as she waved me off the ship, knowing as she always did what I was thinking.

Jason and Neleus fell in beside us as usual, and the language spoken around us seemed harsh and strange, but they both seemed to understand it easily and soon we had rooms at a large, clean inn. It wasn't long after we'd eaten that we were summoned to the palace, and our host nearly fell over himself in his offer to escort us. Having noble lodgers wouldn't do his reputation any harm.

I was weary and wished we could wait until morning to attend to the king but when summoned, you attend. My father would have killed anyone who didn't respond right away. The palace was on a tall hill overlooking the sea, and it was an interesting mix of the white stone of Scodra and the heavy stone I was used to seeing in palaces. Somehow it seemed fitting that here, on this huge sea that would take us where we needed to go, it would be a mix of what we'd had and what was to come.

We entered the throne room, warmed with large fires in hearths that would have fit a man standing tall. Long wood beams were high above our heads and the throne itself was simple. Beside it was a smaller throne meant for the queen, but it was empty.

The king's throne, however, was not. He was far younger than I had expected and not much older than Jason. His thick dark hair was held back at the nape of his neck and his bright eyes were inquisitive and kind. Over his broad shoulders he wore a simply embroidered peplos that went to the ground. He was one of the most handsome men I'd ever seen, and I was taken aback at how my breath caught. Jason glanced at me, one eyebrow raised, before he looked back at the king who had jumped up from his throne and strode forwards to meet us.

"King Chaon, thank you for inviting us to your palace. We bring—"

He waved Jason off and clasped his hand. "Welcome. Gifts can be exchanged later. I should have allowed you to rest and asked to see you tomorrow, but word spread quickly once your men dispersed among my people, and I had to meet the fabled prince on a quest to regain his kingdom. Boats have arrived for many days now from the rivers, with people telling your story." He turned to me and took my hand, kissing it gently. "And the beautiful princess priestess who accompanies him and beseeches the gods on his behalf."

For the first time in my life, I was speechless. I smiled shyly at him, bemused by his compliment and the warm forest wood colour of his eyes. He looked at me for a long moment, until Neleus softly cleared his throat.

He grinned and let go of my hand. "Please, join me for wine and stories."

We followed him not to the dining area but to a large room filled with comfortable chairs and rugs and another roaring fire. On a table in the middle was a jug of wine and various sweets. He nodded and the servants picked up trays and began moving among us. We arrayed ourselves on chairs, and it felt wonderfully intimate in a way I'd never experienced before.

King Chaon raised his glass. "To new friends and stories of heroes. May the Muses guide your tongue."

Taking his cue, Neleus began his story, one I'd heard often now. My part grew and the king looked at me admiringly often. I heard Kip snort softly, and I swatted at her leg. When Neleus was done, the king applauded and poured us more wine.

"To go on such a journey would be a dream come true," he said. "Though I don't envy the fight you may have ahead of you when you return to your uncle with the fleece in hand. I feel certain he wasn't expecting you to succeed."

Jason nodded. "I fear you're right. But he didn't anticipate the gods being on my side or them gifting me with Medea's aid either."

Chaon sipped from his cup and studied me over the rim. "No, I don't imagine he did."

Neleus yawned loudly behind his hand, and Jason rose. "Forgive us, but we've had a long day."

The king stood so quickly he nearly knocked over the table. "Of course. Please, stay here in the palace. Tomorrow we'll have a great feast in your honour."

Jason looked torn and I stepped forwards, placing my hand on Chaon's arm. "If it wouldn't displease you, we have already had our things brought to the inn. Perhaps we could have them moved here tomorrow and stay with you then?" I smiled my most charming smile. "It would be good for the innkeeper's reputation as well."

He looked disappointed but placed his hand over mine. "It is kind of you to think of the innkeeper. I'll have your things brought to the palace first thing in the morning. Please break your fast with me."

I startled when I felt Jason's hand under my elbow, gently pulling me away.

"We would be happy to accept your hospitality, thank you." He bowed his head, as did the rest of us, and we followed a servant out of the palace.

"I think you have an admirer," Kip said from behind me and laughed.

"True. You should watch out, Jason, or we'll lose our ship's priestess to the King!" Neleus too laughed.

I couldn't help but laugh with them. The king looked at me like no one had before, like he desired me and was interested in me. Me. Not in the priestess or the princess, though those roles probably played some part. To be wanted was new and after Jason's recent rejection, it filled a space in me that made me warm inside.

Jason frowned. "Don't jest."

He walked quickly ahead, leaving us behind and was already gone to his room when we entered the inn. I looked at Neleus, who shrugged.

"Sometimes we don't realize what we want until someone else wants it too." He kissed Kip on the cheek. "Come to me if you can."

She nodded and linked her arm in mine as we made our way to our room.

"What did he mean by that?" I asked, mulling it over.

"Truly?" she asked. "Are you so dim?"

I shook my head. "You don't understand. Jason told me on the beach in Skodar he wanted nothing to do with me because only the gods brought us together. That whatever we might feel for one another isn't real. And he has a point."

She looked surprised. "That's why you were in such a mood when we left."

"So you see my confusion."

She stayed quiet for a long time, and it was only when we settled to sleep that she sighed. "Confusion is what happens when the gods take notice of you. Only you and Jason can know what you truly feel, if anything."

I turned over and pillowed my head on my arm. "I like the way the king looks at me."

She laughed. "Like he could devour you? Yes, I should think so."

She was soon asleep, but I knew she'd wake in the early hours and go to Neleus. I didn't mind. She'd be there when I woke as she always was. As I fell asleep, I thought of Skodar. The goddess had said I couldn't stay there. But what if another man wanted my company? What then? Could I stay and be queen? The thought made my heart race, and I spent much of the night tossing and turning, sometimes dreaming of what life would be like if I stayed and others feeling bereft as I watched Jason pull away from shore without me, my heart torn in two.

The next morning, Kip was still sound asleep when I woke, so I dressed quietly and walked down to the harbour, which was already awake with men setting out in ships. Many stopped to stare, and I remembered where I was. I'd left the markings of a priestess behind, and so I appeared as a woman alone and nothing more. It gave me a slight thrill, and I lifted my chin and left the harbour behind to walk along the long, white sand beaches that gave rise to terraced hills planted with olive and citrus trees. It was peaceful the further I went, and I finally sat in the cool sand and watched as the boats made their way to a day of fishing. I'd rarely been alone these many weeks, and it felt wonderful to breathe deeply and not have to speak to anyone, man or god. Perhaps that was what would be best. To live on an island by myself, like my aunt Circe.

I thought of her and her deep ocean eyes and knew I wasn't made for such a life. Even with all her animals, she must be lonely, away from both humans and gods. My father said she'd been sent there to be punished, but it didn't seem like such a bad life, to do as you wished when you wished. Had I been born a man, so many things would be different.

There were many boats here. Different colours and shapes, small and large, painted and plain. And the men on them varied as much, from light-skinned and haired to dark as a night with no stars. Their clothes, too, were interesting. Some wore elaborate headdresses while others wore flowing tunics and sandals. They were like a million spices riding the waves, and my heart thrilled to see it. The cost had been great but to be here as the sun rose, seeing what I did, made it worth it.

Time passed, and I knew we'd be requested to be at breakfast. I wanted to look my best when we returned to the palace and so I hurried back to the inn, laughing at the men who stared and pointed at the woman walking alone through the market. Kip was outside waiting, her hands tugging at her skirt, and when she saw me, her relief quickly turned to anger.

"Where have you been? I thought you'd been kidnapped by the gods themselves."

I hugged her before going inside. "I simply wanted to watch the sunrise from the beach. Nothing more."

She remained irritated and quiet as she helped me wash and dress before doing so herself. I wore the diadem given to me by the god at Skodar and felt the stone pulse against my forehead. It made me feel strong, and I liked the feeling very much.

We met Jason and Neleus at the front door and began our walk to the palace with the servants behind us with our things. Jason took my hand as we walked, surprising me. He rarely touched me.

"You seem to have an admirer here," he said with a smile.

"I hadn't noticed." I grinned when he looked sidelong at me.

We continued to walk in silence, though I could feel he wanted to say something. I could wait, as I knew he often weighed his words before they came out, even though he'd told me that he sometimes spoke without thinking. We were nearly at the palace entrance by the time he turned to me.

"You've become very dear to me." He kissed my hand and waved me inside.

I expected more, and the simple statement left questions gathering on my tongue, but there was no time to voice them as the king's voice boomed out from inside.

"Friends!" He came forward, his arms outstretched in welcome. "I've had our finest breads and cheeses put out. Come join me." He held out his hand to me and I took it. "Priestess, I would be honoured if you'd sit beside me."

I did so, feeling singled out and not at all unhappy about it. The king engaged everyone in conversation, and I was content to listen. He spoke openly with Kip and Neleus, too, which pleased me. I'd always hated the way my father treated anyone who wasn't royalty, and King Chaon's manner suggested a king who valued people.

When the meal was over, Neleus said he wanted to check on the men and Jason wanted to look over the Argo.

King Chaon turned to me. "I would like to accompany you to the temple, if you'd allow it?"

For some reason I glanced at Jason, whose brow was furrowed. He looked at me and then away as he stood and made his exit. It was a response I'd have to analyse later. "I would like that, thank you." I smiled at Kip, who also looked disturbed. "You can go to the marketplace and see if there's anything we'd like, Alkippe. I'll likely be at the temple or with the king for the rest of the day." It was forward of me to say so, but where there was no risk, there was little gain.

His smile told me I'd spoken true. "Alkippe, I'll send one of the palace servants with you to carry your things and show you our city." He motioned and a young man stepped forward and bowed. Kip looked undecided for a moment before she bowed her head and followed the young man out.

Alone with the king, I smiled at him. "Thank you for your kindness."

He tucked my hand in the crook of his arm and began walking. "It isn't kindness if it gives me pleasure. And I didn't think I'd get the chance to spend time alone with you. In my city, it would be considered ill-done to be alone with a princess who had her own escort."

"How do you know I'm a princess?" I asked. He'd greeted me that way when we'd arrived, and I had to wonder now if he'd heard from one of the vessels far more than the story Neleus had shared.

His laugh made me smile. "You don't have a servant's bone in your body, beautiful woman. You carry yourself like a queen." His smile dimmed slightly. "But in truth, tales often come with the ships, and there's been an interesting one arriving from the far sea. They say a Kolchian princess was taken away by a Iolian prince, who killed her brother as well as stole a valuable golden fleece."

To hear I was stolen like some piece of jewellery was vexing; even in story, my power was taken from me. But I nodded as though interested in a tale and nothing more. "That does sound like an interesting tale."

He nodded, playing along. "And to think, I then had a ship arrive in port with an Iolian prince and a priestess of Hecate who looks very much like a Kolchian princess who is far from home."

I remained silent. That he knew who we were and what had happened put our lives in his hands. He could easily call the soldiers and have us placed in custody. My father would pay a handsome reward for us, no doubt. It also meant there had been, or were, Kolchian soldiers in Chimaira.

"I am a young king, as you can see," he went on when I didn't say anything, "and keeping your people happy so that you remain king isn't always easy." We passed beneath a beautiful bower of trees as we made our way up a deeply forested hill. "And in this city where tales come from all over the world, we love our heroes, and tragedies, and stories of the gods." He stopped and brushed a piece of my hair behind my ear. "And in you, we find all of those."

We continued on, and I was still unsure what to say. Were we in danger? In my heart, I didn't feel it to be so. We emerged from the overhanging trees into the bright sunshine on a clifftop, and the view from there was stunning. The sea went on and on, dotted with boats like the ones I'd seen in the goddess's map.

"Princess, I will speak plainly. We don't know each other but the moment you stepped into my palace, my heart sang for you and you alone. Somehow, I know we are meant to be together, that the fates have brought you to me. If you would stay, I would make you Queen of Chimaira, and your father's people would have no choice but to accept that you were spoken for and under my protection."

I searched his pretty eyes for any sign of the gods, but there was none. He spoke truly and I wondered at it. "What if I were a shrew, a nag of a wife you came to despise?" I thought of the blood on my hands. "What if I were violent? What if I'd sinned against the gods and they wanted revenge?"

He laughed. "But when I look into your eyes, I see that you're none of those things."

It showed how little he knew me and how the tales had been spun. Had he been there that day that I slit my brother's throat in front of fifty men, he would not be so quick to invite me to his throne. Although...he was a king. A queen willing to do anything necessary might appeal after all.

I turned to look at the beautiful temple overlooking the sea. "I will pray on what you say, King Chaon. I will ask the goddess for guidance and hope to find an answer that pleases us both."

CHAPTER TWENTY-FIVE
Answers

AT A SOUND BEHIND me I turned to find an acolyte waiting, her head bowed beneath a long white veil. She moved without a sound, and I followed her inside the large open temple with an eye in the ceiling that made it easier to see the gods.

To be queen...the thought went around in my head like a swarm of bees. I stopped before a pool and the acolyte waited while I washed my hands and face, then she led me to a room at the back where incense smoked on an ochre altar. I knelt and soon felt the blessing of the head priestess as she placed oil on my brow.

"May you find the answers you search for."

Her voice was soft and held nothing but the common words we spoke as priestesses, and yet they sent shivers down my back.

I knelt there for some time, my mind whirling with the idea of being queen to a young, handsome king who already knew at least a portion of my story. I would have power and wouldn't have to bend to anyone. And my status as a priestess would mean people would come to me not solely as their queen but for spiritual advisement too. Should Chaon ever become like my father and try to break me... Well, I knew how to deal with that.

I put the thoughts from my mind and called to the goddess, asking for guidance for her servant. When the room grew chill and it became difficult to breathe, I opened my eyes and my heart lurched. Before me wasn't one of the lesser goddesses who had chosen me as a toy, but my own goddess, Hecate, goddess of the underworld and darkness. The goddess I'd dedicated myself to when I was young and looking for escape. Her black eyes were doorways into a world I didn't want to see yet, and I bowed my head.

"Your thoughts betray you, child." Her voice was sibilant, like a snake's. "You are not given to make your own choices. Not yet. For now, you must listen to my sisters and follow as they will. To do anything else would bring only misery, and your role in this story is far from over."

I wanted to weep, to rail at the injustice. "Will I never be free to walk my own path as others do?"

The walls seemed to rattle. "You would cast off the honour of being chosen by the gods so easily? To walk alone without us by your side? Can you not see how powerful it makes you? Beyond that of any silly mortal queen. You *are* power, Medea. You are the goddess's hand on the world. There is nothing greater."

I trembled at the anger in her voice, at the way the sound of her words dredged up dark places full of hollow echoes. "I meant no disrespect, goddess." Of course she wouldn't see how it would be better not to answer to anyone, not even to the gods. Their desire for service meant they couldn't see beyond their own needs. Mine would certainly hold no interest for them.

"The day will come when we will choose someone else and you will understand all we have given you. Until then, you will do as we bid. And my sisters have chosen you to take this journey with the prince of Iolcos."

"But why me?" I asked, knowing it could be foolish.

"You have immortal blood in your veins. You are strong, stronger than most mortal women. You crave power in a way we understand, and you have the ability to use it. You are the weapon we wield in a game you cannot understand."

The words soothed me. I wouldn't have an easy life as a queen here, but I would have a powerful life elsewhere. To know the gods saw me as a weapon worthy of using was intoxicating like the finest wine. I bowed my head until it touched the cold stone. "Thank you, goddess. I will obey with an open heart." It wasn't true, not really, and I knew she would see into my heart and know it. But she would also know that I would obey because of the promise of power she held before me. When I felt her hand on my head, my stomach churned and I nearly mewled like a scared kitten.

"Your head and your heart will battle until the end of time. But you are strong enough to withstand the darkness you must walk through time and time again. For you are my priestess, dedicated to the underworld and to darkness. And that is where your true power resides."

The pressure of her hand left me, and I could breathe again. The room began to warm, and I dared look up. In front of me lay an exquisite dagger made of obsidian and marble, the black blade edges sharp enough to slip easily through skin, the elegant marble handle heavy and beautifully carved. Beside it was a vial and when I held it to the light, the swirling blackness inside nearly made me drop it. I stood, unsteady, with the vial in one hand and the dagger in the other and stumbled from the room into the light created by the oculus above.

The high priestess looked at what I held in my hands and shuddered. She backed away and bowed her head deferentially. "If you would like to prepare yourself and bathe—"

"No. I would like to go back to the palace and lay down."

She glanced at me, searching, and then nodded. "As you wish. I can have an acolyte come with a clean gown for the festival, if it would please you?"

Desperate to lay down, I nodded and turned away. "Thank you." I made my way unsteadily down the path, stopping occasionally to rest against a tree. The weight of the vial and the dagger seemed to drag me down, as though they wanted to go back to the underworld to be with their giver. By the time I made it to the palace, I was sweating and shaking, and I'd never been so glad to see Kip, who sat in the shade waiting for me. She rushed over and wrapped her arm around my waist, and I gladly let her take some of my weight.

"I knew I should have gone with you," she muttered softly.

"We can't know when they'll shake me and when they won't." She was my only friend, my only tie to this world, and without her I'd be lost.

She didn't say anything, just led me into the cool palace to our rooms, where our trunk was already open. After laying me on the bed, she went to fetch servants, who drew me a cool bath in a large copper tub. Once I was in, Kip knelt behind the tub and gently massaged my scalp, and it wasn't long before my body relaxed and I closed my eyes, safe and comfortable.

I didn't remember getting into bed except for how nice the cool sheet felt against my skin. When I woke, Kip sat weaving in the corner and the sun rays were low through the window. I stretched and sat up. "Thank you."

She looked a little surprised. "There's never a need. I'll always be here, you know that." She motioned towards a bundle of material with her needle. "The temple priestess delivered that." She motioned towards another, more vibrant coloured pile. "And Chaon had that brought to you." She tilted her head toward the dagger and vial on the table beside the bed. "More gifts?"

I nodded, not wanting to look at them.

"It explains the odd belt the priestess handed me. It's beautifully worked." She held up a thick band of white leather decorated with lapis and obsidian. "Jason knocked earlier to see if you were okay, and Chaon sent a servant to ask you to dine with him for lunch. I told both you were resting after your visit to the temple, and they said to wish you well."

She waited, as usual not prying but knowing there were things to be said. "Chaon has asked me to stay and be his queen."

Her eyebrows rose. "And your answer?"

"Not the one he'll want. But the one the goddess insists on." I didn't miss the fleeting relief that passed through her eyes. If we stayed, Neleus would still have to go, as his loyalty was to Jason, no matter where his heart lay. I understood, though a flare of jealousy still surged through me.

"I'm sorry," she said. "I do think you would be well matched."

I got out of bed and looked out the window, over darkened olive groves and white houses. "I think so too. But while the gods have hold of me, perhaps no man should be in their path."

"Except Jason."

I shrugged. "He has been chosen too, and so his fate is twinned with mine. But that is the gods' doing and not my responsibility."

She looked thoughtful but didn't say anything further, for which I was grateful. Together we laid out the garments from the priestess and Chaon and put them together so the white of the temple was offset by the beautiful blues and reds of the long peplos given by Chaon. And over them both, I wore the belt from the temple low over my hips, with the dagger slipped into the band that held it securely. The vial I tucked away with my other potions and herbals. I dreaded the day I would be called on to use it, though I had no doubt it would come.

Kip used the remaining material in blues and reds to dress for the festival, and she looked beautiful. I kissed her softly, this woman who stayed beside me and never asked anything of me.

She cupped my face and rested her forehead against mine. "In this world and the next, Medea."

The simple statement nearly made me weep, and I hugged her tightly before we left the room. As soon as we were in the long hallway, we could hear the commotion from below. Music and laughter filled the air, and my spirits lifted. The burden was heavy, but it wouldn't do to forget the excitement life had to offer as I took this quest on behalf of the gods.

Dinner was a lavish affair with roasted swan, and fruits, and vegetables I'd never seen before. Chaon was an enchanting host, conversing with people by name and making them feel special. He was funny and charming, and it was easy to see that his people loved him well. He was the light to my dark, and there was no denying the pull I felt towards him. He would occasionally take my hand or touch my arm, often including me as he told stories of the people around him, who in turn enjoyed telling tales of their king's bravery and good will. He referred to my beauty and power more than once, making me blush.

And throughout it all, there was Jason, glowering from his special place at the table. I'd never seen him in a foul temper, and I admit it wasn't unpleasant to know that he might be jealous of the handsome young king's affection towards me. Or perhaps he was simply concerned that his promised guide might leave him. Whatever it was, it put him in a strange mood, and it wasn't long after the meal he excused himself, saying that Neleus was far better with the tales of our adventure than he.

It irritated me that I felt bad for a moment when he met my gaze before he left, and I saw the jealousy and sadness in his eyes. After he'd bedded Queen Agave, surely he had no say in where I spent my time or with whom. And yet, I couldn't help but feel sorry for him as he left, alone.

But my attention was soon pulled away by Neleus telling grand tales of our journey, including my place in them. King Chaon looked at me with such admiration it made my blood stir. The tales and drinking went on until the morning stars were fading, and Chaon took my hand as we walked outside for some air. Kip and Neleus had long since left together, and this walk through the quiet corridor felt heavy with possibility.

"Princess, I must ask...did the goddess answer you?" He stood close, his hand in mine, his eyes searching.

I did him the courtesy of not looking away. "She did, sweet king. But I'm afraid her response wasn't one either of us wanted."

He looked so crestfallen I couldn't help but cup his face in my hands. "I am the goddess's chosen. I must go where the gods' send me, whether I would or not." Gently, boldly, I kissed him. "Have no doubt, if I could stay with you, I would. I would defy the gods to be at your side, but we both know the penalty would be high, and to lose you because I refused to do as they said would destroy me." They were pretty words, but this time, I meant them.

He sighed deeply and lowered his head to kiss me. "What sorrow, to love so quickly one who has a different path." His hand slid down my arm and tugged on the robe. "The combination of my colours and those of the temple suit you. A woman of both worlds, but not wholly of either."

"And because I am of neither, the rules women must abide by don't apply to me." I took his hand and waited to see if he understood, even though I couldn't voice the desire that grew within me.

He searched my expression, then turned and led me across the courtyard to his quarters. I strode at his side, an equal ready to claim ownership of my body by sharing it with a man of my choice. Desire flowed through me, as well as a sense of disapproval that wasn't mine at all. I ignored the gods and entered his bed chamber.

CHAPTER TWENTY-SIX
Letting Go

I WON'T SAY ANYTHING more of that beautiful night. It has remained with me all these years, a perfect spark of light among the black chaos that came later. It was a moment I returned to in my dreams when I needed to feel cherished. It was a gift from the goddess of love, one I have never taken for granted.

In the morning, breakfast was served in his room, and we spoke only of dreams. He wanted the best for his people and talked of the things he wanted to build. I talked of travel, of being free to roam as I wished. I wanted to see the great pyramids being built in the vast deserts and see how the Amazons trained on their fabled isle. He didn't say anything but I could see the pity in his eyes, because we both knew that only his dream could come true. I held on to the miniscule hope that once the gods were done with me, perhaps I would board a ship and never look back.

After our meal, we dressed leisurely and I took pleasure in his slow, soft touches that left my skin tingling like I'd emerged from a clear lake in the summer sun. He held my hand as we crossed back to my room, and he kissed me softly in front of my door.

"I will never forget last night or the gift you have given me. I leave you now to go to the temple to give thanks."

His smile was sweet and sad, and I kissed his cheek even as my heart broke. It wasn't for what we had, which had been brief, but for what might have been. I bade him wait and ran inside. I took a rare purple gem from my box and came out with it. I pinned it to his robe. "Wear this and remember the woman who gave herself to you and to no one else."

He covered it with his hand and his eyes grew wet. He bowed

his head and left.

Kip was waiting for me inside, her smile wide. "You truly walk your own path."

I laughed, filled with lightness of spirit for the first time in a long while. "And why shouldn't I? The goddess herself told me mortal rules didn't apply to me, and that I'd have to choose and choose again. So last night I chose with my heart."

"I'm not sure it was your heart you were thinking with." She motioned to the steaming bath. "You should wash before we see Jason. He's asked to speak with you before we sail."

The thought dampened my joy, but I shook it off and bathed, laughing and sharing some details with Kip about my night, as young women are wont to do. It was wonderful to feel so free, so mortal.

Dressed in my outfit from the night before, my hair in long braids and my dagger at my waist, I went to the main hall and asked a servant about Jason. He directed me to the garden, and I made my way into the grove of orange trees to find him sitting on the ground, his face turned to the sun. As it often did when I caught him unawares like this, my heart stuttered at his simple beauty. Whether it did so because of the gods or because I truly felt that way, I wasn't sure, and that set it apart from the way I felt towards Chaon. The king had been my choice but with Jason, I would never be certain. "Good morning," I said.

He looked up at me, and there was no denying the pain in his eyes, though he tried to hide it. "Good morning." He stood, pushing himself off the tree, and I saw the dark circles under his eyes.

He started walking and I fell into step beside him. "You wanted to see me?" I asked after we'd strolled in silence for a while.

He sighed and started to speak, then shook his head and said nothing. Then he started again, gesturing vaguely. "You are not mine to keep."

I'd come to understand his short way of speaking that said much. "No. I am not. And yet?"

"And yet." He gave me a quick smile. "I find the attention King Chaon gives you unbearable. I want to tear him to pieces with my bare hands."

It was wrong to like that he was jealous. I knew that, but I couldn't help it. We'd always spoken frankly to one another, and I didn't want that to change. "As I felt when you were with Queen Agave. But we have no claim on one another except that which the gods demand."

He looked surprised, and we walked on in silence again, through the citrus groves ripe with fruit ready to fall.

"In Iolcos, as in much of Achaea, men and women live apart. We come together to celebrate, for rituals and festivals. But much of our time is spent separately."

I waited, sure there was more to his way of thinking and not wanting to rush him.

"Because of this journey, I have learned that the way they do it in Sparta might be better. The women there are much more equal to men. They race and have a say in politics. They speak openly and honestly, like you do."

I liked the idea of Sparta and wished we were headed there instead of Iolcos.

"I've learned, Medea, that you are wise, and strong, and worthy of the respect I'd give any man. Alkippe, too, is wise and sweet, and when asked, she has much to say that is worth listening to." He stopped and plucked an orange, handing it to me. "Will you be staying?"

I began to peel the fruit, the juice running down my fingers, the scent perfuming the air around us. "You know the answer."

He began to peel his own orange and didn't look at me. "But you would if the gods allowed it?"

I considered my reply and decided honesty was best. "He asked me to be his queen. As you've said, a woman must choose her course wisely, because she can't go off and claim glory in war. Yes, I considered staying because King Chaon is kind and light, and my position would be settled, but when I asked the goddess, she told me that my place is by your side, as it has been since you came to my home."

He ate his orange, looking off down the path. "I am glad. I raged through the night, angry that it wasn't me at your side, even though we've never... I don't know how I would continue without you." He turned to me then, his emotion clear in his eyes. "I want you to be happy. But I also want you with me."

There wasn't a kind answer to that, so I simply said, "Perhaps it is possible to be both."

We made our way in silence back to the palace and stopped at the wall overlooking the harbour.

"I'd like to leave by morning. It will be a hard row to Scheria, and I'm still not sure it's a wise idea. But if the goddess sends us there, it's there we will go."

There seemed little else to say that wouldn't cause pain, and so we went our separate ways. He left to see to the Argo's provisions, and I went to Kip, and we left for the marketplace. Unaccompanied, we received more than our share of stares, but I ignored them. I wasn't theirs to order about and wouldn't pretend otherwise. And in my refusal to bow I realized they weren't sure how to respond. If a woman of a lower status refused to live by their rules, she could be beaten and forced into position. But I wasn't lower status, nor was I a normal woman. As Chaon had said, I was a woman of two worlds, and that meant I would do as I pleased. Anyone who wanted to force me to do otherwise would face the wrath of the gods, and surely a woman out of place wasn't worth that.

Kip and I found some beautiful items in the marketplace and traded them well for a few pieces of my jewellery. The market was full of exotic things brought by traders from all over the world, and there were stones and metals I'd never seen, as well as people of every skin tone I could imagine, from night black to fair and light. There were plenty of women, though all were accompanied, and one woman in particularly fine robes asked us to her villa for afternoon wine. She said she'd heard our story and wished to know more about the women travelling with fifty men. It sounded dubious put that way, but Kip laughed and so I did as well.

The afternoon was well spent as she told us tales of the traders who came to the city, and she gladly told us all she could of the Achaeans we were to live among. As we spoke, she scratched things into a tablet, little symbols, and I asked what she was doing. She held the tablet up and explained she was recording our tale, that if you understood the symbols, you would understand what they meant, and they would tell the story. It was astounding, and I begged for a way to learn them. She replied that it would take a long time to learn, and we had only hours, but she gave me the name of a man to speak to in Iolcos, a trader she'd met who had passed through the city last year. They'd grown close, and she felt certain he would teach me.

By the time we went back to the palace, I was excited to begin the next fragment of our trip. She'd described Iolcos as a bustling city with much to offer, full of enormous oak trees overlooking a translucent green sea. I was ready to see it, but Jason said we weren't nearly there yet.

After the evening meal, Chaon asked if I would join him again, but I decided against it and gently told him the gods had gifted us a night and that asking for more might anger them. In truth, I kept seeing the sadness in Jason's eyes and the emotion he couldn't name as he described wanting to tear Chaon apart. We had far to go, he and I, and it seemed reckless to put our tenuous relationship under any further strain. Chaon looked deeply hurt but let me go with a light kiss.

"The gods only know why our hearts don't always understand the way ahead. Jason of Iolcos is a man luckier than any I have known. Fair sailing, princess. You go with my heart."

With a deep bow, he turned and was gone. I wanted to fall to bed and weep, to tear at the pillow and scream at the skies. But I didn't. I sat on the bed with my head on Kip's shoulder, thinking of all I'd seen and done, and how much more lay before me. Emotions were dangerous. They would get in my way and make it hard to be rational. I needed to get a handle on them, so they never ruled me. I'd have to work at it, but I would try. The gods had shown me what it was to feel the emotions of those around me. They were convoluted, chaotic. I would not be that way.

Kip and I made our way to the Argo early in the morning before Apollo had taken his chariot into the sky. The crew were getting settled and Jason gave us a hand into the ship. He squeezed mine and whispered, "Welcome back."

We set sail and though some people waved us off, it was sparse that early in the day. But as we sailed past the palace wall, a lone man stood watching, and when I lifted my hand, he waved.

And so we sailed on, with the men rowing hard towards Scheria. It was out of the way, but they'd had problems with the Corinthians of late and Jason didn't want to get mixed up in their issues, as we'd be stopping at Corinth along our way. But the goddess had been clear, and so the men rowed, bringing us to land as the sun set.

CHAPTER TWENTY-SEVEN
Trapped

WE WERE MET BY the people of the land, and they brought us before the king. A bulky man with poor eyesight, King Alcinous welcomed us as guests. His queen gave a slight smile, and I could see the intelligence in her eyes as she took us in. While Jason's men resupplied the ship and made certain it was ready to put back to sea, Jason, myself, and a sickly man named Typhus attended the king's feast, full of laughter and gentle teasing from a happy people. I couldn't help but think how different it was from my father's table, which was often shrouded in silence and the tension of political disarray. This was very like Chaon's table, though there was more talk of war, and I understood Jason's worry when the mood turned dark at the mention of the Corinthians and their many ships.

After the meal, the king invited us to his private chambers, and I shivered with forewarning. Guards fell in behind us, far enough away that we weren't being escorted but close enough to make it clear we weren't allowed to turn and leave. The queen walked beside him, a pretty woman with a solemn bearing, and it was easy to see the comfortable relation between them. In his chambers, which were simple and centred around an altar, we sat facing him.

"You are welcome in my palace, and you have shown courtesy. But be aware, visitors, that I know who you are. Word has already spread about the witch and her foreign prince. I know you are not married. I know you, woman, have murdered your own flesh and blood and betrayed your father. I will not incur the wrath of the gods by breaking the laws of hospitality, but your presence places me in a difficult position. The king of Aia has promised wealth to the one who returns his daughter."

It wasn't unexpected, given that Chaon had heard of us as well, though here they'd clearly heard the darker, less heroic version. "We mean you no harm, good king, and we too would never betray the laws of hospitality. The things done were terrible, and we'll have blood guilt to settle with the gods. But if you'll allow us refuge, we'll rest and be gone by morning, leaving behind enough treasure to make what the king of Aia would give you pale in comparison."

He raised his wiry white eyebrow and tilted his head to listen to his wife whisper in his ear. Perhaps if I'd let Jason answer it would have been better, but I was done allowing men to speak for me.

Alcinous nodded slowly. "My queen gives good council. You will marry and then I can tell your father that as a married woman, I was not required to send you back to him. If you remain unmarried, I am forced to do so. I am already close to war with Corinth, I will not invite the wrath of Aia as well. You must choose. Marriage or be sent home with your family."

I looked at Jason and saw that he looked as stunned as I felt. We'd been through much already and had grown to care for one another in ways neither of us understood. We were tied by the gods, yes, but we'd come to regard each other as well. But marriage? The trap laid by the goddess was clear, and how I wished we'd sailed past this island and ignored her. But we were here, and her trap was sprung. I'd denied Chaon only to be forced into marriage to the man they'd decided I would be with instead. Perhaps they didn't trust that I would stay at his side unless forced.

Perhaps they were right.

Jason took my hand and said softly, "I would do this, for you. You have given me back my kingdom and saved us from your father's men. You've known the way down every river and have shown us wonders we never would have seen without you. I believe we have more challenges to face and having you at my side surely means victory over those challenges. I will be a true husband, a good one, if you'll have me."

I saw the unearthly light in his eyes. Those weren't his words, and we'd already spoken of what marriage meant to both of us. He knew he'd never truly have my heart. And I felt something not myself trying to force me to respond in kind. When the pain of fighting it became too great, when it felt like my soul would rip from my skin, I nodded assent, unable to speak through the lump of frustrated fear in my throat.

The king clapped his hands together, looking pleased. "Very well. Your father's men search for you even now, so you must do it quickly. Go with my priest to the temple, and he will bind you in the name of the goddess."

We bowed to the king and queen and followed the priest from the palace centre to the house temple, set deep in a cave. He bound our wrists together with a loose rope and said all the necessary things to dictate that we were now married in the eyes of the gods, which only death would end. He cut the throat of a small, pure white goat and splashed its blood across the top of the altar. Together, we added wine and sipped it from the heavy chalice while invoking the blessings of the gods. Red light glowed from the spill, slowly becoming lighter and thinner until we were encased by the god's own blessing. Our hands burned where our skin touched. The priest, his eyes wide with awe, stumbled back and motioned towards a back room, where Jason quickly led me.

We fell onto the mound of furs and quickly shed our clothes, caught in a madness of goddess-inspired lust. I felt the air on my thighs, on my damp sex, on my stomach and breasts. It swept over me, followed quickly by his calloused hands, moving quickly and pressingly over my most tender parts. When he sheathed himself inside me, I cried his name, the fire of desire flaming through me. Over his sweat-glistening shoulder, as we reached our climax together, I opened my eyes and saw, standing in the entrance of the cave, the shadowed figure of a woman, too tall, too wide, too dark. I could see the flames of the campfire outside through the figure's lower abdomen, where the fire was lit within myself.

Jason collapsed on me, breathing heavily, and the shadow

faded into the night.

***

I woke aching and tired, like I'd been running all night. Damp cave walls and the sound of water lapping at the shore reminded me of the night before, and I allowed the tears to fall. Jason stirred beside me and rolled over to look at me, seeming puzzled. Realization dawned quickly, and he looked almost embarrassed.

"You deserved better. It was too quick, too rushed. But..." He shrugged and sighed. "The gods are cruel."

I wiped away my tears and turned towards him, resting my head on my arm. "Why is Iolcos so important? What makes it so interesting to the gods that they get involved in our affairs?" I nearly choked on my words. "Why force us together this way?"

He gently wiped away my tears with his thumb. "I think if either of us could answer that, it would be you, chosen of the gods. I'm afraid I don't have an answer." He twirled a piece of my hair between his fingers. "I hope you won't hate me if I admit that I'm not sorry." At my look of surprise, he smiled slightly. "I told you I hated Chaon for trying to take you from me. I sailed to Aia on my own, and I could make it to Iolcos on my own from here. But the thought of not having you at my side makes me sick, and not because of the gods. You are..." He paused in that way of his, as he searched for the words. "You are extraordinary, Medea. Your power makes me afraid, sometimes. Your words can be harsh, but I always know where I stand with you. There are no games, no wiles to contend with. You are beautiful in your own way." He looked me in the eye then. "I do love you, I think. Not as the bards tell it, not in the frothy foam of Venus's lap, but in a more earthy way, like the fire needs the air to keep burning."

There was no trace of the gods in his eyes, and I knew he spoke from the heart. They were honest words, not pretty or soulful, but true. I could live with that. "And as your wife, Jason, would you try to change me? Would you have me be submissive and lower my eyes when you come in? Would you have me speak only when spoken to? Would you tell me to stay home, behind large walls, while everything happens without me?" I couldn't help the fear and challenge that crept into my tone. My greatest fear was a cage, and it could be I'd unwittingly been placed in one. "Would you betray me with other women when you grow tired of me?"

He got to his knees, the thin blanket falling to his waist. He pulled me up to face him and took my hands in his. "You are unlike any woman I've ever known. I promise you, here and forever, that I will never take your freedom. I will honour you and although your way of being may be challenged in Achaea, I will stand beside you. You will be the woman you want to be, and I will be your protector through it all. I swear it, by the gods."

The room spun and I saw chaos, burning and screaming and ash, and just as quickly, the world righted again. He would be false, eventually. But for now, it was good enough and I would hold him to it. I kissed my new husband, and then got up and dressed. We entered the palace and were greeted with cheers by his crew and by the people who lived at the palace. Kip was smiling, but I saw the sympathy in her eyes when she looked at me. I wanted to go to her, but I was busy accepting well-meant congratulations. I think the crew, even after all this time, felt a little better that I was now a married woman and not an unknown entity in their midst. A woman unmarried and free was a threat, though I've never understood why.

We spent two days feasting and giving thanks, though my desire to do so was half-hearted at best. Jason, though, seemed truly happy. My father's men, informed that I was married, left that day to go back to Egrisi. They wouldn't want me back, but they'd been duty bound to follow my father's orders. Now that I'd been given to someone else like a new cauldron or sheep, they no longer had any claim on me. I was glad, however, that I didn't have to see them. Facing them, men from my own country, was more than my guilt could bear.

I don't know what I thought married life would be like. In truth, I'd hardly thought of it at all. But as Jason and I boarded the ship once again, I thought I should feel different. More humble, perhaps. More willing to accept his lead. But our quick night of passion meant little in the morning light and if anything, I resented the necessity that forced me into another cage. I remained polite to the king and queen and was gracious about the amount of provisions they'd loaded onto our ship, and there was no mention of sending me back to my father. No, now that I was married, I belonged to a different man.

I sat beside Alkippe at the front of the ship and brooded quietly.

"Was it so bad?" she asked softly.

I turned to her, surprised. "You heard?"

"Typhus came back from your meeting in the king's quarters and told everyone. The men feel it was well done, as it will rein in your powers." She shook her head slightly.

"It's done, and the men will see that nothing takes my power from me." The very thought of it made me seethe with indignation. I was not a possession, a thing to be carted from one person to the next. Somehow, I would escape again. In time.

Chapter Twenty-Eight
Family

We pushed away from the dock with no further word from the king. Jason made his way over to me and squatted low to see my face. "You're well, my lady?"

I looked into his eyes and sighed softly. He still looked kind and innocent, and to take out my frustration on him for something he too had no control over would be wrong. "Yes, thank you."

"I would row along the shoreline, but I wondered if you could consult the gods to be sure that's our way?"

I closed my eyes, searching for an answer, and felt it in my depths. "We have to stop somewhere first. The water will take us there."

The tide swept us along, making it so the men didn't have to row, and it wasn't until dusk that the wind died down and the men took up the oars again. Compelled, I stood and looked ahead. A flash of light, like a sunbeam pointing the way, fell on an island ahead of us. I turned to Jason and found him watching me with that same besotted look he'd had earlier when he wasn't in control. Perhaps he was doubting as well, and the gods were convincing him this had been a good idea.

"We should land at that island," I motioned towards it, "for the night."

He gave the command without question, and the men did as he said, though they'd heard me give the direction. The closer we got to the island, the more I felt someone there calling. I searched the shore but saw no one. When we dropped anchor and disembarked onto the soft white sand, I closed my eyes and shut out the din of men moving around me. When I opened them again, Jason was beside me, waiting, docile as a lapdog. "You and I need to enter the forest." I looked at Alkippe, who stood close and looked around, her frown deep.

"We'll be back shortly. This is something we have to do alone."

She squeezed my hand but didn't say anything further. I headed for the path I knew would be in the forest and felt Jason follow me. Immersed in the forest once more, the weight fell away from my shoulders, and I could breathe again. Magic, old and deep, ran through these woods, calling to my own, calling to my heart.

The soft dirt path ended at a clearing where there stood a medium-sized stone house, smoke rising from the chimney. A large lion lay sleeping before the stairs but barely twitched as we passed. I raised my hand to knock, and Jason stopped me.

"We don't know who lives here. It could be a trap. We should have brought some men with us."

I tried not to look as scornful as I felt. "I am a priestess of Hecate, a witch in my own right and one of the goddess's chosen. Do you think I couldn't take care of myself? Have you not been paying attention?" The sting of the men assuming my power would now be under control came out in impatience.

He flinched and dropped his hand from my arm. I knocked and the door swung open.

"Come in, my niece."

The voice was magical, musical, and there was no threat here. When I saw who it was, I began to laugh. "Aunt Circe!"

My father's half-sister had visited us several times in Kolchis. Those were cherished memories; she'd always spoken with me as an equal though I was anything but. She'd taught me much about potions and taken me on long walks to show me what plants to use and in what measures. She'd shown me what it was to be a woman with power, and I'd never failed to appreciate the way my father shrank from her. It pleased me, too, how alike we looked. She was taller by far, as goddesses are wont to be, but she was dark and solidly built like me, and in her company, I knew myself as special and cared for rather than awkward and despised. Her own story, of which I only had pieces, had painted her as an outcast among the immortal nymphs in the court of her father, Helios. Maybe that's why she took so much care with me whenever she came to visit.

She kissed my cheek and led me inside. "I felt you on the waters and the wind whispered your plight." She looked over her shoulder at Jason. "Your road is long."

He tilted his head and gave her a boyish smile. "It is a blessing to meet you, goddess. I wasn't aware my wife had such kin, though she has shown herself to be a favourite of the gods time and time again."

She took a jug from a shelf and poured drinks. "No, young sailor, there's much you don't know, and so very much you'll yet learn."

Her words were innocuous, but the truth of them slid over my skin my like an oil. In her brief glance at me, I saw there were depths to what she meant that would take a lifetime to fathom. She handed us our glasses and led us out the backdoor into a lush garden where wolves and pigs roamed under fruit trees.

Jason stopped and pressed himself to a tree as a wolf approached him. "My lady..."

Circe laughed, and her laugh always made me smile.

"She's only curious. We don't get many visitors. If you weren't welcome here, be certain you'd never have made it onto the shore, let alone to my home." She turned to me and linked her arm in mine.

It was only now as I watched the wonder in Jason's eyes that I understood fully. She was a goddess, one of the immortals, ageless and beautiful. When the goddess inhabited me, he saw a goddess, not a mortal woman. It gave me a power all its own. I saw Circe's lips twitch in a smile and wondered if she could hear my thoughts. As if in answer, she gave my arm a squeeze before letting me go to sit on a bench under a fragrant lemon tree.

"My niece, I know your path leads elsewhere, but I couldn't

allow you to go without speaking to you of things to come." She stroked the head of the wolf who was still watching Jason. "And I would cleanse you of your blood guilt, if you'd allow it."

Jason slid from the bench to his knees and bowed his head. I watched impassively, bemused by his reverence and readiness to kneel.

"Kind goddess, we would very much appreciate your intervention. We did what was necessary, but I admit that it haunts me."

I suppose it made sense. I might have killed my brother, but it had been Jason who had dismembered him, no more or less damnable in the gods' eyes. My time with the other gods on this journey had allowed me to grieve what I'd done. Jason had no such luxury.

Circe smiled gently at Jason. "Yes, I'm sure it does."

The wolf left her side and nudged his thigh, and he put a trembling hand to its head. She watched the whole thing, clearly interested in what was going on. She gave a slight shrug and turned to me.

"I'd like you to stay with me tonight. Jason can return to his men and explain that you'll be here for a day or two, and I'll see they get food and wine. He can return in the morning for the ceremony."

Jason practically jumped to his feet, his relief obvious. "As you wish, goddess." He gave me a brief bow and turned to leave.

"Can you please send Kip to me?" I knew she'd want to sleep beside Neleus, but she'd met my aunt too and deserved to be part of the magic she brought to us. He nodded and then was gone, leaving me with Circe.

She shook her head and gave a deep sigh. "Ah, child. Had I been able to keep you from the journey you're about to take, I would have done so."

"You knew of the oracle?"

"I knew from the moment you were born. The gods sent an old woman to carry the oracle to your father, and she got there before

I did. I would have stopped her if I could, and perhaps things would have turned out differently. My brother always had our father's temper, but it burned brighter for the knowledge of what was to come."

She stood, her diaphanous gown floating around her. Unlike the goddesses plaguing my life lately, Aunt Circe had a more mortal bearing. If you looked closely, you could see her eyes were brighter, her skin softer, and she was more beautiful than a mortal woman could be. But as a nymph, cast out by her family and living on her own, I felt like she was more like me.

"Indeed, child, we have much in common." She plucked a lemon and pulled the skin away slowly, releasing the scent into the air. She let the juice run over her fingers and held it to the wolf, who lapped it off. "And if you were less mortal, perhaps what lies ahead would be easier to bear."

I shivered again. "You make it sound like I'm heading towards a cliff."

She stood and held out her hand. "Come. I want to give you some things that grow only here to take with you when you go."

It wasn't an answer and the lack of one made me cold. I was already trapped in a marriage I didn't want to a man I had complicated feelings for. Through my visions, I knew there was destruction and death but to hear her say so made my heart sink. I watched and listened as she plucked various flowers and herbs and placed them in a basket. She explained what they were for, how much to use, and what to expect. I took it in like a woman reaching for a raft as she's plunged downriver. Knowledge was power, and I would have all I could.

When we returned, Kip was waiting on the stone bench, and when she saw my aunt, she fell to her knees and pressed her head to the ground.

Circe went to her and lightly rested her hand on Kip's head. "Best of us, your road is entwined with my niece's, and for all your days, you'll act as light when she can't find her way through the dark."

What dark? Why would I be so lost? I wanted to ask but wasn't sure I wanted to know the answer. Circe continued inside and Kip looked up at me, her eyes wide. I shrugged and shook my head slightly, then helped her to her feet and we went inside.

A fire burned brightly, and the scent of fresh bread made my mouth water. Circe motioned at the table, and I sat. Kip stood behind me, clearly unsure of her role in front of my aunt.

Circe tapped the table. "Sit, Alkippe. In this house we share our meal as equals."

Food appeared and Circe sat with us as we ate, though she didn't eat herself. When we were done, I decided to take a chance. "Can you tell me about the future, Aunt? Can you prepare me for what's to come?"

Her smile was sad as she looked at me with her multi-hued blue eyes, like the sky at dusk after a storm has passed. "I'm sorry, Medea. It's not my place, and my telling you wouldn't change anything. This is your metanoia, your way to find yourself." She picked up the basket and began putting the flowers and herbs into small jars. "But never forget who you are. Your blood is divine, and you will always have a place here with me, should the fates change their minds and send you back."

I hated the sound of that. Once again, it was as if I had no say in my life. "Are we so controlled by the fates? Is there no way to be free?" The goddesses had already told me as much, but it wouldn't hurt to ask.

She looked surprised by the question. "Darling girl, no one is free. We all answer to someone, and even the gods answer to the time of day as they bring the sun across the sky or move the tides towards shore." She took my hand in hers and electricity surged through me. "It's how you walk the path that matters when it comes to who you answer to. The outcome may be set, but how you arrive at it... Well, that can be your taste of freedom."

I mulled that over as she continued to pull apart flowers and place jars in a row. "But surely no matter what I do, it's what I'm supposed to do if I have to arrive at a particular place?"

She crushed a blossom in her hand and held it under Kip's nose. She sniffed and murmured appreciatively, earning her a smile.

"Think of it this way. At some point, you're going to arrive on a distant shore where you'll make certain decisions. Now, you can take in the world on your way to that shore, seeing all you can and making it a part of you. Or you can sit on the ship with your eyes closed until you get there." She sighed again and looked out her backdoor towards the wolf laying in the doorway. "You'll get to the shore either way, but one of those will make your life better. It's your choice. Do you simply endure, or do you drink every bit of life from the moments you're given?"

Put that way, there was no question. And truthfully, it did make me feel better. "And Jason?"

She huffed slightly. "Sometimes those we travel with are part of what we need to learn about ourselves. If you choose to make him an ally rather than an enemy, or even someone you simply put up with, life will be easier." She caressed the back of my hand with a flower petal so red it was nearly black. "And less lonely." She brought a large amphora to the table. Gold vines flowed around it, so lifelike they appeared to sway in an unseen breeze. "Alkippe, you should sleep. Take the blankets by the fire and rest."

Kip simply gave a quick nod and moved away. She hadn't said a word, but I knew she wouldn't have missed anything. She curled in front of the fire, and I turned my attention back to Circe.

She opened the amphora and tilted it towards me. "Listen carefully. I know your memory is excellent. I'm going to show you some spells you're going to need one day."

I didn't ask for what or why. She wouldn't tell me, and in truth, I wasn't sure I wanted to know. If things were truly awful in the future, I'd beg her to stay here, to live out my days among her wolves and birds, free and peaceful. But what I'd already experienced told me I wasn't ready for that yet. I loved being in new temples, meeting other people, and being free on the water as it swept us onward.

I concentrated and asked questions. I could feel the power at my fingertips, the way nature would come alive and transform into something useful and deadly.

By the time dawn broke, my eyes ached and my back was sore from being bent over the table for so long. She placed the amphora onto a shelf before sitting with me again. She gave me a hot drink and held my hand as I sipped it.

"Jason will be back soon, and I want you to understand." She frowned and traced the lines on my palm. "I can cleanse you of the blood guilt you took on when you killed your brother."

I was going to defend myself, but she shook her head.

"It was foretold, child. The paradox is that although there was no question you would do it, you aren't relieved of the consequences of doing so." She tucked a piece of my hair behind my ear and studied my face. "You are stronger than I was when I left my family home. Your grandfather's fire and your mother's water will make you burn and flow through life, setting it alight and moving around any obstacle in your path."

I liked the sound of that. Very much. "I feel the water like a lover, knowing how it will move. Poseidon gave me the gift. The old gods, so old we don't remember them, spoke to me of balance and emotion."

She smiled. "Don't lose sight of the light, Medea. You're going to be tested beyond most mortal women's capability, and your fire will burn hotter because of it. But remember your father's fire and how he had no water to temper it. Burn without control and you'll lose those you love."

I knew words of prophecy when I heard them, and although hers didn't tell me of a specific event, there was a warning in them, much as the other gods had warned me before. "Can I call on you? When I start to lose my way?" I'd never considered praying to my aunt before. She was so real, so kind. So unlike those who used me.

She looked out the window. "You can try. But you're going to be a long way from me, and I don't live on Olympus where the gods hear all mortals' prayers. Remember this, though. The goddess you serve is the right one, and she's also the goddess of crossroads. Seek her guidance and know that hubris is always a downfall." She squeezed my hand and then let go and stood just as Jason appeared outside. "Let's begin."

Jason came to my side, and once again, I saw the flitting fear in his eyes. His new wife had spent the night in the company of a goddess, and there weren't any tales to help him handle that. I liked the feel of his fear, of his awe. It made me tingle. When I met Circe's eyes, I could see her understanding, but I also saw the warning in them. I tempered my reaction and flexed my toes against the cool floor to ground myself.

We followed her down a path to a small sacred lake surrounded by unnatural beauty, and of the rites themselves, I will say little. They're revered and only to be performed by a god or goddess who has the right to take away blood guilt. I can safely say I wouldn't want to go through it again, though it was never offered, no matter the amount of blood on my hands.

We returned to the goddess's house after, and Jason was subdued, his fair brow furrowed. What he saw or felt during the rites I can't say, as we all go through our own memory and repentance. I felt lighter, and the memory of the good times we'd had and my brother at his sweetest replaced the bitter tang of his death and the feel of his blood soaking my hands.

Alkippe was waiting in front of the fire and looked up when we entered. Her eyes searched mine, and she gave me a small smile at whatever it was she saw. Circe handed her a basket and then turned to Jason and me.

"Take care of these potions, child. They'll see you through to the end. And remember my advice."

She looked at Jason, and I felt him take the smallest step back.

"You are what the gods have made you. That will have to be

enough."

It was hardly the inspiring speech he was probably hoping for, and I could feel his disappointment. Still, he bowed his head graciously.

"Thank you, goddess Circe. My wife is indeed lucky to have a relation such as you, and I count my blessings that you saw fit to lift our blood guilt."

She placed her hand on his head. "You have much to learn and so very much to see. Take courage that you are the first of a generation, the hero who will begin an age of heroes."

Clearly, that made him feel better.

He stood taller, his shoulders back, his eyes wide. "I will do all I can to earn that title."

She glanced at me, but I couldn't fathom the thought that went through her head.

"Yes, I'm sure you will."

The words were empty, like the ones the temple priestesses said every morning when reminding people to pray and give thanks. I had so much to consider from this unexpected visit, so much to ponder.

She folded me into a hug that brought tears to my eyes. She was the last of my family and from this point forwards, I would be utterly alone. Except for Kip, but she wasn't blood. I held my aunt tightly.

"Be strong and remember who you are," she whispered into my hair. She released me and stepped back. "Safe journey."

Dismissed, Jason led the way out of the house, followed by Alkippe. I walked out and turned around at the edge of the trees, but her house was shrouded in swirling mist. My aunt Circe had gone.

I followed Jason and Alkippe down the path towards the boat. It was loaded and ready to go, and there was no question the men were ready to leave the island fabled for its lone inhabitant. I turned my face towards the sun as we pulled away from shore. If we were headed into darkness, I would take what light I could.

CHAPTER TWENTY-NINE
Corinth

WE SAILED FOR CORINTH, and Jason's behaviour didn't change towards me at all. He was still kind and attentive and pointed out things of interest as we sailed past Ithaka, where the young King Odysseus was said to be cunning and fast, and his young wife was beautiful and one of the most loyal wives in the world. That her beauty and loyalty were seen as her best traits made me roll my eyes, and Jason laughed when I pointed it out. Soon after Ithaca, the men rowed us into a new, wide river that Jason said was the Gulf of Patras. On one side was Epirus, which we'd been sailing down the coast of for some time. On the other was Achaea, though that was far smaller and divided into many states. The men had been rowing hard and for a long time, slowing sometimes to shout to another crew on a passing ship, and although they were exhausted, their spirits were high. For many of them, this was homecoming as we passed their places of origin. Neleus asked if we should make port, but Jason said no. He was concerned that once the men got ashore, it would be hard to get them on the Argo again, and so he pushed them to continue well into the night.

Looming over us was Mycenae, a palace with enormous walls, higher than any I'd ever seen. Torches flickered along the walls, both at the top and the bottom, highlighting how large they were and making the palace seem otherworldly. At the far edge was a large, dark temple.

Jason was leaning on the rail beside me and saw where I looked. "The temple of Hades and Persephone. The Nekromanteio Acheron."

He didn't offer to stop so I could pray, and I didn't ask. It was a story I disliked, that of a god tricking a woman into marrying him so that she had to give up half her life in the sunlight to rein over the underworld at his side. It wasn't a temple I should set foot in, as I wouldn't have the patience or veneration that would be expected. And given what I'd learned of the women's fashion there, where they bared their breasts to show their fertility, I was eager to move on.

So it was we came to Corinth when Apollo was waking the sun. It was already busy, though, busier than any port we'd yet been to. Houses crowded the shoreline and the palace, like Mycenae, was well lit. The crew, exhausted but happy, quickly made the ship ready and left. Jason and I, followed by Kip and Neleus, made our way to shore.

"King Creon lost his wife in childbirth several years ago," Neleus said. "They were true to one another, and he vowed never to love another. He dotes on his daughter and is said to be a fair king, but he's ruthless when there's something he wants. That's part of why they're fighting with Scheria. He wants more trade with them, but they don't feel they get fair prices."

We came to a strange contraption pulled by horses. Jason got in, followed by Neleus, and they helped us in. I held on tightly as the horses lurched forwards after Jason told the driver our names and where we wanted to go.

"Chariots are common here," Neleus said and grinned. "You'll come to use them often. The cities are large, and the roads dirty."

I was thrilled. I'd heard of them in tales but riding in one was completely different. The wood was simple, and it was necessary to bend the knees so the bumps and ruts didn't cause discomfort, but it was superior to walking. I felt like a hero as we bounced along and people got out of our way. And it soon became apparent how useful the chariot was as we ascended a steep hill towards the castle. We entered through a simple stone gate large enough for two chariots to pass side by side and then took more steep, winding paths past houses that grew larger the higher we went, until we eventually reached the palace. Walking it would have been exhausting, and for any invading army, it would be impossible to attack the palace unseen.

The red and blue columns on either side of the heavy wood doors were delicately painted with white flowers. Large stone walls were covered with woven tapestries and candles lit the area even as the morning sun filtered into the passages. The main door opened, and a large man with a full, curly beard and a bushel of grey hair stepped out, his arms raised in welcome.

"Jason! You return."

Jason leapt from the side of the chariot and took the older man in a hug, kissing both his cheeks. "You said I would, and so I have. With the fleece, as well."

The three of us left the chariot, and it was all I could do not to faint. This place had been in my visions. Burning, screaming, chaos, and death. So much death. Nothing like the happy, busy place it was now. Kip took my arm, and I used her strength to steady myself. I lifted my chin, ready to face whatever destiny had brought me here.

Jason turned to the three of us, still holding onto the older man's arm. "King Creon: my wife, the princess Medea of Egrisi, her servant Alkippe, and my commander, Neleus."

I doubt if anyone else noticed the brief frown that crossed Creon's brow before he greeted me with all due ceremony, praising my beauty and lineage, though he likely noticed nor knew of either. His hand in mine was calloused, showing that he wasn't a soft king, but one who practiced with the sword. It was his eyes, though, that captured me. While his expression was schooled and polite, his eyes were hard and cunning and not so different from my father's. I shuddered and pulled my hand back as soon as possible, and his eyes narrowed slightly when he looked into mine.

"It seems you have much to tell us, boy. Come and rest, and we'll feast your return tonight."

Jason's exuberance was that of a young boy, and I wouldn't

do anything to dampen that, but I wanted to leave this place at the first possible moment. When he turned to me, I smiled and lowered my eyes so he wouldn't divine my repulsion, my desire to be elsewhere. To anyone else, I would simply look like a good wife. No one need know the darkness here was coming.

"As you know, women and men live separately here in the palace. You'll have your own rooms, as will I, but we can come together for meals and overnight." Jason walked backwards, as though eager to be away but not wishing to offend me.

I nodded, grateful for the reprieve from my new husband and keeper. "Enjoy your return."

Neleus was having a quiet word with Kip, and he looked at me with a kind smile before following Jason and Creon inside. Two young servants led Kip and me through long dark corridors of heavy stone that made it hard to breathe. Our rooms, however, were open, light, and large, and the panic dimmed. I requested that the servants draw the shades, as I was exhausted and wished to sleep. They did so, their eyes downcast all the while, and when they were gone, I fell naked into the sheets. Kip lay beside me, her head pillowed on her arm.

"Are you well?"

I sighed. "Terrible things will happen here, Kip. It's a place of death and destruction."

She pondered that in a long moment of silence. "Is it going to happen soon?"

I concentrated on the images I'd seen before, on the chaos and terror. "No. Not for a while yet, I don't think."

She turned on her back and closed her eyes. "Then enjoy the quiet while you can, and let it be what it will be when the time comes."

She stroked my forearm lightly. It was a simple way to look at it and sometimes, her advice worked. But she couldn't know what it was to see something so dire and know it was coming at you like Poseidon's trident aimed at your chest. Kip's touch, though, relaxed me as it always did, and I soon fell asleep.

***

A gentle knock at the door woke us hours later, and Kip got up to open it.

A servant stood, head bowed, waiting. "The king has suggested that the princess might wish to attend the temple before tonight's feast, to ask for good food and laughter and to bless the house."

So, Jason had told Creon I was a priestess as well as a princess. Unless all women were expected to pray at the temple? I didn't wish to put a foot wrong but asking outright wasn't an option. I couldn't look foolish in front of the servants. "Yes, thank you. Where can I bathe?"

"If you would follow me, I will take you to the Pirene."

I looked back at Kip, who simply gathered our clothes. We followed the servant down yet more corridors to an open square. The fountain was the largest I'd ever seen, with beautiful marble columns in a row and numerous caves behind them. Clear water spilled from each one and into a large pool in front of us. The servant led us into the largest of them, which was lit with torches so that the water was as green as spring moss but clear to the bottom. Heat rose in light swirls of mist.

"The gods gifted us this water made of the tears of a woman who grieves always for her lost son."

The servant's voice was soft, her tone respectful, and I appreciated the information. "Are all the caves full of hot water?" I asked as Kip removed my shift.

"No, princess. This and the one beside it, but the other three are cold. The gods provide both hot and cold so we may have luxury and stay in good health."

Kip began to shed her shift as well, and the servant finally looked at us directly, her eyes wide. "I'm sorry, princess, and no disrespect meant, but servants do not bathe in the Pirene."

I admit that I'd forgotten how others would see Alkippe now that we were among those who lived by such rules. "She sees to my needs and is always by my side. She is my companion, not my servant." I allowed no hesitation to enter my tone, even though I was worried I'd offend someone and cause trouble. I wouldn't have Kip treated like a common slave no matter what they thought of me, and it was better to show them who I was now than to have them expect me to behave as they did. Also, I didn't wish to be alone in this strange new place. I needed Kip with me.

The girl swallowed hard, her eyes down once again. "Yes, princess. As you wish."

Kip smiled at me and continued to disrobe. Together we lounged in the deliciously hot baths until a servant brought us a strange, curved piece of metal with a long handle. When I looked at her questioningly, she blushed prettily.

"The strigil is used to clear the skin. After a journey such as yours I thought, perhaps..."

"Show me," I said, intrigued.

She knelt beside the bath and leaned forwards. After cupping a handful of water and letting it flow over my shoulder, she placed the metal edge against my skin and pressed as she slid it from my shoulder to my waist, a motion she repeated in smooth lines across my back. My skin tingled pleasantly, and she shifted to the side to show me the blade, which was full of the dirt and sweat of my travels. She then rinsed it in a large, wide mouthed vase and motioned for me to turn. She repeated the process over my chest and stomach, and Kip grinned when she saw my nipples tighten, though she covered it when the servant glanced at her.

"If you would lay beside the pool, I would do the rest, princess. It would be my honour."

She knelt on the hard, wet stone as I climbed from the water, steam rising from my body. I lay beside her, and she made quick work of the back and front of my legs, and when I moved back into the hot water, I felt refreshed and tingled all over.

"Will you attend to my companion, please?" My tone left no question as to whether she would, and Kip gladly underwent the same treatment, though I felt certain the servant wasn't quite as gentle with her.

When she was done with Kip, she said, "If you'll follow me?"

We left the water and walked naked through a roughhewn doorway to another cave. The water was far cooler but felt exceptional on my newly scrubbed skin. There, she poured scented oil in her hands and cleansed me from neck to foot before I moved to another pool where she used the strigil once again. Strangely both energized and relaxed, I lay on a long couch and waited while she repeated the process with Kip, who looked as I felt when she joined me.

"While we have been here, your clothes have been brought to your room. Shall I bring them here, or would you like to go back to your rooms?"

"Back to our rooms, thank you." We wrapped ourselves in heavy linen robes. She looked slightly surprised but bowed her head and led us back through the maze to our rooms. Perhaps it was unseemly that we walked through the halls half dressed, but I couldn't bring myself to care. Once in our room, I asked that we be left, as my companion could dress me. In truth, I wanted to talk freely and to dress in my own time with Kip's input. Once again, she looked discomfited, but she bowed and left.

I flopped back on the bed. "I want one of those metal things to use every time I bathe from now on."

Kip sat beside me. "Medea, I'm worried."

I sat up on my elbows. "Okay, I won't make you use it all the time."

She shook her head. "You call me companion and ask their servants to treat me as one of their betters. But they won't see me as such, and it will cause resentment."

She was right, of course. But I didn't care. "You are no less worthy of respect than Neleus at Jason's side. You sail with me,

JJ Taylor

you give me council, and you hold my hair when I'm sick after my visions." She went to protest but I stopped her. "If it causes you grief among them, we'll discuss it when we've stopped travelling. But in the meantime, you're the companion of the princess, Jason's wife, and I'll not have it said otherwise."

She took my hand and smiled. "And how do you find it, being Jason's wife? I wanted to ask on the ship, but it seemed too hard a subject for men's ears."

I allowed the tears to come, and she squeezed my hand. "You know how I felt about marriage. How I feel about it. But Jason has sworn to be true and never to chain me, even though their ways are different from ours." I brushed away my tears and sat up. "How do I feel? I hate the thought of it, even though I could do worse. I hate that my choice was taken from me, and not by the king, but by the gods who told us to go to the island. They give me power with one hand and take it from me with the other."

Kip got up and began gathering clothing, laying out options, before she turned to tame my hair. "I cannot understand, Medea, what it is to be a toy of the gods the way you are. But if any woman in the world can handle it, you can."

I turned and hugged her to me, my oldest and only friend. Then we looked at the clothes laid out.

"I like the idea of Chaon's. That you wear both items to show the different parts of you."

"Even to the temple?" I fingered the soft blood-red material he'd given me.

"Maybe especially to the temple. You're no longer a maid, but you're still you, and you still want to be seen as you. That means always showing who you are the moment someone looks at you."

It made sense, and I wanted these people of Jason's to know I was, as the goddess Circe said, no ordinary mortal. And so I wore the deep red beneath the white peplos with slits up the side that showed the red clearly. Around my waist I wore my dagger and white leather belt, and on my brow, the purple diadem. My hair was held back in thick, intricate braids, and I used a small piece of coal to highlight my eyes. The necklace, the deep black stone shot through with white, seemed to glow against my chest. Kip nodded in approval, and I took a deep breath as we entered the hallway to find a servant waiting.

The servant stared at me, her eyes wide, until Kip laughed a little and broke the spell. The servant ducked her head and turned, leading us through corridors that climbed gradually and soon became steeper, until it turned to stairs. At the top was a door with intricate markings and a bowl of water beside it. The servant dipped her fingers in the water and touched her forehead before opening the door, but I chose not to follow her lead, not knowing why she did it and unwilling to do anything in ignorance.

The door opened into the hot, bright sunshine at the very top of the hill. The temple was enormous, built on two floors. In front of two large columns stood a statue, a likeness of the goddess.

"The temple of Aphrodite Encheios, princess."

I studied her for a long while, moving around to see her in different light. In one hand, she held a long spear and in the other, a shield. But it was turned backwards, her head tilted so she could see herself reflected in its surface. The goddess of love in armour was a strange combination, and yet it called to me. Love and war, and seeing oneself through the eyes of another... The thoughts floated and escaped as they came and went, to be plucked and studied later.

Eventually I realized a priestess was waiting and I went forwards. She bowed slightly, looking at my diadem and my belt. To an ordinary person they would be pretty things, interesting because of being unusual. But a temple priestess would understand well their origin and significance, and this one clearly grasped it in an instant. She bowed a little lower.

"Princess, I am Phryne. I was given to understand you were a priestess dedicated, but I'm afraid I didn't understand that you were chosen. Please forgive me."

"There is nothing to forgive. We're far from home and here to give thanks for the long journey."

She looked over my shoulder at Kip. "And is your servant dedicated to the goddess as well?"

I looked at Kip and raised my eyebrows in question. She'd served me at the temple of Hecate, and because of that, she'd been part of the rituals and was allowed to participate. But she wasn't dedicated, and so had no real need to be here. She gave a small shake of her head.

"No, my companion is not dedicated, though she has long been at my side, even in the temple, and understands my...relationship with the gods."

She frowned. "Will she be coming into the temple with you now?"

"No. But if you have a guide, someone who can explain your ways and what is expected of us so we don't offend gods or people, it would be welcome."

"We have scholai in abundance." She smiled, and it opened her expression greatly. It seemed I'd said the right thing. "I will send out one of our priestesses, and she will take your companion to the common room where they can speak freely." She looked at Kip. "Please ask her anything at all. If she does not have an answer, she will find someone who does."

Kip nodded and stepped back into the shade to wait. I took a deep breath, aware in a way I hadn't been in other cities that I would be alone once she wasn't at my side. When she turned to lead me inside, I noticed that the priestess's peplos was slit down the back, all the way to her waist.

"Are you familiar with our goddess, priestess?"

"The goddess Aphrodite I've heard of, yes. She gives the gift of love. I've never seen her in armour though." We entered a barren room with a single door. There was an altar with a wooden bowl of water and nothing else. She dipped her fingers in the water, touched her forehead and her breast.

"Love can be our fiercest emotion. A mother's love will make her leap in front of a lion to save her child. A man will do everything to protect the family he loves. The bards would have you believe love is desire and passion, and while that is true, it is also dark and can force us to see that in ourselves which we want to look away from."

Her words sent chills down my spine, as if she was an oracle. But she was simply explaining the goddess she served, nothing more. "And the water?"

"Blessed by the goddess. We touch our third eye and our heart, so that our minds and hearts may be pure as we enter the temple to receive her blessing."

It was sensible, and I did so, but touched the water to the purple diadem on my forehead instead. It was a gift from the goddess, and the waters of another goddess could only be a blessing.

Satisfied, she led me around the altar towards the door.

"Do people not leave offerings?" I asked.

She hesitated. "People venerate the goddess differently here." She opened the door, and we stepped inside.

CHAPTER THIRTY
Service

THE VENERATION OF APHRODITE in Corinth was all about sex. It was far noisier than any other temple I'd ever been to, making me wince. Laughter abounded from common rooms where men sat with courtesans on their laps, both women and young men in various states of dress, playing their parts. Some were openly having sex in front of an appreciative audience, while others ate and drank as they were served by slaves wearing little more than a piece of cloth wrapped around them for modesty, which was more alluring than if they'd been naked.

The priestess cleared her throat lightly, and I realized I was gaping. I followed her through another doorway, where it grew quieter. Here were rooms, some with doors open, some closed, but the sounds coming from them commonplace enough. We entered an empty room with a small altar in the middle that had various items on it, as well as food and drink.

"As a married woman, you are prohibited from enjoying any of the courtesans and paying respect to the goddess in that way. But here you may enjoy yourself, releasing yourself into her arms and giving thanks for the passion she provides to your bed."

I thought of the people I'd seen on my way in. "And my husband? As a married man, is he too prohibited?" I knew the answer but had to ask anyway.

"Like Zeus, men are led by their passions, and so are expected to release them more often than a wife is capable of providing. It keeps them from thinking about war, and so love keeps the peace of our city."

"And the temple priestesses? Are they given to this life, or do they choose it?"

She folded her arms, and I saw the intelligence in her eyes she probably kept hidden from most.

"Some choose, some are slaves. In Corinth, it is considered an honour to serve the goddess in this way, and it is possible to serve only for a number of years. The temple provides marriage gifts to the girls who leave to wed, and they often marry well." She bowed her head and backed towards the door. "When you're done, I will be waiting in the dining hall."

She closed the door behind her, and I stood there for a moment, bemused.

Finally, I moved to look at the items on the table. There were phallus-shaped things covered in soft material, as well as ones made of smooth marble. There were many sizes and shapes, and some items I had no clue what to do with. Truly, I didn't wish to do anything with any of them. This was too strange, too far from my understanding of the goddess. And yet, when I thought back to the first time I saw Jason, when he entered my father's hall, and I was overwhelmed with desire for him, it made sense. So, too, did it make sense when I thought of the night before, when I'd been overcome, and we'd crashed together in a rush of god-inspired passion. Mostly, I thought of my one night with Chaon and the unfettered passion we'd shared. This goddess was powerful in her own subtle way.

I knelt before the altar and placed my hand on my breast. *Aphrodite, goddess of love and desire, I am here to thank you…*

The words stuck in my throat. Thank her for what? Forcing me to feel things that weren't true? For making me desire Jason so that I would marry him and continue playing the gods' game? For what? Denying the goddess could be catastrophic, as they weren't known for their patience, but to thank her would be a lie. I waited, trying to find the words. She wasn't responsible for our safe journey either. My mother and the goddess I served were responsible for that, as was my grandfather, Poseidon. The other goddesses, ancient and wise, had gifted me along the way. Aphrodite. What was love to me?

The earth trembled under my knees, and I opened my eyes to see some of the things fall off the altar. It stopped, smaller than the earth shakings I'd felt in other places, and I closed my eyes once more, trying to find a place inside me to pray to this goddess. In the end, I had nothing to say, nothing to offer. I touched my head and heart respectfully and left the room.

Had I known what would come of my affront to the goddess, if I'd had any idea at all what she could do to me when I thought I was powerful, would I have done differently? I don't know.

Regardless, I didn't know then. I left and went to find the priestess. She looked puzzled, probably because I didn't look like I'd tumbled myself, but she didn't ask any questions. At least that was one similarity. What you said, or didn't say, to the gods was between you and them.

***

Neleus has become our tale spinner. Jason is too shy to do the travels justice, at least as far as entertainment goes. I grow weary of listening to the story of our journey, which grows with each telling. But this time, it included the happy tale of our marriage, destined as we were to be together. I did my best to look both maidenly and delighted with my new prospects, though my hands remained clenched so tightly in my lap my nails left bloody half-moons in my palms.

The story, however, was becoming well-known and had reached them before we got there. Men at the table shouted for the part about the nymphs, and the clashing rocks, and the women who needed husbands. I knew this tale would outlast us, leaving our names written in the stars for centuries to come. In that way, I would not be forgotten. Nor, however, would my reputation, and there was no question I was a curiosity, looked at by both the men and women with respect and no small amount of suspicion. Neleus never downplayed my part, although he did ascribe the murder of my brother to Jason. A woman capable of that kind of violence would be profane and force me into outcast territory with no way back, and I understood that, though it angered me.

When the tale was done and all applause given, the table turned to individual conversations. Young Glauke, Creon's daughter, turned to me. "To be married to such a hero as Jason, you must be so grateful to the goddess. He's so handsome and strong and will provide you so many sons!"

She was vaguely pretty in a simple way. Her hair was the colour of mouse droppings, her small nose and her wide eyes unremarkable but not disagreeable. Like her father's cleverly concealed cunning, there was more to her than her simple words and girlish romanticism. There were questions in her eyes and jealousy on her lips. She wasn't that much younger than me, and yet I felt a lifetime older.

"Yes," I said, "It is an honour."

"Is it true that the gods themselves drew you together?" She sipped her wine and looked at Jason with desire.

"It is true. From the beginning, we were bonded to take this journey together, and now we are bonded in truth." Whether I wanted him or not, whether it had been my choice or not, he was my husband now, and I wanted to scratch at her for looking at him the way she did. It was worse than how I'd felt with Queen Agave. The queen had been in pain and in need of solace. But there was something else in Glauke's eyes. She, too, wanted power, and she was happy to take it as a princess who would be queen.

Glauke leaned towards me, like a girl conspiring for gossip. "But how? As a priestess and a princess from so far away, how can you be a wife as well? Are you not pulled in all directions and unsure how to act in our culture?"

"You're a princess. I simply have one more calling than you do. And Jason understands the desire of the gods for me to be who

I am, who they created me to be. I can learn your ways, I'm sure. They don't seem all that difficult." It came out a little sharper than I intended, and I tried to soften it with a smile.

She drew back, her eyes narrowed. "True." She turned to speak to the person on her other side.

Dismissed, I could breathe again. Jason was laughing with Creon and Neleus, and the king caught my eye and nodded slightly. I understood then. He had planned on marrying Glauke to Jason after he regained his throne. Together, they would hold the isthmus and the north coast and stand together against invaders, maybe even Mycenae. By marrying me, Jason had upset the plans he likely had no idea were in play.

So where did that leave me? A priestess of power, chosen by the gods themselves, married to a prince trying to regain his throne. A princess in my own right, disgraced by the murder of my brother. A woman from a faraway land who needed to learn the way these people thought and acted. One friend in the world, no family other than Jason's. I grew despondent until Kip squeezed my hand.

"Your face is dark as a moonless night," she whispered, smiling for those around us. "If you would have these people on your side, you should do as your mother did and play your part."

She was right. I thought of my mother and how gracious she was, and how people adored her, and I tried to do the same. I spoke with the people around me, asking questions and listening for clues about how they lived. In return, I answered questions about Egrisi and what we had to trade, things the sailors around me were very interested in. Soon I lost myself in discussion of trade and routes, of the towns we'd come across along our journey, and about the earth shaking, which was happening more frequently here too. Once the men lost sight of the fact that I was a woman, conversation became more interesting and intense, and I enjoyed myself thoroughly. From the corner of my eye, I saw Glauke growing more agitated, and I admit to spurring the conversation on solely for the sake of irritating her.

Eventually, Kip asked if she could retire, and I saw Neleus waiting at the door. I smiled at him and warmed when he smiled back. He, too, accepted me as I was, though he didn't have the challenge of being married to me. I kissed Kip's cheek and wished her fair sleep, though I doubted she'd get much. It wasn't long before Jason stood, and I joined him for the walk back to my room. Once there, he hesitated.

"I can sleep in my own room, if you wish."

He looked so young, so unsure of himself, and it pulled at me. I took his hand and led him inside. Our coming together that night was slower, less rushed, and I allowed myself to focus on nothing but the way his hands felt on my skin and the way he looked in wonder as my body arched into his touch. I showed him what I liked. My time under the covers with Kip had allowed me to understand my body, and now, so did Jason. After we'd slept, I woke him and learned what he enjoyed, taking my time to taste his skin, feel his hardness, see what made him catch his breath and cry out. This was a form of power I understood better now. I would go back to the temple and give thanks tomorrow.

After, we slept against one another, his muscular leg pressed against my softer one. When I woke, he was gone, and Kip wasn't back yet. The sun was only beginning to caress the sky, but I couldn't sleep any more. I rose and wrapped myself in a robe before I left our room and walked out to the terrace overlooking the city far below and the sea far beyond. I stood lost in thought, thinking of all we'd seen and done, and how much more there was ahead. It wasn't long before I felt someone join me, but to my surprise, it wasn't Kip.

"Your majesty," I said, bowing to Creon.

"We both know you're my equal. There's no need to bow to me in private," he said, leaning on the rail beside me.

"You're a king. I'm a princess from far away, as your daughter mentioned last night. I'm hardly your equal." I was *more* than his equal, but I wouldn't say it aloud.

"I spoke with Jason yesterday privately. He told me about you being the gods' chosen, about the gifts you've been given, and the things you've done to help get the Argo this far. Woman or not, god-chosen is beyond any king."

"He must have great trust in you," I said.

"He has been like a son to me. After his mother hid him away, I went to see him sometimes while he was being raised by Chiron. I've always felt a connection to him, and I wanted to see him well." He turned to look at me, the sunlight glinting off his grey hair. "You understand I had hopes?"

I nodded. "Your daughter."

"Yes." He sighed. "But the gods had other plans, and mine are nothing in the face of theirs." He tapped the railing with his fingertips, his brow furrowed. "You frighten me, Medea, and I've never been afraid of anything in my long life. There's something about you, something I cannot understand. A woman who needs no one, a woman of power who could kill her own brother, not with poison, but with a knife like any warrior...but a woman, just the same. A woman not just one god, but many, have touched, one who uses their powers without breaking. And you speak of war and trade and negotiation like a man. I can't help but admire you."

"I was told by the gods that I am neither immortal nor mortal, that I exist somewhere in between, and so the rules of man don't apply to me." I doubted he'd ever had so honest a conversation with a woman. "You're uneasy because you have no power over me."

"I could order you killed. Then Jason would be free to remarry."

I nodded again. "You could. But would you defy the gods that way? Knowing what you do, would you face their wrath by killing one who does their bidding?"

He pondered the question, a look I couldn't decipher in his eyes, and I decided I would wait until someone else tasted my food from now on.

"No." He shook his head slowly, his eyes still on the horizon. "Right now, I would do no such thing. And it could be that another suitor comes for my daughter who would be as fitting."

The implication was clear. For now, he would leave things as they were. But if things changed, so would his plans. "Understand, this, King Creon," I said, but the voice was not my own. This time I willingly let the goddess speak through me, and I looked at him directly. "If you interfere, the gods will punish you in ways you cannot imagine. I am theirs and belong to no man. Jason has made his choice. Abide by it and live well."

The goddess left me abruptly as usual, but I stood firm though my knees trembled. Creon stared at me, his eyes wide with fear, his grip on the railing white. "What are you?" he whispered.

I turned away to look at the sea. "I am Medea. Priestess, princess, chosen."

He left me then, hurrying away, and I sank onto a bench. I had a feeling we were far from done with each other but for now, it was enough that he truly understood. I closed my eyes, breathed in the fresh morning air and drank in the sunlight on my face. I was power, the immortal in a mortal body. My path might be laid for me, but I would revel in the world, just as Circe had told me to.

Chapter Thirty-One
Apollo's Grove

That afternoon, the meal was set in the garden. Kip and I had spent the morning speaking of what she'd learned about Achaean ways, and it fit with what little we'd found out elsewhere. Corinth, it seemed, was the only city where Aphrodite was worshipped in this way, and men came from cities far and wide to worship at her temple, where the priestesses, courtesans, and slaves were well-versed in the art of love. As Jason said, women and men lived in separate quarters but still spent time together throughout the day, as we did now under the late autumn sun.

Glauke wore Mycenae fashion, one I found distasteful. The full skirt with bright colours was fine, but the top covered her back and shoulders and was cut in an open square in the front, baring both breasts, which were adorned with ochre painted designs to look like flowers. It seemed backwards to me, that they should want their women to be kept hidden behind closed doors, and yet to bare themselves as a way to sell their virtue as child bearers and wives. It was a fashion I wouldn't be following. Fortunately, as a married woman, I wouldn't have been expected to even if we were staying in Corinth, which we weren't. Kip assured me that women in Thessaly were more commonly attired.

"Your gifts will weigh down the Argo so that she won't sail," Jason said to Creon as he helped himself to more wine.

"There aren't enough gifts to do justice to such a young hero as yourself." Creon turned to me, his eyes guarded. "And to you, of course, my lady, chosen of the gods."

I tilted my head and smiled slightly but said nothing. Sometimes it was wiser to stay silent, especially when I wanted to start conversations that were ill-advised.

"When I get my kingdom back, I will throw a feast like never before seen!" Jason raised his cup. "And you will be my guests of honour."

Creon smiled indulgently but then leaned forwards, his expression serious. "Beware, Jason, of your Uncle Pelias. Your people have been unhappy under him, but he rules with a heavy hand. His son is a hard, angry young man. They have little honour, and rumour is they put anyone who opposes them in any way to the sword."

Jason set his drink down. "Have you heard aught of my mother and father?"

"No. As you know, Pelias threw them both out of the palace, and I heard they found friends in the city, but I've learned nothing else."

"I will find them and restore them to the palace." Jason looked at me. "You will get along well with my mother. She too is wise and kind."

I smiled, this time with genuine pleasure. I liked that he spoke of me that way in front of others. Glauke, silently pretty, seemed less happy about it.

"I'm off to my loom and my women, if you'll excuse me. The heat of the day isn't good for my skin." She gave Jason a winsome smile and left without looking at the rest of us.

"When will you sail?" Creon asked.

"Tomorrow, I think. We could stay longer, and I'm sure my men would be happy, but I want to finish what I've begun."

Creon nodded. "Wise, and you don't want your men getting soft before the journey is done." He squeezed Jason's forearm. "Remember that you are always welcome here, son of my heart. I am your ally, always."

Jason's eyes grew wet, and he returned the gesture. "Thank you, Father. You know I feel the same. If we need to face Mycenae or Cythera, we will do it side by side."

The earth began to tremble, and the noise grew. We held onto the table, and Creon turned to look at the palace, where there were shouts and cries as the shaking grew and pieces of rock fell from the walls. When it stopped, there was a long moment of silence.

Creon released the table and shook his head. "Medea, do you know why the gods shake the earth this way?"

I wished I had some wisdom to impart, but I wouldn't answer for the gods. "I know only that it is happening everywhere. Jason told you of the cities we visited?" I waited until Creon nodded. "From my home in Egrisi to here in Corinth, the earth shakes. If the gods are angry, it is with all men and not only one city."

He blanched. "If they are angry with us all, then we have little hope." He motioned towards the sea. "Men who call themselves the Sea People arrive and say the mountains that rise from the sea are smoking and sending bleeding earth from the tops back into the water. The mountains grow angry and shoot the earth into the sky, where it falls onto ships unlucky enough to be near. And then the waters grow restless. Sometimes I wonder if that's when we feel the earth shake, when those mountains break open."

It was an interesting idea, one that had occurred to me before, and it was easy to see how they might be connected. But where did the gods fit in, if at all?

Creon pushed himself up from the table. "Those are questions for the gods, I suppose. If you get any answers from them, I hope you'll let us know." He looked at me, and his smile was almost genuine. "Now I must go make sure no one inside is hurt. Let my servants know if you need anything at all to sail tomorrow."

Jason, Neleus, Kip and I sat talking for a while longer, and it was nice to have a moment of calm with the three people I cared about.

"We'll send all the cargo to the other coast, and the coastal slaves will put the Argo on a rolling cart that sits in deep ridges in the land. They'll pull the cart across the isthmus and put the Argo back in the water on the other side. It will save us weeks of sailing through dangerous waters." Jason used the water from the cup to draw the map on the table.

It was ingenious, and I hoped to see it myself. "And will we travel the same way, by chariot?"

He nodded, looking deep in thought. "We will. It's a long way and not terribly comfortable, but it's better than walking."

Neleus stood. "We better see to the provisions and the movement if you want to go tomorrow. Can we bring anything from the market for you? Or do you want a chariot to go yourself?"

Kip looked surprised. "I thought we weren't allowed to go without an escort?"

He laughed. "Believe me when I say the tale of Medea the witch has spread and no one will bother you. But we can send a servant with you anyway, to carry your things and so you don't get lost. It's a rabbit warren down there."

I'd been called a witch before, and I would think of it later. I turned to Kip. "Would you like to go? I've no wish to see more of this city, but I don't want to keep you."

Her eyes searched mine, looking for answers to what I was thinking, but I didn't give anything away. "I'd like to, yes. And I think we have a few small things to trade for the coin they use here, which would be good for the rest of the trip."

That made sense, and I was grateful for her forward thinking. "Then take one of the servants with you and do what you will. Be safe."

She and Neleus strolled away, talking, and Jason turned to me. "You don't like it here?" He looked crestfallen.

"I'm eager to see your home." It wasn't an answer, but he accepted it.

"Then I will see you tonight, wife." He grinned, making me smile back, and then turned to follow Neleus and Kip.

I sat in the sun a while longer, thinking of Creon and his daughter, of being a wife. And now, a witch. The term wasn't one we used often in Egrisi, but somehow it fit like a perfectly made cloak. A witch, someone who performed spells, who healed the sick, who spoke to the gods. Not a Pythia who gave out words mixed with omens but someone who caused things to change. I liked the term very much and added it to my list. Princess, priestess, witch. *Chosen.*

I should have gone to the temple. I was alone with time to spare, but I couldn't bring myself to do it. I should have thanked her for the gifts of passion that came to my marriage bed, as surely many women weren't as lucky. But I couldn't let go of the anger I felt at being used, at being filled with desire long before I even knew the man I now shared my bed with. I thought of what I might have had with Chaon, of a life unfettered by gods and expectations, and I couldn't go to the temple. Instead, I unpacked our trunks and aired our clothing from the trip, carefully rewrapped the trinkets and jewels, and folded the clothes given us on our journey. Each brought a memory, and the afternoon passed quickly as I immersed myself in moments past. I sat on the thick rug, spread the gift from the gods before me, and took the time to hold each one, concentrating on the advice they'd given me along with those gifts.

When I was done, I was relaxed, my shoulders eased. I felt the need to be out in the open where I could pray the way I knew best. Not surrounded by walls with the moans of pleasure around me but in silent contemplation. I took my dagger, my diadem, and moonstone, and I asked a servant where the nearest cave was or a temple open to the sky. She looked at me like I'd become a Chimera, but she led me through the castle, past the men's quarters and the house temple to a grove at the back.

"Apollo's sacred grove," she said and backed away.

It wasn't dedicated to the goddess, but it would suffice. Surely Apollo wouldn't mind me using his sacred area to pray. I wandered through the sun-dappled trees and came to a small patch of grass in the setting sun. I knelt on the warm grass and bowed my head, and I prayed from the truest part of me. I prayed to Hecate and asked her to help me tame and mold the destructive parts of my being. I asked the harvest goddess and those even older ones I'd met along the way to help me, to guide my hand, to keep me wise and tempered so I didn't do anything rash. I prayed for balance and for a place inside myself where I could be at peace with the path laid before me.

Each of the goddesses heard me. I felt their immortal touch slide over my soul, touch my heart and mind. Power suffused me until I felt as strong as the trees, as deep as the earth, as full as the sky. I wept openly at the beauty of life and my part in it. Resentment washed away, and I collapsed on my side, curled around my items, as spent as any lover. I don't know how long I lay there basking in the pleasure of my experience, but I started at the touch on my shoulder and saw that it was dark.

Phryne from the temple knelt beside me, her expression one of concern. "Medea, can you hear me, child?"

Child. No one had called me that in so, so long. But to her, I must still look like the young girl I'd been when I left Egrisi. I blinked against the torchlight held by a servant behind her and shivered against the chill air. Slowly I uncurled, and with her hand against my back, I sat up. "How long have I been here?"

"Long enough to give the servant watching you a fright when you lay down and didn't get back up." She chafed my hands and blew on them to warm them. "She was afraid to disturb someone who had clearly been speaking to the gods, but when night fell, she worried you were ill and came to me."

I began to shiver harder, and she helped me to my feet, my body protesting after being curled up for so long on the hard ground. "I must thank her." I wrapped my arm over her shoulder, and she held my waist as we slowly made our way back inside and to my rooms. When we opened the door, Kip came rushing over and helped get me to the bed.

"Bring a bath of hot water for the princess."

Phryne helped Kip undress me and put me under the covers.

"Where on earth have you been? I've been frantic with worry."

Kip tucked the cover around me before she moved to my feet

and started rubbing the feeling back into them. If Phryne was surprised by Kip's sharp tone, she didn't show it. But I couldn't answer with my teeth chattering, and I looked at Phryne.

"She was praying in the sacred grove. The servant said the trees began to sway like they were dancing, and she heard the sweetest music though there was no one else there." She smoothed my hair back. "Medea lit up like the sun and moon combined, dark and light swirling around her until she was part of them both. After, she collapsed to the ground and didn't move."

So that's what someone else saw as I prayed. I wished I could see it that way. It sounded impressive. That servant was probably already telling her tale, and it would get back to those who doubted. Would that make things easier or harder? I had no time to think on it as the bath was drawn and ready. Together, they helped me into the steaming water, and I nearly cried out with relief as my skin began to thaw. I closed my eyes and let the warmth flood through me.

"Does this happen often?" Phryne asked.

"Too often for my liking." Kip laughed gently. "It happened when she was a girl. She'd get visions of things about to happen, and those came more often as she got older. When Jason came, so too did the goddess, who rides her like a beast when she wishes Medea to do her will."

I laughed at the image of a goddess riding me like a donkey.

"And then on our travels," Kip said, a hint of sadness in her voice, "it seems the gods of every village we came to wanted to speak to her or through her. She's been given gifts, from knowing which way the rivers will flow to having a sense of what will happen in the future, as long as it isn't hers."

"To be a god's chosen is to live a hard life," Phryne said.

At that, I opened my eyes. "Have you been so chosen?"

She tilted her head. "When I was young, Aphrodite herself came to me in a field. She loved me and showed me how love and passion could make the world better. Ever since, I have served in her temple and trained others how to sacrifice in her honour."

"And so you forsake finding love of your own." I nodded and slipped deeper into the water. "We sacrifice ourselves for the honour of their use."

"And we gain a measure of power and independence other women covet." She smiled at me, understanding. "Now that you are safe and warm, I will leave you. I hear you leave tomorrow, and I will ask the goddess for safe travels for you all." She went to the door and stopped to look back at me. "I think, however, we will meet again."

I had that feeling too. When she was gone, Kip let out an exasperated breath.

"I was worried you'd fallen off a cliff or been turned into a swine for refusing the goddess of love. I was worried some man had taken you away, or that Creon had murdered you and dumped your body down the hillside."

I reached out for her hand. "I'm sorry to have worried you, Kip. I meant only to pray before we left, but it became more than I warranted."

She snorted. "It seems so."

She let go of my hand and went to a pile of items on the table. She held up various pieces of lovely cloth and jewels that she then packed away. They were gifts from Glauke, and Kip knew I wouldn't be interested. "I've set out your travel clothes for tomorrow. Is it strange that I'm looking forwards to being back on the Argo?"

I got out of the bath, and she towelled me off and helped me dress. "I feel the same. I dislike this city. Something about it feels dark, like Hades has his hands cupped and is ready to pour the waters of the Styx over it."

She shuddered. "Even more reason to be ready to leave. Are you hungry?"

"I'm famished." So we went to find leftovers. As we made our way to the kitchen, servants scattered before us, heads bowed and looks of awe in their eyes as they stole glances at us. It made me smile, and I jerked when Kip pinched me.

"Hubris will get you turned into a goat." She laughed when I rolled my eyes. "And if they knew how you snore and how bad you smell after three days on a boat, they wouldn't look at you like you'd fallen from Olympus."

As always, she grounded me. Chastened, I felt the earth under my feet again. "You smell as bad."

We laughed and she linked her arm through mine, before we went and found fresh bread, cheese, and wine laid out in the dining hall. Jason and Neleus entered not long after we sat to eat, and they joined us for food, having been all day working on the Argo.

"You've created quite a stir among the people here," Jason said, eating a large chunk of bread. "They say you're the most beautiful woman to grace the palace and rival even Aphrodite in your power."

Neleus made a warding symbol. "Not that Medea herself would say such a thing."

To compare oneself to a goddess was a good way to get turned into a snake-haired monster, and we all knew it. Women always paid the price when it came to matters of the heart, and for men's idiocy as well. "Of course not. I've never been a beauty, and I know it. I prayed and the gods answered. The servant saw what she wanted to see, nothing more."

"Nevertheless, if you stayed here, you'd be as renowned as the oracle at Delphi."

"Where is she? Is she near here?" I'd grown up with stories of the oracle who lived at the Delphi temple, a wise woman who was never wrong.

"She's across the water, not even a day's row. If we stayed another few days, you could see her, but there won't be time before we leave tomorrow." Neleus ate like he hadn't had anything in weeks.

"It's best to stay away from her," Jason said. "Knowing your future doesn't keep it from happening. And even if you try, it will still turn out as she says, probably because of the things you've done to make it *not* happen."

That was true, and I agreed. "I wouldn't ask her anything. I want to meet her, to see how she lives with the gods speaking through her. I want to know how she does it."

All three of them laughed, though I didn't understand why. I looked at Kip for explanation.

"Only a woman who speaks to the gods and can tell the future herself wouldn't want to know what the oracle has to say to her. It's hard for us mortals to understand."

I understood and heat rose to my cheeks. I concentrated on my wine.

"A woman of this world but not of this world." Jason kissed my hand. "We are not making fun, Medea. We laugh with you, not at you."

I sighed and relaxed. "Thank you."

We spent the rest of the meal discussing the route we would take, and when Jason learned I had no directions from the goddess, he went on with his plan. We would have to make several more stops as we wended our way through the islands towards his home, and I was looking forward to the time we had left on the Argo.

We went once again to our separate rooms, where Kip left with Neleus to Jason's room, and Jason went with me to mine. After we'd done enjoying one another's bodies, I turned towards him. "When you retake your throne, will your people accept me as their queen?" The question had been playing on my mind since Glauke had mentioned me being a foreign princess.

He looked surprised. "Of course they will. Kings marry women from many different cities to cement bonds. By marrying you, I've created a bond with the Sea of Marmara and Aia. You and I know that we will never trade with your father's people, but your status as a princess of that great city will never be denied. And with the story of all you've done for me and with me to help me regain my throne,

I have no doubt that my people will love you."

His words made sense. So why did I have a sense of fear? Why did it feel like mist instead of land? There was no reason to worry him, and so I curled next to him and slept in his embrace, letting his heat warm me. My dreams were mottled with sunshine and darkness, with shadows sliding into light and overcoming it. I heard cries and heat seared my skin as I ran through the night, looking over my shoulder with tear blurred eyes.

I woke sweating and alone when Kip quietly came into the room. Seeing me awake, she opened the curtains, looked at me and sighed.

"A bad night?"

I nodded and stretched the tension from my shoulders. "Visions, but not visions. Dreams, but more real than that. I don't understand them."

"Nor do you need to." She pulled the covers back and helped me from the bed. "As we said last night, there's little point in knowing because you can't change anything. Your father tried to avert the prophecy given him and likely caused it instead."

The same thought had occurred to me in that discussion, but I hadn't voiced it. "How long do we have?"

She gathered towels and wrapped me in a robe. "Enough time to visit the Pirine and wash before we're shipbound again."

We hurried to the baths and though there were a few other women there, we didn't stay to talk. We bathed quickly, though I did let a servant use the strigil on me so I was extra clean. I loved the tingling sensation it gave me as I moved into the colder water to wash off, and by the time we made it back to our room, the trunk was gone. We dressed and made our way to the hall for bread and wine before the journey.

Phryne surprised me when she came in and offered me a bag. "Food and drink for your journey." She kissed my cheeks and touched my forehead and breast. "Be well, Medea of Aia."

Her thoughtfulness touched me, and I hugged her. "Thank you."

She left quickly, and we were soon on a chariot and underway. The trip was bouncy and uncomfortable, but I loved it and hoped I'd have one of my own in Iolcos. Kip seemed to enjoy it and hung onto Neleus, laughing all the way. Jason's crew was already at the port with the Argo, which had been moved overnight. I could see the deep ruts in the ground where they moved the cart through and was impressed.

We set sail mid-morning, and I pushed away the sense of darkness ahead, turning instead to face the sun.

CHAPTER THIRTY-TWO
Warning

THE COASTLINE WAS SIMILAR to what we'd seen coming down the other side of Epirus, but as we skirted the islands, the water changed and became beautifully clear, like a green jewel turned to liquid. Dolphins jumped at our sides, playing and rolling in the wake. The islands were sun-baked but covered in trees and had white sand beaches that made me long to lay on them. We sailed first to Akron Sounion, where an ancient temple looked over the water. It had been abandoned, but still I climbed the hill to kneel there, pulled to its lonely position overlooking the vast sea.

I knelt in the late day sun and felt the wind slide over me. She was still here, the goddess who had been cherished. My vision swam and the world tilted, and I saw the temple as it would be again. First dedicated to the goddess of wisdom and wild things and later, to the god of the sea. Both were fitting, and I was glad to know it would come to life once more.

An invisible caress touched my hair, lifting it from my shoulders, and I smiled at the feeling of playfulness surrounding me.

You are no longer a maiden, but your heart is young. Remember to run in the grass.

There was no goddess with me, but I heard her anyway, and I promised to remember her words. There were no gifts or warnings. And when the vision faded, I didn't have the sickness I usually felt. A vision of something good to come was a rare gift in itself. I gave my thanks and asked for the safety of all of us travelling together, then made my way back to the ship.

There is little to tell of our other stops except to note their beauty. On one side, we passed the Attic and Boeotian lands, and on the other, the islands of Euboea. The river was wide enough to sail through easily but not so wide we couldn't reach either side quickly. In Chalcis, we stopped to leave offerings at ancient tombs said to house the spirits of ancient warriors, but it was in Kynos, which belonged to the Locrian king, Oileus, where we first had a sense of what we would be facing when we got to Jason's home.

As always, we gave our names when we arrived at the port of Opous, and more than one person stopped to stare before scurrying off. Jason frowned and looked to Neleus, who shook his head, scanning the crowd as he did so for possible danger. It took some time before a servant from the palace showed up but instead of taking us to the palace, he took us to an inn near to it.

"What is this?" Jason asked.

"The King of Locris wishes you fair sleep and requests your presence to dine in the morning light." The servant bobbed and bowed, backing down the street.

We were left standing on the steps of the inn, baffled.

"The king won't receive us. That's a bad omen, Jason." Neleus held open the door for the rest of us to enter.

The innkeeper was gracious enough but didn't stay to talk, and the four of us spent a restless night in the same room, deciding that staying together was safer than sleeping apart. In the morning, we dressed quickly and found a servant waiting outside. Once again, we were led away from the front gates and around the side. Jason's jaw clenched, and Neleus kept his hand on his sword. We entered the palace through a back entrance that came in off the gardens, which was better than the servant's entrance but not by much.

The palace was small in comparison to others, but it was clean and airy, unlike the inn, which had been stuffy and dark. Instead of being shown to the throne room, we were taken to the king's private rooms. He struggled to his feet, his thin grey hair matching the lines in his face.

He held out his hands. "Prince of Iolcos, please forgive the rudeness of my hospitality."

Jason took his arm in greeting, still frowning. "What is going on, King Oileus, to treat your guests so?"

The king waved us to chairs and a servant poured wine. "You have been gone a long time, son of Aeson. When your uncle Pelias sent you on your quest, he never expected you to return from the perils you would meet."

I waved away the wine, as did Neleus. We'd been brought in under cover and should anything happen to us, no one would know. It was important to keep our wits about us. I noticed that although Jason accepted his glass, he didn't drink.

"I thought as much, but that doesn't explain your behaviour."

The old king sighed. "He has already had word of your return, and storm clouds hang over Iolcos. He rages and threatens anyone who helps you to get the rest of the way. He's built a mighty army, and my small city would not survive an attack. But my friendship with Aeson and the laws of hospitality required that I meet with you to tell you what I could."

It was practical and canny. By meeting with Jason in secret, he made it so that Jason wouldn't hold it against him when he retook his throne, but he also kept Pelias from knowing he'd helped Jason at all.

Clearly, Jason understood this too. He set down his glass and clasped Oileus's arm once more. "Thank you for explaining. We will set sail right away and avoid bringing down my uncle's army on you, and when I take my kingdom back, we can talk about how to be better friends."

The old king sighed again and wished us fair sailing. Before we left the room, he called out once more. "Jason, beware. Pelias is old, but he will not give you Iolcos back without a fight. He is cruel and devious, and lies drip from his lips like honey from the gods. He would handsomely reward anyone who made sure you didn't come home."

Jason glanced at the wine, of which no one had drunk, including Oileus. "Thank you for the warning, friend of my father."

We left the way we came in but went straight back to the Argo to find all the men already aboard. As we set sail, they told us the rumours they'd heard as well, and it painted a grim picture. The mood dampened, and we sailed quietly, passing ships but hailing no one. Jason came to stand with me at the rail.

"I fear I may have put you in danger." He picked at a splinter of wood as he stared out at the water.

I couldn't help but laugh. "Do you?" When he looked at me, surprised, I shook my head. "Why do you think the gods sent me with you? Why do you think they've given me the powers I have?" I put my hand over his. "Think, husband. The gods want you to have your throne, else they would not have brought us together. You say you have put me in danger, but it is the other way around. You have brought danger with you."

He gave a short, sharp laugh. "Truly, I had not considered that. What advice do you give?"

I thought about it before answering. "First, we must stay alive long enough to get to the palace. That means the crew of the Argo must go with us, to be celebrated as the heroes of the quest for the golden fleece. It will mean we have their swords at the ready." I moved slightly closer. "You trust all of them completely? They would not take a reward for your life?"

He gripped the railing. "Each and every one I would trust with my life."

"Good. You will need to." Unbidden, the black vial left to me by the goddess came to mind. "He will not simply step down, and you will need to be ready for that. I will learn what I can from the women in the household, and we will plan from there, once we understand how things stand."

He raised my hand and kissed it. "You are a gift."

I knew in that moment there would come a time he would not think so, but it was a feeling and nothing more, so I dismissed it to concentrate. As we sailed around the river bend, I saw Jason looking increasingly worried.

"What is it?" I touched his hand and he smiled slightly, then looked again at the water.

"Talos is a creature who guards the entry to the bay of Iolcos. We lost a good many men when we came through on our way to your land, and if the goddess wasn't with us, I'm sure the Argo would have been pulled apart."

I'd heard tales of giant creatures, the kind heroes fought, but I'd never thought to see one beyond the snake who had guarded the fleece. "What does it look like?"

He went on to describe it, the memory of its monstrous visage clear in his words. It was a giant made of bronze, invulnerable to every weapon, who could wade into the water and tear boats apart with its bare hands. When they'd passed before, it had raised the waters and made them crash down again, throwing many of Jason's men overboard. If it hadn't been for a ray of light that blinded it, giving the Argo enough time to move beyond it, they would have perished.

"And what is your plan to get beyond it this time?" I pictured the monster as looking much like my father's bulls and wondered what tricks could be used.

"I don't know. I suppose I was hoping the goddess would distract him again." Jason looked over his crew. "I don't want to lose any more men, but perhaps the sacrifice is required." He spoke softly, only to me, and I liked the feeling of having a co-conspirator.

"Let me pray to the goddess for guidance. Perhaps I can help." I squeezed his hand and appreciated his grateful look before he went to walk among his men.

I sat beside Kip and closed my eyes. A monster, no matter what it was made of, lived, and as such, it could be killed. Surely he wouldn't let this ship pass a second time, and words were unlikely to soothe a beast born for destruction. I continued to think, letting my mind wander, until Jason moved quickly to my side.

"There, on the shore. You can see the sun shining off his armour."

I stood and stared at the unfamiliar shore, and sure enough, the creature of bronze stood at the edge of the water, his hands open over the waves lapping at his feet. I leaned on the rail and studied him, but he never moved. His helmeted head was turned towards us, but his eyes were dark holes and nothing more. I closed my eyes and pictured him and heard the voice whisper what I needed to do. I bit my lip at the instruction I received knowing the action ahead was one I'd have to be brave enough to venture. But I remembered who I was, what I'd been given. Nothing could stop me.

"Row to shore. Here, nowhere near him, and let me off. Then row back out onto the open water and wait for my signal."

Bemused, Jason shook his head. "That's insanity. I won't leave my wife on an island with a monster."

I turned to him and felt the goddess rise. "I am more than a wife. Do as I say, and we'll survive this."

His jaw worked again as he looked into my eyes, and then he turned away and gave the order. No one spoke against him, but I could feel their confusion. And in more than one face I saw the hope that he would leave me there. They'd come to respect me to some degree, but the bonds we'd forged these many days at sea were pulling tight as Jason sought to bring me to their land as queen.

Kip gripped my hand. "What are you thinking? What if he leaves you behind? What if you're killed by that thing?" She held my hand to her face. "What would become of me? What would I do without you?"

I caressed her cheek and lifted her chin. "Look at me."

She did and flinched away at what she saw in my eyes. I wondered what it looked like to have a goddess look back you from this distance.

"They will not leave me, and I will not leave you. Have faith." The boat bumped the shore, and I walked quickly away. At the gangplank, I turned to Jason. "You swore to be true."

He nodded, but his gaze stayed on the water. "When you give

the signal, we'll come straight back to pick you up." This time, he took my hand and kissed it lightly. "I made an oath to the goddess, and we are meant to be together. Have no fear."

The words were hardly a romantic bard's song, but they made me smile anyway. I turned away and swiftly made my way to shore and into the cover of the trees and granite-lined cliffs. Behind me I could hear the boat pulling away, and I moved silently through the trees until I was behind the bronze creature. Up close, he was far more unnerving. Easily three times the height of a man, he was built like an oak tree, and there were no chinks in his armour. But unnatural light glinted off his ankle, and I understood. I crouched low and moved slowly up behind him, aware that he was looking at the Argo where she bobbed, unmoving in the water. My head barely came to his knee, and I knelt behind him in the soft, warm sand. Everything was brighter, sharper, and I knew I wasn't alone.

Still, it was with trembling fingers that I reached out and found the bolt at his ankle, the only part of him made to be removed, the part a god had used to fill him with the icy ichor of Olympus. I took it between my fingertips, closed my eyes and drew on the goddess's power, and pulled until my muscles felt like they would tear.

With a groan and screech, it pulled free. I lost my balance and fell back onto the sand before I scrambled back further on my bottom. Green ichor spilled from the hole into the sand and steam rose where it fell. The creature turned slowly towards me, his hands still poised to raise the ocean. His eyeless stare fixed on me, and he took a step forwards before his knee buckled and he went down, causing the earth to rumble and the sand around me to jump. He reached out to grab me, but the other knee went, and he fell forwards. I was only steps beyond his head when he fell facedown before me, unmoving, his bronze armour turning to granite. The sand beneath the oozing pool turned to lime green stone.

I stood, allowing the men on the ship who were cheering to see me standing there over the giant I had defeated. Yes, it was with the goddess's help and knowledge, but I'd had the courage to do it, and I wanted them to see it, to remember. On impulse, I took an empty vial from one of the many small pockets in my skirt and went to the hole in the giant's leg. Drops still fell, and I held my vial under them to fill it with the life force of the gods. Once the vial was full, I placed it in my pocket and turned to the boat. The men stood waiting, staring, and the rush of power once again made me dizzy. The boat waited for me offshore, the plank lowered so I'd hardly have to get my feet wet. On board, the men bowed their heads as I passed, and Jason swept me up in a hug that made me laugh.

"The goddess brought us together and because of you, all of us will make it home." He set me down and kissed me tenderly. "You are a wonder, priestess of Hecate."

I smiled at him, but the power infusing me had yet to wane, and I wanted free. He seemed to sense it and set me down beside Kip before he went to give orders to move us to the next section of the trip.

Kip hugged me fiercely. "If you weren't glowing like something out of a temple right now, I'd say that was foolish. So I'll simply say I'm glad you're back."

I turned to the rail and watched the land slide by. Foolish was probably right. But the monster had been waiting for a warrior, for a man. He'd never suspected a woman. Perhaps this was where the goddess had chosen well. No one ever considered the goddesses less than, and yet mortal women were often underestimated. Those who underestimated me would find they'd made a grievous mistake.

I had tasted power. I had taken control over my life and chosen to live the life of adventure. No one would take it from me, and I would do everything and anything to keep my place in this world.

CHAPTER THIRTY-THREE
Homecoming

"It's a long way to Iolcos yet, but to stop again seems foolish. Do you agree?"

He was asking me if the gods were speaking, but they weren't now that Talos had been defeated. I said yes and hoped it was the right answer.

"Men," he turned to the crew and raised his voice. "You heard the whispers on the wind and know what we row towards. We sail with fair tides and to dock anywhere before Iolcos could bring consequences. I ask that you conserve your strength, and that we row straight home."

There was general agreement, and several men left their oars to rest. We would move more slowly, but we would make it to our destination. Kip and I slept huddled together as the evening wind was chill, and there was little to see as we passed the dark shores in the night. So it was we came to Iolcos, Jason's home, at the witching hour when my powers flooded through me, and I knew things here would set our course to come.

Before we docked, Jason turned again to his crew. "I will be under threat here, as will my wife. I ask that you guard our backs but draw no attention to our awareness of the danger. Celebrate and be yourselves but keep your sword hands free. You have been brave, admirable companions, and I love each and every one of you like my own brother. You will take your parts of the treasure we have brought back, as I promised."

Neleus stood at the back of the ship, his voice raised so we could hear it at the front. "You have been our leader, our prince, and it has been an honour to sail with you. We will be by your side to the end." The men cheered him, echoing his words, and Jason smiled at them.

"May the goddess bless us as she has this far."

We docked at Iolcos, our long sea journey over, our next one just beginning.

***

They were waiting for us, even though we shouldn't have arrived for another day or two, which suggested a network of spies along the route. Jason was heartily welcomed back, and much was made of him as he ordered the chest containing the golden fleece brought with us to the palace. Chariots were lined up and when Jason saw there weren't enough for the crew, he laughingly ordered more for the rest of the heroes of the Argo, and he refused to leave until they were all ready to go, except for three he left behind to guard the cargo.

The procession led up the hill to the palace, flickering torches lighting our way and making my eyes water as images not of this time warred with what I was trying to see now. The goddess pushed against my skin, making me raise my eyes to the heavens to tell her I understood, to let me breathe or she would crush me. The feeling subsided enough that I became aware of my surroundings once again.

It was hard to gauge what the palace looked like in the dark, but if I could have stayed outside the door bigger than two men standing on each other's shoulders, I would have done so, for the foreboding was heavy on my neck. But our chariots raced through, and there was no escaping my future. *This* was what the goddess had brought me here for.

We were shown to elegant, well-furnished rooms. Before we separated, I pulled Jason close, as a wife might do, and whispered in his ear, "Eat and drink nothing until tomorrow. Sleep with your sword ready. I can feel the darkness here like a cloak."

He kissed my cheek and said loudly enough for others to hear, "Yes, my wife, I will come to you in the morning."

He went into the rooms across from mine, and the other Argonauts spread into the rooms further down the hall. We would be safe, if only for this night.

Kip and I fell into bed exhausted, but dreams plagued me, and I woke wishing I was back on the Argo. Kip waved the servants off and told them we'd be rising late, which gave us time to speak in private while we bathed and dressed at our leisure. She braided my hair and helped me put on the double robes I'd taken to wearing as Chaon had suggested. Before we left the room, I closed my eyes and prayed for guidance so I didn't let her, or Jason, down.

I went across and knocked on Jason's door and Neleus answered, letting us in. Jason looked tired. "You are well?" I asked, looking around the room.

He motioned towards a thick tapestry hung on the wall and I understood. There would be someone listening on the other side. Palaces like these always had bolt holes where people could listen in to conversations not meant for them.

"Yes. You?"

"I'm looking forwards to seeing the kingdom you've described throughout our trip. Can we explore? Or are we to have an audience with your uncle first?"

Kip and Neleus watched us from the kline, where he sat with his arm around her shoulders.

"My uncle has said he has urgent business this morning but will be glad to feast our return tonight. So we can explore, yes."

What was his uncle planning that meant he wouldn't do his host duties and meet with us? He'd known to expect us, but he had likely hoped someone would kill us before we made it this far.

The four of us left, walking like we had nowhere to go, and several Argonauts joined us, saying they also wanted a tour of the palace they'd heard so much about and had travelled so far for. There was plenty of laughter and jesting, but every man was armed, which would have been an affront to the king, if he'd been willing to see us. Jason took us through the palace, showing us the courtyard and gardens, the olive groves, and the temple. I realized that he was finding his way; he wasn't raised here and had no idea of the layout. It was clever, as no one could bar him entry, and we could divine the way the palace was positioned.

Outside, we saw the walls, arranged twice around in a loose circle with houses in between. As I'd seen elsewhere, the houses became larger and more elegant the closer they got to the palace, which had a stunning view of the sea and everything around it, much like that of Corinth.

"No way to approach unseen, and once inside, trapped like a rat in a maze unless you know the secret exits," Neleus said softly and several of the men nodded.

A servant gained our attention. "The daughters of Pelias would be delighted to entertain the heroes of the Argo for the midday meal, if you would be so inclined."

The men laughed and joked about their appetites, but there would be little eating or drinking unless someone else tasted things first. I suggested it should be the princesses themselves, but that remark was met with good-natured scoffs. We made our way to the long, open dining hall and spread out at a table full of food and drink. At the head of the table waited Pelias's daughters.

"Be welcome, cousin." The taller one with lank dark hair kissed Jason's cheeks. "I am Hippothoe, eldest daughter of King Pelias. This is my sister, Alcestis. I'm sorry our mother, Queen Phylomache could not join us, but she is assisting our father with his business."

Jason's raised eyebrow was the only indication he'd found issue with the titles she'd given her parents, who, now that he'd brought the fleece back, were no longer royalty because Jason and I were now rightful king and queen of Iolcos.

"I'm sure she is, cousin. Thank you for laying out food for us."

We sat, and two of Jason's men took food. They'd volunteered to test it for poison, but it turned out there was no need. Using the magic the goddess had given me, I looked over the table and saw shadows, oily and dancing, above the few things that had been tampered with. "Wait," I said and moved along the table. Whenever I touched a dish, the Argonaut near me moved it to the floor, along with two jugs of wine and one of water. There was still a great amount of food on the table, so they could say that if they'd meant to poison Jason, they would have poisoned it all. This way, they could blame it on the cooks.

I returned to my seat and pulled a dish of sweet pears to me. "This looks perfect. Thank you."

The younger sister, her blue eyes much like Jason's, stared at me, her face pale and her hands trembling. Her sister, too, looked ill but far more poised.

"There was something wrong with those dishes? I'm sorry, we haven't met."

I stabbed at a pear and smiled sweetly at her. "I am Queen Medea, King Jason of Iolcos's wife and dedicated priestess of Hecate. The food was tainted, but no matter. I can see what others cannot."

Neleus tried unsuccessfully to cover his laugh, and Jason sat back in his chair, arms folded, a grin on his face. Dishes clattered and conversation surrounded us, and Jason spoke to us of his time on Mount Pelion and how much he loved to run in the forests. The princesses continued to look at us, stunned into silence and out of their depth. When the meal ended, we made our way outside and played games in the sunshine until it was time to dress for the evening's feast.

"How did you know?" Jason asked, his mouth close to my ear as we returned to our rooms.

"The goddess showed me. There were shadows over the poisoned food." I wished I could take credit, that it was something I knew without divine help, but it had come through me, and that was enough. I'd felt the stares and admiration of all around me, and the power of it made me dizzy.

JJ Taylor

He wrapped his arm around me and pulled me close. "As you said, we were meant for one another."

I hadn't said that, not exactly, but I let it be. I told him I would meet him in the dining hall for the feast, and he inclined his head, not bothering to question me. I washed and dressed carefully for the feast in my finest Kolchian robes, with my jewels and the gifts from the gods showing. I had arrived a princess, but I would enter as a queen.

We made our way to the dining hall after the bell had rung, and when the door opened to admit us, quiet settled as they stared. I lifted my head, determined not to show my heart pounding and the way my palms grew wet with fear. *Priestess, princess, witch*, I reminded myself. No, that wasn't right. Priestess, *queen*, witch.

Jason stood and I saw the goddess in him, lighting him from within, making him look every inch the hero in love. "I present my wife, Medea of Egrisi, priestess of Hecate, beloved of the gods, and the reason we made it to celebrate here today."

A cheer went up from the crew, and others applauded politely. I made my way to Jason's side, and he took my hand and faced the older couple at the table. "Medea, my uncle, Pelias, son of Poseidon and Tyro, and his wife, Phylomache. And their son, Acastus."

When I looked at the queen, I saw my mother. Not that they were similar, because she was as dark as my mother was fair, but because of the look in her eyes. She'd long ago given up joy and the desire to live, and her body was a shell, moving day-to-day until she could escape. Even the shadows of Hades' hearth would be better. Her smile was thin and wan, and I don't think she really saw me.

And when I looked at the king, I saw my father. Angry, suspicious, cunning, and determined to keep what was his, even though it didn't belong to him. He was a tyrant with a nice smile and eyes that sang of cruelty. Death shrouded him, and the goddess's rage seared me from the inside.

He kissed my cheeks. "Thank the goddess you found our

wayward prince."

Jason stiffened beside me, and I squeezed his hand. "We've thanked the goddess many times to get here and still, she guides my hand." I said it sweetly but saw the threat register in his clenched jaw and false smile.

"Let us eat and hear the deeds of heroes!" Pelias called out and the hall responded with cheers.

As always, Neleus rose to tell the tale of our journey, but he'd changed it somewhat. There were still the funny bits, but he made clear Jason's role in leadership and thoughtfulness, in his strength against foes, and in accomplishing all the tasks he'd had to face to get the fleece and bring it back. He ascribed to me the qualities of a queen and priestess who remained calm and did what I needed to, including the tale of Talos, guardian of the port.

Phylomache looked more interested now and smiled shyly at me. Her daughters, seated beside her, stared with innocent wonder. But Pelias's son glowered with envy and rage. He barely showed it, but I could see it, coming in waves from him as he ate. The son of Aeson had returned, and it meant dire things for his family.

When the meal was done, Pelias stood, and I doubt anyone but me noticed how white his knuckles were as he held up his glass.

"To Jason, who has brought the fleece home to its rightful place." After the cheers subsided, he turned to us. "I swore before Hera I would return the throne to you if you brought back the fleece, and you have done so. I will not be forsworn. Come the winter festival, before the goddess and the people, I will step down and make you King of Iolcos."

The cheering was deafening as the crew pounded on the table, as did many of the nobility in attendance. The winter festival was still a moon cycle away: why wait? When Pelias met my gaze, I knew he was saying what needed to be said to honour the gods, but he had no intention of following through. Jason would be dead before the winter festival if he could manage it. He was simply buying time.

JJ Taylor

The feasting went on late and when we retired, Jason joined me in my bed, both of us having imbibed too much fig wine. It dulled my mind but heightened my senses, and I fell into his touch and the way he felt under my hands.

CHAPTER THIRTY·FOUR
A Wedding

Today. I seek joy in the coming darkness.

I SMOOTHED OIL OVER the wrinkles in my hands, irritated at the way my youth has abandoned my body even though my mind remains as sharp as it was when I was first chosen by the gods so long ago. It isn't worth thinking about and yet, at times I rail at the injustice of it. With a sigh I set the bottle down and turn to other thoughts.

The battle at Troy is causing its own type of earth-shaking. The people of the Anatolian peninsula are fleeing the destruction. There are tales of glorious battles, of gods interfering in fights, and of petulant heroes. Medus sends word that he and Dioscorus are camped beside the great hero Achilles, who spends more time in his tent with his lover, Patroclus, than he does on the battlefield, but when he does fight, he is an unleashed beast.

But Priam's walls hold, even as his people in the villages flee. The war is set to continue for a long time, with neither side inclined to surrender.

Men and their stupid pride. I laughed at myself, for I've been guilty of that sin for most of my life. Even now, I was proud of the palace changes I'd made, of the relationship I was building with the farmers, and the fact that we had enough food and water to take in those fleeing from Troy. I allowed them to set up their own village on the outskirts of Aia, so they could keep their ways intact. There was no threat, and the possibility of their gratitude outweighed any concerns there might be.

I made my way outside into the warm, moist air and let it fill me as I walked to Kip's villa, tucked behind the queen's quarters in the palace. I greeted her husband with a kiss. Neleus would always be Kip's first and most beautiful love, but the man who had begged her to be his wife not long after we'd returned to Aia was kind and charming, and he loved Kip like the sun loves the sky. I was happy for her, though I occasionally missed her company in my bed.

She smiled and nodded to the seat across from her when I entered. I sat and poured myself a cup of honeyed wine. I tilted my head when I looked at the needlework in her hands. "A new robe?"

She shook it out and held it up. "A wedding dress for your niece."

I'd forgotten about Chaliope's daughter and her soon-to-be wedding. "With Medus gone, I can't leave the throne unattended. I'll have to miss—"

"I've already arranged for the wedding to be held here. They arrive next week." She shook out the dress again and examined her stitching.

I leaned back and closed my eyes. "What would I have done without you?"

"Died in a ravine. Been eaten by wolves. Fallen overboard and drowned. Been turned to a particularly ugly flower after you insulted one too many goddesses." She grinned. "Your life would have been ruined."

I laughed. "True enough. I was bad enough with you to temper my darkness. Without you..." I shrugged.

"Without me, you might have gone on to challenge Hera herself and won. You might be sipping ambrosia on Mount Olympus while sitting in the lap of Apollo."

I grimaced. "He can keep his ambrosia and his lap. I've had more than enough of the gods for one lifetime."

We sat in silence for a while, birdsong the only sound. "Do you think my sister resents me?" I asked.

"If she did, she wouldn't allow her daughter to be wed here, and she'd thank the gods you couldn't go there." She gave me the look she always gave me when she thought I was being stupid. "What happened took place long ago, and your sister knows you loved her."

I nodded and sighed. "Thank you, Kip. For being the best thing in my life, always."

She threw a ball of yarn at me. "Don't get weepy. We're too old for that now."

I stood and moved to the door. "Have you already made the necessary arrangements with the kitchen?"

"I gave them basic instructions so they could begin gathering what food they could find without starving other people. I'm sure you can give better direction." She bit through a piece of thread and grinned at me.

As I went back to the palace, excitement began to course through me. A wedding was a perfect reason to celebrate, to bring the people together, and to give them something other than warfare to think about.

I made my way through the palace and held to a wall as the earth shook. I waited patiently, very nearly used to the tremors now. Though our walls shook and the forests swayed, it was rare there was any real damage here. We had news of far worse happening elsewhere, and those were reminders of the destruction and death I'd encountered on my journey so many years ago. People in need flooded the coastlines, and more were coming all the time. I welcomed them but told them to spread out among the communities beyond the palace walls so as to not put more pressure on the already slight stores in and around the palace itself.

The latest travellers had brought word from the battle at Troy, where the gods were as much part of the war as the humans swinging the bloody swords. I shuddered, glad to be far from anywhere the gods were using as a game board.

Being queen suited me as I'd always known it would. I gave the orders and they were carried out, much as they'd been when Medus was a boy and not yet ready to rule. But his shadow had always been there, overlapping mine, reminding me there was someone waiting to take that power from me.

Now, I spoke with the kitchen servants and discussed what was possible for my niece's wedding and all the celebrations we'd have leading up to and after it. I didn't want them arriving to a ramshackle, poor palace that could barely feed its own people. I would go hungry myself before I'd allow anyone to think my kingdom wasn't flourishing under me.

"My queen." Medus's advisor bowed low in front of me. Now that he had no charge, he seemed a ghost haunting the palace.

I inclined my head for him to speak. I'd never liked him, but Medus had wanted to keep him. Likely because he was useless.

"I thought you would want to know that your princely son has joined the fighting at Troy. The Aia soldiers have joined with the great heroes of Greece. I'm sure he will bring great honour to his father's name."

I arched my eyebrow. "And to his mother's, to be sure."

He flinched and bowed yet again. I wanted to bring up my knee and crush his nose, but my aching joints wouldn't allow that kind of thing anymore. Instead, I decided to remove him from my sight. "I have need of someone to take messages to certain kingdoms for me. Messages to the queens who also rule while their husbands are fighting for the honour of a man whose wife wanted someone younger and more pleasing."

He blanched and took a step back. "Yes, my queen. Of course."

I waved him off. "I'll have the gift offerings and messages ready by morning." In truth, there was no need. I'd already sent messengers to the two most important queens. But I wanted him out of the palace, and if it were true that Medus was fighting and could potentially survive, I wanted as many allies among the women as I could find.

Kip was there when I got back to my rooms, and she shook her head as she continued to stitch when I told her my plans. "You would have just killed him before."

"Now I can send him with other young people who are eager for adventure and who might find homes elsewhere along the way instead of starving to death here."

She frowned and examined a stitch, her old eyes meaning she had to move it here and there to see it well. "That may be well done, though I hate to think of it."

I didn't have a response. I sat in the window seat looking out over the crystalline waters of the river so far below. An old stirring reached me, and I wondered what was coming at us.

CHAPTER THIRTY-FIVE
Planning

My youth, as I learned my purpose.

THE DAYS PASSED IN hot, arid Iolcos and the season soon turned as Persephone was called back to Hades. Plans were made for the winter festival. The days and nights grew cold, and there was even snow. Kip spent more time with Neleus than me, but I was fine with that. The goddess was beneath my skin, always, and I waited and watched. I spent time talking with Phylomache, sometimes with her daughters present, sometimes alone, and she slowly seemed to come back to life. There were bruises on her arms and face on occasion, and red rage flooded me when the king would speak to her sharply. She and her daughters were under his hand, but the queen spoke of a time when he was young when he'd been full of joy and light, when he'd laughed freely and loved well.

"But the temple accident changed him." Phylomache wiped away tears, and her daughters comforted her.

"What happened?" I asked, keeping my voice steady though my hands shook on my needlework.

"He went with a scouting party to see if a city was plotting against his father. Fighting broke out, everything got out of hand. The temple was raided, and his stepmother was there. She'd left his father and dedicated herself to Hera, and he killed her for it there in the temple. They say her blood ran down the steps and into the gutter."

The answer was laid at my feet. All this, the journey, Jason, the gifts...they were all to avenge Hera's priestess. Killing in the temple was punishable by death. Killing a priestess was punishable by the gods. There would be no forgiveness.

Phylomache told her daughters to go to the washroom and get more cloth, and they left obediently. When they were gone, she turned to me.

"You understand this is a farce?"

I nodded and set down my sewing. "I do. I'm yet to understand my part in it."

"But you do have a part to play. Otherwise, the gods would not have brought you here." She bit her lip. "I'm glad you have come."

Strangely, I was too. She was trapped, much as my mother had been trapped, much as I feared being trapped as well. Marriage to a cruel man made life unbearable, and I knew she worried for her daughters. "Whatever is to come, remember your own strength. For you have plenty to have survived as long as you have."

She smiled that small, sad smile I was becoming accustomed to. Her daughters returned, and we went back to talk of small things. The girls became brave enough to begin asking about my life as a priestess and how I'd known about the food. "Did you know it was poisoned?" I asked. They said they had a feeling, but their father had given the instructions, and they had no idea which food was tainted. I believed them. They were too submissive to carry out anything so dishonourable.

As the days went on, I told them about the gifts from the gods, what it felt like to be god-ridden, and how I understood the winds and tides as I understood how to sew. The girls asked as many questions as they could think of, and Phylomache smiled indulgently. It would have been considered rude to ask so many questions of a stranger, but I didn't mind, and Phylomache was clearly pleased with their open curiosity. Jason, always with some of his men beside him, practiced with his sword in the courtyard and learned as much of the politics as he could.

Pelias's son, Acastus, was always there, lurking in the shadows, his malevolent glare trained on everyone but his mother, whom he softened for whenever she was in the room. And it was Acastus who sat with us at mid-day meal one day, lounging and looking as though he had nothing important to say.

"Have you spoken with your father yet, Jason?" he asked, eating a grape and looking innocent.

Jason leaned forwards. "I've asked Pelias several times where my father is, but he continues to not answer me. Do you know?"

Acastus stared at us, chewing like an animal from the field, and finally he leaned closer. "I do. And I think it's wrong to keep you apart." He stood. "Come. I'll take you to him."

Jason glanced at me, but I had no answer. There was no feeling of danger, but something was wrong. Several of the crew were nearby and fell into step behind Jason, and no explanation was given. It was obvious why Jason went about guarded and no one had questioned it, for to say something out loud is to acknowledge it, and no one from the palace wanted to admit that his life was in danger.

I followed, at the back and out of the way, so I could use what the gods had given me to see more fully. When we headed down the stairs and into the gloom, it became clear where Jason's father was.

Indeed, Acastus stopped in front of a cell door and motioned for the guard to open it. "My father couldn't afford the kind of rebellion a king who is no longer king could raise, so your father has been residing here."

The stench when the door opened was enough to make my eyes water, and several of the crew gagged and covered their noses. Jason, though, stepped into the cell and cried out from inside.

"Medea! Come!"

I wove my way through the men who remained on alert and went into the dim, dank cell. Jason knelt beside an old man who lay curled on his side on the floor, his robe in tatters and grime thick on his skin. His eyes fluttered as he held Jason's hand, but he quickly faded out of consciousness again. I knelt and touched his neck to feel for his pulse, then pulled back his eyelids and lips to see how close to death he was.

"Get him moved to a room and have a bath drawn. I will get my herbals and meet you there."

Jason nodded and slid his arms beneath his father, picking him up like a child who weighed nothing. He didn't stir, simply hung limp in Jason's arms, even when tears landed on his face.

Acastus wasn't there when we exited the cell. I feel certain that if he had been, Jason would have ordered him killed and thrown in the cell to rot. As it was, his grief mixed with his rage, and he seemed far away as we parted so I could go to our rooms for my things.

Kip was there when I went in and helped me gather the things I needed, and she ran with me to the room where Jason's father lay. Two of our crew stood outside the door on guard, for which I was grateful.

Jason had already stripped off his father's disgusting clothing, and servants were filling a copper bath with steaming water. I carefully mixed some of the herbs I'd been given by Aunt Circe in oil and water, and Jason held his father's head as I dripped it into his mouth.

The servants bathed him. It was clear to see they still revered the old king, as they were gentle with him and cleaned him well. He became alert a few times but seemed not to understand what was happening before he was gone again.

Jason's fury was wearing a hole in the thick rug as he paced, swearing and promising revenge. I wondered why Acastus had made this move. Was he hungry for war, or did he know that in a fight, Jason couldn't win? Did he hope to trick Jason into doing something foolish?

"Husband," I said quietly as he passed me again. He stopped to look down at me, as I remained at Aeson's side. "Revenge will be ours but let the goddess do as she will."

He stared at me, reading my eyes, and finally gave a curt nod.

"As you will." He left, and I saw Neleus glance at me before going after him.

The plan was already forming in my mind when Aeson finally opened his eyes and looked around the room late that night.

"Jason?"

I soothed his brow with a cool cloth. "I will send someone for him." I motioned to Kip, who slid from the room to retrieve Jason.

"I thought I heard cows, and the sirens were calling me. How I wanted to go to them."

His eyes watered, and I could tell he didn't see me. I tipped the mixture I'd created to his lips, and he drank, but not as deeply as when I gave him water.

He grasped my hand the moment Jason entered. "They killed them. My beautiful wife, my strong son. They killed them both." He began to sob like a child.

Jason knelt beside him and took his other hand. "Father, I'm here. No one harmed me, and someone will pay for what they've done." Tears scored his cheeks.

I stood to stretch the aches out of my back and left them to their reunion. Back in my room, I fell onto the bed, too exhausted to even undress.

When I woke, I wasn't alone. Jason slumbered beside me, his face drawn and his arm heavy across my waist. I wondered what it would feel like to have a parent treated so. Had it been my mother, I would have burned the palace down without a thought, but Jason's father had sent him away as an infant to keep him safe, and so the bond wasn't one of closeness. Was it pride that his own blood had been so reduced? Certainly, Aeson had been in a pitiable state.

I shifted, and Jason opened his eyes to look at me, not moving his arm.

"I thought you might have stayed with him through the night." I brushed hair from his eyes.

"I was too exhausted, so Neleus took over and I posted men outside the door." He sat up like a man with the world on his shoulders. "Pelias had my mother killed, and when they put my father in that cell, they told him I'd been found and killed too. If I'd known he was in a cell when I came here the first time." He glanced back at me. "Your potions may have saved him, but I fear his mind is broken."

I got out of bed, pulling my robe around me. "It may be true. And only the goddess can help the mind. I have no potions for that." I poured us water before sending a servant for breakfast. I returned to the bed and pulled him back to rest against the pillows.

"Would you have revenge, now that the morning has brought light to the darkness?" It was a calculated question. I needed to fully understand his frame of mind to know my next move. Even though I understood now that the goddess had brought me here for this purpose, I didn't want to misstep with Jason and end up impaled on a sword myself.

He took my hand and stroked it absently. "I remember them. Even though I was only a child when they sent me away, I remember my mother's kind smile and her light eyes, and I remember my father throwing me in the air and telling me I'd be a hero one day." He wiped at his tears. "Pelias took them from me, and then he took them from each other. He destroyed us. I would have him know what that feels like."

I nodded, allowing silence in case he had more to say, but he went quiet. "And would you take that revenge yourself?"

He let go and ran his hands through his hair in frustration. "Do I kill Acastus and allow Pelias to feel my pain? Or do I kill Pelias for the dishonour he's done all of us and reclaim my throne? If I do that, I'll have to face Acastus and whatever army backs him, and I fear I don't have enough men to do so. If I were to kill them both, would the people accept me? Could I do it quickly enough to take control, even with my few men?"

The plan that had been forming in my mind the night before began to solidify. "I have an answer from the goddess, if you would hear it."

He turned to me, his eyes wide. "Truly?"

There was a knock at the door, and the servants entered carrying the morning meal. I waited for it to be set up and motioned Jason to the table, which I'd moved to the middle of the room, away from any ears pressed to the walls.

"You know of the gifts I've received from the gods?" I slathered butter on my bread and poured us both wine. When he didn't move to eat, I pushed the bread to him. "You'll need your strength."

He nodded wearily and began to eat, keeping his eyes on me.

"I could use one of those gifts to...speak with Pelias, in my own way. And at the same time, you could have a conversation with Acastus. That way, we would be correcting their behaviour at the same exact moment, after which you would be free to see to other matters." It seemed silly to speak in riddles, but to say outright that we would kill the current ruler seemed foolish.

Jason sat back, chewing thoughtfully. "I think that discussion would work well, if we were able to speak to them both when they weren't busy."

I raised my glass and smiled wryly. "To discussions of worth."

That day, we stayed close to Aeson, speaking to him when he was awake and to one another when he slept.

"He will be expecting a fight," I said, speaking of Acastus. "You must be careful."

Jason continued to stare at his father's weathered, sorrow-filled face. "I will be, and I won't do it alone."

"Tomorrow, then, after the evening meal. I will need to do some things throughout the day." I made a mental list of the things I would need, aside from a trip to the temple for guidance. The other lives I'd taken had been out of necessity. My brother would have killed me had I had taken his life first, and Talos was a monster, and all heroes killed monsters. But this... Where did this fall? Was I a hero, despite being born a woman? Or would this be seen as an atrocity against the gods *because* I was a woman? I was reminded once again of the goddess's words to me. Mortal rules did not apply.

"Do you need aught from me?" he asked, barely looking at me.

"Time, as much as I can have, for once it is done, there will be no turning back." I squeezed his arm, hard. "You *must* be certain, and you must follow through."

He frowned, looking affronted. "They have dishonoured my family, my throne, and my kingdom. I will do what is necessary."

Satisfied but not completely convinced, I let go and stood. "Then I go to make my preparations. I will see you after it is done tomorrow night." At that point, he would be king, and I would be queen. My breath caught at the thought.

He nodded and turned back to his father, and I left. Kip, waiting outside, fell into step beside me. Her eyes were dark, her jaw clenched, but she said nothing until we were back in my room.

"The filthy bastard of a whore." She stomped to the wine and poured us each a glass. "Why keep him alive at all? Why not kill him and be done with it?"

I drank deeply and closed my eyes. "People in power like having people who cower beneath them. They like how it feels against their skin, that kind of fear and brokenness."

Kip stared out the window. "It's revolting and a crime against the gods."

I told her of Pelias's crime in the temple, and she trembled.

"Is that why we're here?" she whispered.

"I think it is. Hera may be angry at what happened in her temple, but on Jason's behalf, I'm equally angry about Pelias's abuse of those around him. I have no issue with implementing the goddess's justice." It was true, and it seemed I'd come to that conclusion without knowing it. "I have to decide how to go about it. I need to go to the temple."

We finished our wine in silence and made our way through the palace to the temple above and behind the gardens. It was chill, and we wrapped our robes tightly around us. Once there, the head priestess met us at the door. Her dark eyes searched my face as she blocked our way.

"I come to seek council from the goddess," I said, trying to remain polite.

"You bring darkness and suffering." She sighed and moved out of the way. "But it is already foretold, and there is no changing it."

Kip and I moved inside the warm temple, lit by an altar fire.

The priestess motioned to Kip. "You can pray and sacrifice here." She moved towards the back and looked at me. "There is a private room for you, priestess of Hecate, bringer of darkness."

I tilted my head, liking the moniker.

Kip grasped my hand and leaned close. "It could be a trap, Medea. Be wary. He's already killed in one temple."

I kissed Kip's cheek. "The goddess brought me here to do her will. She won't leave me now." They were bold words, given how unreliable the gods could be, but I believed it. I followed the priestess into a large dark room with a fire burning incense that filled the space. Before she turned to leave, I stopped her. "You said my coming was foretold?"

She leaned against the door like she had no strength. "I am the oracle of Iolcos. When I sensed darkness, I made the journey to Delphi to more fully understand. She said Hecate's witch would come to deliver Hera's justice, and when I saw you arrive, I knew it was time."

She looked tired and defeated, and I felt for her. "I do what the goddess demands, nothing more."

"As do I." She smiled slightly and left me alone.

I knelt on the warm stone and shivered. Now that it was upon me, now that I understood what I was to do, fear filled my heart. What if I wasn't strong enough? I bowed my head and called to Hecate and to Hera, asking for them to be at my side.

The now familiar breeze caressed my skin, and I looked up to find them both on the other side of the fire. Too large for the space, too powerful, too imposing, I shook under their gazes.

"Daughter, you asked for us, and we are here. You will right the wrongs and be our hands, letting mortal men know they will not disrespect us in our own temples, that they will not push us aside in our own cities so they might feel more like gods themselves."

The words were fire in the air, smoke filling my lungs, the pressure of cave walls crushing me. "I will do as you ask," I said, keeping my eyes on the fire to keep the fear from eating me alive.

"This is power, child of darkness. This is woman's power, which no man can compete with if you wield it without hesitation. You will be our hand on the world, and men will fall before you."

My heart sang from their promises, and I wanted to rush from the room and take up a sword to kill everyone in my path. But that wasn't me, and it took a moment to understand that.

"Use what we have given you. *All* that we have given you."

And then I was alone. Bereft and deeply glad they were gone so I could breathe once more, I lay down on the warm stone, my faced pressed to it as I knew what had to be done.

CHAPTER THIRTY-SIX
Cowardice

I MADE MY WAY through the palace, touching the walls, looking at the tapestries. I still felt outside myself, the world a surreal painting and I a flat person against a landscape.

At the entrance to the king's chambers, I was stopped by a guard.

"I bring gifts to the king and wish to speak with him." I stared him down, and he turned to lead the way to the king's receiving room. I shivered against the cool breeze flowing through the hall and nearly smiled at the mumbling of the guard, who said there must be a window open somewhere.

He left me, and I had the servants set up the items I'd brought with me. When Pelias entered the room, he frowned, quickly taking it all in.

"What is this?" he asked after nodding to me.

"A demonstration and an offer." I smiled and sat at the table, though he'd not invited me to do so. His eyes narrowed, and he sat across from me.

"I doubt any offer would interest me. I already have a wife." He looked me over, making my skin crawl. "Although a barbarian mistress would be interesting."

If anything solidified my desire to kill him, it was the way he looked at me then, but I smiled. "Any woman should be so blessed. I'm not here to offer myself, but rather to give you a gift from the gods." I motioned to the servant, who brought forwards a doddering, barely breathing ram. "Because you are a canny ruler who must see to believe, I have brought a way to prove the gods' benevolence." I stood and held up two vials. "The blood of

Talos the giant and a special potion from a more ancient goddess than any we know." I motioned, and the servant set the old ram in the enormous cauldron I'd also had the servants bring. Water splashed over the side as the ram disappeared beneath it. I said the words I knew by heart, the incantation to the goddess for life and strength, and I dropped in small amounts of each vial. I knelt beside the cauldron and prayed, and then stood and reached in.

I brought out a lamb, pure white fleece dripping, its tiny pink nose twitching, and held it aloft.

Pelias jumped from his seat and ran to the cauldron. He thrust his arms into it and searched. "That can't be. There is no such gift."

When he came up empty and turned to me, I handed him the lamb, which he took with wonder. "As I said, a gift from the gods. They offer you this gift, Pelias. If you step down from the throne with no blood shed, they offer you the gift of youth. You can start life again as a young man and make the world your own."

He stared at me, the lamb still clutched in his arms. I could see his thoughts whirling as he weighed his options and tried to find the trickery. Finally, he set the lamb down and it leapt away, past the stunned servants who shied away from it. He motioned to the seat, and I sat opposite him once more.

"I have no need of youth. The gods give no gifts without a heavy price, and I have paid mine. I have no desire to pay more before I move to Hades' domain."

I hadn't thought it would be so easy, but I'd wanted to try it this way first.

"I have promised to step down at the winter festival, have I not?" His gaze was shuttered, but there was no denying the malice in it.

"You have." I waited, wondering if I could say anything else without tipping my hand. "But power is a precious thing, and it's a rare king who would walk away as you say you will."

"Then perhaps I am a rare king." He stood and left without another word.

I waited, thinking, and then turned to one of the servants. "Bring me another old ram and get the princesses. Bring them here." It didn't occur to me that they wouldn't do as I bid, even though they weren't my servants. They soon would be.

He hurried off and I waited, thinking of what to say and praying again for the goddess to guide my hand. When the princesses entered, looking around fearfully for their father, I felt the heat of the goddess invading me as the room grew bright. The girls looked at me and shrank back.

"Come, princesses. I would never hurt such beautiful and sweet creatures." My voice boomed in the room, and they moved closer, shaking. "I have a gift from the goddess, but your father is too stubborn to see it. I believe you could convince him."

I hated using them this way. I hated their fear, their vulnerability. They were good girls, sweet and kind, and this would destroy those traits. But the goddess was speaking, and I had no choice. I turned to the man with the ram and bade him put it in the cauldron, then I dismissed the servants and told them to leave us. Once again, I used the two potions, said my prayers, and out jumped the lamb.

The princesses squealed over the cute little thing, exclaiming the goddess's praises.

"The gods would give your father the gift of youth, so that he might be kind and strong like he once was, before he desecrated the temple. But he is proud, and wilful, and will not accept. Will you make him as he was before, so he may be the kind of king people love?"

The girls said they would do whatever they could, and how happy their mother would be to have the man she'd once loved back.

"For it to work, he must be in this sacred cauldron, and he must be fully submerged. You must cut him to pieces so all of him fits, and he will come out, just as the lamb has." The words choked me, and bile filled my mouth, but there was no way to stop the goddess from using me.

The girls went silent and continued to caress the lamb. Eventually, the eldest girl spoke softly. "If the goddess wills it, then we will do it." She looked up at me, and I could see the fear and understanding in her eyes. "We follow the goddess where she wills."

I set a gleaming knife on the table, the edge sharp in the firelight. "The goddess hears you, but the gift is only available today, now. You must call your father to you and do it before sun sets."

I left, the vials in my pocket. There would be no rebirth for Pelias.

The goddess left me, like the sun leaving the sky at night, and I sagged against the wall in the hallway. My legs trembled, and my eyes watered. Slowly I made my way back to my rooms, wondering if Jason had finished with Acastus. When I opened my door and saw Jason sitting there, his head in his hands, I knew.

"You didn't do it." I sank into a chair.

He swallowed hard, his stare far away. "I'm not a killer. He sat at the table, unarmed, and refused to pick up a sword. He said that as long as his father lived, he had nothing to fear, and he knew that I would kill him in a fair fight. If I wanted to kill him, I would have to do it the coward's way and take his head from him there at the table." He looked at me pleadingly. "I am not a coward, and I will not disgrace the gods and my name by killing an unarmed man."

I sighed and let the weight of his stupidity ground me. "You should have taken his head when you had the chance. He will not be unarmed when he comes for us now that his father is dead."

He jumped up, knocking over his chair. "You killed him?"

"He is dead." I could feel it, that certainty. The goddess's satisfaction ran through me. I couldn't say I'd done it, but it was by my words it was done, and so I was as responsible as whoever had wielded the knife.

Jason ran to the door and called to his men. "Seal the doors. Watch for Acastus's men. Pelias is dead." He closed the door and turned to me, his expression grave and fearful. "I should have killed him."

I was tired to my soul, and I should have handled everything instead of leaving him to do his part. "But you didn't. The gods wanted this. It is why we were brought together. You have failed them, and we will both pay the price."

His eyes widened, and he had that look of fear I'd seen several times since we'd set off on this path together. Why the gods had chosen him, I would never understand. He was kind, and gentle, and not made to be the man of legends.

I stood, pushing on the table to keep myself up. "Acastus will come for us, and we have little time. Get your men, gather what you can, and get to the Argo. If we don't leave soon, we will not live till morning."

He left to do as I said, and I began to gather our belongings, though I kept dropping things. I heard the door open and shut and looked over my shoulder. "It is done?"

The queen nodded, tears sliding down her face. "My girls will never be the same. They came to me right after."

I shook my head and continued what I was doing. "No one ever is after the gods get hold of them." I turned and faced her. "For what it's worth, I'm sorry. I do as the goddess bids, nothing more."

She nodded again and sat in a chair, letting the tears fall. "I'm thankful they spared my son. I will make sure he's a better ruler than his father was." She looked at my bag. "You have little time."

The door opened and Kip slipped in, her eyes wide. "The girls—" She saw the queen and bowed her head.

"Speak freely."

Kip turned to me. "They cut the king to pieces. The servants said they went into a frenzy, screaming at him that he'd never touch them or their mother again. That the gods could have him. They put him in the potion, but they seemed to know he wouldn't be coming out of it reborn, as the lamb was." She touched the queen's shoulder but didn't say anything else.

The queen pushed to her feet and went to the door. "I will buy you what time I may. Goddess protect you." She hesitated before she left. "I will sacrifice in her name and thank her for sending you."

"You have an opportunity, Phylomache. Step into the light.

Wield the power of a queen and don't allow anyone to take it from you or your daughters ever again. You must change things if you wish them to change."

She looked at me for a long moment, and then took a deep breath as she left the room.

Kip pushed me into a chair. "You're no good if you don't have the strength to make it back to the Argo."

She moved around me like the wind, filling our trunks and bags, packing anything of value we might need, and then she got some servants she'd become friendly with to get our things and load them onto a chariot. Together, we climbed into the chariot and headed down the steep, dark road towards the harbour.

Behind us, shouts and torches flared into the night sky. The bell began to ring, and I heard the pronouncement from the walls.

"King Pelias is dead. King Acastus reigns! Find the son of Aeson and bring him to justice!"

I shivered, and Kip let go of the chariot with one hand to pull me close. I wasn't concerned about Jason making it back to the ship. I knew he would, that our journey together wasn't finished, much as I deeply wished it was. The sound of chariots behind us told me that the crew of the Argo was with us, and when we got to the ship, the men moved quickly. Kip and I stayed out of the way and watched as the flames lit the road from the palace. Jason rode up on a chariot and leapt from it before it had fully stopped. Together, he and another of the crew carried Aeson aboard, laying him at the front with Kip and I, who tried to make him comfortable.

Chariots raced towards the harbour, men in armour shouting for us to stop, demanding that the murderer of the king be brought before the gods for punishment.

"Go!" Jason yelled, and the Argo pulled away from the dock as the first chariots were arriving.

A few spears were cast our way, and one even stuck in the side of the ship, but Jason pulled it free and held it as we moved away from shore into the blackness of the night. It was all for show. They didn't get in the boats and follow us, and I knew the queen had told her son to let us go. Our work was done. And then I understood why Acastus had shown us Aeson. He'd known it would drive Jason to revenge, and that he would get his chance at being king. He'd played his hand well, and so we left what should have been ours. I couldn't help but wonder why the goddess had allowed this to happen.

"Jason? Where would you have us go?" Neleus asked.

He leaned on the railing and stared out into the night. "Medea?"

I stared into the night. They could go to Hades for all I cared, but I asked the question and received the answer. "Back to Corinth. We'll be welcome there."

Jason didn't respond, and Neleus shrugged and gave the crew the order.

Eventually, with the men subdued and silent, Jason turned to me. "I don't deserve to be king if I can't take what is mine."

Any other wife would have found soothing words, spoken of things that were meant to be, but I wouldn't lie to him or coddle him. "You had your chance, and you chose wrongly. Now we go where the gods take us."

He flinched like I'd struck him and turned away. I let him go, too tired to say anything more. Sometimes, there simply weren't any more words.

CHAPTER THIRTY·SEVEN
Shadows

By THE TIME WE reached Corinth, Aeson was upright. He still spoke nonsense, but he looked better. When we docked, he managed to walk, slowly, on his own. Soldiers escorted us to the palace, once again in chariots. On our arrival, Creon stood at the door, waiting.

"I expected word that you'd taken the crown." He clasped Jason's forearm, his gaze searching. "But you arrive in the dead hours and looking haunted instead." He looked past Jason to me and frowned. "And your wife looks like the gods are pulling her apart."

It surprised me, his astuteness, and I nodded slightly to acknowledge it.

"If you would give my men leave to find a place to sleep, I will explain."

Jason looked at me, as though unsure what else to say. I looked back, impassive. We'd been close, and we'd had the gods' blessing. He'd squandered it, and now we were in open waters in an unsteady ship.

Creon gave the orders to find bunks for the crew and took Jason by the arm. "Come. We have spiced wine that will warm you, and the fire is high."

We made our way into the more intimate living space, and I stood in front of the fire. Kip took my salty, damp cloak off and replaced it with a blanket before doing the same for herself and settling in a chair in the shadows by the fire.

Creon glanced at me and then at Jason. "Surely your wife would be more comfortable in a hot bath and bed than in here, speaking of men's affairs?"

I couldn't help but raise my eyebrow at that, and Creon flushed. "When you hear the tale, you'll understand there are no affairs in which I'm not included because I have breasts."

Jason gave a small, humourless laugh. "She speaks true, and she knows part of the story I have yet to hear."

Creon motioned, and we sat around the fire. All except for Neleus, who remained standing by the door. I understood why. If Creon reacted badly, we might need to fight our way out.

"You warned me," Jason said softly, turning his wine between his hands. "I thought maybe honour would guide him, or fear of the gods at least. But he was planning to kill me before the winter feast."

"I'm not surprised." Creon sipped his wine. "So you had to strike first."

Jason nodded. "We came up with a plan. Medea dealt with Pelias, who was in disfavour with the gods. I went to deal with his son." He sighed and dropped his head.

Creon frowned and looked at me. "What could a woman do that a warrior couldn't?"

"Women are capable of far more than you allow for." I debated telling him the truth and decided on a version of it. "During our time there, I showed his daughters magic given me by the gods. I turned an old ram into a lamb, so they would understand how important it was to stay virtuous and to give the gods the respect they deserve, unlike their father." I sipped the wine and saw Kip shift in the shadows, her eyes wide. "They begged me to make their father young again, but I refused, as only the gods hold sway over men's lives. They stole my potions, cut Pelias into pieces, and put him in my cauldron."

Creon choked on his wine.

"But they are not god-touched. They have no power, and so it didn't work." I shrugged. "It was my intention that night to go to him, to use the gifts from the gods to persuade him to give up the palace without bloodshed. He refused, and I left him with his daughters. The gods had their revenge."

There was silence after my somewhat altered tale. Jason looked like he might be sick. Creon's eyes were narrowed as he watched the fire, and I knew he was calculating the threat we'd brought to his feet if anyone from Iolcos came for us. I knew as well that he was debating the truth of my tale and my part in it. If I killed one king, why not another?

Finally, he turned to Jason. "And his son?"

"Acastus lives." Jason scrubbed at his face tiredly. "When I went to cut him down, he was surrounded by men. I couldn't get past them, and my chance was gone. I had to run as news of Pelias's death moved swiftly." He looked up, his eyes brighter. "If I had an army, perhaps I could move against him. If you were to support me—"

Creon was already shaking his head. "I'm sorry, my son. My army isn't nearly as strong as the one Acastus has put together. Even with your crew added to it, we could not take Iolcos." He reached out and grasped Jason's arm. "But I meant what I said before you left. You are my son, and you are welcome here. If any Thessalonians come for you, we will fight beside you. From here until Hades claims you, you can consider yourself Corinthian."

Tears fell down Jason's cheeks, and goddess help me, I think I hated him in that moment. I hated his cowardice, his unwillingness to do what had to be done. I hated his deep feelings, his openness, his lies to save his pride. I felt the knife cutting through my brother's throat, and the vehemence I felt towards Jason in that moment was much the same.

I stood. "Thank you for giving us safe harbour. I would like to sleep, if I may."

Creon stood and motioned to a servant. "Take the princess to her chamber."

I followed the servant without a backwards glance. If I looked at Jason again, I might scream curses at him, and I would not debase myself that way in what might be our new home.

We entered my room to find a bath had already been drawn, and I gratefully shed my clothes and sank beneath the hot water, letting it sluice off the salt and disappointment. Once I was in bed with Kip sleeping soundly beside me, I began to wonder what was next. I was married to Jason, yes. But what did that mean? It had happened in a moment of necessity, and I was more than a wife. I couldn't go back to Egrisi, at least not yet. In my soul, I knew the time would come when I would return. But it was far off. We didn't have to stay here, though. We could get back in the Argo and sail on, to places yet unseen. We could pray for guidance and continue to explore the unknown together. And if he didn't wish to leave? Could I go without him? A woman travelling on her own was unheard of, but a priestess had more freedom. If I were to travel from temple to temple to learn the ways of the gods, would that work?

The more I considered it, the more excited I became. I had done my duty by the gods. Pelias, who had transgressed against the gods by defaming their temple, was dead. Surely I was of no use to them now, and freedom would be mine. In the morning, I would go to the temple and pray for release. Satisfied, I slept.

I slept late, and when I woke, Kip was gone. I lay thinking, and then opened the door and asked the servant outside my door to find Kip. I dressed slowly in my priestess robes, donning the gifts given me by the gods. Kip came in with two other servants bearing food and wine. She dismissed them and pushed me into a seat to eat.

"Anything overheard?" I asked.

"There are doubts about your story, and there's a feeling that you took the knife to Pelias yourself, as you did your brother." She spread honey on warm bread and chewed thoughtfully. "That makes them fear you, and the princess has already gone to the temple to pray that your evil eye does not fall on this palace."

Fear could bring power, but it could also bring ruin. "And Creon?"

"Glad to have Jason back. He's worried that you're out of control but sees your usefulness." She pushed a piece of bread at me.

I ate without tasting anything and looked at her. "Alkippe, I need you to answer me truly when I ask you something."

She set her bread down and frowned. "Always."

"If I left here, if I ran and never stopped, would you come with me? Or would you stay here with Neleus and live a happy life?" It was an unfair question, but I needed to know if I would be alone.

She picked at the bread, rolling pieces between her fingers before she dropped them to the plate. "I've thought of that several times."

"And have you come to an answer?" My heart pounded in my chest. I hadn't known how desperately I wanted her at my side, how much I didn't want to leave by myself.

Tears welled in her eyes, and she brushed them away. "I would always choose you, Medea. We've been with each other since we were children, and I wouldn't let you go into the world alone."

"But you'd miss him. It would break a part of you." It was true, but I needed to say it out loud to believe it fully.

She nodded. "Yes."

I stood and pulled on a cloak. "I'm going to the temple to pray for guidance." I caressed her cheek and wiped away her tears with my thumb. "If it came to that, maybe he would go with us."

She shook her head, smiling sadly. "As I feel about you, he feels about Jason."

I left, making my way to the temple. There was no need for placating words between us, and as much as I wanted freedom, I didn't want to hurt my dearest and only friend either.

Once I was at the temple, I noticed how several of the priestesses pressed themselves to the wall as I passed, how they didn't make eye contact. Only Phryne gave me the kiss of greeting and took my arm as we made our way towards the private sanctuary at the back.

"It is too cold for Apollo's grove, but if you need to go there instead, we can get you a thick cloak. If the goddesses don't speak to you here, that is."

As always she spoke kindly, and she couldn't have known how much I needed her kindness that day. "Thank you. I believe they will hear me."

She lit the incense and glanced at me. "May I stay?"

I was reminded of priestesses in other temples who wished they were spoken to the way I was, and I nodded. To serve blindly all your life is hard for some. I knelt on the stone floor and breathed deeply, clearing my mind. I called to the goddesses I served, to Hecate and Hera, to old goddesses and to any who would answer.

We are here, daughter.

A chill wind blew through the room, making me shiver. *I have done as you asked, divine ones. The man who wronged your temple is dead, and you are avenged.*

You did well, child. You are the greatest mortal priestess of your time and will be treated with the respect due to kings.

Am I free? Can I leave here and see the world?

Laughter, cruel and emotionless, echoed off the walls. *You are devoted to the gods, and we still have need of you. When you are no longer needed, you will know.*

It was foolish, but I couldn't help myself. *You said I would have freedom and power if only I did as you said.*

The floor shook, and I barely kept my balance. Fear rattled through me, shaking me like dead leaves in a winter wind.

You dare question the gods? We will take it all away. All your power, your ability to see, your understanding of the water and men's minds. You will be left here to rot, a woman with no standing and nothing to offer.

Bile rose in my throat and tears burned my eyes. *No! Please. I meant no disrespect.* I couldn't say more without lying outright. But their threat was enough to keep me from saying more. Warmth slid up my hands, and I opened my eyes. Hecate, her wise, dark eyes looking into mine, held my hands in hers.

You are darkness, Medea. Seek balance, always. We are beside you, in you, with you. Have no doubts and use what we have given you.

In her eyes, I saw myself. Not a woman to be set aside. Not one to bare my breasts and bow to every man who walked past. No, I was far, far more than the world knew to understand, and in that, I was a goddess of darkness, like the one I served. Mysterious and misunderstood, I would stand tall no matter where I was. I cried and bowed my head and felt her hand caress my hair.

And then they were gone, their absence sucking the air from the room. I heard a whoosh of air behind me and looked back to see Phryne sitting against the wall.

"For the first time in my life, I'm glad the gods have ignored me." She stood, using the wall to support her. "Wine?"

I shivered and pulled the cloak around me. "Please."

Together we made our way to the dining area, and novice priestesses quickly brought wine and bread.

Her hands shaking, Phryne poured for us both. "Did you get the answers you sought?"

I considered the question. "I'm not sure. I have to think on it."

She nodded and sipped her wine, her eyes closed. "I saw her. At the end, the goddess." Her eyes opened, and they were full of tears. "She was so beautiful, so...so..." She shook her head. "I don't have the words."

I could think of several, but I kept them to myself. We sat in silence for some time, me pondering what the goddesses had said, Phryne staring into the fire, lost in her own thoughts. She startled me when she turned to me.

"You could be high priestess here."

I frowned, not understanding. "You are the high priestess."

"But the gods don't speak through me. They speak through you. And when people come to pray, you could give them real answers, give them something that matters."

I shook my head, exhausted. "I don't want to be high priestess. I want to be..." *Free.* "I don't know. But it isn't that." There was no mistaking the relief in her eyes, though she tried to hide it. She'd been worried about losing her position, and in that moment, I'd made a loyal friend without intending to do so.

"I am at your disposal. Whatever you need, come to me and I will help."

I smiled at the genuine offer. If she understood what I was, what I could do, she wouldn't be so quick to say so. "Thank you. There may come a day when I need your help. For now, I'd like to go to sleep."

She had a novice escort me back to my room, which was good because I was stumbling, I was so exhausted. Talking to gods saps one's strength more than fighting in a war, I'm sure.

After sleeping for several hours, I asked that my meal be brought to my room. I had no desire to face Creon, nor his daughter, or anyone else looking for answers. I was nearly done eating when Jason knocked and entered. He looked tired but not as downtrodden as he'd been the day before.

I motioned to the table. "They eat well here. Help yourself."

He thanked me and sat down, picking up an apple. "Thank you."

I tilted my head. "For?"

"For killing Pelias. For not unmanning me before the crew, though you had every right, and any other warrior would have called me coward without a thought." He set the apple on the table and rolled it absently under his hand. "I don't have my kingdom, and that is my fault and mine alone. But as always, you said you would do something, and you did it." He finally looked at me, and his eyes were full of tears. "The gods only know why I couldn't find it in me to do what I needed to when the moment came. Why would they allow me to falter?"

He was pleading, his hands upturned, truly wanting an answer. None came to me from a divine place, but I answered anyway. "They wanted Pelias dead. Once that happened, they turned away.

The gods are only interested in what serves them." He'd called me a warrior, in his own way, and I liked the way that felt. I was certainly more suited to it than he.

He held his head in his hands and wept. "Then any courage I had was false, given only by them in the first place. I had no right to rule if I couldn't be strong enough to take what was mine without the gods' intervention."

A different sort of wife would have consoled him. She would have fed him pretty falsehoods about the fates and destiny, and she would have held him to her breast.

I was not that sort of wife. I drank my wine in silence, letting that speak for me. There was truth to his words, and I would not make them false by denying them. "And now?" I finally asked. "Will we stay here? Or will we sail on?"

He seemed surprised. "Sail on? To where?"

So it hadn't even occurred to him. Granted, he hadn't had much time to think about it. "Anywhere we wish. We could board the Argo and set sail to distant lands. We could go in search of treasure and kingdoms we've yet to see."

"You would do that? Go without a home, without lands of your own? No family?"

I studied him, my hopes slowly falling to ash. "I had no home or lands of my own, nor family, the moment I left Egrisi for you. Sailing on the Argo would not change that."

He blanched and sat silently, thinking. Eventually, he shook his head. "I can't ask my men to go back to sea without any end in sight. They've already been away from their families for too long. The earth shakes, the crops burn, illness spreads. And..." He hesitated. "I am not a sailor, Medea. You've seen it. I enjoyed it, yes, but my heart is here on land, among the trees and animals, with people who care about me." He reached out and took my hand in his. "Will you give it a chance? See if you can be happy here with me? There are many places to explore, and I will show you them all."

I stood, pulling my hand away. "We are married in the eyes of the gods. If you stay, then so must I."

His expression fell, and he nodded. "If you are truly unhappy in the years to come, we will seek another home, I promise. But I believe we could be happy here, and in Creon's palace, we will be safe."

I stared at him, nearly uncomprehending. "And you will not try to take your kingdom back from Acastus? You will simply give up?"

He shrugged. "I have no army. No money. We will be living here by the king's grace. What would you have me do?"

I shook my head. "It's not for me to say, and I won't say anything further if you have made up your mind. As you said, if you aren't willing to fight for it, then you don't deserve it." I turned away and went to the window, dismissing him.

The chair scraped back. "Creon would like to speak with us, if you have a moment." His tone was distant and flat.

For a moment, I missed the easy feeling between us that had built on the ship, the sense that it was okay I'd given up everything and everyone for him. But it was only for a moment as I looked out at the crowded city spread below. "If the king wishes to speak with us, then we should go." Had I been queen, I could have told the king to go sing in Hades.

I walked beside Jason to the common room, where Creon and Glauke were sitting at a table. They rose when we entered, and Glauke embraced me.

"We will be sisters now," she said and kissed my cheek.

I smiled and nodded. "Thank you."

Creon motioned to the table, and we sat with them. "Medea, I understand you went to the temple today?" At my nod, he continued. "They say the building shuddered and a cold wind blew through the halls, and there was no question that the gods were visiting."

I nodded again, unsure where he was going with his questions.

"Then the gods themselves will agree with my decision to offer you hospitality, and to turn you away would be an afront to them."

He smiled and clapped Jason on the back.

I understood, then, though I don't believe Jason did. He was building himself a cushion. If anyone demanded retribution for Pelias's death, Creon could distance himself by saying he was respecting the gods. It gave our place in his kingdom validity, and no one would gainsay it. He was shrewd, and I wondered if I would ever grow to like him.

"There is a beautiful villa behind the palace, at the back of the gardens." Glauke leaned forwards, her pretty light hair falling over her shoulders. "It has been empty for a long time, but we think it would be perfect for you."

Jason smiled at her. "That is very generous, princess, but surely living here at the palace is too great a gift for people with nothing to offer. Had I not given the fleece to Pelias, I would gladly have given you that and more."

"Nonsense!" Creon slapped the table. "You're a fine warrior who completed a grand quest. Your name will be remembered by men for generations. Taught by Chiron himself, you will be my right hand, helping me fend off the grasping Mycenaeans." He tilted his head at me. "And you bring with you a wife of power, one who speaks with the gods, a woman of strength and beauty and unusual standing. She brings to us the god's blessings. You both have much to offer."

They were words of flattery, though there was a semblance of truth in them, and I liked that he had acknowledged that I wasn't like other women, even if he didn't mean it as a good thing. "Then we would be happy to accept your kind offer," I said.

"You and I can see about getting the villa fit to live in tomorrow morning, if you'd accept my service," Glauke said.

"I would appreciate that very much, thank you." In truth, I wanted little to do with her. There was a shadow attached to her, a feeling that made me want to put whole mountains between us. The connection between us felt twisted and dark, though I could see she didn't feel it at all. I shivered. *She will.*

CHAPTER THIRTY-EIGHT
An Impasse

TOGETHER, GLAUKE AND I walked quickly across the garden, past a beautiful stone fountain to a large villa in the trees. It was slightly overgrown, but I could see the beauty in the murals hidden by the vines, in the red pillars and thick stone steps. Inside it was dusty and dark, but after we opened the windows and let the sunshine in, the walls brightened. It was nicer than many of the houses we'd had on the palace grounds in Egrisi, and my frustration at being stuck in the city began to fade.

The group of servants who had come with us began to clean, and we directed them throughout.

Glauke linked her arm through mine. "Will you be happy here, Medea? It must be so different from where you're from."

"It is, and it isn't. We wouldn't allow sexual servants in the temple, but our palace is much like yours, except it's surrounded by trees so large you can barely see the sky in the middle of summer." The words brought a strange longing to see my home, and I pushed it away.

Glauke frowned. "I can't imagine not being able to see the sky, or to be so hidden from the view of the gods."

I laughed. "Do you think trees stop them from seeing you? I assure you, they can see you always, wherever you may be. I've spoken to them in caves, on the water, and in the forests. They are truly everywhere."

"Then," she said, "perhaps they are in the temple with the sexual servants."

Surprised at her wit, I laughed, and she laughed with me. The shadow that stretched between us remained, but until I understood it, I had no choice but to ignore it. That or risk offending her by avoiding her presence. "Yes, mayhap that is the case." We left the villa to the servants and made our way through the cold rain back to the palace, where we warmed ourselves by the fire with bread and wine. "Tell me more about your city."

She told me tales of gods who had been there, lovers who came together and were torn apart, of kings and queens of the past. "And now, there's tension with Mycenae."

I nodded, finally interested in what she was saying. "Creon mentioned that. What builds the tension between your cities?"

"Mycenae is wealthy. The palace is twice the size of ours, and their citizens double ours. They also have an army rumoured to be one of the best in the world. They force us to pay them taxes, to send tribute every year. If we don't, they threaten to take the city, and our army isn't strong enough to stand against them. In return, they send servants and slaves to the temple and in the lower temples in the city, but since it's many a Mycenae man who comes to pray, it still serves them well." She poured more wine. "I'm glad I was born to the palace and not to the commoners."

"And are you betrothed yet, princess?" I had no idea what made me ask, but I felt the need.

She shook her head, a pretty blush spreading over her cheeks. "There have been suitors, but my father hasn't felt any of them worthy. He waits to make a proper alliance."

"And if you could choose, is there a suitor you would have chosen for yourself?"

She stared at me, puzzled. "Why would I choose one for myself? Is that not my father's job? He knows best, after all."

I wanted to shake her, to tell her the world could be so much bigger. "But is there one you liked the look of?"

She smiled shyly. "In truth, there was one. He was quietly spoken, handsome, and gentle. But my father said he had nothing to offer and sent him away."

She wasn't interested in a strong warrior type like her father.

That was interesting, and something I would think on later. Knowledge was always worth having, as you never knew when it would become useful.

She leaned towards me. "Is it true you defied your father for love of Jason?"

That wasn't how I would tell the story, but the look of hope in her eyes made me soften. "The goddess came to us and made our hearts sing for each other and no one else. I could do no less than what he asked, and I couldn't bear to see him leave without me." It was true, in a way.

She sighed and drew circles in her wine with her fingertip. "I hope the goddess visits such a love on me one day."

The shadow darkened so I could barely see her and screams and smoke filled my senses for a moment. They cleared, and she was looking at me with concern.

"Are you feeling all right, Medea? You looked...odd."

"Visions sometimes come to me, though I can't make any sense of them. The goddess speaks in riddles, showing me shards of a puzzle that doesn't come clear until things come to pass." If I was going to live here, there was no sense in pretending to be less than what I was.

Her eyes went wide. "Are you a Pythia?" she whispered.

I laughed, and it sounded harsh in the big room. "Hardly. Pythias hand out riddles that are never wrong, and there's no sense in asking them questions because there's no way to change your fate; you only know that you have one." I sipped my wine, thinking. "I get a sense of things, sometimes pieces that tell me which way we should sail, or where it is we need to stop. I can feel people, sometimes, and know what type of person they are." I sighed. "Sometimes it's nothing but terror and destruction."

She sat back. "What if an oracle could make sense of the chaos for you?"

"What good would it do? What they say always comes to pass. If they were to tell me what caused the smoke and screams, there would be nothing at all I could do to stop it. What good is knowing?"

She frowned again and sat thinking. "I've never thought of it that way."

"Men want control of their destinies. They want to think they have a say in what will happen, in the way they will live and die." The wine began to taste bitter, and I pushed it aside. "But if the gods are paying attention to you at all, then you're nothing but a child's toy in their hands. Comprehending what they'll do with you is seeing the ocean about to sweep over you and knowing you'll drown."

"I see you're making the princess laugh with joy," Jason said, entering from a door behind us. "You're far too young to sound so old, my wife." He kissed my hand and sat beside me.

I forced a laugh. "My apologies, princess. I can become morose when contemplating the gods and their power over our lives. I suppose it's expected when you speak with them as I do."

She laughed too, also sounding forced. "I cannot begin to imagine what that must be like, and I find myself in awe of you, Medea. I hope to learn from you all I can."

Once again, the shadow shrouded her, and this time I turned away. "Have you been to see our villa?" I asked him.

"I was hoping to walk with you so we could see it together," he said, standing and holding out his hand.

I took it and smiled at the princess. "Do you mind?"

"No, of course not. Be well."

We left and made our way over the wet stones to the villa, and to my surprise, Jason continued to hold my hand as we walked. We walked through the villa, talking about where we'd put things and the view of the palace. We stopped at a large room with a few of the trees beyond.

"This would make a nice nursery." He turned from the window and looked at me.

I froze, wordless, and stared at him.

"I would like children, one day. Would you?"

"I...I've never thought about it."

He laughed. "Most women have thought about it long before they're your age, but it doesn't surprise me you haven't." He came forwards and took my hands in his. "We were brought together by the gods, and maybe we'll have strong words for one another sometimes. The gods know you're not an easy woman, not soft and pliable, but I love your strength. I think our children would be the best of us both."

I continued to stare at him, speechless. He kissed my hands and led me back outside.

"You don't have to answer me. Now or ever. But I wanted you to know what was in my heart."

I didn't say anything else, not during the walk back, nor when we separated inside the palace, he to talk to Creon, and me to my rooms. Kip was waiting for me there. I'd given her leave to spend time with Neleus while I was busy with the villa and the princess, but I was glad she was back.

"He wants to have children," I said, throwing myself backwards on the bed.

"Yes, that's often the way of things. Marriage, sex, children, old age, death." She counted them off on her fingers. "Many people want those things."

I sat up on my elbows. "Do you?"

She shrugged. "I'm a servant to a woman with a maddening desire to be free in a world of men. I try not to want things."

Her words stung, though I wasn't sure why. "You could marry Neleus and have a horde of babies."

"And maybe I will, one day." She tugged me to a sitting position and hugged me, letting the matter drop.

We ate together that night, talking of the city and the people in the palace, and it was good to have my friend back. With her, I had a home. As I went to sleep that night, I thanked the gods for her and for giving me a place to live. I could make it work here. I would, if that's what the gods wanted. Kip would be happy with

Neleus, and I would learn to be happy with Jason, who was, in his very simple way, a decent man.

I would learn.

Chapter Thirty-Nine
Ten Years in Corinth

"Don't put that in your mouth," I uttered the refrain I seemed to say a million times a day. I picked up my daughter and pulled the stone from her little hand. "You can't eat rocks, child."

She laughed and pressed her head to my shoulder, and I took her inside and laid her down to sleep through the afternoon heat. Her brother, one year older, was already curled into a ball, sound asleep. Though Jason and I had tried for a child for many years, it had only come to pass four years ago. I found I very much enjoyed being a mother, to my surprise. These little beings who were so dependent on me, who cared for me because I cared for them, who wanted my love and cared not a whit for the politics around us. Not yet, anyway.

I made my way out to the balcony and accepted the cold glass of water Kip handed me.

"Ten years, and I still can't stand how hot it gets here," she said, fanning herself.

"That's because it gets hotter each year." I went to sit in the small fountain we'd had put in five years ago, letting my feet cool off in the lukewarm water. Kip came and sat beside me, pulling her skirt up to her knees as well.

"You were screaming in your sleep again last night," she said.

"The same dream. Blood, and fire, and smoke." I shook my head. "The same dream I've been having since we made our way here."

"But?"

She knew me so well. No one else would have known I was holding back. "But it's getting stronger. The feeling of something terrible about to happen sits on my shoulders, pushing me to my knees."

"Is it time for your trip?"

I'd been putting off my trip to Delphi for nearly ten years. I had no desire to know the future, to speak to someone who likely had less power than I did. She would tell me something I couldn't do anything about, no matter what I did. "You know how I feel about that."

"Everyone knows how you feel about that. But what if she tells you that there's something you can do? Or will do, to make things better?"

I laughed. "When do they ever tell someone something good?"

"Fine. Then go so you can get away. See what's on the other side of the water. Pray in a different temple. Once, there was a time you couldn't wait to see how another chosen one spoke to the gods." She threw a pebble in the pool. "Maybe they have answers you haven't received about the weather and earth shaking."

In that, she had a point. The ground shook too regularly now, almost every day. Not always very strong, but enough to make people wary of putting breakables on shelves. And the heat had become truly unbearable. As had happened on our journey here, the crops had been dying off, starved of rain and scorched by the sun. Water was becoming scarce. People were leaving the city and seeking cooler places in the mountains or even further beyond them. Corinth was restless, and tempers were high. Fights broke out over small things, and large issues often resulted in death. "You're right. Maybe if I can bring back some answers, Creon will stop looking at me like I've grown snakes from my head."

She laughed. "Once you became the one who advised the dying on how to approach Hecate in the afterlife, you had no chance with the old morosoph."

It was a position I'd come to love, and it provided me with the freedom and power I'd craved. The gods had held up their side of our bargain, and although I wasn't as free as I'd wanted to be when I was younger, I was content, if sometimes lonely. The people of Corinth came to me for ailments of all kinds, from childbirth to fevers and broken bones. They came to me to ask of love and marriage but those, I turned away. The herbs from Circe and the potions from the temples I'd been to had come in useful over the years, helping me gain that freedom and respect I'd always craved.

I had Kip and Phryne, the high priestess, but I'm made no other true friends beside them, not in all these years. I remained an outsider, a woman of the gods. Useful, but feared. Glauke had her group of hangers-on, women who tattled and spoke of inane things. She'd been sweet when she was young, but she'd grown into a woman with a sharp tongue and hard eyes. Her father had probably been whispering in her ear, refusing to let her marry anyone who wasn't fit to be her equal in his eyes, and it had given her a sense of herself that was wholly unjustified.

I frowned when that thought led me elsewhere. Jason had been spending far, far too much time in the palace since Eriopis was born. He'd delighted in his son, Tisander, but even he seemed to have lost his shine. The boy sometimes asked after his father and cried when I said he was busy. I'd taken them to Jason in the palace several times, but when I saw he was with Glauke and not Creon, I'd refused to leave them there. I disliked the way she looked at my children, like they were vermin caught in the pantry. Once, several years ago, I'd heard her tell one of her servants to make sure the *barbarian witch* wasn't coming to dine with them. Ever since, I'd made my excuses when I was invited, which became ever more infrequent. I'd been close to Jason's father, Aeson. He'd never fully recovered his wits, but we'd spent many easy evenings by the fire, and I was sorry when he left for the next world. Jason, after his initial burst of familial duty, had kept his distance from his father, ashamed of his failure to regain the throne his father had lost.

I spent much of my time at the temple, and truth be told, I let the children come with me. They were coddled and watched after by the women serving there. They were safe, and I could sit at the side of the dying and alone and help ease their transition to the underworld. Phryne was happy to let me take on that part of her job, as it was one she found distasteful. But as a priestess of Hecate, with my potions and magic, I didn't mind it at all. I enjoyed the darkness and silence that came with the soul departing the body.

I stood, shaking the water from my feet. "I will go today."

Kip looked up at me, shading her eyes from the sun. "I'll watch the children. Be safe."

I squeezed her shoulder. "Thank you, sweet friend." When she and Neleus had wed, they'd moved into a smaller villa near ours, and I'd never seen her so happy. She still spent her days with me, and I was happy to share her with someone who made her smile so. For years, they'd been mine and Jason's companions, spending many nights drinking too much wine on the balcony. But then the war with Mycenae had come. Jason and many of his crew had joined with Creon's army and fought against the might of Mycenae.

Neleus had died in Jason's arms on the battlefield, and when Jason came home, a piece of him was forever broken. Kip had mourned deeply, torn apart in grief, and I'd done all I could to help her, from giving her sleeping potions to holding her as she wailed to the sky. She'd slowly crawled from her despair and had moved back in with me when I'd become pregnant with Tisander. Jason had been attached to me then, reaching out for me in his grief, and I'd been there for him. By the time our daughter had come along, his grief was nearly healed and instead of reaching for me, he turned away, spending more time at the palace instead.

I didn't understand it, and I didn't like it. I didn't care what he did with the women at the temple, and I'd heard that plenty of them had helped him pray, but if he disrespected me outside our bed with a woman not from the temple...that was different.

I changed into my priestess robes, donned my jewellery, and went to the palace. Jason, Creon, and Glauke were sitting in the shade of the portico, drinking wine. He barely glanced at me when

I moved to his side.

"Wife. Would you like some wine?" His tone was flat.

"No, thank you. I'm taking a boat to Delphi to see the Pythia."

At that, he looked up at me, as did the other two. "You hate oracles."

"I'm having visions too strong to ignore, but I'm not sure what to make of what I'm seeing." I held onto the chair as the earth shook beneath my feet, the low rumbling of the earth something we were getting used to. "And I'm going to see if they have any understanding of the earth shaking or the crops failing."

Creon tilted his cup to me. "A fine idea, Medea. You're always watching over us."

I narrowed my eyes and smiled at him. "Always." I looked at Jason. "The children are with Kip. Perhaps you'd like to see them while I'm gone?"

He nodded, staring into his wine. "Of course."

He wouldn't, and we both knew it, though I couldn't understand why. I turned away without further comment and made my way to a chariot, where a servant took me through the city to the docks. There was a single boat reserved for trips across the lake to the harbour at Delphi, and it was often in use in the cooler months. Right now, it bobbed gently, the rower resting in the bottom with his head under a thin piece of material to shade him. I tapped the boat with my foot, waking him.

"I need to go to Delphi."

He sat up and moved aside. "Of course, princess."

It pleased me to hear that old title used. "I haven't been called that in some time," I said after I'd settled in the boat and he'd shoved off.

"It wasn't long after you got here that we met, and I'm not surprised you don't remember me. My name is Sicarus." He smiled shyly, one tooth missing at the front. "My wife was having a terrible time bearing the baby, and I was afraid I would lose them both. But you showed up, and you gave her one of your potions, and you told her stories of your home to keep her mind occupied. When the baby was born, she wasn't breathing. But you prayed over her, and now she's a fire spirit who runs circles around both of us."

It was a touching story, and I vaguely remembered it, but I'd helped a great many women in birth. "I'm glad I could assist."

He pulled hard at the oars. "They're my life. I owe you everything."

"You owe me nothing. I'm a hand for the gods, nothing more."

"But it wasn't their hands mixing the potions or telling the stories. It was yours."

I let it go. If he wanted to believe that, I would let him. "How far is it to Athena's temple once we reach the harbour?"

He frowned, thinking. "Not more than half a day's journey, probably less. You can see the top of the temple from the harbour, and I'll take you into the inlet at Itea. The way along the Kirra Delphi is steep, but you can get a chariot at Itea. It's too far to walk in this heat, and there are cliffs that are unstable because of the earth shaking." He slowed and looked towards the mouth of the gulf that led out to the sea. An enormous boat was entering, painted with bright eyes at the front and ocean waves along the side. A drumbeat pulsed across the water.

"Who are they?" I asked, feeling a pull towards them.

"The Sea People."

I remembered them from our adventure. "Truly? I've heard much of them over the years. I even saw them from a distance, once, many years ago. I didn't know they were coming here."

He spit over the side of the boat. "They're a strange mix. People from all over who have no land and who prefer to live at sea, taking what they can wherever they stop."

That sounded like freedom. It was a word I hadn't thought much of these last ten years. But that was what they had, to a truer degree than I did. Now, it nearly hurt to think of it.

We docked at Itea, and he pointed out the path to me. He promised to wait for me no matter long it took.

I hired a chariot driven by a woman, which was strange, but

she explained that only women were allowed into Athena's inner temple. Men had to go to the main temple at the palace. It was an interesting difference from Corinth, but I was far from there now, and as we made our way higher up the steep mountain and the edges fell away on one side and grew ever taller on the other, I felt even further away. The air grew cooler and the trees a little greener, less parched than they were far below. Mist hung between the mountain's thighs in the distance and the beauty made my heart ache. This felt more like Egrisi than anywhere else I'd been in Thessaly and a strange desire to go back swept over me. We passed the palace, and it was surprisingly busy. People lounged on terraces built against the massive craggy mountain side, chariots moved every direction, and the temple to Apollo stood sentinel over it all, massive pillars facing the valley before it.

We went further, until the path began to go downhill. The chariot driver stopped and pointed. "Down those steps between the trees, and you'll find someone else to take you to the temple."

I thanked her and paid her extra, and with a quick smile, she set off back to the harbour. I turned and followed the white stone steps carved into the mountainside, down into an almost hidden valley. At the bottom, I looked up and couldn't see the path above, nor the temple or palace. It was as though I'd dropped into another world, one that was quiet and smelled of sun-bleached pine. A temple priestess bowed to me and walked ahead, not speaking. I followed her past several small buildings, all beautifully built of stone and wood, to a temple that stood by itself in the middle. It was round, which was something I'd never seen, and I liked it instantly. Pillars set on a plinth encircled a room hardly bigger than my room at the villa, but it was cool and scented inside. I took off my sandals and washed my feet before walking in further.

"Medea, priestess of Hecate. We've long waited for you to come."

The voice came out of the shadows, and I moved towards it. At the back, sitting on massive stone was the Pythia. Her grey hair fell in soft waves to her waist and her unseeing eyes looked towards me, milky and clouded. Her hands, long bony claws, reached for me, and I took them.

"So much destruction. Do you see it?"

I knelt before her, wanting to lay my head in her lap. "From morning to night, I'm aware of it, and my dreams are overrun with blood and terror."

She nodded, releasing one of my hands to stroke my head. "To be a god's chosen is a heavy burden."

For the first time I was with someone who truly understood that, and I began to weep.

"I know, child." She stroked my head. "Remember this, always. For those of us chosen to serve, there is no other path. What happens is what was decided would happen long ago, because time for them is different than it is for us."

I wept, not saying anything, simply glad to be in a place where I felt I belonged and was understood. Why had I waited so long to come?

After a time, she sighed. "You were once told you would have to choose and choose again. Those choices are yours to make, and soon you will choose so that your path is set before you once more."

"Will it be my fault?" I whispered, already knowing the truth. "The blood and fear. Will it be my doing?"

She nodded slowly. "In some ways, yes. But the gods are starting again, making us understand how small we are. Your part in it is a winter leaf buried under snow, nothing more." She paused. "And yet, you will be remembered for what is about to come."

"If I knew—"

"You know better, Medea. It will happen whether you know it beforehand or not. Let the gods do what they will, and remember you are their hand."

From the moment I'd met Jason, those words had been with me. To be remembered, just as the heroes were remembered. The hand of the goddess, doing her will. But there was an ominous feeling beneath her words, as gently as they were delivered. I remembered my conversation with Kip. "And the earth shaking and sun scorching? Is that the gods starting over?"

She nodded again, in a way that left no doubt she understood things no one else could. "It is, and there is no stopping it. Some will survive, some will not. Nothing is forever. You were told once about balance. Dark times come, but there will be light again."

She stopped talking, and I knelt there until my legs went numb and I grew tired. She never said another word, even when I kissed her cheek and thanked her. I was given a small, plain room in a nearby home, and I lay awake looking at the ceiling. As I suspected, she hadn't told me much I hadn't already known, but she seemed to be forgiving me for whatever it was I was about to do. The Pythia was the voice of the gods as I was their hand, and if she was forgiving me, then so were they. It was small comfort. I finally fell asleep, and with no children to worry over and no husband to wonder about, I slept well.

CHAPTER FORTY
Destruction

THE GROUND BEGAN TO shake in earnest, harder than it ever had before, waking me in the blackest hour of night. The roaring of Hades' domain rumbled through the ground and into the air. I stumbled outside and pitched to the ground on my hands and knees, watching, horrified, as the craggy mountainsides began to rain down boulders on the houses at their base, crushing them and whoever remained inside. The temple swayed behind me, the roof falling as the pillars toppled over, sending clouds of dirt into the air. All around me were screams and pleas for the gods to help us. But the gods were no longer listening, at least not to prayers for help. I stayed on my hands and knees, waiting for the land to stop moving, feeling like it was jarring my skin from my bones. When it stopped, I climbed shakily to my feet and looked around, stunned at the damage. None of the buildings around me had escaped damage, and the one I'd been sleeping in was buried under rubble. Had I not come outside, I would be waiting on the bank of the Styx.

I moved from pile of rubble to pile of rubble, sometimes helping a priestess out, sometimes seeing there was no point in trying. Once I'd done what I could, I climbed the broken steps leading up to the main road, and I nearly dropped to my knees once more at what I saw.

The mountainsides had collapsed on the houses, knife-like slivers of mountain slicing through the city, demolishing everything. Compared to the city, Athena's temple area had hardly been touched. The silence, deep and dense, was sickening. Crying could be heard here and there, though the cries for help should have been loud.

But there was no one to cry out.

I made my way back to Athena's temple, praying for guidance and for those who needed help, but I was alone in the darkness under the full moon. Torches surrounded the Pythia's home, and I went towards them. Priestesses knelt beside her prone, bloodied figure. Wheezing, bloody froth came from her mouth as she lifted her hands.

"It has begun, my daughters. Help those you can and stay by each other to keep yourselves safe." She wheezed and coughed, and a priestess stroked her brow with a wet cloth. "You must leave this place. We serve the gods who created us and who make our lives what they are. Do what you have trained to do. Athena, great earth mother Gaia, watch over our daughters who serve you. Make them strong enough to survive what will come."

Her hands fell, she gave a last long breath, and was gone.

The priestesses began to weep and wail, grieving for their leader. But I had already used all my tears, and it was time to move forwards. Had the earth shaking hit Corinth so hard? Were my children safe? I had to know. I climbed back up the hillside and picked my way through the rubble to the chariot stand at the far edge of the city. Remarkably, one chariot remained intact, and I tethered to it a horse I found locked in the stable. The journey back to the harbour was slow and dangerous as I navigated around rockfalls and earth that had fallen away where the path once was. By the time I made it to flat land, my hands were shaking with exhaustion. The horse looked worse than I felt, and when I could see there would be no getting the chariot through the rubble of the city before me, I got out and untethered it, setting it free. It didn't run, but it would go where it wanted when it had rested, and I felt better for that.

Slowly, I picked my way through the rubble, helping where I could, but always moving forwards. I promised to pray to the gods for answers, and said no, I didn't know why this had happened. Anger pulsed beneath the fear, and there were no few looks sent my way that suggested their need to take out their emotions on someone, especially someone meant to help protect them. The waters were higher when I reached the harbour, and Sicarus waved to me from where he held the boat to a pillar of the dock. I hurried over and he helped me to board, then set off right away.

"I'm glad to see you're well, princess. Did Athena protect her temple?"

I shook my head, swallowing at the image of the crushed city and the dead Pythia. "The gods won't save us now. Delphi is destroyed."

He stopped rowing and stared at me, horror etched in the lines of his face.

"Please. I would make sure my children are safe."

He began rowing again and said nothing else until we reached Corinth. But the harbour there was gone, replaced by water that ran in from the gulf, flooding the city. He rowed in, past the houses where people perched on their roofs, holding their children tightly. Some began to call him but when they saw me, a robed priestess aboard, they stopped. None of them expected help from a priestess in the temple of Corinth, and that enraged me. Worship had been turned into something ugly here, and it served the people in no way. Still, I let Sicarus row on, desperate as I was to see my children.

He stopped rowing and pointed. "The water reaches only to the lower groves. I'll get you as close as I can." He manoeuvred past a cluster of houses and bumped against something.

I looked over and saw a group of bodies tangled together, floating face down. I turned away and asked the goddess what misery she'd heaped on these people but got no answer. Sicarus gently moved the bodies away and kept rowing, but he looked ill.

He got near to a house that butted up against the hillside, and the path to the palace was behind it. "I fear I can't get you any closer, princess."

I nodded and leaned forwards, placing my hand to his chest.

"May the gods bless you, Sicarus, and if you have need of me again, I will be at your side."

He took my hand and kissed it. "We are all at the mercy of the gods now, princess. Be well."

I got out and managed to climb onto the roof on my hands and knees, then scuttled along the top until I got to the end. I lowered myself into the murky water that went up to my waist and moved clumsily towards higher ground, slipping and sliding so that I was wet through by the time I made it to the path. I looked back, but Sicarus was already gone, helping others move from their roof tops to land as well. I began to climb, stepping around rocks and fallen trees, until I finally saw the torches lighting the villas below the palace.

Phryne came out of the dark and wrapped her arm around me, helping me to the nearest house, which happened to be hers. I'd been there many times over the years, a place of sanctuary and calm, as it was now.

"How has the palace fared?" I asked, gratefully accepting the towel and dry gown.

"Still standing. Delphi?"

I shook my head but couldn't find the words to say anything else.

She swallowed hard. "After the earth shaking, the water came in so fast, like Poseidon himself was riding dolphins into the city. No one had time to get out."

I struggled to my feet. "I need to get home."

"I'll walk with you. I want to check on the temple."

Together, we made our way up the hill to the palace. She squeezed my hand once before we separated, her to the temple, me to my home. When I opened the door, Kip rushed to me and threw her arms around me.

"I was so worried you wouldn't come back to me," she said into my neck.

"I very nearly didn't." I told her what had happened at Delphi, and that the Pythia was dead. I looked in on my children, who were sleeping peacefully with no idea that the world outside their door was drowning.

**

Come morning, the palace was overrun with people from the city begging Creon for help, for answers, for hope. He sent his army to help the survivors, and sent women to the temple to pray, not on their backs but on their knees, their arms full of offerings. I wasn't surprised when he called for me, but I refused to go. I stayed beside my children, watching them play, and his irritation was clear when he arrived at my door.

"When a king calls, you obey." He looked down his nose at me.

"When a god destroys a city, you realize how small a king is," I said, not looking away.

"What did the Pythia say?"

"She died." I liked the way he flinched. "She said the gods are starting over, and there's nothing we can do about it."

His face turned the red of late autumn leaves, blotchy and ugly. "So you give up? You stop praying on the people's behalf? What kind of priestess are you?"

I stood, letting my loneliness, my rage, my desperation loose. "I am Medea, priestess of the dark goddess, Hecate. I am Medea, princess of Egrisi, granddaughter of Helios, beloved of Poseidon who loved my mother. I am like no priestess or woman you have ever known, and if you do not understand that by now, Creon, then you are more ignorant than a fish on land."

He raised his hand as if to hit me, and then seemed to rethink it. I was as tall as he, and I didn't look away or cower. He backed away, malice coming off him in waves like the ones swamping the city below.

"You will be sorry, witch. I will show you that you're like any other woman. You brought misery to my city, and I will ask the gods to show you your rightful place."

He stormed off to the palace, and I sighed and sat on the balcony. It was time to move on, with or without Jason. There was no love lost between us anymore, and Corinth was going to be gone soon. I should go before it was too late.

CHAPTER FORTY-ONE
A Choice

MY SKIN CRAWLED WITH foreboding, shadows dancing along the edges of my vision. Screams and death surrounded me, sometimes in reality, sometimes in my mind, often mixing together so I wasn't certain where to place my feet. I grew irritable, snapping at every little thing, and felt myself descending into madness. I prayed, I begged the gods to make it stop until it so consumed me that I couldn't breathe and had no notion of where I was at any given time.

I was lost, and the gods were letting me wander into the fields of venomous asphodel with no guide.

Three days after Creon's visit, unable to stand the desire to rip off my skin and throw it from the balcony, I made my way on foot to the market at the harbour, pulled to see what it held. People blurred together, turning from selling their wares to screaming and bleeding on broken streets. I pushed through them, past them, desperate to get to the water.

I stumbled to a halt at the dock and closed my eyes, blocking out everything but the scent of the water, the sound of it lapping against the wood. My mind began to return to me, and the shaking in my limbs eased as I felt the old ebb and flow that still spoke to me. I breathed deeply, feeling rooted to the ground, and realized I'd walked all the way here with no sandals on. I looked at my feet and saw they were dusty and bloody, and then they began to throb. I hobbled to a stone wall and swung my legs over the side, letting my feet dangle in the water. The sting of the salt made my eyes tear, but soon they were clean, and the throbbing eased.

"Medea?"

A familiar voice made me turn, and my heart leapt at the sight. "Chaon!"

He rushed to me and hugged me awkwardly, as I remained sitting over the wall. I pushed away and turned to embrace him more fully.

"I heard of the powerful witch in Corinth and wondered if it was you. How the gods have blessed me this day." He held me at arm's length, his gaze penetrating.

He was older now, as was I. Grey peppered his hair and faint lines were appearing at his eyes, and I loved him even more. What did he see when he looked at me? The body of a mother, not a maid, a few grey strands appearing in my hair as well. But the way he looked at me was as he'd looked at me when we'd met so long ago now.

"Why are you in Corinth, Chaon?" The shadow that followed me hovered nearby.

He sighed deeply and sat on the wall beside me. "The earth shaking and the drought have driven us to find a new home. There's no water and the crops have died. Fever spread, and I lost many of my people." He caressed my hand gently. "The Sea People arrived at the moment when there was no hope. I'd sent all I could, but the food was gone and the wells had run dry. I didn't have enough ships to take everyone away, but they made room for us, and we abandoned our home."

"And are you Sea People now as well?" I asked.

"Some are. Those who like living at sea and going from place to place. Others, like me, prefer land and hope to find a home one day."

Breathless, I clasped his hand to my breast. "You could stay here, in Corinth."

He smiled sadly. "Corinth is a stop, nothing more. You see the destruction of the earth shaking." He kissed my hand. "You, of all people, know it will get worse. No city is safe."

I began to weep, and he pulled me to him and held me as I wept like I rarely had before, letting my frustration and loneliness fall with my tears. My tautly strung body ached as I sobbed in his arms, and he said nothing.

"Is it so bad, princess?" he murmured into my hair when I'd finally cried myself out.

"I was forced to marry Jason or be sent back to my father. We have children, and I fear he loathes us all now." I swallowed hard, but let the words come. "I hate it here. I hate what I'm becoming. I hate the people. I hate him." Had there been actual venom in my words, people around me would have died painfully.

He turned me to him. "Then leave with me. Bring your children, and come with me, Medea. Be with me, as we were meant to be."

Was it possible? Could I do so? The gods had kept me in check for so long, and the visions were so consuming, I wasn't sure what I could and couldn't do anymore. If I prayed on it, I was asking permission, which might not be granted. But if I didn't ask, if I simply left...

"Yes. I will come with you." Laughter filled me, and I let it slip out. "When do you depart?"

"Tomorrow morning. We were only meant to stop briefly. Will you be here at sunrise? I will gladly accept your children as my own."

"You never married?" I hated the thought of him with anyone else, but to expect him never to love was absurd.

"I did. A princess from another town along the river. But the fever took her a few years ago, and we never had children." His tone was missing the passion of someone deeply loved, and it made me glad.

"I will meet you in the morning." I slid from the wall and waved down a chariot. "We will start life anew, as Persephone brings the spring."

He kissed me and made my knees weak. "Until morning."

I got in the chariot and barely noticed anything on the way back to the palace. My feet continued to ache, but it was nothing to the joy consuming me. The gods were rewarding me for all I'd done, and I would take this chance at love and freedom and never look back.

At the villa, Kip was waiting and looked up warily when I came in. I rushed to her and hugged her fiercely. "Gather our belongings and help me pack the children's things. We leave in the morning." I turned and began piling items in my arms, taking them to the bed and tossing them in heaps.

"What do you mean we leave? You're married. And where are we to go? How will we pay our way? Women can't travel alone."

I reached beneath the bed and opened a chest full of money I'd been building up over the years. "We have the funds. Chaon is in the harbour and has asked us to leave with him, to start over somewhere else. Us and the children." Kip stared at me, and I could see that she was wondering if this was one of my fits of madness. I didn't blame her. "I promise, I'm here right now, all of me. The gods have given us a gift."

She turned and ran into the other room, dragging out trunks for our things. "We will have to slip out under cover. I'll find a chariot driver who can hold their tongue." She began folding the children's clothes haphazardly.

Together we made quick work of what we wanted to take, and when the children came back from visiting their father at the palace, subdued as they always were after seeing him, they looked around in surprise. I knelt before them, taking them in my arms. "My loves, we are going on an adventure. Would you like to go on a big boat and see dolphins and many other magical creatures?" Their sweet choruses of yes made me smile, and my heart was lightened. "You must go to sleep now, because we must leave very early in the morning."

Tisander twirled a piece of my hair, as he was prone to do. "Will father be coming too?"

I glanced at Kip, who shook her head slightly. "No, my love. This is an adventure for the three of us. Is that all right with you?"

His little face brightened. "Yes, Momma."

I tucked them in, kissing their heads, my heart bursting with love that I'd never felt for any other creatures on earth.

Kip left to find us a chariot, and I finished packing. When there was a knock at the door, I froze, ice spreading from my chest. But I held my head high and opened it slightly.

I was knocked to the floor as it was slammed all the way open, and two guards took hold of me. I fought and twisted, kicking over tables and managing to draw blood from one of their noses, but then one brought his fist down hard on my head, and the world went dark.

***

I woke in darkness so complete I couldn't see my hand in front of my face. Visions swarmed around me, mixing with the scrabbling of rats in the pitch black. I felt around me and sat up, quickly vomiting as my head spun and my stomach rebelled at the pain. When I was done retching, I slid away from the wet spot and felt my way to a wall, which I leaned against.

This would be Creon's doing. Panic surged through me as I thought of Chaon, waiting for me at the harbour. Would he stay? Would he think I'd changed my mind? The possibility that they knew about him, that spies had seen us together, made my stomach churn again. Would they kill him?

I got to my knees, unbalanced by the storm of fire and chaos of screams surrounding me.

Please. Please don't abandon me. Please hear me and help me.

We told you we would continue to use you. Your powers have grown, and you have been respected, as we said you would be. Now you will repay us again.

No! I pounded the floor with my fists. *No! You must let me go to him. Let me take my children and leave. Take your gifts away, I don't care. You have ruined my life.* I doubled over as it felt like someone was crushing my throat. I clasped at it, trying to breathe. I was being kept from saying anything more final.

They were gone, and the visions overwhelmed me. Fire singed my skin, and terror made me scream as something chased me through crumbling streets. From a distance, I heard the creak and groan of a metal door scraping open, but I couldn't see past what was to come.

Someone grabbed my shoulders and lifted me, dragging me from the cell into the light and up the stairs, but still I saw nothing and was barely aware of my surroundings.

I was pushed to my knees, the visions faded, and I could see once again. Creon and Glauke sat on their thrones. Before them, Jason stood looking down at me.

"Chaon has been informed that you are married. They set sail an hour ago." His eyes, once kind and thoughtful, were hard and distant.

"You don't want me." My voice was parched gravel. "Let me leave and be happy."

He shrugged. "If you weren't trying to take my children, I would have let you." He squatted in front of me. "Where have you hidden them?"

Thank the gods. Kip must have seen the mess when she'd come back and had an idea of what had happened. And of course, the children would have woken. "They were in bed sleeping when you abducted me."

"Then where would Alkippe have taken them?" He grabbed my hair and forced my head back. "I will find them."

I stared at him, refusing to show any fear, and with a grunt, he shoved me away.

Standing with his arms crossed, he looked down at me. "Creon has offered me Glauke's hand, and I have accepted. I will set you aside, barbarian princess, and marry one of my own. In this way, we'll appease the gods. I will be king of Corinth, and you will leave the city, *without* my children, who will be raised in the palace."

I looked over his shoulder and knew from the look in Glauke's eyes that my children wouldn't live long enough to grow up here. He was setting me aside, and yet he'd sent Chaon away, only to dash any chance of freedom or happiness. "How dare you?" I stood slowly, pulling myself to my full height, silently calling on the goddess to come to my aid and hear my words. "You promised the gods to be faithful to me. You swore an oath to always be at my side, to protect me. Are you an oath breaker, Jason of Iolcos, son of Aeson? I know you're a coward, but I never thought you would openly offend the gods."

He blanched slightly, but Creon stood. "You cannot be forsworn to the gods when married to a barbarian. Sacred oaths only apply to our own, not to others."

They swam before me, swaying and twitching, and rage like I'd never known filled me. I let the goddess come, let her take over, and Jason stepped back quickly. Glauke gasped, and Creon stepped in front of her.

"You are forsworn, Jason of Iolcos, son of Aeson. You will know the god's wrath. Creon of Corinth, you have forgotten the warning provided you when we arrived."

I turned away, walked from the room. Not as myself, but as the vengeful goddess who would not be denied. The rage felt cleansing, burning as it did through my soul, erasing my fear and replacing it with the purity of fire. Together, we went to the villa. I went into one of my trunks and pulled a wedding dress from it. I'd made it for a young woman who had died before she'd gotten to wear it.

From a high shelf, I pulled down my old box of potions, mixtures I'd created and been given on our journey to Iolcos. The black potion that swirled with shadows and the blood of Talos combined with other potions I'd been given, and we mixed them in a cauldron that bubbled and smoked with a fragrance as sweet as spring but as black as a moonless winter sky. And it was death we cleansed the wedding dress with, dipping it in and coating it well, and when it came out, it was dry, and only I could see the sickly green tinge to it. Deep down, part of me rebelled at this, but the larger part of me, the part attached to the goddess of darkness, revelled in it. I wrapped it in linen.

I rang a bell, and an older child came running. "Take this to the princess. Tell her Medea said she was deeply sorry, and she hopes this will bring peace and passion to her wedding bed."

He took it without question and ran off.

CHAPTER FORTY-TWO
Death

I WENT TO THE balcony overlooking the garden and waited... The goddess and I waiting for the carnage to come. I'd once been told that mortal rules didn't apply to me. In that moment, I understood.

It wasn't long before Glauke's shrieks of agony cleaved the air, and the goddess inside me rose up, vindicated. Together, we watched from a distance as she ran into the garden, tearing at the gown that clung to her, the poison seeping into her skin and melting it away. Blood trailed behind her and seeped through the gown in places, creating a gruesome patchwork. She tore at it, pulling away sections that ripped off more skin. I leaned on the railing and watched in fascination as Creon ran to her, grasped the back of the gown and tried to pull it off. But when he touched it, his hands stuck to it, and as he tried to break free, he stuck to her, and soon their screams mingled as they tumbled together into the fountain, trying to wash it off.

The water turned inky red and spilled over onto the stones as they splashed and writhed. Jason stood at the edge of the monstrous scene, tears streaming down his face, his arms outstretched as though to help, but there was nothing he could do but watch as the people he'd chosen over me, the ambition he'd decided was more important than our marriage and his vows, of our time together, were turned into a messy wet pile of entrails and effluence.

The water stopped churning, and the silence turned to wails as the servants began to lament the passing of the king and princess. Jason fell to his knees, never looking away from the horror in the fountain. In the deepest recesses of my mind, I saw the boy I'd once helped steal a golden fleece, one who'd looked at me with awe and, in his own way, love. That boy was gone, turned into a bitter man whose cowardice and self-loathing had turned toxic. I turned and got my cloak and what money I could hold in pouches on my person. I left the palace through an unguarded door in the wall behind our villa and soon found an abandoned chariot. I placed my meagre belongings in it and rode off. The goddess stood straight and tall, riding as one who knows the world is nothing but a speck of mildly interesting dust in the palm of her hand.

And then the earth shifted. It shook so hard, the chariot slid and slipped off the side of the road, throwing me into a ravine. It shook so hard, it rattled my teeth, and it was then the goddess left me, dirty and holding onto the ground, hoping it wouldn't open and swallow me, taking me to Hades where I'd just sent the souls of two people. Stone crashed and people screamed as it went on and on, and when it finally stopped, I couldn't hear anything but the pounding of my heart. On my hands and knees, I clawed my way back to the road and gasped.

The city was destroyed. Fires raged throughout, and smoke and dust covered the stars. Cries and pleas for help rose from the rubble. I began to run, climbing over rocks and buildings when I couldn't leap them. I skirted bodies, broken and bleeding in the dirt. Some dead, some dying. My children were in the lower temple, I was sure of it. Kip would have taken them away, to a place where they would be safe.

I heard my name being muttered and called out along the dark and broken streets. I slowed and looked around and saw the angry faces of the people I'd been helping all these years.

A woman I'd once helped through the fever screamed at me. "You killed the king and princess. The gods are punishing us for what you've done!"

She was joined soon by others, and I backed away, tripping over debris. "The gods themselves killed the king and princess for telling Jason to disobey them." They didn't hear me.

And behind them, standing on a pile of rubble, was Aphrodite in her armour. The goddess I'd turned away from when I'd arrived here was finally making me pay the price, using the Corinthians fear and desperation against me. They were her punishers, just as I'd been the goddess' hand for so long. I had insulted the goddess of love, and now she was exacting her revenge.

I turned and ran, and the mob came after me, howling like a pack of rabid, injured wolves. This was the terror, the running I'd been having visions of all my life. This moment had been my destiny since I was a child. I ran, down one street and then another, making my way to the temple. Once there, I took the steps two at a time and fell inside, gasping. Priestesses slammed the door shut and barred it behind me.

Kip ran to me and helped me up, dragging me into a room that hadn't fallen apart.

Phryne was there with her arms wrapped around my children, who clung to her until they ran to me. Kip slumped onto a bench, and a priestess tended to a small wound on her leg.

"The temple is no longer safe, Medea." Phryne moved to the window and pointed. "Your friend Sicarus waits for you at the Pieta harbour. You have to make it to the boat, and he will take you away."

I grasped her hand. "Come with us. There is nothing for you here."

She seemed undecided until there came a pounding at the temple door. She nodded and whirled to pick up her cloak. "We'll leave through the back."

We followed her out the back of the temple into the smoke-filled darkness. Tisander held my hand and Phryne carried Eriopis, who was too small to get over the rubble. We moved as silently as we could, Kip behind us, keeping watch. We were nearly there when torchlight showed on the path ahead, and then as quickly behind us. We were trapped between them, and we pressed together, animals hunted with no way out.

The mob was quickly on us, hurling stones and curses as we

turned down another street. They were close, too close, and then I heard Phryne cry out. I turned and reached for her, but she was pulled backwards into the crowd, my daughter still in her arms, and I heard her screams. But far, far worse, I heard the cries of my daughter, which were quickly silenced.

I shrieked and leapt forwards, pushing my body against the crowd, Kip tightly pressed behind me, and then Tisander was ripped from my grip. I searched for him, shoving and pushing at the crowd, who tore at my cloak and gown. Someone grabbed my wrist from behind and pressed a dagger handle into my palm. I raised it and began hacking, screaming for my children as my heart threatened to beat out of my chest, and my pulse pounded in my ears.

And then the goddess filled me, and my screams shook the rubble. The crowd fell back, silent and wide-eyed. In the middle of the empty space created were three bodies. My children and Phryne, who lay with her body curled around them as though she'd protected them to the end.

My heart shredded into pieces that burned black as coal. I lifted Phryne and my son as easily as though they were pillows, and Kip picked up the tiny, limp body of my daughter.

I looked at the crowd, hatred spewing from me. "Run, Corinthians. Run for your lives, and never return to this cursed place."

I stared at the faces of Phryne and Tisander as I walked to the boat, no longer afraid of those chasing me, no longer afraid of anything in the world. The worst had already happened, and only the goddess inhabiting my body kept me from dropping to my knees in anguish. It would come, but not now.

Sicarus, wide-eyed and trembling, reached out and took Tisander from me, and I laid Phryne in the bottom of the boat. Kip boarded and kept Eriopis in her lap, cradled as she wept and tried to wipe the dirt from my beloved daughter's cheeks.

As we were pulling away, the dragons on the front of the boat lit by the burning fires of Corinth, Jason ran to the shore and dropped to his knees.

"Why?" he screamed. "Why would you kill our children? Why would you murder innocents?"

From far away, I realized I was already being painted as the monster, but I didn't care. I let the goddess speak for us. "The day I helped you steal the fleece, you swore to respect me always. You swore it again later, and again when we married. I told you never to cross me, never to cross the dark goddess. You have paid for your sins against the gods, and you will never be the man you might have been. You will die alone, forsaken, a coward among men who despise you."

The curse was clear and terrible, and there was no question it wasn't me casting it, although I would have done so if I'd had free will. He wept and wailed, and his sorrow followed us into the dark night, where the flames of burning Corinth soon faded into smaller fires. And as they faded, so too did the goddess.

It was then I began to weep. I held my children to me and sobbed over their still bodies. That the goddess of love would be so cruel shouldn't have been a surprise, but still I cursed her as I held their cooling little bodies. I'd forsaken her in her own temple, and now she'd taken all I loved in the world from me. When the boat bumped against a dock as the sun was rising, I finally looked up.

There on the shore was a small, simple temple built into the hillside below a mountain. There was nothing around it, just a cove with steps that led up to a path in the hill.

"The temple of Hera." Sicarus looked at me with tears in his eyes. "A good place for them, I think."

He helped me out as I refused to let go of Tisander, and behind me, Kip brought Eriopis. Sicarus carefully managed to bring Phryne, and we carried them to the temple. A single priestess waited, her eyes sad.

"The goddess said you would be coming." She turned, and we

followed her to three tumuli. Two small and one large. "She told us what to arrange."

We lay my children on fresh linen and used the bowls of water to clean them, readying them for the afterlife. Reverently, the priestesses did the same for Phryne. Prayers were said and gifts were laid with my children as we placed them in their graves.

Kip held me tight as my sobs threatened to tear me apart. When the ritual was done, she led me away, as I couldn't bear to watch them put dirt over my children. Sicarus hugged me and kissed my cheek in parting. I clutched his hand.

"Thank you for saving us. May the gods care for you."

He nodded and said nothing further as he got in the boat and rowed away.

Kip and I went to a small, simple room, where we lay down, and she held me as I screamed and raged throughout the night. The price of my freedom had been too high.

CHAPTER FORTY-THREE
Return

THE MORNING DAWNED CLEAR and bright, infuriating me. How could the world go on? How could Apollo allow the sun to shine? Did they not feel my devastation? Did they not understand the never-ending depth of my grief? My hatred? My despair?

Kip sat beside me, grief written in her eyes. But with a heavy sigh, she stood. "I'll get us breakfast. And then we need to decide what to do."

I couldn't understand her words. What did she mean? I couldn't do anything but let my grief rage through me until I was able to join my children. I had nothing, *was* nothing. Yet, I couldn't weep any more. Numbness began to set in, and I hugged my knees to my chest, looking out the door at the water. Smoke rose in the far distance, which meant Corinth was still burning. I hoped it burned to the ground, along with everyone in it.

Kip came in and set a tray in front of me, and then left me to my thoughts. It was past noon when she returned with lunch, replacing the untouched food in front of me.

"Sicarus returned this morning. He searched the rubble of our villa and found the chariot you abandoned on the road. He brought as many of our trunks and belongings as he could, including the chest of money. I gave him much, for his time as much as his thoughtfulness."

I nodded absently. Clothes and money would do me little good now.

Kip took my hand. "Medea, we cannot stay here. The people of Corinth will flee, and some may come here. We need to get further away from the city."

I stared at her blankly.

She sighed and stood. "I'll make arrangements, but I don't know where to go."

Gods, how I wished I knew where Chaon had gone so we could follow him. But he hadn't said where they were headed, and so he was truly lost to me. "Athens." King Aegeus had come to visit Corinth once, and we'd spent much time walking in the gardens together. I'd been blunt with him, telling him of my place as an outsider and mentioning the understanding that I would never be safe.

She nodded thoughtfully. "The king promised he'd take you in if you ever needed him."

She left, and once again I fell into a dream state as I remembered my children. Holding them when they were born, listening to them cry and laugh, and watching them play in the autumn leaves. I'd been unsure about becoming a mother, with all the ties that bound one to a single place, but they'd become my heart. I felt their little souls entwined with my own and knew where they were each moment of the day. The thought that they were gone, that they'd been ripped away from me... I retched, my bile mixed with my tears as my body tried to empty itself of the horror and anguish. How could I not break apart from the rage consuming me? How could the earth not burst to rubble as I screamed? The cruelty of the gods was beyond reason, and I would gladly slip into madness to release myself from the nightmare my world had become.

I slept, trying to ease the pain, and when I woke, dawn was breaking over the water, casting long pink shadows. Kip pulled me to my feet and wrapped my cloak around me. She took my hand, and we left the temple to climb the steep path to the hillside. A chariot waited, in it our trunks. The driver didn't look at us as we got in, and Kip tapped him on the shoulder. The driver hit the horse's flank and we were off, leaving the temple behind. I looked back at the last place my children would ever go, but the temple was completely hidden from view, almost as though it belonged to a different world.

I sat awkwardly on a trunk, wrapping my arms around myself, as we made our way to Athens. There is little else to tell of that journey, which made our bodies ache and required us to sleep on the ground overnight, only our cloaks beneath our heads. It was still winter, but it wasn't cold, not like it had been when I was young. I stared at the stars and raged at the gods and kept silent.

When we arrived in Athens, I was taken aback by the noise and crowds. Here, too, it was clear buildings had fallen because of the earth shaking. But unlike Corinth, it hadn't completely fallen, and people were at work repairing the buildings that could be saved. Looking down on it all was the palace, built on a high bluff with an impressive temple beside it. The chariot climbed the steep hill at the back because at the front were an incredible number of steps.

At the back gate a guard stopped us, and Kip announced my name. He sent a messenger into the palace, and we waited. My voice seemed to have left me, along with my desire to live. I didn't care whether we were admitted or turned away to live on the streets. The fact that I wasn't brave enough to kill myself so I could be with my children made me rage even more. The messenger returned, and we were admitted to the palace. The driver took us right to the front steps, where servants waited to take our belongings. Two female servants led the way into the palace, and Kip and I followed.

In the clean, open palace I slowly became aware of my own state. I was covered in dirt, my peplos ragged and torn, my cloak filthy. I looked like an urchin, and I couldn't have been further from the proud princess priestess I'd once been. The throne room doors were flung open, and King Aegeus strode forwards to meet us. He took me in his arms and pulled me close.

"Ah, Medea. To see you in this way breaks my heart." He held me at arm's length and studied me. "My servants will take you to the baths, and we will talk tonight."

I nodded dumbly and turned away, and I heard him stop Kip and speak to her. I didn't care what they were speaking of. I followed the servant down hallways and stairs to baths steaming below ground, lit by torches and scented with pine. I held still while they stripped my clothes from me and helped me into the warm water. I let them wash me, my hair. I was vaguely aware of Kip nearby and at one point, I reached for her, and she quickly took my hand. I accepted the comfort of her simple touch, a reminder that I wasn't entirely alone in the world.

Once we were clean, dry, and in new clothes, we once again went to the throne room where King Aegeus was waiting. I sat beside him and accepted a chalice of wine.

He took my hand, his eyes serious and kind. "I cannot tell you how sorry I am for your loss, Medea. To lose a husband is one thing, to lose your children is to lose your soul."

I let the tears slip and didn't wipe them away. I also didn't mention that Jason wasn't dead. He was simply dead to me.

"You can stay here with me in Athens for as long as you wish. I have no queen to be jealous, no daughter to worry. I lost my son long ago when he was stolen from the palace."

I nodded and stared at my plate, picking at my food and drinking more wine than I should to numb the pain. Kip led me to bed and slept in the room attached to mine.

***

Time passed, as it does. The ache of losing my children dimmed, though it stayed with me always. For many months I refused to speak, hardly ate. I couldn't pray. My brutal anger at the gods who had planned this all along wouldn't allow me to say words to them which I'd regret. Eventually, though my children's loss remained an open wound in my heart, I began to live again. Aegeus asked me to marry him, and I said yes. He'd been told Jason was dead, and I let him believe that. I knew in my bones I would never see him again and wasn't worried. Shortly after we were married, I was pregnant. Aegeus doted on our son Medus from the moment he was born.

But I...I found that I was unable to love this new child in the same way I'd loved the others. I loved him, yes, but with a distance I hadn't felt with the others. Perhaps I was protecting myself from the anguish that comes with loving too much. Or perhaps it was angry Aphrodite, keeping me from feeling the love a mother should have for her child.

I ruled beside Aegeus as his queen, and I revelled in it. And, as I'd thought would happen if I'd stayed with Chaon, I was seen as more than queen. People came to me for advice, for potions, and to see if I knew what their future held. I never told them that, even if I saw anything. I wasn't a Pythia and had no desire to be sought as one. I refused to go to the temple most days, unable to put aside my rage at what they'd taken from me. But I enjoyed mixing the potions for sickness or childbirth. Occasionally I even went to people's houses to help. I never forgot Sicarus's kindness and sought to make the people around me love me as much as he had.

The gods rarely spoke to me while I was in Athens. I rarely spoke to them either. We were no longer on good terms, but I still did their bidding when certain mortals crossed my path as part of the Olympian games. Fortunately, that was rare.

It was when Theseus, a hero of men, came to the palace that I knew my time there had ended. He was much like Jason when I'd first met him. Young, strong, bull-headed. But in his eyes was ambition and intellect Jason had never embodied, and when he looked at me and Medus, there was cunning I understood well. It wasn't so different from Creon's or Glauke's. One night, on a whim, I slipped poison into his drink and hoped that would change what I knew to be my path.

But when Aegeus saw Theseus's sword, he cried out and hugged his long-lost son to him. The sword had been stolen when Theseus had been taken, and the poor couple he'd grown up with had saved it for him. The cup with the poison in was dashed to the ground by Aegeus in his eagerness to embrace his son, my hopes of a calm, happy life, with it. I was still chosen of the gods, and I knew with the powers they'd given me that my time here was done.

This time, though, we did not flee in the dead of night. I told Aegeus that I feared for our son's life, as ambition and first-born sons are not a good combination. I told him that the goddess herself demanded that I leave and return to my homeland. It wasn't true. But he accepted it with tears in his eyes and said he'd never understand the ways of the gods, nor of those they used so hard. He made me promise to send Medus to him one day when he was grown, so that he could make a man of him. I smiled and kissed his cheek and said goodbye.

I didn't love him. He was kind, and steady, and had taken me in, for which I was grateful. But love was beyond me now, that particular goddess one I reviled above all, and I wanted true freedom. On the day we set sail for Egrisi, I let the pull of the tides fill me and set me alight.

The journey home was made in a different world than the one I'd set sail in so long ago. Crops had failed everywhere, and cities were left smoking and abandoned when they could no longer support their people. Trade slowed until it ceased almost entirely, and the earth shaking had become a daily occurrence. Even Athens was nearly deserted as people sought cooler climates with more water. I was glad to leave the parched, desperate land, and when we rounded the beautiful islands and the coast of Anatolia, my soul began to sing. We entered familiar territory, my heart raced, and I pointed out landmarks and special places to Medus, who looked on in mild interest. My son was far different from my other children. He could be petulant and demanding, needy and bratty. At times I didn't like him much, though I loved him dearly. I coddled him, often afraid of something happening to him, so perhaps some of his behaviour was my doing. Guilt often swamped me when I looked at him now and felt...nothing.

But when we arrived in Egrisi, he caught hold of my excitement and ran up the path ahead of me to the palace.

"If your father is there?" Kip asked, looking around us. Servants carried our trunks of clothes, jewels, and offerings.

"He isn't." I shrugged when she looked at me. "I still know things, sometimes. I don't know who is here, but it isn't him."

She nodded and didn't say anything else. At the palace, guards stood at the front doors, but when I announced my name, they let us pass. I walked down the familiar halls with their familiar scents and patterns, and it felt as though the world had stopped. Nothing had changed. Until I got to the throne room and found my aged Uncle Perses sitting on the throne. Hunched and wrinkled like linen left in the sun, he glared at me through cloudy eyes.

"You do not belong to this place any longer, murderer of your father and brother."

I raised my eyebrows. "Brother, yes. Father?"

"He died of grief after what you did. When they hung your brother's pieces from the tree, he sat against the trunk, screaming at the gods and slipping into a madness that eventually took his life. Your mother skulked back into the sea, forsaking him as well." He shook his gnarled finger at me. "You brought nothing but despair and darkness to this city."

I'd long known about my mother, who had left soon after me and had sent a message of love during my voyage, but it felt like a fitting ending for my father. I smiled and moved next to him, placing my hand on his cheek. "Uncle, you say the kindest things. I'm so glad I got to speak with you before you left us to go to Hades."

He turned red and began to speak, but the poison coating my palm, made of the ichor from the giant Talos, seeped in quickly and he tumbled from the throne, choking, his eyes bulging as he gasped his last breaths. I watched impassively and when he was nearly gone, I stepped lightly over him and sat on the warm throne. "Yes, this will do nicely." I patted the smaller throne next to me. "Sit, Medus. This kingdom is ours now."

He did as he was bid, though for once he appeared properly frightened as he stared at the still-twitching corpse of the former king. He looked at me, wide-eyed, and sat silently, on the throne that was still far too big for him. I smiled at Kip, who smiled back.

"My queen." She bowed low and then laughed, and I joined her.

"Tell the servants to remove the body, please, Kip. And tell them to find us suitable rooms until the queen's quarters are ready." I slowly peeled the beeswax covering from my palm, careful not to touch the poison coating the side that had touched Perses's face.

I was finally home. I was finally free.

CHAPTER FORTY·FOUR
A Gift

Today, when I remember what love is and my paths become one.

"Medea!" My sister ran to me, her arms open wide.

I received her gladly and hugged her to me. "Chaliope. It's so very good to see you."

Behind her entered her family, a brood of children followed by her laughing husband. They were light, and laughter, and beauty, and for the smallest moment, I was deeply envious. But that time had passed for me, and my sister deserved the joy in her life.

She introduced me to the nieces and nephews I hadn't met on her previous visit several years ago. The one to be married looked so like my sister it took me aback. And, like my sister, she was light and sweetness. Her husband-to-be would arrive the following day with his own group of people.

That night, the dining hall was filled with laughter and conversation as it hadn't been in my lifetime. They shared the tales they'd heard about me, and I told them whether or not they were true, and possibly embellished somewhat in order to make the children gape. No one brought up the rest of our family and for that, I was glad. It would have cast a shadow on what was otherwise a perfect night.

When everyone else had gone to bed, Chaliope walked back to my room with me, and I poured us water instead of wine. We sat before the open window, letting the night breeze cool us.

"This room has changed so much." Chaliope didn't look away from the window, and her voice was soft.

"How so?"

"It doesn't feel sad anymore." She turned to me, her eyes serious. "Mother was always so sad, wasn't she? I can't seem to remember her smiling."

I thought back to the last time I'd seen her, when she'd told me she'd always love me. "She smiled when she looked at you. She loved us. You because of the beauty and light, and me because she knew that my road would be hard."

"And Father?" she asked.

"I don't believe she ever loved him, not truly. She was told she would marry him, and she did so. But after I left—"

"After you left, so did she. I was alone with Father when he went mad. I was betrothed, but he wouldn't let me go. I was all he had left."

It hadn't ever, in all these years, occurred to me that I'd left my sweet, beautiful sister alone to bear the brunt of what I'd done. She hadn't mentioned it the few other times I'd seen her. "Gods, Chaliope. I'm so very sorry."

She accepted my hand when I reached out to her. "I was angry with both of you for a very long time. In a way, I could understand you leaving. You were always too much for the world, and this was a cage you needed to fly from. But then..." She swallowed hard. "But then Father told us what had happened, and he brought the pieces of Absyrtos home." She turned to me, tears in her eyes. "And instead of staying to grieve, Mother left. She walked into the water and swam away."

I let her cry, guilt eating at me. "I can't imagine how hard that must have been."

She shook her head. "You can't. Uncle Perses was even worse than Father, and when he came to help, the palace descended into shadow."

"Perses told me that Father died after he went mad. You say so as well?"

She laughed hollowly. "Father died of a sword in the back one night when he sat with Absyrtos's corpse in the trees. Perses wasn't strong enough to do it himself, but I have no doubt he had it done. He was beyond saving, and Perses saw an opportunity."

My father had been murdered by his own brother. There was a theme in our family, but gods willing, it would die with me.

***

"We have enough food and drink, but I'm sorry it isn't more lavish." I looked at the table, the meagre fare paltry in comparison to the tables I'd been at in other palaces.

"Aunt Medea, it's a feast. You have more resources here than most places."

My niece hugged me and gave me a bright smile as she went off with her women to prepare for the night's feast.

Chaliope and I sat down. "What news do you bring?" I asked, pouring us watered-down honey wine.

"The war at Troy grows as more young men join. The walls remain strong, and from what I've heard, the moment Helen arrived, Priam began stockpiling food in preparation for a siege. They have enough to last, and they have gardens that grow fruit and vegetables." She sighed and leaned back. "But everywhere else, things grow worse. The crops have died, and the riverbeds are drying up, while the coastlines flood with undrinkable water. Mycenae, Athens, Corinth, even the Minoan palace of Midas— they're nearly deserted. Without trade and enough food, the people have fled. Disease spreads quickly, and many ports have stopped ships from docking for fear of illness. The sky is dark with ash and burning winds."

I nodded. These were much the same reports I'd been hearing from those we were taking in. "Trade no longer comes here either. Even the Hittites keep to themselves."

"What will you do?"

It was a good question, and one I'd been working on for many years, given what I'd seen on my way to Iolcos and since. "I'd hoped

I'd done enough by building dams and moving people away from the city. But we've had disease here too, and even the forests are brittle and like to burst into flame at any moment."

"But you don't want to leave." She tilted her cup at me.

"Medus has gone to join the war at Troy. I'm the queen here, and I'm enjoying it." I didn't tell her that Medus had gone at my urging. She'd only just forgiven me my other sins. "But if we stay, I fear my people will starve and die like those in other cities."

"We're lucky that Alaca Hüyük is small enough that we don't need to worry as you do." She reached for my hand. "You make a good queen."

I had no reply to that. It felt odd, like a snake about to bite. "I'm considering telling the people to move on. To spread out as they have at the big cities and find their own space."

Chaliope nodded. "Where would you lead them?"

"Maghara."

She looked surprised. "There are hardly any settlements in the area, and it's too dense to farm."

"Farming isn't working anymore anyway. People will have to find a way to live, and the forest and caves will provide shelter from the heat. The lake is fresh and deep, fed from the mountains, which means drinking water."

"I think that's an excellent idea. How can we help?" Chaliope's husband came in and sat beside her.

"It's rude to lurk on other people's conversations." I smiled to take any sting from the remark. He was one of the few good men I'd met. "I'd like assistance helping people get ready for the journey. It isn't long if you're travelling light, but people will be bringing their belongings."

Chaliope reached out and took my hand. "You mean to leave Aia completely empty?"

I sighed deeply. Until that moment, I hadn't made a decision. "No one will be forced to go, and some may choose to stay behind. It could be that they're better off once most everyone else leaves.

But if I'm going to save the people, we must move further inland where we can shelter from the storms. The Kaska have become a problem as they attack small villages. The caves would give our people a way to stay safe. I sent several soldiers to look at the area, and the trees there remain healthy. Perhaps because it's protected by the mountain alongside it."

He nodded and poured himself some wine. "When do you want to begin? And have you spoken to the Amazon queen?"

"Not until it cools down. People will die in the heat walking up and over the mountain if we try now. But by Penelope's return to Hades, we should be ready. I've sent word to the Amazon queen, but she's also fighting at Priam's walls. The gods only know why."

"Then we will send soldiers to help."

It was decided, and I admit to a weight lifting from my shoulders. Now we could act rather than wait for our turn into the River Styx.

"A boat has arrived, my queen." My advisor bowed as he stopped inside the doorway.

Chaliope stood. "That will be our new son-in-law. Will you come to the docks with me?"

I laughed. "I don't think the queen can run to the docks to meet the ships anymore, sister."

She tugged at my hand. "She can if she wants to."

I shook my head. "Very well."

We laughed and told stories of the times we'd run down that forest path as children, spying on the traders and merchants, winding our way through the markets and stealing the odd piece of fruit. Then, it was moist and the moss soft under our feet. Now, crushed pine needles under the chariot's wheels released the scent of memories gone brittle.

The dock was busy with sailors unloading chests and goods, but they came to a standstill and then bowed low when I appeared.

"Please continue as you are," I said loudly, pleased that my presence had the effect it did.

Everyone resumed, and Chaliope, her husband, and I went to

greet my niece's new husband. His eyes were kind, and his smile was wide, and once again it seemed my sister's family had escaped the curse of our history. It was good to feel love once again, to be reminded I wasn't a ship foundering at sea, waiting for a wave to overtake it. There was much laughter and jesting as we directed servants where to take the various trunks and gifts meant for the temple. For perhaps the first time in my life, I felt part of something instead of outside, looking in.

"Medea?"

The voice was soft, almost awed. I closed my eyes. I would know it anywhere, at any time, even if I heard it in Hades. I couldn't make myself turn around, afraid it was a trick of the gods.

"Medea. It's truly you."

I saw Chaliope looking at me, her eyebrows raised in question. That meant she'd heard it, and it wasn't a hallucination. Slowly, I turned.

My knees went weak, and I swayed. My sister caught me, holding me up. "Chaon?"

He laughed and leapt towards me, taking me in his arms and swinging me in a circle like I weighed nothing. I held him tightly, afraid to let a breath of doubt come between us.

Finally, he set me down and held me at arm's length. "By the gods, I can't believe it. I'd heard tales of a beautiful and deadly queen, but last time I had word, you were queen in Athens. Rumours abound and often have little truth, or the truth has changed once we arrive in a place. I didn't dare believe..."

I cupped his face in my hands and stared into his beautiful eyes that had once made me feel like I was meant to be in this world. "I've been home many years now. Why are you here?"

He nodded towards the boat. "Once I left the boat, I took my people to Alaca Huyuk the home of the prince who is here to marry..." His eyes widened. "Your niece?"

I laughed, and for perhaps the first time in my life, I thanked the gods honestly with the very depths of my being. "My niece."

I took his hand in mine and introduced him to my sister, and then practically dragged him to the chariot. "We'll meet you back at the palace!" I called to her and was glad to see her laughing, though she looked bemused. We'd spoken sporadically over the years, but I'd never told her about the only man I'd ever loved. His memory was one I held closest to my heart, refusing to sully it by trying to explain what we'd had together.

Chaon held me close as we made our way to the palace, and when we made our way to the door, he stopped, frowning. "I don't want to ask, lest my heart be torn apart once again. But I have to know... Are you married?"

I laughed freely. "I am not. Aegeus set me aside after I left and has married a young woman half his age who will most certainly outlive him." I didn't speak of Jason, as he wasn't worth mentioning. Chaon searched my eyes for a moment and didn't ask the obvious question.

He grasped my hands and looked to the sky. "Thank the gods."

Hand-in-hand, we went inside out of the intense midday heat, and I had servants bring food and drink to my private dining chamber. We spoke for hours, catching up on the many years and miles that lay between us. I told him of the death of my children, and he wiped away the tears that escaped, and I held his hand when he spoke of his son who was stillborn, and his wife who died minutes later. Like Chaliope, he told me of the desperation faced by city after city, as food became scarce and water turned to dust.

"I travelled with the Sea People until I got to Lycia. But they needed to spread out too, and some of my people had expressed a wish to keep searching for somewhere better. I could have stayed in Lycia, but I've never been able to settle. I felt pulled, always, to keep searching."

I nodded and told him of my own plans to get my people to safety.

"And you?" he asked, caressing my hand with his. "Where will you go?"

As I looked into his eyes, more deeply lined now, I knew my heart had been his all this time. "Would you stay here, with me?"

He tilted his head. "If you want to stay here, yes. My people can go with yours, and I'll stay here with you." He leaned forwards, looking into my eyes. "But is that what you want?"

What did I want? It wasn't a question I'd asked myself since I'd left Corinth. Even in Athens it was more about survival than desire, about power rather than love. Now, the goddess was gone, and my love sat beside me.

"I need to consider." I kissed his hand and smiled when his eyes darkened with a desire I knew well. "But in the meantime, we have a wedding to enjoy."

The feast that night was made better for the laughter and celebration of love. At one point, I moved into the hall, into the shadows and watched. I closed my eyes and simply listened to sounds that had never echoed in these halls before. Joy, laughter, camaraderie. Tears filled my eyes, and I cursed the old age that made me sentimental.

Kip came out and put her arm around me. "I can't believe he made his way back to your side."

"I never thought to see him again. After Corinth…"

She squeezed me tighter. "The past is gone, Medea. Live for the future you've wanted all your life."

I turned to her. "But where will that be? And what about you? Shall I drag you off to travel the world once again, sleeping on the floor of ships without knowing where we'll stop?"

She snorted. "My bones wouldn't survive." She kissed my cheek and cupped my face. "Paths diverge and come together again. Chaon is proof of that. Perhaps you should pray on it."

Since the goddess had left me, I hadn't been back to the temple, but her suggestion sounded right. "What would I have done without you all these years? I think you may have been my truest love." I let the tears fall, and we hugged one another for a long moment.

She smiled at me sadly and then went back to join the merriment inside, as did I when I'd composed myself. There would be time yet to decide my path, which I'd already thought was set. The gods never seemed to let me walk a straight road.

Tonight, Chaon would sleep beside me, and I would know peace. Tomorrow, or maybe the next day, I would pray.

CHAPTER FORTY-FIVE
The Wind Calls

THE WEDDING CELEBRATION WAS uninterrupted by gods or man. The right sacrifices were made at the temple, the young couple pledged themselves to one another, and the feast went on until the sun rose again the next day. Exhausted and with sore heads, most people slept the day away, emerging only after the sun had begun to hide behind the mountains. Chaon and I stayed in bed most of the day, telling one another tales of our travels and the people we'd known.

It was as though no time had passed between us. I lay comfortable and secure beside him, no pretence or barrier between us.

"Have you found what you wished for?" he asked.

I nodded slowly. "I came home, and I'm queen. I have power and freedom to do as I wish."

"And have you given more thought to what it is you still wish to do?" he asked softly, looking at our entwined hands.

"I'm going to the temple to pray about it today."

He nodded. "Wise, to seek answers from the gods you've served for so long." He placed his hand over my heart. "But remember to ask with this and not your head."

I laughed, touched by his sentimentality. "I promise."

We dressed, teasing and touching like we were young again, and then made our way to the dining hall, where many others had gathered. After the meal, I excused myself and made my way through the forest to the temple. It wasn't an auspicious day of any kind, no festivals or days dedicated to any of the gods. In a way, that suited me better as there were no distractions. I went to the altar and the rest of the priestesses left me to pray alone. I poured a libation of wine and placed a bowl of fruit, a great gift in these hard times, on the altar. Then I knelt and bowed my head.

If you would hear me one last time, I would seek your counsel. A breeze picked up dry leaves and spun them around the room, and I smiled at the old feeling caressing my skin. When I opened my eyes, she was there, the goddess I'd been dedicated to in my youth. Hecate, the goddess of darkness and contemplation.

She looked down at me, her eyes black pools. *We haven't left you, child. We simply give you what we promised. You may always call.*

A sob, sudden and unexpected, escaped me, and I realized in that moment how empty I'd felt without their presence. *I don't know what step to take next. Would you guide me?*

No. Your will is your own now. What you do, you do with your heart. The breeze swirled more leaves. *But you wanted freedom and to see the world, once. Living in a cave or in a palace alone is a cage of another kind, is it not?*

Tears streaked down my face. The breeze was gone, the leaves stuck once again to the stone floor. I was alone, and I knew what I wanted to do. Not because anyone or anything else demanded it but because *freedom* was calling. And I was finally free to answer.

***

It took two months to ready the people for the journey to Meghara. Once I'd announced the plans, my people were quick to begin making preparations, and bands of them travelled separately into the mountains towards the lakeside caves in the forest. The first group took with them building materials for homes outside the caves, and the next sections took food. Women and children were the last to go.

The leaves were changing colour by the time the city was empty, and I admit to sentimentality as I walked down the empty market streets and past areas which used to heave with business and men arguing over heroic tales. Things left behind allowed memory to drift into the wind, scattered and forgotten. Would someone, one day, find these things and wonder who they'd belonged to? Or would time turn them to dust, leaving no trace of my kingdom, my people? Would we turn into tales told in firelight to frighten children?

I swallowed against the emotion welling in me. I knew full well I'd done what I needed to do, and I'd even sent a message to Medus at Troy, so that should he come back from the war, he'd know where his people were. But deep down, I knew he wouldn't return. The lack of ache at his loss made me ill. What kind of mother, *person*, was I to feel nothing?

But there was Chaon, who filled me with love and peace. Perhaps because Medus was born of scheming and necessity, I felt little for him. Or maybe I resented, to some degree, that he lived when my other children didn't. Whatever the reason, it didn't matter now. I returned to the palace, melancholy and thoughtful, but I brightened when I saw my sister standing beside Kip on the balcony.

"We thought you'd been lost in the mists, never to return," Chaliope called down.

"There will be stories of other women who do that one day." I laughed and made my way to them, giving them both the kiss of greeting before we sat to a late day meal.

"Is everyone gone?" Kip asked, pulling a honeyed fig from the bowl.

"It's so empty. Like life was simply sucked away by the tides. Some remain, who can't imagine leaving their home."

Chaliope sighed. "I suppose it was always going to come to this."

I frowned, confused. "What do you mean?"

She waved vaguely towards the city. "Part of our family has always been cursed, and that kind of darkness spreads like mud, smothering everything it touches. It makes sense that this place gets left behind to be scrubbed clean by time."

It was the most poetic thing I'd ever heard my sister say, and it touched me deeply. "Perhaps you're right, my love." I turned to Kip. "When do you go?"

We'd had a long talk after my visit to the temple where I'd received my answer, and through many tears, we'd agreed it was time for us to part. I didn't want to be caged, and my people were already figuring out how to make their way in this new world. They didn't need me, and in truth, I no longer needed them. I'd had the power I'd wanted all my life, and now I could give it up. I would always need Kip, but her place wasn't on a ship facing an uncertain future. Her place was beside her husband and as a matriarch to our people. For the first time in our lives, we were on separate paths.

We'd talked long into the night, remembering the journey of our youth. The bloodshed, the gods riding me like a beast of burden, the ego I failed to rein in more than once... I held her, and we cried. She'd been my everything for so long. My closest friend, my deepest love, my safe place when the world collapsed around me. We'd faced gods and monsters, kings and crises side-by-side, and letting her go felt a little like it had when I'd lost my children so long ago. We grieved as we lay in bed beside one another for a final time, letting go of the most precious parts of ourselves so that we could move into the next, and final, journey of our lives.

I met her gaze and knew she too was thinking the same even as she answered my question.

"We leave after you set sail. I want to make sure you don't frighten like a hare and go running off into the forest." She smiled, but there was deep sadness in her eyes.

"I've always envied your desire for adventure, just like the heroes feel." Chaliope's eyes were bright. "And to travel with the Sea People, seeing the world! Can you handle such excitement in your old age?"

I laughed and swatted at her. "I'm not as old as I felt not long ago. We're sailing south. The people have heard of a place called Rhodes, with fair winds and beautiful coasts, and that's where we'll go first. After that?" I shrugged, filled with excitement for the unknown. "We'll go where the winds take us."

Kip looked thoughtful, whereas Chaliope looked as she had when we'd spoken of these things when we were children.

"The earth shaking has become worse, and the Sea People have said the flaming rocks flying from Poseidon's hearth are making the oceans unstable. If you have any gifts left from the gods on our first voyage, be sure to use them." Kip, always practical, tapped at the table.

"I've already packed them and will have them ready." I would miss her desperately, and part of me had wanted to beg her to come. And I have no doubt that if I had done so, she would have joined me, even though her heart remained behind. Her husband would have joined us too, but it was well known he had no stomach for boats and often vomited over the side even when it was docked. They would have been unhappy, and loath as I was to lose her, I couldn't ask it of her. But neither could I stay. The wind itself called me, and my mother's people in the water were waiting to welcome me back. My blood sang, and I couldn't wait to be underway.

CHAPTER FORTY-SIX
Remember Me

"Do you like our space?" Chaon asked, his arm around my waist.

I looked at the small berth where we would sleep, below deck on the ship decorated with enormous blue eyes to see where it was going. My trunks took up a large section, but they would serve us well. I had enough gold and gems to barter with for a long time, to keep the whole crew fed for as long as we could find food for sale in our travels.

"As long as I'm beside you, it's perfect."

We went back into the sunshine and onto land. I hugged Kip hard, letting my tears fall in torrents. How could my heart break like this and still let me live?

"Promise to send word whenever possible," she said, holding me and crying into my shoulder. "And make sure to give the war at Troy a wide berth. The gods are active there, and you don't need that dirt in your life anymore."

I laughed and cried at the same time. "I promise."

I finally let go, said my goodbyes to the few people left, then turned to Chaon.

He smiled and took my hand. We boarded and set sail with the sunrise pointing our way across the water. Once again, I was headed towards Greece, but this time there was no death chasing me nor ahead of me. My time on this world wouldn't be much longer, but it would be the happiest of my life, that I knew. I'd chosen once again, and this time, the choice was mine and mine alone.

There is little else to tell you now. We sailed night and day, stopping where we could, living off the land. Storms, fierce and violent, raged across the water, forcing us to land for long stretches at a time. The Sea People were kind, and from every city I'd known and several I'd never heard of. All were from lands parched or drowned, with nowhere else to go. And so, they roamed together, and I was one of them now. Landless, without family, without a title, I was freer than I'd ever been, and it raced through my soul, and I sang with the birds and flew with the clouds, swimming with my ancestors as the waters parted before us.

And beside me, always, was Chaon. We loved, and laughed, and slept, and we shared our sorrows and fears. One day, at open sea, a crater that looked barely noteworthy began to froth red fire, and we were safely away when it shot that fire and rock into the air, to come crashing down into the sea with a hiss and steam that created a dense fog all around it. It was magic of its own kind, and I revelled in it, even though the volatile nature of it meant destruction. As we watched it recede in the distance, Chaon told me it was much like the woman he'd known so many years ago, explosive, beautiful, and deadly. I laughed, pleased with his memory of me but grateful that part of me was in the past. Now, I was prepared to watch and learn, rather than own and control.

I prayed and sometimes got a response. I used what powers hadn't left me, and those worked well throughout the voyage. One night I woke, sweating, from a vision.

Jason, aged and wizened like a grape in the sun, sat in the sand against the ruined hull of the Argo. Alone, he raged at the gods until, with a great crack, the prow of his ship broke from above, crushing him.

My heartbeat slowly returned to normal, and I lay back. Chaon hadn't wakened, and I was glad for the silence, broken only by the water lapping at the sides of the ship. I'd dreamt a part of this many years ago, but I knew what I'd seen had only now come to pass. Once, I would have rejoiced at his gruesome and lonely end. Now, I felt nothing but pity. The young golden boy who'd been kind and thoughtful had deserved better. The older man who'd turned bitter and allowed that bitterness to blind him, didn't.

And so, my story ends. I'm here, where I belong. I've had power and freedom. I've known love, loss, and laughter. I've seen more of the world than any other woman of my time, and I've wielded the power of the gods in my hands. I've taken and given life. Will people remember me? Will you tell the story of the princess, priestess, and witch who had to choose and choose again?

I think you will. And so, I will remain with you always, a reminder that you walk the path of the gods, but how you do so is up to you.

Other Great Butterworth Books

Fragments of the Heart by Ally McGuire
Love can be the most thrilling adventure of all.
Available on Amazon (ASIN B0CHBPHR6M)

Here You Are by Jo Fletcher
Can they unlock their hearts to find the true happiness they both deserve?
Available on Amazon (ASIN B0CBN935ZB)

Stunted Heart by Helena Harte
A stunt rider who lives in the fast lane. An ER doctor who can't take chances. A passion that could turn their worlds upside down.
Available on Amazon (ASIN B0C78GSWBV)

Dark Haven by Brey Willows
Even vampires get tired of playing with their food...
Available on Amazon (ASIN B0C5P1HJXC)

Green for Love by E.V. Bancroft
All's fair in love and eco-war.
Available from Amazon (ASIN B0C28F7PX5)

Call of Love by Lee Haven
Separated by fear. Reunited by fate. Will they get a second chance at life and love?
Available from Amazon (ASIN B09CLK91N5)

Where the Heart Leads by Ally McGuire
A writer. A celebrity. And a secret that could break their hearts.
Available on Amazon (ASIN B0BWFX5W9L)

Stolen Ambition by Robyn Nyx
Daughters of two worlds collide in a dangerous game of ambition and love.
Available on Amazon (ASIN B0BS1PRSCN)

Cabin Fever by Addison M Conley
She goes for the money, but will she stay for something deeper?
Available on Amazon (ASIN B0BQWY45GH)

Zamira Saliev: A Dept. 6 Operation by Valden Bush

They're both running from their pasts. Together, they might make a new future.
Available from Amazon (ASIN B0BHJKHK6S)

The Helion Band by AJ Mason

Rose's only crime was to show kindness to her royal mistress...
Available from Amazon (ASIN B09YM6TYFQ)

Of Light and Love by E.V. Bancroft

The deepest shadows paint the brightest love.
Available from Amazon (ASIN B0B64KJ3NP)

An Art to Love by Helena Harte

Second chances are an art form.
Available on Amazon (ASIN B0B1CD8Y42)

Let Love Be Enough by Robyn Nyx

When a killer sets her sights on her target, is there any stopping her?
Available on Amazon (ASIN B09YMMZ8XC)

Dead Pretty by Robyn Nyx

An FBI agent, a TV star, and a serial killer. Love hurts.
Available on Amazon (ASIN B09QRSKBVP)

Nero by Valden Bush

Banished and abandoned. Will destiny reunite her with the love of her life?
Available from Amazon (ASIN B09BXN8VTZ)

Warm Pearls and Paper Cranes by E.V. Bancroft

A family torn apart by secrets. The only way forward is love.
Available from Amazon (ASIN B09DTBCQ92)

Scripted Love by Helena Harte

How good can a romance writer be if she doesn't believe in happy ever after?
Available on Amazon (ASIN B0993QFLNN)

What's Your Story?

Global Wordsmiths, CIC, provides an all-encompassing service for all writers, ranging from basic proofreading and cover design to development editing, typesetting, and eBook services. A major part of our work is charity and community focused, delivering writing projects to under-served and under-represented groups across Nottinghamshire, giving voice to the voiceless and visibility to the unseen.

To learn more about what we offer, visit: www.globalwords.co.uk

A selection of books by Global Words Press:
Desire, Love, Identity: with the National Justice Museum
Aventuras en México: Farmilo Primary School
Times Past: with The Workhouse, National Trust
Young at Heart with AGE UK
In Different Shoes: Stories of Trans Lives

Self-published authors working with Global Wordsmiths:
Steve Bailey
Ravenna Castle
Jackie D
CJ DeBarra
Dee Griffiths
Iona Kane
Maggie McIntyre
Emma Nichols
Dani Lovelady Ryan
Erin Zak

Printed in Great Britain
by Amazon